In his wildly entertaining new novel, Erin, *Joe Harrington gives us a fast-paced murder mystery for our times.*

Structured as a series of mini-cliff-hangers and filled with up-to-the-minute details, Harrington takes us on wild ride through San Francisco, a city he knows, loves and celebrates. I loved it!

—Stephen Flaherty, Manhattan, New York
Multiple Tony winner and composer of numerous musicals, including
Anastasia, Once Upon an Island, Ragtime and *Rocky*

Whether it's true crime or fiction, Joe Harrington's deep Irish roots have gifted him with a unique storytelling voice.

Erin, *set in San Francisco, is the latest example of his literary strength. It has more twists and turns than that city's serpentine Lombard Street — a thoroughly entertaining read.*

— Steve Cottrell, Florida
Political Columnist, *St. Augustine Record*

What I love about "Erin" is the strength, intelligence and humor of the female characters. What a range in ages: landlady Angela, 96; psychiatrist Sarah, 30; and the homicide detective Erin, 46.

This is the only murder mystery I have ever read that had such a strong subplot, in this case the current national political reality.

— **Diane Lewis,** East Bay, California.

Not only is this a rip-roaring murder mystery, it also has the bonus that it mocks the President of the United States with politically satirical drawings.

A fun romp, made me think of Damon Runyon's use of crazy yet human characters.

— **Bryon Snyder**, Tucson, Arizona

A fun, exciting story featuring cops, priests, and a tiger! This mystery/ political satire has it all.

— **Patricia Diaz,** PhD, Boise, Idaho

For over a decade I've read Harrington's weekly column called Movies and Madness *in the English magazine publication* The Puerto Vallarta Mirror. *The contents of the columns involved his opinions on current films and political events.*

I've read Harrington's true crime books. When I learned he had written a novel I was interested to see how he made the leap between these genres.

He brought his research abilities in non-fiction into his fictional world and did it seamlessly — blending real life political events into his deadly tale.

The novel Erin *is one wild ride. I'm originally from Wyoming and loved the chaotic action that takes place in a dump called the Triple M Saloon, especially the antics of the owner, called with good reason God's Own Bookie.*

— **Bernie Candelaria**, Puerto Vallarta, Mexico

ERIN

The Bizarre Murder Case
that Created Her Terrible Secret

JOE HARRINGTON

ISBN: 978-1-948638-14-2

Published by Fideli Publishing, Inc.
119 West Morgan Street
Martinsville, IN 46151

www.FideliPublishing.com

Other books by Joe Harrington

Eye of Evil — St. Martin's Press

Profiles in Murder — Dell Publishing

Justice Denied — Plenum Publishing

Death of an Angel — Quantum Entertainment

An Execution's Odyssey — Pegasus Publishing

Mauled — Fideli Publishing

Dedication

to my lovely,
loving wife
and best friend
Lorraine

and the three children
who not only give me joy,
but make me laugh:
Erin, Damon and Devin

Acknowledgements

Tom Durkin: editing

Bob Crabb: political drawings by the monk

Matt Regan: cover illustration and Angela's drawings

Author's Note

One of the inspirations for this story was a tragic incident at the San Francisco Zoo on Christmas Day 2007. Out of respect for the teenage boy who died and the two men who were mauled, details of that horrific event have been altered regarding names and dates.

Prologue

It's a Sin to Tell a Lie

"Bless *you*, Father, for *you* have sinned," Erin said, "now take off the Roman collar you've disgraced, waive your bullshit Miranda Rights and confess."

"Are you joking?" Father Mario asked.

"I don't joke about felonious behavior."

"What are you talking about?"

"I have evidence the monk's alive."

"Impossible."

"Come into the light and I'll show you."

The priest and the homicide detective left the dark confessional booth.

The nave was empty save Erin, the priest and the statues of long-dead saints: Patrick, Cabrini, Peter, Elizabeth, Joseph, Mary, Theresa, Augustine and Jude.

Subdued cones of light revealed the fourteen Stations of the Cross that lined opposite walls. Behind the altar an overhead golden glow illuminated a life-sized replica of Christ on His cross.

Erin said, "If we sit across the aisle from each other we don't need these." She removed her N-95 mask.

"I see you're dressed for success," the priest said.

Erin was wearing tennis shoes, gray gym pants and a windbreaker. Her red hair was tied into a ponytail using a yellow bandana.

"Don't try horseshit misdirection," she said with a cold glare. "I'll answer one question, but from now on stay on point. I'm dressed for a brutal and exhausting run once this meeting is over because I know I'm going to want to get a rancid taste out of my mouth."

"Not exactly a good attitude to celebrate the Fourth of July."

"A day that might end *your* independence." Erin opened her briefcase, removed a single sheet of newspaper, slid it across the aisle and pointed. "Proof the monk's alive."

The priest picked up the large single sheet of newsprint and saw:

San Francisco Chronicle · Independence Day, July 4, 2020
SPECIAL EDITION
Is the Monk, aka Friar Tuck, Still Alive?

Happy Independence Day from Friar Tuck

Six weeks ago, in May, Trump stated: "Vaccine or no vaccine, we're back. Whether it's an ember or a flame, we're going to put it out. But we're not closing our country."

That's the president of the United States telling Americans you're free to go on working and dying.

The priest crumpled the paper into a ball, tossed it back across the aisle and said in an unemotional voice, "I see a cartoon. So what?"

"You reported the monk died last Christmas. If he did, how could he draw this? There are coffins on one side of the Justice Scale, moneybags on the other and Trump, with his finger pushing down on the money scale side, making a decision on when to open the country. The country wasn't closed last Christmas."

"On my oath as a priest, the monk is dead."

"Why are you lying? We've been friends for twenty years, since I was a rookie cop and you the PD's chaplain back—"

"Erin, we *are* friends and—"

"A half a year ago," she said, "on the front steps of this church, the monk collapsed. I helped *you* give him last rites. An hour later *you* claimed he died. *You* stated he was cremated. His artwork in today's *Chronicle* and a direct quote from the president proves the monk's alive and that you're a Goddamn liar."

"Glare at me all you want; a newspaper's not proof."

"There's the monk's handwriting."

"Could be a forgery."

"Our PD's handwriting expert did an analysis. It's Friar Tuck's."

"Experts make mistakes."

"So do priests," Erin replied as she opened her briefcase and removed a document. "This search warrant gives me total access to Saint Jude's rectory, church, basement and crypt."

"What?"

"Let's start with the church basement."

"My lawyers need to review and approve this alleged legal document."

"They can review anytime, but I've the legal right *now* to inspect anywhere I Goddamn feel like inspecting on Saint Jude's property. I'm heading to the cellar."

They donned N-95 masks, went behind the altar and down a stairway leading to the church basement. A single row of four bare bulbs dimly lit the vast interior.

Erin said, "It's freezing."

"Who heats a basement?" he replied in a muffled voice.

"Get six feet away so we can remove the masks."

He did so and they both took off the N-95s.

She pointed at a door with a padlock. "That wasn't here last Christmas. I recall an archway leading to the crypt."

The priest shrugged.

"Why's the crypt secured?"

Father Mario shoved his hands into his cassock.

"Open up," Erin demanded.

"Don't have a key to the padlock."

"You're lying, but no problem," she said, removing a small crowbar from her briefcase. With a firm yank, the detective pulled the padlock's screws from the door.

She fumbled about, found a switch and turned on the lights.

The crypt lit up, flooded with a soft, luminescent glow.

"Warm in here," she said. "Why heat the crypt? It's a rhetorical question. I know why this place is heated. Where's the monk?"

He shrugged.

On the wall to the right of the entrance there hung a 75" flat-screen television. Facing the TV was a metal folding chair and a bed.

Erin said, "Bed looks expensive."

"A Baldacchino Supreme Bed. Cost six million."

"Must be comfortable."

"I wouldn't know," the priest stiffly responded.

"None of this was here Christmas, when I was down here investigating multiple murders."

Against the far wall was a small, yet elegant kitchenette, a large refrigerator and marbled double sink. To the left were five ancient stone caskets, behind them a purple curtain. She pulled the drawstring and a bathroom was revealed.

In the center of the crypt, on a table, was a large stack of drawings chronicling President Trump's activities since last Christmas.

An easel in the center of the room held a canvas.

"I don't get it," Erin said. "What cause can't the saint save?"

"Saint Jude's the patron saint of hopeless causes. Obviously, Trump is the lost cause even the saint can't redeem."

She waved a hand. "Also obviously, your fabulously rich attorney pals bought this stuff for Friar Tuck, who has lived down here since you falsely reported his demise."

"They wanted him to spend what little was left of his life in luxury. Didn't work; he slept on the floor."

"Finally, an admission he lives," the homicide detective said in a deadly tone that held no hint of jubilant triumph. "But where is he?"

"Died around dawn this morning. I told the truth when I said he was dead."

"*Now* you told the truth, but you've been lying for months."

The priest shrugged.

Erin's eyelids closed to slits. "That's the third time you glanced at your watch. Why?"

He smiled a tight smile.

"Son of a bitch, you're buying time. You know what pisses off a cop?"

"I assume the same thing that pisses off a priest."

"Lying. Why in fucking hell didn't you tell me—"

"You promised your mother, the day before she died, that you'd stop swearing. Why the foul mouth?"

Erin looked stunned, then sputtered, "Another delaying tactic. Yes, I did promise Mom, but I forget when I get angry and right now I am fucking furiously pissed."

"Why so angry?"

"Because you've betrayed me. You promised you'd keep our secrets."

"I didn't betray you."

"You gave the *Chronicle* the monk's latest artwork."

"I did not. Your landlady did."

"Angela? How did she get the drawing?"

"She was here this morning. She assisted me with Last Rites. She must have lifted the drawing then."

"Why give it to the newspaper?"

"She felt Friar Tuck's last effort was an appropriate epitaph."

"Why didn't you stop her? If you had, I wouldn't be here."

"Angela told me *after* she'd dropped the drawing off."

"She has to know the danger to all of us, including her."

"She's bereaved; she loved the monk. She was only thinking about honoring his work and sticking it to the president. After I confronted her, she apologized and wept."

"Where's the monk body?" Erin asked.

"A hearse retrieved it a few hours ago."

"How are you going to explain a fresh corpse showing up of a man you pronounced dead months ago?"

"He's already cremated, meaning no proof *when* he died."

"DNA can be performed on the smallest of bone fragments. Results might provide a timeframe."

A soft chime sounded three times.

"What the hell was that?" she asked.

Father Mario pulled a cell phone out of his cassock, looked at the screen, put it back in his robes, and smiled at Erin.

"Goddamn it," she said, "what message did you just get?"

"DNA *can* be run on bone fragments and that would be absolute proof that the monk just died. But, at the Golden Gate Bridge, Angela has just sent Friar Tuck's remains over the rail, through the wire mesh of the suicide prevention net, and into the deep waters of the San Francisco Bay. Now all that's left are some drawings any competent artist could have created by emulating the monk's style and signature."

Erin frowned, shaking her head from side to side.

The priest said, "You should be relieved. I know why you're reacting the way you are. You saw the newspaper's drawing and came to the erroneous conclusion that not only was the monk alive, but that I had betrayed your terrible secret."

Erin's jaw clenched.

"Then you come into my church, swearing and furious, with rage based on an assumption that I had stabbed you in the back. You couldn't be more wrong."

Erin's face relaxed.

The priest continued, "I remember what I was doing back then, on the day both our secrets were born. I consoled a devastated grandmother who had just lost her grandson; a teenager savagely ripped apart by a Siberian tiger."

"Afterwards you got drunk at the Triple M Saloon."

"With good reason," The priest stood. "I'm headed for the saloon."

"Triple M's closed."

"I have the key-code to the backdoor," Father Mario said. "We can discuss my secret and how it led to your secret and why the two are married. We need a plan, damage control, and a solution to the devastating problem facing us."

"I keep thinking about how it all happened and if there was anyway to have prevented these disasters."

Chapter 1

The First Disaster = A Tiger Escapes

Sunday, December 22, 2019, The Triple M Saloon

The pub was arguably the worst dive in San Francisco. The front of the building was a ramshackle combination of different materials: unpainted splotches of stucco, mold-covered bricks, scarred wooden swinging front doors, and windows so filthy that peering through them was like trying to x-ray fog.

The interior was even more a disgrace to probity as much as to sanitation. The twenty-five-foot, L-shaped bar hadn't received varnish in decades. Deep gashes penetrated the mahogany plank, evidence of pummeling from dice boxes. The black-and-white checkered floor was missing half its tiles, exposing a dirty, pitted and stained wooden sub-floor. Three overhead fans moved only when the front doors swung open and a breeze floating in forced them to turn. Opposite the bar, four booths ran along the north side of the saloon.

The place was in startling juxtaposition to the pastoral scene it looked out upon: the eastern end of Golden Gate Park, three miles from the Pacific Ocean.

There was one touch of dignity: a pleated, scarlet velvet curtain on the rear wall that hung floor to ceiling and was over eight-feet wide. Above the curtain was an oaken sign with etched words in emerald green: *God's Own Bookie.*

When asked why the bar was called the Triple M Saloon the owner, Max, would shout, "For money, money, money." He was a bookie. The tattered bar a front, hiding the real action in the backroom poker parlor and upstairs sport's book. The cops from nearby Park Station either ignored this illegal activity or participated. Max cared not a whit if his bar lost money. He charged far less than any other joint in The City. He loved having cops as patrons as it guaranteed the Vice Squad would leave him alone.

The only customers in the bar were Paddy, a retired police officer and Father Mario.

The priest asked, "Where's your sister? Erin told me she'd meet me at five."

Erin entered the bar and said, "It's only three after five."

"Late's late," the priest said.

She ordered ice tea for herself, a vodka on the rocks for her brother, and said, "Want one, Father Mario?"

"Of course, but I'm buying, time to celebrate your promotion to Homicide."

Father Mario was the police department's psychiatrist and chaplain. He had an office downtown in the Hall of Justice but rarely went there. Each weekday he would get to the saloon by nine, unless other priestly duties were required. Cops had no problem coming to see him for psychological counseling in the Triple M, but wouldn't be caught dead seen going into his official shrink's office. The rear booth served as his impromptu workplace.

The bar's doors swung open and the head of the Homicide Division entered. Captain Fitzgerald was a diminutive man, wearing a three-piece charcoal suit and a silver tie. He said, "Max, turn on the TV. A tiger's escaped."

Max turned on the television. The 55" flat screen flickered to life with the five o'clock news. Lead story was Nancy Pelosi stating that Congress had no choice except to bring impeachment charges against the president.

Max looked at Fitzgerald and said, "Tiger?"

"Wait for it, just heard about it over my police radio."

As if on cue, the television lit up with the message, "Breaking News."

Over the next half hour, as off duty cops from Park Police Station trickled in, horrifying events taking place at the zoo unfolded: tiger escapes; teenage boy killed; another young man mauled; police arrive; tiger shot; *coup de grace* administered to animal by a police captain; injured man taken to San Francisco General Hospital.

Erin noticed Fathers Hillman and Lewis, two of the five priests stationed at Saint Jude's, the local parish, coming out of the backroom poker parlor. Both men were in their fifties. Hillman was a distinguished looking African, born in the Kingdom of Lesotho. Lewis had good looks inherited from his Brazilian-born mother.

Captain Fitzgerald, Erin's new boss, said to her, "I've been scratching my tired, old Irish head trying to figure out what case should be your first assignment. Can't let you have a high-profile murder, or even a drive-by shooting. Maybe you could figure out who murdered the unfortunate tiger."

She snapped, "Police captain at the scene executed the tiger. Case closed."

"Erin, when you clench up your lovely Celtic face, coupled with your eyes smoking with anger and your red hair flaming with fury, it makes you look truly awful. Your mug is all pinched with hate and loathing."

Erin said, "You did everything you could to prevent my promotion."

"Just your promotion to my homicide."

Erin noticed the priests Hillman and Lewis, who were also lawyers, whispering. She thought, *they're pissed. Why?*

She headed for the restrooms. As she passed the two priests she slowed and heard Lewis mutter, "Mauling is disastrous."

Erin thought, *disastrous? Not tragic?*

The two priests were rich.

Disastrous meant money, not death.

The newscaster said, "More at six involving the tragedy at the zoo."

"More?" Paddy asked. "What else possible is there?"

Chapter 2

God's Own Bookie

Max held up an ancient brass skeleton key and said, "I'll show you." A hush fell as the dozens of patrons watched.

Max entered the storeroom and returned with a short step-ladder. He went to the rear wall and pulled the drawstring on the scarlet, velvet curtains. Two black wooden 2' x 8' doors appeared, now bracketed by the crimson curtains. Using the key, he opened an ancient lock and slid the two doors sideways behind the red curtains. A large blackboard, 4' wide and 8' high appeared.

Above the board was a replica of Michelangelo's *Creation of Adam.* Instead of the full shot of the bearded image of God reaching His hand toward the equally outstretched hand of a naked man, it depicted a close-up of the two hands, forefingers outstretched.

There was one alteration from the famous iconic image of God giving life to Adam. A $20 bill floated between both hands, making it unclear whether Adam was receiving, or, as bookie Max liked to say, paying off a bet.

Max climbed the ladder and, using chalk, wrote: *Pool. Ticket 5 bucks. Entry must have date and hour. Closest to when a plaintiff attorney's hired to represent tiger's victims and sues the zoo wins. Vig: 10% to the SPCA.*

God's Bookie blackboard was only used for pools involving a sensational crime in San Francisco, national politics or the Catholic Church. The vig was the "vigorish," the lubricant to the house, or, in Max's case, a charity of his choice.

Over the years pools were run on myriad issues such as which cardinal would succeed John Paul II aka Cardinal Ratzinger. No one won the contest as no bettor considered any South American cardinal, but most Catholic clients were delighted when the Italian from Argentina became pope.

On the last presidential election most of the Triple M' civilian customers bet on Hilary and most cops, who hated politicians and figured they would get screwed no matter who won, bet on Trump.

The vig went to Duffy's, a dry out clinic. Max explained his choice with, "I predict this president is going to cause a rise in alcoholism."

Chapter 3

Landlady Angela

The doors of the saloon banged open and an ancient, tiny lady, looking like an emaciated version of Queen Victoria, pushed through a shopping cart filled with groceries. She saw the open scarlet curtain, squinted at the blackboard and called out in a voice that was in amazing contrast to the size of the lungs from whence it came: clear, dulcet, throaty and full. "Max, I'll take all twenty-four hours on the day after Christmas."

The old lady pointed a bony finger at the attorneys Lewis and Hillman and said, "Even bloodsucking, bottom feeding lawyers might have a tad of propriety left and wait until after the birth of Christ."

Father Lewis said, "Don't bet on it."

Max collected $120 from Angela and gave her a receipt.

Angela pushed her shopping cart into the corner and sat next to Erin.

Max poured a liberal shot of Campari over some ice cubes, twisted a slice of lemon peel over the drink and set the glass in front of Angela.

Angela was Erin's landlady. She owned a pair of Victorian flats three blocks south of the saloon. She lived in the lower unit, Erin the upper.

A group of just off-duty fireman came in and bellied up to the bar.

The two women moved to the rear booth.

Angela pointed, "Oh joy, it's Sarah."

Standing at the open bar's swinging doors was Sarah, one of the SFPD's psychiatrists. She had high cheekbones, sapphire eyes and a dazzling smile. She was half Ethiopian and half Jamaican with skin of Carmel cream. Her mane of jet-black hair resembled a lion's and her lithe body moved with the flowing grace of a jaguar.

The crowd in the bar wolf whistled and clapped and gave thumbs up.

Sarah had on Riedell's Phaze skates with the 951 boot resting on the PowderDyne Reactor aluminum Plate complete with Bone Swiss bearings, Ragar Zodiac wheels, plus a jam plug.

She wore purple bellbottom pants and a tight yellow tank top which had on the back the words: *Titanic's* Di Caprio's not king of the world — *Roller-ball's* royalty Jonathan is!" The front of the tank top read, "I am woman, hear me roar!" Underneath was a picture of a male lion except the face was that of Sarah.

She called out, "Attention everyone, I still love running, but needed diversity and have taken up jam skating. I will now demonstrate some simple moves like windmills, flares, jackhammers, crickets, turtles and halos. Now move the hell out of the way and behold my majesty."

Bar stools were tossed on the bar top. Men joined the furniture and stood on the plank. Others crowded into booths.

Sarah placed a G-Project G-BOOM wireless Bluetooth Boombox by the door and turned it on.

Blow by Beyoncé began as Sarah flowed around the floor changing from various styles: break dancing, gymnastics and modern dance.

Angela gasped, "She's a ballerina. Talk about the essence of grace."

Sarah finished with a twirling pirouette, joined Erin and Angela, and said, "Angela's the one pushing a grocery cart, but Erin's the one who looks like a bag lady."

"Just finished my run, that's why jogging togs."

"Think you're going to seduce someone in that sloppy outfit?"

"What make's you think I'm looking to seduce someone?"

"You're a woman," Sarah said, "you're single."

"You're a woman," Erin fired back, "you're single."

"I'm a woman," Angela said, "and I would love to seduce someone."

"You're in your Nineties," Erin said.

"So what?" the old lady said.

"There's nothing like it, "Sarah said, "watching that fire light up in the guy's eyes, knowing what's coming, but wanting to hold him off and to tease, tease, tease as the frenzy to sate his lust builds, not only in his loins, but his heart and mind."

"Oh, God, "Angela said, "you're killing me. I may be old, but my memory works fine."

"Last night," Sarah said as she tossed her head back arching her neck, "my latest got me so fired up I thought my eyeballs had rolled back so far in my head that I was staring at my brain."

"My friends," Erin said, "you know I've been divorced for six years."

"So?" Sarah and Angela said simultaneously.

"I've been off men for a long time."

"You actually have some looks left," Angela said. "You still might catch some guy's eye. Like Max. He's, forty-eight, only a couple of years older than you, and you look thirty not forty-six. Hell, Sarah looks twenty, not thirty."

"You're so sweet," Sarah said.

"Plus," Angela said leaning forward, "our bookie is in great shape, rugged good looks and owns his own business."

"I am a cop," Erin said, "he's a bookie."

"I'm a cop," Sarah said, "and I've fantasized about nailing God's Bookie and getting him to roll his eyeballs back in his head."

Angela said, "So have I."

Chapter 4

Five Outcast Priests

Two other priests stationed at Saint Jude's entered the saloon. Monsignor Mulheye, sixty, and Friar Tuck, fifty-five, were, like Mario, Hillman and Lewis, dressed in the robes of priesthood.

San Francisco's Archbishop Dooley had dumped four of his rotten apples into one impoverished parish. The fifth, Friar Tuck, was not a lay priest, but a former Trappist — an Order that took a vow of silence. He had been given the boot from the monastery for talking too much and given a roof over his head by the priests at Saint Jude's. As a gesture of camaraderie to his fellow priests, the monk wore a cassock rather than the brown robes of a monastic.

Erin noticed Father Hillman ordering two double Beefeaters straight up and thought, *they usually don't drink.*

She once again sauntered to the restroom and managed to pick up another snippet of conversation. From Father Lewis she heard, "Spin."

Erin washed her hands. As she returned to the bar she saw Friar Tuck and Monsignor Mulheye seated in the rear booth. The monk was sobbing; Mulheye's face stricken. She realized that, because they both loved animals, they must be consoling each other over the events at the zoo.

There was no direct link, at least not one Erin was aware of, between the five priests and the tragedy at the zoo. But it was obvious that, with the exception of Father Mario, four priests were affected.

She watched as Friar Tuck went to the God's Bookie blackboard and studied it for a moment. From his black cassock he withdrew a small aspersorium, a vessel for holding holy water, removed a tiny, delicate brush, dipped the bristles into the vessel and sprinkled holy water on the blackboard.

Erin thought, *welcome to the Dark Ages.*

Max examined the betting slips he'd taken in the previous half hour. He went to the blackboard and wrote: Pot = 245 bucks.

Erin's brother Paddy called out to the clientele, "Have you heard about the tiger?"

Late comers admitted they hadn't heard the details.

Paddy stood, waited for the crowd to stop talking, and said, "Out at the zoo a tiger escaped its *supposed* inescapable confinement. To figure out what happened one has to think like a tiger. The animal has unbelievable hunting ability. When ready to attack the instincts of uncountable millennia take over. This is a predator who likes to strike from behind, using claws to rip the frail throat from a prey. Imagine, just imagine being born in the wilds of Siberia."

Father Mario said, "The tiger was born in San Diego."

Paddy continued, "No matter where the tiger was born, her instincts aren't lost just because she was a cub in a zoo, her instincts are to hunt and kill. At the San Francisco Zoo there's a Big Cat Grotto that contains four large outside enclosures labeled A, B, C and D. Her home was grotto C."

Erin watched her brother's face. Normally shallow, flaccid, dead, but once a story began to unfold, once the bottomless bullshit began, it became animated. The regulars of the bar allowed him unfettered access to their undivided attention, mainly because when he finished he would buy the house a round.

Paddy said, "The human smell the tiger sensed was not the stench all cowards feel as it oozes out of the pores of their quivering flesh, betraying the trembling and nauseating cowardice they try to shamefully hide.

"No, those prey who came each day to the edge of the zoo's Grotto C felt no fear as they where protected from an animal's lust for blood by a deep dry moat." Paddy paused, then roared, "But this tiger was free, free—"

"Show some respect," Father Mario called, "a kid was killed."

Unfazed, Paddy continued. "Let's move to that teenager's point of view. He's with a friend. Suddenly, for whatever reason, the tiger's no longer contained, it's loose. Imagine being that teenage boy. I've stood in front of the big cat grottos. I've heard the incredible roar of those wild beasts. The back of my hair went up. My throat constricted. My heart palpitated. My mind flooded with dread. And I was on the safe side of the moat.

"Imagine no separation between you and a tiger and possible death in an instant from joyously rampaging fangs and claws. Yet this teenager acted to save his friend. He's as brave as any soldier who threw himself on a live grenade to protect his comrades. He deserves the highest medal this land can give."

Paddy paused, searching for inspiration, then added in a booming voice, "He was swept into Heaven on the wings of our Maker's loving angels."

Father Mario asked, "What if the kid wasn't in the State of Grace?"

Paddy's face blanched, then the white flushed into a blotched combination of reds and purples as he shouted, "Fuck you, Mario."

Chapter 5

President Donald J. Trump

Max's main function, besides booking bets and pouring monstrously large yet cheap drinks, was crowd control. His patrons allowed Max to rule with an iron fist because expulsion meant the economic reality of either drinking at home or spending at least twice as much per drink anywhere else in town.

After Paddy yelled "Fuck you," Max said softly, "Mario, enough interrupting. Finish your story, Paddy."

Paddy's tale ended with, "The tiger was shot by a policeman and fell to the pavement. A police captain drew his revolver, carefully approached the fallen, yet still breathing creature of God's limitless imagination, and, placing the muzzle of his weapon behind the quivering left ear, delivered a lethal death blow."

No bar patron spoke for ten seconds.

Paddy bought all a drink.

In an attempt to get rid of the awful image of an animal being slaughtered with a coup de grace to the brain, the bar crowd began talking about the upcoming football playoffs or President Trump's latest outrageous statement.

Erin knew each priest's position on Trump.

Hillman and Lewis, financial members of the top tier, cared not a whit about a vow of poverty as secular priests did not take one. The two priests were 100% for The Donald and that juicy drop in corporate tax. They felt no conflict with the position of the firm of Hillman & Lewis LLC versus Jesus' comment to render unto Caesar that which is Caesar's because they knew far better than the government on what to do with their money.

Before the 2016 election, Monsignor Mulheye had been a solid fan of Bernie Sanders and had pled with people who misunderstood the difference between a Nationalist Socialist, aka Nazi, and a Social Democrat, aka one who believes in mailmen/librarians/Social Security etc.

Father Mario had kept his own counsel about the contentious president.

Erin knew what Friar Tuck thought, even though he never vocalized an opinion. He had a talent for using a brush to create images that spoke more than a thousand words.

The police had tired of wasting their time arresting the monk for violating the graffiti laws of The City because if they had continued to enforce them on the monk they would have had to arrest, under the Fourteenth Amendment's equal-under-the-law's concept, hundreds of Hispanic/artist teenagers in the Mission.

Especially since Friar Tuck, after the immigration flap and the separation of kids from parents, meandered over to Saint Patrick's on Mission Street and drew the stricken faces of one hundred Hispanic children on the sidewalk in front of the church. The monk had then drawn on the steps leading to the church entrance the faces of horrified parents, arms outstretched. On the second riser from the top step he had penned, "What you do to the least of My brethren you do unto Me."

On the top riser was: POTUS, you will be reminded of those words once you face your Maker."

Chapter 6

A Sexual Eruption on Hold

Erin asked Angela, "Do you have plans for Christmas dinner?"

"You bet," the old lady said, "sexual plans."

"You telling me you're sexually active?"

"Remember the gardener I use every three months to mow the lawn?"

"You mean the six-by-eight-foot, burned-out pathetic example of a lawn in front of our place?"

"That's not all the old fart's servicing. Having *him* for Christmas dinner."

"Our *gardener*! How old is he?"

"Eighty-five."

Homicide Captain Fitzgerald, standing behind the two women, interrupted with, "Eighty-five and he gets it up?"

"Fitz, he can't get it up," Angela answered, "we only cuddle. I think about my dead husband when I'm holding the gardener. What I like is the resurrection of memories in my dreams."

"Dreams?"

"Hot, hot, hot. My husband was a randy old fart. I could walk into the kitchen wearing a garbage bag and he'd start drooling."

Erin noticed Friar Tuck and Monsignor Mulheye leaving the saloon.

Angela continued, "I love cuddling and thinking of my love. In my dreams I am no longer an old lady, but a young, flirtatious girl who tries to catch the eye of a handsome Italian man. He talks to me and I pretend I am not interested, but my body yearns for him with intense, white-hot aching interest. I want him to overwhelm me, to ravish me."

Erin, feeling empty, ordered a vodka martini.

Pointing at the glass of liquor, Captain Fitzgerald asked, "Aren't you on duty tomorrow?"

"So?"

"An easy case might come up I could assign you to, you being someone with no experience at all at murder investigation. I'd think you'd want a clear head."

"Right now I want a *blurred* head."

Angela told Fitzgerald to bug off, waited until he had moved down the bar, then said, "Erin, are you suggesting you're not sparking some cop down in the property room? You must crave captivating some man?"

"I've been sexually inactive for about six years, since my divorce."

"Six years? Six years! I pity the poor guy who unleashes the sexual fire broiling inside you waiting to erupt."

Chapter 7

The First Amendment

Erin told Angela she needed some air and walked outside. She noticed a large crowd across the street and wandered over. The throng contained members of the media from local newspapers and television stations.

Monsignor Mulheye ordered the crowd to stay back.

Friar Tuck was on his knees drawing a sidewalk painting. A few tiny angels were on the edge of the drawing, some dancing, some playing instruments like flutes or harps. Under the cherubs the monk entered the words: "The First Amendment guarantees a free press."

Monsignor Mulheye held up a piece of paper and said, "Members of the media, as you know Friar Tuck does not speak; I will read his words. Trump is denying credentials to members of the media who won't let him get away with his countless lies. I denounce the president and his ongoing deceit by burning this symbol of the country of my birth, which I once fought and killed for. My right to burn this flag is guaranteed by the Supreme Court."

Friar Tuck removed an American flag from a bag, bundled the Stars and Stripes into a ball, and then poured a can of lighter fluid over the cloth.

Television cameras rolled as the monk reached into the bag again and withdrew spray cans. Methodically walking around his sidewalk creation he sprayed into the air a wild concoction of swirling and intermingled colors of red, white and blue, much of it ending up on his black cassock.

He dropped the three cans, raised his arms towards the sky, removed a lighter from his cassock, snapped a flame and tossed it on the American Flag.

A breeze swept out of the surrounding trees and caught the billowing smoke causing it to swirl about the monk. The flag lit with an explosion of blazing colors that swarmed with convulsions of smoke that all danced together like a tango of violent, vivid shades of red and blue that clashed with equally angry wraiths of the fog's swirling smoky whitish grays.

Friar Tuck stared heavenward with arms outstretched embracing the heavens.

Erin walked over to Monsignor Mulheye and said, "Thought he was going to ignite himself."

"He's a mystic, not a fanatic," the monsignor said.

"What's this about killing for his country? I thought he's been a religious since young."

"His first calling was as chaplain attached to the U.S. First Armored Division during Desert Storm. He was there during the battle for Medina Ridge — largest tank battle in America's history."

"That's when he killed?"

"No. After that fight, this in March of ninety-one, there was a cease fire in the Gulf War. But then an insurgency broke out called Sha'aban Intifada. The Iraq army, the Republican Guard and the MEK faced off against the SCRI/Bada, Dawa and the Peshmerga. This was Arab against Arab — with all religions in the region involved. Two hundred thousand died in five weeks. The rebels were put down and Saddam Hussein went nuts creating a bloodbath against all rebels."

"I vaguely remember this," Erin said.

"Have you seen the movie *Three Kings*?"

"Yes, big fan of George Clooney."

"Remember the scene where the Iraqi soldier executes a woman?"

"I do. Brutal."

"That's what set the monk off. He saw a Republican Guard shoot a mother and baby. Should have given Last Rites to the fallen, instead, picked up a dead soldier's weapon and went bonkers. Killed s couple of dozen soldiers. They didn't fight back because Saddam had ordered no attacks on the U.S. during the ceasefire. They ran and Friar Tuck chased them down like dogs."

"My God."

"A Biblical bloodbath. Because he was a priest he was not court-martialed, just dishonorably discharged. He suffered from Gulf War Syndrome but was unable to talk about his war experiences. A friend suggested he join a Trappist monastery. He was fine for awhile, then suddenly couldn't stop talking about all the men he killed. That's when he was asked to leave the monastery."

"And ended up at Saint Jude's. I've heard Archbishop Dooley is tight-fisted. Why did—"

"The law firm of Hillman and Lewis pay the monk's salary. They are the ones who really protect Friar Tuck."

Chapter 8

The Second Disaster = I am Padre Pio

The commotion at the Stanyan Street entrance to Golden Gate Park ended after Friar Tuck sank to his knees, rolled on his side and shrank into the fetal position.

The media, knowing when a show was over, left.

Erin, Monsignor Mulheye and Friar Tuck returned to the saloon. She joined Angela. The monk and Monsignor Mulheye went to the rear and joined Fathers Lewis, Hillman and Mario.

***

There was one man inside the Triple M Saloon who never mentally referred to himself by his given name. When he was young his grandfather died and his grandmother came to live with his family. She was religious: daily Mass, daily communion, daily rosary. She constantly told him that he would become a priest, an officer in the ranks of the soldiers of Christ.

When he brought home friends from school his grandmother called him names like, "My sweet darling," or "My gentle boy." He told her she was embarrassing him and she said she would think of a nickname.

She told him of an Italian priest who had become a canonized saint. Padre

Pio's extraordinary abilities included spiritual insight and the stigmata: bleeding from the hands, feet and side replicating the five wounds of Christ.

His grandmother told him, "From now on I will call you Padre Pio." She stayed true to her word right up until the day she died while he was in his second year at the seminary.

Her constant referral of him as Padre Pio became entrenched in his mind. So much so that he began to refer to himself in his thoughts as Padre Pio, sometimes in third person, sometimes in first.

About him people were talking about the tiger attack about how did the animal get out and why did it attack the two victims.

He thought, *the tiger wasn't driven by hunger. Those animals were fed every day at two in the afternoon. The mauling happened a few hours later.*

He knew animals act in a certain way, programmed into their natures. No rabbit ever slashed the throat of a prey. A tiger did not hunt unless hungry, or when in search of food for its young, or when teaching its babies to hunt. None of those applied to the death at the zoo.

He remembered reading how excited the zoo personnel were when they tried to get Natasha pregnant. He had gone to the zoo to watch.

Tony the Tiger was relentless; Natasha equally enjoying the sexual romp. Tony and Natasha put on a physically monumental show combined with the sound of the lustful roaring of frenzied animals in heat.

It was a savage copulation to watch.

It was a violent copulation to watch.

And it was a wonderfully moving copulation to watch.

Animals, Padre Pio thought, *cannot sin.*

The tiger Natasha was four-years-old, barely an adult, and now her life was snuffed out. Why? Because of the negligence of humans who created an artificial cage that could not correctly hold the incredible beast within.

Chapter 9

A Drunk's Torment

The Triple M Saloon emptied out by ten, only customers left were the five priests, Paddy, his sister Erin, Angela, Max and the night bartender Charlie.

Erin watched Father Mario kill his drink and order another. She said, "You should slow down. Never seen you even tipsy before."

Father Mario said, "A couple of hours ago I had to tell one of the parishioners of Saint Jude's that her grandson was mauled to death by a tiger. How do you console someone for that? God's will? Shit happens? Que sera sera? Suck it up?"

"Sorry," Erin said, "I didn't know."

The swinging front door's crashed open and a disheveled man lurched to the bar. His slurred words hissed, "Son of a bitch; where the hell am I?"

Charlie recoiled from breath fetid with the stench of garlic and liquor floating across the bar top. He said, "You're in the Triple M Saloon."

"Gimme a shot of whiskey."

"You've had enough."

"Never enough." The drunk stared about the bar. "What the hell is this? A religious convention?"

"Do you need a cab?"

"I need to confess."

Charlie waved at the five priests huddled at the other end of the bar. "Take your pick." The clerics, all in their cups, started to head toward the bathroom.

The drunk pointed at one of the priests and hollered, "Need to confess."

As that is a request no priest can deny, the chosen priest led the drunk to the rear booth.

The man yelled, "Been a long time, forget what I'm supposed to do."

"How long since your last confession?"

"Haven't a clue."

Max ordered Charlie to raise the volume on the television.

Angela asked, "What are you doing?"

"Drowning out the guy's confession."

"Turn the TV off," the old lady said, "I want to hear this."

The drunk bellowed, "Thinkin' 'bout killing myself."

"Why?" the priest and Angela asked.

"Daughter died."

The priest said, "I'm sorry. I know—"

"You don't know shit," the drunk sobbed. "Virgin like you never had a child, never loved a child, never lost a child."

"Amen to that," Angela said.

The priest choked on the awful combination of sickening smells coming at him. He held a corner of his purple stole over his mouth and nose.

The drunk yelled, "My daughter ODed on meth supplied by that SOB she shacked up with. If I find the bastard, I'll slit his throat."

"Murder is *the* most serious offense against—"

"All I think 'bout's revenge."

"Revenge is—"

"Fuck you!" snarled the man and staggered out of the bar, leaving a lingering foul air, a mixture of cheap bourbon, stale garlic and blistering rage.

Chapter 10

The Third Disaster = Death by a Lake

Monday, December 23, 2019 , Ten Minutes after Midnight

Padre Pio stumbled into his humble room. The air was stifling. He changed clothes, then staggered a few blocks to Stanyan Street.

Above him the night sky was clear, stars dazzling.

At the western end of Haight Street, where it abuts Stanyan Street, there is a double staircase leading to a horseshoe-shaped pathway surrounding a small meadow. Nestled in a thick grove of trees was Golden Gate Park's Alvord Lake. Shaped like a run-amok amoeba, it sent out watery fingers into groves of trees. Four paths came at the lake from the main points of the compass, and each was illuminated by lampposts.

Padre Pio went to the lake's edge and splashed water on his feverish face. He sat on a nearby wooden bench,

A young boy walked towards him. There was no adult with the child.

Padre Pio stood and called, "Are you lost?"

"No."

Padre Pio noticed that across the lake a strange glow was pulsating in the darkness of a pedestrian tunnel.

He asked, "How old are you?"

"Ten."

"I can help you find your parents."

"My parents are drunk."

Padre Pio thought, *is this really happening? Or am I dreaming? Or having the DT's?* He asked, "I can help you get wherever you're going."

"Gimme five bucks for a cab."

A vision appeared in Padre Pio's mind. *This boy's soul's already lost. Drunken, uncaring parents. Panhandling. The kid will start stealing, unless he already has. Candy, then more and more expensive items. Cars by the time he's sixteen. Armed robbery by eighteen. Prison. Sodomy. Released. Rape, more robbery, and then murder.*

"Five bucks. You're a priest. You're supposed to help people."

Padre Pio noticed that the pulsating fiery glow in the tunnel had disappeared.

Did I imagine the flame? Like a keyhole to Hell. Am I imagining the boy?

The boy said. "What's a lousy five bucks to *you?*"

"I don't have five dollars."

The boy pointed. "Look at the drunken priest, he pissed himself."

"Shut up!"

"Shove this up your ass." The boy raised his right hand and extended his middle finger, thrusting his arm skyward.

Padre Pio swept an arm out, sending the boy sprawling.

The boy screamed, "I'm suing your ass off!"

Padre Pio grabbed the boy by the shoulders.

"Help, he's touching my pee pee!"

What? What!

He shoved the boy, sending him tumbling to the ground.

Padre Pio's right hand found the child's throat and squeezed. His left hand blocked the boy's arms as they flailed about. The child's fingers snagged Padre Pio's Roman collar and tore it away. That white, horseshoe-shaped symbolic badge of religious authority fell to the concrete and rolled unnoticed under a bench.

Padre Pio let the boy go.

The child shouted, "Fuck you!"

Padre Pio punched the small face. The boy flopped backward, hit his head on the bench, rolled sideways and slumped to the ground. A pool of blood spread out, a crimson river flowing from a deep gash to his skull.

Padre Pio's breath came in ragged puffs, exploding into the dead air. He cradled the broken body in his arms and went to the edge of the lake. He sat down and splashed water on the boy's face.

No movement.

He stood, spilling the body into the water. One of the boy's tennis shoes had fallen off during the struggle. He absentmindedly picked it up and wandered from the lake.

What just happened?

Was that a dream?

A hallucination?

Or did I accidentally kill a child?

Chapter 11

"You're an Idiot"

In Erin's bedroom was a large birdcage containing a scarlet macaw. She had named the parrot De De because it only spoke that one word. The bird was flightless; she never closed the cage door. The pet would sleep inside the cage but spent the rest of its time hopping around the apartment.

Each morning the parrot, at quarter to five, would jump on the window-sill and screech its name over and over.

Erin slid out of bed, slipped on a jogging outfit and made herself a power protein drink.

Her home, a one-bedroom, one-bath unit, exemplified minimalism. After her divorce six years earlier she decided to shun obtaining things. Her combination front room/kitchen had a small sofa, a tiny TV, a stereo and two plants. In the bedroom she had a queen-sized bed, an end table and small reading lamp.

Her front room windows faced Golden Gate Park's west end parking lot, Kezar Stadium and the Park Police Station.

On a living room wall were four Monet prints: *Morning on the Seine; A Cart on the Snow Covered Road; Tree in Flower near Vetheui,* and *Springtime at Giverny.*

In her bedroom was one more Monet, an oil of his wife Camille with child. Each morning after her run, while getting ready to shower, she would look at the tranquil setting of a mother knitting with a small girl at her feet and think, *I could have had that and tossed it away.*

In her bathroom, taped on each side of the mirror, were a dozen small photos of her landlady Angela doing something outrageous, like at a Baptismal Fount grinning while filling a hipflask with Holy Water.

Her phone rang. She listened, and then dashed downstairs.

Erin arrived at Alvord Lake.

Paddy pointed at a small, body on a bench.

"Why did you call me instead of 911?" she asked.

He shrugged.

"Paddy, didn't you learn anything as a cop?"

"I—"

"Ever heard of 911?"

"I thought—"

"I called Park Station. The lab and uniforms are on their way. Did you move anything?"

"I moved the body."

"Crap, you moved the body? Did you touch anything else?"

"No."

"Which path did you use to enter the area?"

"The pedestrian tunnel under Kezar Drive."

"You hit the Triple M every morning. The tunnel's in the opposite direction."

"I arrived at the bar too early. I took a walk."

"When did you find the body?"

"Six, just before I called you."

"To sum up: you entered the water, put the body on the bench and phoned me?"

"Yes."

"You're an idiot."

Chapter 12

Material Witness Report

Erin led her brother to a nearby picnic table, sat down, and took a tape recorder from her briefcase. She said, "While we're waiting for the uniforms, forensic and lab teams to show up, I want you to explain what happened this morning. What you saw, what your heard and what you did. Understand? A material witness statement, no Paddy bullshit exaggerations."

He nodded as he took the tape recorder from Erin. He waited for her to return to the crime scene. Once alone, he spoke into the tape recorder:

"I was a peace officer for thirty years. After spending three years in traffic control, I spent twenty-seven years riding a horse in Golden Gate Park telling teenagers to go somewhere private to make love, telling winos to sleep under the bridge instead of under the stars, and watching the park's flowers blossom.

"My sister is a homicide inspector. When I found the body I phoned her.

"I woke up this morning and rummaged around the refrigerator, vainly looking for a bottle of vodka.

"No vodka. Triple M time. I left my apartment.

"I stopped in front of the saloon. Not open yet. I stared at a garbage can crammed with the refuge of the bar's business: broken shards, cigarette butts, soggy napkins. One orchid, colors faded but glorious considering its surroundings, rested on an empty can of tomatoes juice. The bright, butter color and clean white column gleams among the blackish coffee grounds along with squeezed and already rotting green limes.

"There is just enough of a crack in the swinging front doors of the Triple M to peek inside. I squinted through the opening at the wall clock. I received the horrifying message that it was five a.m., not six.

"An hour to kill before relief arrived. I decided to walk. I ambled up Kezar Drive. Through the mist I saw the vague outline of the Conservatory of Flowers, a building spun from a spider's web of delicate latticework, strips of wood and glass, and its cupola, like an ornate wedding cake, thrusting into the dark sky.

"I walked through a tunnel and stood beside Alvord Lake. I come here often. Trees and natural ground cover gave visual protection from the surrounding streets. At night, when traffic dies down, the lake could have been in the tranquility of a giant preserve instead of in the center of a major city.

"I saw the neon sign of the pub go on. I circled the lake and saw a small body lying in the shallow water. The concrete sides of the artificial lake were slippery with moss. I fell in. Cold water cascaded over my arms and face as I grabbed at the body.

"I placed the body on the bench and headed for the Triple M. Why I thought I had to call my sister instead of central dispatch is beyond me. My only excuse is that I had a hangover that would disable an ordinary man. Once in the bar, I borrowed the house phone and called Erin.

"She's now directing uniforms to seal off the crime scene. She looks like hell. Her hair's mussed, tangled in knots. She has on her jogging gear. I always thought of her as an attractive woman. At the age of forty-six she still has a shapely body, with high cheekbones and devilish, twinkling eyes.

"Except now she just looks really pissed."

Chapter 13

To Lead or Not to Lead?

A police officer said to Erin, "Lab and photographer are waiting for you. And Captain Fitzgerald just arrived and is waiting for you by the bench."

"Any ID on the victim yet?" Erin asked.

"I called to see if Park Station received any missing person's reports last night. They had none. They're checking with the other precincts now."

Erin went to the bench.

Captain Fitzgerald bent over the corpse and began a running commentary, talking into a tape recorder: "Body's face down, right profile visible. There are bruises on the throat. Left arm under torso. Legs fully extended, mouth open with the tip of the tongue protruding. No tearing on the clothes. The boy is wearing a plaid shirt, Levi's, white sweat socks and one tennis shoe. The clothes on the victim are damp. That is because Paddy, who found the victim, moved the body from the lake to the bench."

Erin asked, "Are you taking this case?"

"You got the call, not me."

She noticed two reporters behind the yellow police tape. She had called in the crime on a hard-line phone. Paddy used a hard-line at the Triple M. No call went out over a police radio.

How did reporters find out?

She went over to the waiting media and asked.

"Captain Fitzgerald, as a courtesy, phoned us."

Of course, have to have media here in case I screw up.

Erin said to the crime scene photographer, "I want at least six photos of the body from different vantage points. I want shots of the surrounding area, the paths and the pedestrian tunnel, and an overall of everything."

She examined the mouth of the victim and felt a knot form in her stomach. Even before seeing the marks on the neck, she knew this was not an accidental drowning. There was no white foam at the lips and nose that forms from gas in the windpipe and other air passages during drowning.

Captain Fitzgerald asked, "Any word from the coroner's office?"

"They can't get anyone here yet, working on minimum staff because of Christmas week. And there's been a drive-by shooting with multiple deaths."

"With the body in a full state of rigor mortis, what kind of estimate of time can you make?"

"Normally it takes around sixteen hours for the entire body to become involved. This water is awfully cold, so rigor could have come on at a faster rate. An educated guess is between eight and midnight last night."

A police officer said, "Five children have been reported missing since last night, the youngest fifteen. They're checking on the day before."

"Erin," Fitz asked, "does this dead kid look fifteen to you?"

"Years younger."

"What do you think happened?"

"There are grooves and abrasions on the neck that were caused by one hand. I assume the other hand was used to block the thrashing of the arms and legs of the victim. But, from the amount of blood by the bench and the vicious gash on the back of the head, it's obvious he hit his head on the bench and bled to death."

She touched the neck of the child. "Lividity confirms the original estimate. This happened last night, between eight and near or just after midnight. Postmortem lividity is advanced. Pressure doesn't produce blanching."

Captain Fitzgerald asked, "Where did you learn about lividity?"

"From one of your books. I've read them all." *Plus,* she thought, *you learn a hell of a lot in a hurry when you walk in on someone you love and the blood is settling throughout their body.*

"Then you know you should start a quadrant search of the area."

"You *are* officially assigning me this case?"

"Let me call Brendan." Using his cell phone, he contacted the deputy police chief and explained the situation.

Captain Fitzgerald listened, then disconnected. "The boss said, unless you feel some conflict of interest over your brother's participation in this, and also the potential he might be the perp, then Brendan will let you lead. Your call."

"I'll lead."

Chapter 14

A Dangerous Case

Erin asked, "Captain, you actually think Paddy might have done this?

"Many times the person who reports the body is the killer."

"The body was in rigor when Paddy found it. The boy was dead hours before he came on the scene."

"Unless Paddy did it last night, and, worrying, came back this morning to find the body and report it to throw suspicion from himself. And I don't like his showing up at the Triple M an hour earlier than usual."

"Why not?"

"Anything out of the ordinary raises suspicions. People are creatures of habit. Paddy broke his routine this morning."

Erin's voice raised a notch. "Paddy? You can't be serious."

Captain Fitzgerald pointed and said, "My, oh my, what do we have here?" He knelt by the bench and, using a tweezers, lifted a Roman collar. He held it up in front of Erin and grinned.

She knew from the gleam in Fitz's eyes that the Roman collar was *potentially* his ticket to rid homicide of the uppity female who had dared to taint the pure male domain of his homicide department.

Erin was not the first female homicide detective, but Fitz had managed to drive every one of them into other departments.

Fitz was such a fixture, achieved by skill, insight, brilliant detective work and longevity, that he always took the sensational cases. Let the other grunts in homicide handle the wife who shoved a butcher knife into her old man's throat because he complained the pot roast was overcooked. Let some other flunky handle the drug war that led to the killing of three unknown immigrants, aka drug mules, sans green cards, passports or visas.

He liked the limelight from a crime with no risk, like the tiger mauling. He had a nose for cases that stayed on the front pages of the *Chronicle*.

She said, "There's no connection between that collar and the dead kid."

"Yet."

She thought, *Fitzgerald mentioned Paddy breaking his routine last night. But so did five priests.*

Hillman and Lewis' norm was to play poker from around four until seven and then leave. Monsignor Mulheye and Friar Tuck rarely came into the saloon, and, when they did, usually had ice tea or, if a drink, rarely more than one. Last night all five were blitzed.

I know because I didn't leave until nearly ten. Paddy was so upset about the teenager getting mauled by the tiger that it took me hours to calm him down. When I left, all five priests were drunk. All acted out of the norm. None of them have stayed that late or drank that much in the past.

Should I ask Fitz for help?

She knew Captain Fitzgerald's record. Every cop in homicide knew. An average of forty on-site homicides a year for twenty-one years meant he had been in charge of over eight hundred murder investigations. Toss in another four hundred or so he had assisted on, like this kid case, and he had been involved in over twelve hundred murder cases.

In his book on crime-scene investigation he had stressed over and over: Nothing can replace the crime scene once it has been disturbed and always concentrate of the "why" of a crime.

Paddy disturbed the crime scene. The why of this crime might end up linked to the Roman collar. If so, the scenario changes into a dangerous case.

Chapter 15

The Fourth Disaster = A Devastating Clue

Erin figured Fitz didn't actually believe a priest killed the kid. But what if? Talk about a lose-lose situation. The last thing she wanted was to handle a case that ended up with tossing some deranged priest into the legal system, followed by endless appeals and a languishing embarrassment to everyone.

Archbishop Dooley wouldn't like it. The mayor wouldn't like it. The police chief wouldn't like it. Catholics in the police department and general public wouldn't like it. *No one* would like it.

A kid killing's a nightmare for a detective. Couple it with Holy Mother Church and the nightmare became living reality.

Which is why Fitz's wearing a smile that's wicked.

Erin had watched him in action. He knew the press. She figured he had already realized the media would go bananas over her, a reasonably good-looking, blue-eyed twist. With high cheekbones and a dead hero policeman father, killed in the line of duty. What copy.

If they only knew the truth about Dad's gruesome death it'd make for even more sensational copy.

Erin instructed a lab technician to tag-and-bag the Roman collar.

Captain Fitzgerald said, "Not so fast, lass. You're not as familiar with the inner workings of the archdiocese as I am. Archbishop Dooley's favorite saying is, 'Take care of the pennies and the dollars will take care of themselves.' Our religious leader believes in central purchasing. Every article used or needed by a priest comes from a central warehouse. And every item that went out had, somewhere on it, as a matter of inventory control, a stamp with the name of the parish and its purchase order number."

He held up the collar. Stamped on the inside in small, precise letters was SAINT JUDE 1189rc. He pointed, "The rc stands for Roman Collar."

Erin said, "Last night all five priests were right across the street. All five had opportunity. But that collar could have been lost earlier in the evening and have nothing to do with this death."

"Maybe, maybe not. Not one priest has an alibi for any of the others."

"Captain, how do you know that?"

"I called Charlie, last night's bartender, while you conducted the quadrant search. All five priests left the saloon last night at different times and all near midnight. He mentioned your brother left around the same time."

Erin thought, *Paddy kill a kid? Paddy's not a doer, he's a recorder.*

She knew getting him to turn off the fire hose nozzle of his bursting imagination was impossible. Bad enough most witnesses, even those with the imagination contained in a head of cabbage, had trouble remembering things accurately. And essential to any murder investigation was accuracy.

I have real worries about Paddy that have nothing to do with this case. Christmas Eve is coming and with it the resurrection of the horrible memories involved with Dad., Each year Paddy gets more and more withdrawn.

I have to be more understanding and gentler with him.

Chapter 16

Who, What, When, Why?

Erin walked to the picnic table, picked the tape recorder and listened to Paddy's statement.

"For fuck's sake, an orchid?" she said. "Who cares that you saw a friggin' orchid this morning? I need a witness statement *period*. Who, what, when, where and, if you know something, the why. Nothing else."

"I was trying for thoroughness."

"Forget thorough, be precise."

Shit, Erin thought, *swearing at Paddy's not exactly gentle or understanding.*

She opened her briefcase and removed a notebook and pen. "Please Paddy, this is important. Write down what's applicable to this case. Just who, what, when, where and why."

She rejoined Fitzgerald.

Paddy wrote: What? Dead boy. Who? A Roman collar.

He glanced down at the crime scene. Captain Fitzgerald was by the bench looking at the body.

Paddy scribbled: I hate that guy. His nickname is Fitz the Fuck.

My sister's pissed. Fitz is grinning like an Irish barkeep at the close of day on Saint Pat's. Whatever I'd done in phoning her, instead of 911, isn't going to be good for her.

I don't understand what all the fuss is about over the Roman collar. I figure a priest had a heat-on last night and lost his collar.

Right now there's a glint in Fitz's eyes that would make me fold a full house. I think I know what's going on. He's dumping this case, a kid killing, with all its terrible ramifications, the press, the TV, the Catholic Church and the pressure to produce, into Erin's lap.

The evil S.O.B. couldn't get around Affirmative Action to keep Erin out of homicide. Instead, he's going to use the death of this kid.

Erin's eyes changed with the light and her emotions. The day we buried our dad was overcast, with the kind of fog San Francisco gets in the summer. Her eyes looked like a forest fern shimmering with dew on a wet morning. The day she married that asshole cop who shit all over her for years, her eyes shone like they were drenched in champagne.

Now her eyes are lit up like they're on fire. I know the look. It's her *I'm angry, I'm pissed, I'm getting fucked look.*

And it's Fitz's fault.

Paddy wrote in block letters, I HATE THAT EVIL ASSHOLE.

Chapter 17

Fitz the Fuck

Fitzgerald walked over to the picnic table and purred in a thick Irish brogue, "Great to see you again, Paddy."

"Not great to see *you*."

"Is that any way to treat the grand friend who landed you your cushy job in the park so many years ago? Plus who pulled your family name out of the muck and mire of scandal?"

Paddy shifted uncomfortably on the park bench. He did owe Fitzgerald favors, one being saving his life. Three years after joining the force Paddy was directing traffic in the Financial District. Two gunmen robbed the Bank of America. They ran out into the street and discovered that their driver had panicked and driven off with their getaway car. Paddy pulled his gun, but couldn't fire. They would have drilled him if Fitz hadn't of screeched up in a squad car and shot both of them.

After the incident, Fitz went to bat for Paddy with the police chief explaining it was not only a hazard to Paddy's health, but every other cop on the thin blue line to keep him a patrolman. He finagled a transfer to the mounted patrol in Golden Gate Park, a job Paddy had stayed on until retirement.

Captain Fitzgerald glanced at the last thing Paddy had written and said, "*I hate that evil asshole*? I assume you mean me."

"Yes. What do you want?"

"You found a wee body. Did thirty years of police service ever transfer the knowledge of what that means?"

"Nope, never worked a homicide."

"Any good homicide detective knows half the time the bum who reports the crime is the criminal."

"What?"

"Or did you think I'd swallow the Roman collar you planted by the bench?"

"What?"

"A Catholic lad like yourself trying to throw suspicion on a religious."

"I know why Erin's pissed and you've been preening and prancing. You're going to smear my sister by crapping over *me*. Think I'm guilty, read me my rights and arrest me."

"Ah now, you must have learned some police procedure while you were clopping about the park on that grand stallion. I can't throw your lazy Irish ass in custody. Not yet, anyway. But I'm keeping me eye on you as I amass the facts and clues that will bring you to justice."

Captain Fitzgerald raised his voice to the level of an evangelist and delivered his oration towards the two reporters standing behind the yellow police tape. "You ought to be ashamed of yourself, you, the brother of a prominent homicide inspector. Poor Erin straddled with a bum for a brother. Watch your backside, lad, it has my eyeballs glued to your shoulder blades."

The head of homicide walked a few paces, then shouted, "Paddy, I know where to find you when I want. Now get the hell out of here."

Paddy headed toward the Triple M Saloon, entered and said to Max, "I've wondered for years about Fitzgerald's nickname. I'm now personally finding out why he's called Fitz the Fuck."

Chapter 18

Accident, Manslaughter or Murder?

Erin stood by the yellow police tape and studied the scene.

What happened? Either the boy and killer knew each other or else they met by accident.

She asked the lab tech if he had gotten prints from the dead boy.

"Yes. To get prints from the boy, because of the submersion in water, I had to inject paraffin under the skin to smooth out the surface."

"Have you dusted the Roman collar?"

"Only found one print on the collar. Matches the forefinger of the dead kid."

"One print?"

"Yep."

She faced Fitzgerald. "Why only one print? Why isn't there a print from the person who wore the collar? But the print does affirm whoever was wearing the collar was with the kid. The youngster must have snagged it during the struggle and whoever was wearing it didn't notice."

Captain Fitzgerald said, "That makes it mighty short odds that one of the five priests at Saint Jude's killed the kid."

She said, "That fingerprint proves Paddy's innocent."

"Maybe."

"Maybe?" Erin said as her face flushed. "That fingerprint proves whoever was wearing that Roman collar was with the kid."

"What should be bothering you is why toss the body in the lake? Visualize the scene, recreate, become the killer."

"Killer fights with the kid," Erin said. "It appears the kid was shoved, fell backwards, hit head and bled to death. Meaning this might have been an accident. But why pick the kid up, move ten feet, and toss the body into the shallow lake?"

"Think, Erin, think."

"Not to hide the body. Lake's not deep enough."

"Then what's another possible explanation?"

"Unless the perp thought the boy was still alive and carried him to the water to try to revive him."

"What can be inferred from the body left in the lake?"

"Killer splashes water in an attempt to revive. Showing remorse. Then just dumps the body? A heartless, callous act. Dumping the kid doesn't make sense if the reason for going to the lake was to revive. Puzzling."

"What else?"

"The missing tennis shoe. This was a *kid*, apparently lost in the middle of the night. Maybe his shoe fell off somewhere else?"

"Visualize what the kid was doing," Fitzgerald said.

"Why was the kid in the park in the first place? This is a young boy; nine, ten. There's no evidence in the surrounding area of the boy being dragged here. No evidence of a struggle anywhere except by the bench."

"Meaning?"

"Two scenarios: If they knew each other they arrived together. Or, the killer and the boy did *not* know each other and met accidentally by the lake. That makes more sense, but then no motive. If they came together, they knew each other and the motive could be anything."

"What's your gut telling you?" Fitzgerald asked.

"They met accidentally and got into an argument. Adult grabs kid's throat, the abrasions on neck. Adult lets him go, then pushes kid, who hits his head on the bench and bleeds out. Adult tries to revive. No luck. Adult leaves. If this is correct, then no premeditation, but an accident is still out because of the initial confrontation. That would leave manslaughter, but not murder."

"Voluntary or involuntary?"

"Voluntary is defined as either in the heat of passion, in self defense, or sudden quarrel. Neither of the first two appears to apply here. But the last does: during a sudden quarrel."

Captain Fitzgerald said. "In some criminal cases everything that is obvious is just that: obvious. In others everything that is obvious ends up convoluted beyond belief. Keep an open mind. Wait until you have as much information as possible. The autopsy might prove this *was* murder."

"How?" Erin asked.

"The abrasions on the neck. If, while throttling the lad, the perp broke the kid's hyoid bone, and then the kid fell back, hit his head, and died that would be considered by a prosecutor to file a charge of murder."

Chapter 19

Music to Sooth a Troubled Brain

Padre Pio tried to think of a happy song, something to alleviate the dread in his heart. Part of his personality manifested itself in the songs he heard in his mind. The lyrics in his head were not *a cappella,* they were accompanied by a symphonic orchestra, complete with strings, woodwinds, percussion and brass.

He knew the old High Mass, with its wonderful music and Latin verse, was rarely heard anymore. Churches were now filled with the music of guitars played by teenagers who only knew three chords. No more did *Credo in unum Deum* fill those in attendance with awe and inspiration.

Not only religious chants filled his mind, however. Love songs also reverberated inside his skull.

Padre Pio would sit inside the Triple M Saloon and listen to people argue, watch hatred in their eyes, feel the disgust sweating out of their pores and in his mind would peal, "We kiss in the shadows, afraid to be seen."

Sometimes, while sitting at the bar staring at his drink, the strains of Beethoven's *Moonlight Sonata* soothed his thoughts. Or Handel or Ravel or Brahmas or The Beatles or U-2 or Hip Hop. No matter. As long as the music filled its resonance between his ears, he was content.

He knew the world he lived in was artificial, but didn't care because he also knew it was a world he had created as a defense against the real world — the terrible, suffering hatred and putrid, rancid venom of what usually constituted personal relationships.

His musical library covered a range including such diversity as, "I love you for sentimental reasons," to "Sash me and momma you die."

But the music playing most in his head was the music he had grown up with. In the ruined remains of his brain rambled the notes of some of the greatest composers who ever lived. Franz Schubert battled with Frederick Chopin for best top ten on the chart in his mind.

Every so often the brawl erupted over any logical chronological realm and, when that happened, he might hear Elvis Presley's guitar in a dueling battle with Itshak Perlman's violin, or Amadeus Mozart fighting a piano duel with Victor Borge. Those battles by musical giants could, when he heard people argue, help smother the vitriolic verbal excrescence.

But now the battle was with himself.

A boy was dead.

He remembered nothing from last night — alcoholic blackout. Except when he woke up he discovered he had lost a Roman collar. Even more damning was the small, red tennis shoe he found on the floor of his small room. He had tossed it into his closet.

That red tennis shoe had triggered a flash of memory: a child falling backward, slamming his head against a bench, then an oozing stream of blood and lifeless unseeing eyes.

He knew all too well how efficient the cops could be, especially when a case riled them. And the death of a child always riled them.

Padre Pio wondered, *how long before I see an accusing finger*?

Chapter 20

Lividity in Action

Erin watched the CSI do their job gathering evidence and thought, *just like a CSI team had done after my Dad died.*

Her father had been, like Paddy, a horse patrolman — his exclusive beat the zoo, helping with internal security and bolstering public relations with the patrons; especially young children.

Erin remembered.

Decades ago, on Christmas Eve, a year after her mom died of cancer, she had stopped by her dad's house for a visit. The drapes were drawn, lights off.

She phoned Paddy, "What time did Dad leave work?"

"Never came to work. I figured he was feeling so down about the anniversary of Mom's death he decided to stay home."

She said, "Get over to Dad's house ASAP."

Erin found her father in the master bedroom. He was on the bed in full uniform, chin tilted back, mouth open, back of his head gone, brain bits and skull fragments spread all over the pillows.

She sat on the edge of the bed, held his hand and watched the blood settle throughout his body, blanching the upper, discoloring the lower — lividity in action.

She phoned Fitzgerald.

Fitzgerald had stood at the end of the bed and said, "This can't happen, not to this man. His kindness over years to those who visited the zoo made him one of the police department's best public relations figures."

Following his orders, she and Paddy carried their father's body to Fitzgerald's automobile.

Fitzgerald told them he would take it from there. They were to meticulously clean the master bedroom and they were to say nothing, "Not to a friend, not to each other, not to a priest. Forever. Understand?"

They had both nodded, too much in shock to argue.

She learned the next morning her dad was found at the rear of the parking lot behind the San Francisco Irish Cultural Center near the zoo.

Fitzgerald took command of the investigation. After a grueling and thorough investigation — which never actually took place — he told the press that a great policeman had been slain in the line of duty. The hero who died had learned a gang was selling heroin near the zoo. He personally tried to stop this outrage by attempting to lure the two heads of the organization into a trap. It failed and he gave his life because of his dedication. And then the killers had dumped the body, *dumped*, in a parking lot. The department would not rest until the perpetrators of this heinous crime were brought to justice.

She remembered asking Fitzgerald why he chose that spot. He answered, "The body needed to be dumped because forensics wouldn't add up if I tried to make it look like your dad died where his body was found."

"Why next to the Irish Cultural Center?"

"Always a huge amount of people involved when a cop gets murdered. I thought, while I was at it, I'd throw some business to the Center's bar and restaurant."

Two weeks later a shootout resulted in a cop seriously wounded and two drug dealers killed. Fitzgerald announced conclusive evidence had been found. A bullet from one of the dead men's gun matched the one found in hero's brain.

Erin had told Fitzgerald, "You can't be serious."

"I'm deadly serious, lass. I know as well as you do those two bastards didn't execute your dad. He took care of the formality himself. I do know, however, these two assholes murdered an entire Columbian family, a rival bunch. The kids, ages four and seven, who were slaughtered weren't part of the family business. I also know I was never going to prove it, at least not in a way that would stand up in court. So I hang a murder on them that they didn't do. So what?"

"It's against the law."

"How perceptive you are."

"I can't let you—"

"You mean you and your brother are going to come forward and admit to participating in covering up a suicide? That's fraud, first degree felony if I remember my criminal codes correctly, which I always do."

"But—"

"But nothing. Besides, we need someone complicit and punished in your dad's death. Otherwise the criminal elements might get excited and think they can get away with killing policemen."

Chapter 21

The Media

Captain Fitzgerald took Erin by the elbow and led her away from the steward and lab techs. "You see those two fellows standing behind the yellow tape? Do you know what fucks up most cases? The media. They romanticize, they fantasize, they do just about any fuckin' 'ize' it takes to sell papers or attract viewers to the five o'clock news."

"*You* phoned them."

"I called them when I thought this was just a kid killing, before I knew about the dead kid's fingerprint on the inside of a Roman collar."

"You called the press to screw me over."

"Ah, you *are* indeed insightfully fuckin' perceptive. But now you need assistance. This is delicate, what with the almost certainty a cleric is involved."

"You don't think I can handle interrogating a priest?"

"What an attitude you have. Chip on the shoulder. Belligerent. First off you don't interrogate, you interview. The boys in the press know the difference, I can assure you. Unless you know beyond a shadow of a doubt the person's guilty, and you can prove it in a court of law, you call what you're doing *interviewing* a witness."

She nodded.

"I'm going to go over there to diffuse the situation, and buy you time. Get on with your crime scene investigation."

Captain Fitzgerald walked over to the two reporters. "Appears the poor lad slipped, hit his head on yonder bench, staggered to the edge of the lake, became unconscious, rolled into the water and drowned. 'Tis a pity."

"What about keeping an eye on Erin's brother?"

"Just having a wee bit of fun at the lass's expense, but nothing to it."

He sent them on their way saying, "Do you think if there was anything more to this case, a kid dying, and the front-page potential involving lads like you, I'd assign it to a rookie homicide detective? A *female* rookie homicide detective?"

Chapter 22

How to Don a Roman Collar

Erin asked the lab technician, "Is there any evidence of sexual assault?" The man shook his head. "There are defensive wounds; the kid fought back. If there was an attempted sexual—"

"Look around," Captain Fitzgerald interrupted. "This is not the preying grounds of a pedophile. Too much light. Too many paths for a pedestrian to unexpectedly arrive. The autopsy, I'm positive, will not reveal any signs sex was part of this crime."

Erin drew a hand across her throat, signaling the CSI to pack it in.

Captain Fitzgerald asked, "Your thoughts?"

"Why haven't this kid's parents reported him missing? If the boy was older I wouldn't place such emphasis on it, but this is a youngster. This is indicative."

"You think the parents might have done it?"

"I said indicative, but of what? Uncaring parents or homicidal parents?"

Captain Fitzgerald glanced at his watch. "I'm calling the corner's office. I want the autopsy done today. I'll let you know when. Take a break for an hour."

She nodded.

"Go home. Shower. Put on something appropriately professional. I'll pick you up at the saloon. Hold Paddy's hand, he's probably traumatized."

"At ten the autopsy?"

"No, later. At ten we'll go to the Chancellery Office."

"*We'll* go to the Chancery Office? I repeat, is this your case or my case?"

"Your case, which is why I want you with me. But I'll handle that prick

Archbishop Dooley."

"Prick?"

"Yes, and make that fuckin' prick. I explain later."

As Erin jogged home she thought, *last night I was with all five priests in the saloon. All five were drunk.*

She realized whatever had affected those priests last night could lead to depression, which could lead to drinking, which fueled anger.

Being sad, depressed and drunk were not mitigating and extenuating circumstances for manslaughter.

She entered her flat, had a quick shower and then thought about what she should wear. She decided on a Kasper Brown suit set. She buttoned the white blouse up to her throat, put on the jacket and looked in the mirror.

Perfect, she thought. *Modest, professional. I'm meeting the archbishop,* can't be sporting a plunging neckline and tantalizing cleavage.

Erin parked in front of the saloon, started to enter, then noticed a garbage container. She went over and looked inside. *Paddy's right,* she thought, *that orchid is in marvelous juxtaposition on its bed of trash.*

She snapped a photo with her Smartphone, entered the saloon, sat beside Father Mario and asked. "Where's Paddy?"

"Restroom," Mario said. "He told me what happened across the street."

"I told him to keep his mouth shut."

"That's like asking Rush Limbaugh the same thing. Impossible."

She asked him to show her how he donned his Roman collar.

Father Mario demonstrated, using only the tips of his fingernails, explaining, "This prevents soiling the white."

"I've noticed most priests rarely go anywhere wearing cassocks; why do you guys at Saint Jude's always wear them?"

"We're mavericks. When the rest of the clerics go one way, we go the other way. There's camaraderie at Saint Jude's, a fellowship of outcasts."

Chapter 23

The Rebel Parish of Saint Jude's

Erin asked, "What's life like at Saint Jude's?"

"Do you know the history of my parish?"

She shook her head.

"The parish house, or, as we priests call it, the rectory, is about fifty yards away from Saint Jude's. The church and rectory were financed by five miners who hit it rich during the Gold Rush. Behind the altar, in the sacristy, there's a staircase giving access to the basement and a crypt."

"What's a sacristy?"

"A room behind the altar where vestments are kept and priests dress for services. It was once one huge room, but a few years ago was divided in half — one room for the clergy, one for the laity assistants, separated by a bathroom."

"Was the parish house built at the same time as the church?"

"Yes, the rectory was originally an old folk's home for the five gold miners. Back then, the pastor's home was located in the sacristy. But after the last surviving miner died and was buried in the church's crypt, the priest moved out of the sacristy and into the parish house. Upstairs, five bedrooms, each with a private bath; downstairs, a foyer, two consulting rooms on the right, a common area to the left, with kitchen and dining facilities behind. Off the kitchen's pantry is a staircase to the basement area."

"Housekeeper? Cook?"

"We had a full-time housekeeper awhile ago, but she left us. Now we have a woman come in once a week to clean. As far as food, Hillman and Lewis always eat out. Friar Tuck eats at the soup kitchen. Monsignor

Mulheye loves to cook. I join him sometimes, but usually get something delivered here to the saloon."

"I read in the paper that there's a shortage of priests. It's so bad that some pastors serve two parishes. Yet Saint Jude's has—"

He held up his hand to stop her. "Our leader Dooley may have an accountant's brain, but his thirst for vengeance needs to be quenched as bad as President Trump's. Dooley wouldn't dare spread us five mavericks out among his Diocese. Better to lump us all in one place."

"Understood," she said.

"There's a truce now. We at Saint Jude's do what we choose and the Archbishop usually ignores us except for an occasional empty threat. The parish is so small and parishioners so old, his Eminence figures our contamination level is at a minimum."

"You're pariahs."

"No, rebels."

Chapter 24

Slingshots and Ball Bearings

By mid-morning a large crowd had gathered at the Triple M Saloon. Having just gone off-duty from working overtime, police who had secured the crime scene across the street, along with most of the forensic and lab teams, were in the bar. In addition, so were all five Saint Jude priests, Erin, Paddy and Max.

Erin punched in a number on her cell and asked Sarah to meet her at 5:30 that evening at the saloon.

Sarah said, "Great, love that dump."

Erin disconnected and glanced at where the five priests were huddled in a booth. All were drinking black coffee or green tea. She thought, *all nursing monumental hangovers.*

On the saloon's television local news came on. The anchor said, "Today, in *The New York Post*, an unnamed source stated ball bearings were found in the tiger grotto at the San Francisco Zoo and slingshots were found in the car belonging to the two men along with a bag of marijuana and a half-filled bottle of vodka."

Angry bar patrons muttered things like, "That mauled dead kid got what he deserved," or, "Prison's too good for the one that lived."

Erin called out, "Something doesn't make sense. Don't rush to conclusions."

Paddy said in a loud voice, "Erin's wrong, this answers the question of why the tiger picked that moment to escape from its enclosure."

"Dear sweet Mary, mother of God," Father Mario moaned, "here we go again."

Undeterred, Paddy continued, "Picture the situation. Two males, ages seventeen and twenty-one, go to the zoo. They sit in their car in the parking lot and smoke a joint. They drink warm vodka. Their brain functions are slightly fucked up. But they're young, resilient. They enter the zoo and past the Serengeti with its zebras and giraffes."

Paddy waved at the gathering of patrons around him. "You have to think like the tiger, not the kids. The tiger's name was, hmmm...?"

"Natasha," Erin reminded him.

"Ah, yes, Natasha. The Siberian was four years old. Bred in captivity. But once a tiger, always a tiger. Imagine being that magnificent killing machine."

Chapter 25

Natasha Fights Back

Natasha dozed.

She had never stalked the freezing timbered wastelands of Siberia, never roamed a vast wilderness staking out her domain with claw marks on trees, looking for a mate, nursing infant cubs.

From birth she padded about the confines of her cell in San Diego, then padded a similar confinement in San Francisco in an area masquerading as her natural habitat: scrubs, bushes, concrete rocks, concrete walls, and dry moat — all trying to mask she was in prison.

Her fangs never ripped a throat; her claws never slashed a prey. Her mind never knew the joy of the hunt, pursuer and pursued, heart pounding, beating faster and faster, closing in on a prey fleeing in terror.

Day in and day out, week in and week out, month in and month out, she ate a slab of dead horsemeat served precisely, without fail, at two in the afternoon.

In sleep her mind was filled with visions of satisfied bloodlust. She could sense the victim's heartbeat, each throb coming faster, with fear overriding all as Natasha closed in for a death lunge.

She hungered, but the hunger was in her mind and heart. She hungered, not because her belly was empty, but for the fulfillment of what she was. Her hunger came from emptiness far beyond any need for nourishment.

She eyed with a wishful, bloodthirsty longing the humans who arrived every day and, from a protected distance, waved and flashed bright lights and gawked and called meaningless sounds to her.

Back and forth she paced. To and fro. Pacing, pacing. Without purpose.

Trapped.

Two hundred and forty-three pounds — young, healthy, fearless -- trapped.

Endless days of nothing to do.

Endless nights with nothing to do.

Wait for dead meat to be served? *Served*! Then eat the lifeless flesh and drink the tepid water.

She longed for the slash her extended claws could deliver, carving flesh, then joy sinking fangs into a quivering neck. Followed by the taste of fresh, hot blood washed down from a stream's cold, clear rushing water.

A breeze formed over the nearby edge of the Pacific Ocean and wafted across the Great Highway, sloughed through the entrance of the zoo, meandered through the artificially recreated savannah and headed toward the big cats' compound.

The scent of two humans, including the smell of blood pumping excitedly in their bodies, filled Natasha's nostrils. The smell triggered her saliva glands, firing off red-hot signals: blood, alive, prey.

Suddenly, pain. Sharp. On a rib.

Another pain, left hind leg.

Natasha glanced wildly about. Where? Where? Where?

More pain, right shoulder.

Shapes. On the wall. Beyond reach.

Noise — like a hyena's high-pitched cackle.

Natasha backed frantically to the rear of her artificial enclosure. She saw two males at the rail above the wall.

Movement... round... shiny... arcing...

Move!

Something clanked on the concrete floor. Another missile arced toward her. Pain. Noise. Pain. Laughter.

Enraged, she bolted forward, flew over the edge of the plateau and landed amidst the undergrowth cluttering the moat floor. She moved with eons of inbred stealth, edging closer and closer to the moat's wall. Once there, she launched upward toward the source of her agony, shattering the air with a growl that grew into a gigantic, primeval, ravenous, voracious, outraged roar.

She hit near the top of the wall and dug her claws into the aging concrete, found purchase, and thrust herself upward, turning a somersault in the process.

She faced her tormentors.

"And that," Paddy said, "is why Natasha became pissed enough to escape her escape-proof cage."

Captain Fitzgerald walked into the saloon.

Erin asked, "Paddy, why would the boys go back to their car to get rid of the slingshots? Shouldn't the slingshots have been found next to the dead kid?"

"Besides," Captain Fitzgerald added, "no ball bearings were found in Grotto C. Whoever was the spin doctor on this one should be working for the Trump White House."

Patrons began moving away from Paddy, some divvying up the newspaper, while others went down the bar a safe distance from the Kipling wannabe.

Erin patted her brother's shoulder. "Grand story, well told."

"And," Paddy said, "sadly full of crap."

Chapter 26

New God's Bookie Pool

Erin watched her brother walk to the rear and sit in alone the last booth. *I worry about him so much. He worked with Dad out at the zoo for years. He was somewhat happy back then, or as happy as he has ever been. He's been alone for so long.*

He was so handsome in high school. The gals flocked like bees to honey. He dated them all. Then he changed completely. Withdrawn, a loner. Back then gregarious, now? Only when he tells a story.

I have to watch him closely. The closer we get to Christmas Eve the more depressed he gets. If he ever kills himself it will be my fault.

Angela walked into the bar, slammed a ten on the plank and said, "Coffee, black."

Max nodded.

The old lady asked, "What's this world coming to? Kid killed almost on my doorstep."

"Your flat's three blocks away," Erin said, "not exactly on your doorstep."

"Not safe for kids or old ladies anymore."

Erin stifled a laugh. "A couple of weeks ago you shot some poor guy in the face with wasp spray."

"Much better range than pepper spray or a stun gun. You have to get too close to use those things, but a full can of wasp spray? Range at least twenty feet."

"The guy wasn't a mugger."

"He looked like a mugger. Better safe than sorry."

"I repeat. He wasn't a mugger."

"What part of better safe than sorry do you not understand?"

"He could sue you."

Angela shrugged. "I'd say a wasp just stung me. I was trying to make sure it wouldn't again. The guy got in the way of the battle."

"You'd lie under oath?"

"Doesn't everybody?" Angela sipped her coffee. "Paddy told me there was a Roman collar found next to the dead kid."

Goddamn my loose-mouthed brother.

"Priests as killers," Angela said, "what a world."

"You're acting like five Roman collars were found across the street."

"Where there's smoke, there's fire."

News came on the television. Swirling around Congress's looming impeachment, the media managed to segue into President Trump's problems involving women in his life, like the porn star Stormy Daniels, were being reviewed. As usual, the Access Hollywood clip involving Trump bragging about how he could just walk up to a woman and grope her privates because he was a star was played.

Friar Tuck slammed his fist on the bar top. He opened his satchel and took out a can of black spray paint. The former Trappist went to the rear wall and sprayed, "Donald Trump. This disgrace shall no longer be known as POTUS. Because of his outrageous behavior towards women I rename him PATASS."

Captain Fitzgerald said, "Max, just heard a law firm in Walnut Creek has been hired to represent the boy the tiger killed."

Max said, "No one had ten o'clock. Erin, you had eleven o'clock so you've won $585 — less $58.50 for the S.P.C.A."

Max retrieved his stepladder. He went to the blackboard and erased the last pool. He stood studying the empty expanse of the blackboard. He wrote: "Who does the lost Roman collar belong to? Monsignor Mulheye 5 to 1; Father Mario 5 to 1; Father Hillman 5 to 1; Father Lewis 5 to 1; Friar Tuck 5 to 1. Vigorish: 10% to CFF."

Angela asked, "Max, what's CFF?"

"Compassionate Friends Foundation is a nonprofit, volunteer-based organization committed to providing emergency support to families in crisis after the death of a young child from any cause."

"I am familiar with CFF," Father Mario said, "They meet at the Taraval Police Station. Very worthy of help."

Father Hillman bet a hundred on Father Lewis, who did the same thing in reverse.

Mario tossed a ten on the bar. "Friar Tuck."

A few minutes later, Max went back to the blackboard and changed the odds to reflect the wagering: "Monsignor Mulheye 14 to 1; Father Mario 3 to 1; Father Hillman 4 to 1; Father Lewis 4 to 1; Friar Tuck 2 to 1. Pool total: $1,575.00."

Max said, "If it takes a while before we find out whom that collar belongs to, this could end up a monster pool. If there's no winner, I'm refunding half of everybody's money. The other half will go to CFF."

Father Mario said, "Comforting to see at least a few people think some other priest could be the killer besides yours truly."

Angela bet fifty dollars on Mario.

"Angela," Father Mario said, "you think I'm the murderer?"

"You bet your holy black britches I do." She grinned. "Well, maybe not, but it's worth fifty bucks just in case."

Max said, "The pool's not on *who* killed the kid, rather on which priest *lost* his collar."

Chapter 27

A Decent Bookie

Erin said, "Captain Fitzgerald, what possible motive is there for killing that child? None of the seven deadly sins seem to apply. Lust's out, no forensic evidence. Greed? Kid had no money. Envy? Of what? Gluttony, sloth, pride? But there must be a motive."

"Maybe wrath," the head of homicide said.

"At a kid?"

"Opportunity, means and motive are the cornerstones of solving and later proving a crime. Means here is easy: hands to attempt to strangle, then used to shove the victim causing him to hit his skull against the edge of a wooden bench. Opportunity's also easy: Last night all five priests were sitting in the Triple M Saloon within a hundred yards of the murder site. We may not learn the motive until the perp is caught, but wrath's as good a guess as any."

Fitzgerald glanced at this watch. "We have to leave in ten minutes and go to the Chancellery office."

Erin decided to have a quick talk with the priests.

She corralled Father Lewis and said, "I have to ask you some questions about last night."

"Talk to my lawyer."

"Who is?"

"Father Hillman."

She asked Father Hillman if she could question Lewis. Hillman said, "Got an arrest warrant?"

"No."

"He will not talk to you."

"Will you talk to me?"

Hillman answered, "Talk to my lawyer."

"Whom I assume is Father Lewis."

"You assume correctly."

"And I further assume he will advise you not to talk."

"Of course, unless you have a warrant."

Erin said, "I feel like I'm caught on a Mobius Strip."

"A Mobius Strip or Band is what good lawyers try to accomplish on cross-examination — leading people in un-orientable circles."

"For maximum confusion," she said, "When the news about the tiger escaping came out, you and Father Lewis seemed upset."

"The definition on upset in unhappy. I might have been unhappy at the news of a tiger mauling someone."

"The definition of upset is also disappointed or worried. Neither of which would apply to the news involving the tiger."

"Which is why I used the word unhappy," the priest said, "rather than disappointed or worried."

"I overheard several snippets of conversation between you and Father Lewis. Words like 'disastrous' and 'spin.' Curious to what they refer to."

"Eavesdropping may not be a crime, but it is certainly rude," Father Hillman said as he excused himself and joined Lewis.

He's hiding something, Erin realized. *Or if not certainly obfuscating.*

She cornered Mulheye. "Monsignor, when did you leave here last night?"

"Around midnight."

"Did you walk back with one of the other priests?"

"No, alone. We may live under the same roof, but we lead solitary lives."

"Meaning?"

"Meaning we observe each others space. Last night I did not head directly for the rectory, I walked to Oak Street and then took a stroll through the Panhandle."

When she asked Friar Tuck what he had done when he left the saloon last night, he shrugged and went to the Men's Room.

She asked Father Mario.

"I drank more than usual," the priest answered. "Telling a grandma her grandkid is dead by lethal tiger mauling can lead to severe overindulgence. When I left here I was a bit confused and headed down Stanyan instead of up Haight. I went up to Cole and headed north. I vaguely remember meeting Paddy in front of his apartment building. Then I somehow managed to get back to the rectory and pass out. That help?"

"Can't seem to learn anything concrete."

"Maybe you should ask Max."

"Why? He doesn't know anything."

"I meant ask him to dinner."

"What?"

"Everyone needs someone, even you."

"He's a bookie."

"Hardly a Class A felony. And you're in homicide now, not Vice."

"Angela suggested the same thing to me."

"She's a smart old lady."

"I've too much on my plate right now to start dating."

"File it away for consideration in the future," Father Mario said, "You could do far worse. I personally know Max's a decent guy."

"Is there such a thing as a decent *bookie*?"

"Yes, the unusual man who's also known as God's Bookie."

Chapter 28

More on an Unusual Bookie

"Back to work," Erin said, "when did you leave here last night?"

Father Mario answered, "I left here right before midnight."

"Who else was here?"

"Paddy left right before me. Around midnight. I do remember arguing with my fellow inmates of Saint Jude's."

"Which ones left before you?'

"Erin, I was well in my cups or 'liquored up,' as your brother likes to phrase it. We all left within a few minutes of each other. I vaguely recall I was the last to exit."

"But you don't for sure remember?"

"I doubt if any of us remember clearly. We started mixing our drinks. We ended up drinking stingers. I do recall we were all upset about the kid killed by the tiger. I remember we had a spiritual conversation, which you civilians might call as a 'get-in-your-face' theological argument about God seemingly not caring about those born in his image."

"What side did you take?"

"I'm sure the others went on about freewill, which means I'd have attacked with what bull freewill is — once a sophist, always a sophist."

"Wouldn't your life be easier if you just conformed?"

Max, eavesdropping, interrupted, "Conform? Mario? Did *Christ* conform?"

Erin blurted, "When did you become an advocate of non-conformity regarding religion?"

Max answered, "Since I was kicked out of a monastery."

"*You*? A monastery? Why?"

"My dad owned a bar," Max said. "I used to run the football pools for him. I entered the Order of the Brothers of Mary. The pope died. I ran a pool on who the new pope would be."

"Monks take a vow of poverty. What was the cost of the ticket?"

"A half pint of milk. All they gave us teenagers was a lousy half pint of milk each day. Back then I could polish off a half pint with one Oreo cookie."

"Focus," Erin said, "Max, the pool on the pope."

"Back then there were eighty-seven cardinals, so I sold tickets for each one. The dean of discipline found out I charged a twenty percent vig instead of the normal ten percent. He kicked me out. I learned great lessons that made me a better bookie. Like don't make book in a monastery and think you're going to clear a profit."

Captain Fitzgerald said, "Erin, our religious leader Dooley awaits."

"In a second," Erin said, "Max, you said lessons. What else was learned?"

"Treat everyone honestly, even if they screw you. If they screw you, never book another bet with them."

"Bravo," Mario said. "No broken arms, legs, no bullet to the head. Max, the sensitive and unusual bookie."

Chapter 29

Archbishop Dooley

Erin slid into Captain Fitzgerald's car and asked, "Why does the Chancellery office insist on such accuracy for something as inexpensive as a Roman collar?"

"The Chancellery office doesn't insist on it, Dooley does. Altar boys have a tendency to lift them. They're small, not like stealing a cassock, and they're symbolic."

"What are we trying to accomplish this morning?"

"First you need background on Dooley. For starters, I always call him Your Eminence."

"He's an archbishop, not a cardinal."

"You're correct. I give him a verbal promotion because it fans his ego. He dreams of getting the red hat. A dream that's impossible because of his past."

"Why?"

"It's a wise thing to know something bad about the person you need something from."

"Enough with the suspense. What's so bad in Dooley's background?"

"He's from the old country. The same way blacks and Hispanics try to use boxing to get out of the slum; Dooley saw the priesthood as a way out of Bogside, Belfast. Born in one of the poorest ghettoes in Ireland, Dooley realized early the only thing he'd get in life if he stayed in Bogside was a brick to his teeth."

"How old was he when he left?"

"Let me tell this my way. He was an altar boy by six. For years he cleaned the sacristy, scrubbed floors, shined windows and polished chalices. His campaign launched against his pastor had one goal and one goal only: A written request to allow him into the seminary in Dublin. He accomplished his goal and left years later, right on schedule. *His* schedule was two years short of ordination. Dooley's dream was to get to San Francisco and finish training in that rich diocese."

"I don't hear anything about Dooley thinking he had a vocation."

"You won't. His cost-accounting brain realized the advantage of offering a diocese an almost-trained seminarian. He shipped out as a cabin steward on the luxury liner *New Hope*, jumped ship in Nova Scotia and crossed into the United States illegally at Niagara Falls. The first train that came by was headed west and Dooley took it to San Francisco. He immediately presented himself at the Chancellery office, showed his transcript from Trinity College and was accepted at Saint Patrick's major seminary."

Captain Fitzgerald lips turned into a wry smile. "Figuratively speaking, Dooley's a wetback, literally an illegal. No green card. No passport. That's why he never visits Rome or any other place outside the United States. And you can't become a cardinal unless you go to Rome. And you can't go to Rome without a passport."

"Why has Dooley extended such rage towards the five priests at Saint Jude's?"

"He has thin skin regarding misappropriation of funds. Fifteen years ago, Father Hillman was treasurer of the diocese. He took monies from the church's coffers and invested by backing various attorney friends involved in contingency cases. They settle the case and get thirty-three percent or go to trial, win and get forty-five. Then those attorneys would pay a high interest fee to the church's savings account."

"Is that legal?"

"Yes, he *was* the treasurer. This worked fine until Hillman backed the wrong lawsuit — one an insurance company fought like it was WWIII. It sucked up so much money the banker called Dooley and asked him what was going on. No matter that there was finally a settlement and the funds returned with interest. Hillman was cast out, banished to Saint Jude's Parish for taking the risk."

"Friar Tuck?"

"He's at Saint Jude's courtesy of Hillman and Lewis, not Dooley."

"Father Lewis?"

"The archbishop hates unions. Construction and maintenance costs continually bleed his coffers. Father Lewis formed an organization called P.U.F.F., Priests of the United Financial Front, a union that demanded higher pay for clerics and got it — hence Dooley's wrath."

"Monsignor Mulheye?"

"He was once in charge of the diocese cemeteries. He made a mistake, a whopper, screwing up the burial of a couple of caskets that resulted in a lawsuit and got him cast him into San Francisco's secular version of purgatory."

"Mario?"

"Dooley must think Mario's the worst priest in the archdiocese because he's been at Saint Jude's the longest — twenty years. Back then he started marrying divorced Catholics and ended up at Saint Jude's. Ever since he's continued marrying divorced people."

Chapter 30

A Quid Pro Quo

They arrived at the Chancellery and were shown into the archbishop's office.

The room was opulent, done in deep maroon and gold colors.

Captain Fitzgerald said, "It's kind of you to see me without an appointment, Your *Eminence*."

"What can I do for you?" Dooley asked. The barked question was matched in tone by graying arched eyebrows hovering over hooded blue eyes.

Fitzgerald introduced Erin and filled the archbishop in on the tragic event that unfolded that morning in Golden Gate Park.

Dooley said, "You haven't told me what you want."

"How did a Roman collar end up under a bench next to a dead kid?"

Archbishop Dooley's eyes became slits. Only a tiny horizontal line of thunderously stormy sapphire peeked out. "You're not implying that—"

Captain Fitzgerald held up a hand, "Glory be, no. But still—"

"Maybe an altar boy?" the archbishop suggested.

"You mean pinched one out of the sacristy to play priest."

"You agree that there're other explanations for the collar being there."

"Miracles are possible, Your Eminence."

"Did you dust the collar for prints?"

"Yes. One print, the lad's," Captain Fitzgerald answered. "I have another problem. With the exception of Father Mario, who is a chaplain in the police department, I don't have fingerprints to compare on the priests."

"Compare with *what*? You said no other prints were found on the collar."

"The bench needs a complete analysis. It is now at the lab. Do you mind if I ask the other four Saint Jude's clerics for their cooperation?"

"Of course I mind. What if the press finds out? That Roman collar has certain possible, err..."

"Implications," Captain Fitzgerald completed. "Erin and I have kept the existence of the Roman collar to ourselves."

"That's a relief. The media can be cruelly exploitive in cases like this. No one reports on the tremendous volume of charity..."

Erin tuned out the commercial. The press hadn't found out yet. And, even though a lot of people currently drinking in the Triple M knew about the collar, they were priests and cops. The priests wouldn't say anything and the cops hated the media. Even so, the information on the Roman collar could be contained for awhile, but not for very long.

She watched Fitzgerald. He was not really listening to the archbishop either, but occasionally said, "That's wonderful, Your Eminence."

She knew he'd gotten what he wanted. The archbishop was informed and would not forget who informed him. The quid pro quo was the archbishop would look the other way when Fitzgerald surreptitiously obtained fingerprints off the priests.

They left the Chancellery.

"Autopsy at two this afternoon," Captain Fitzgerald reminded Erin. "Until then I want you to gather as much information on those five priests as possible. I'll drop you back at the saloon. They were all there when we left. I'll pick you up at a quarter to two. Then tomorrow morning, I—"

"Tomorrow's Christmas Eve. I usually spend the day with Paddy."

"Who gives a flying fuck what you usually do? You're in homicide now. Time is of the essence. Get ready to work your ass off."

Chapter 31

Preparing a Practical Joke

Captain Fitzgerald dropped Erin off and she entered the Triple M Saloon.

Angela said, "Erin, come with me. I need your help."

The two women went up the street to Saint Jude's. Angela said, "I want you to go to the top of the tower, the one on the right."

"Why?"

The old lady didn't answer. She removed from a large bag a small, black box, some paraphernalia and a flashlight.

Erin asked, "Flashlight? It's almost noon."

"Dark up there."

"I won't do this if it's sacrilegious."

"Just a practical joke to usher out the old year," Angela said and explained what she wanted Erin to do, then added, "There's a ladder under the first stairwell. I'll keep watch in the church, to make sure no one knows you're up there."

"How do I get into the stairwell?"

"The door's lock's been broken for years."

The two women entered the church. Erin slipped unnoticed into the right alcove, grabbed the stepladder and climbed the stairs. When she arrived at the top of the belfry she lit the small flashlight and turned it upward to seek the beam Angela told her about.

She was startled to see an immense face staring down at her from the dome above. It took her a moment to realize it was a portrait of the Cheshire Cat from *Alice in Wonderland*, except superimposed on the feline's face was that of Donald Trump. Underneath the face were the words: "Curioser and curioser, why does no one believe me?"

Erin followed Angela's instructions and, standing on the stepladder, rigged up the strange assortment of small electronics on top of one of the support beams. She made sure they were hidden in the shadows.

The last thing she did was run a wire on top of a beam to an air vent. She removed the air vent, clamped a device on the outside brace, and reinstalled the vent.

Erin returned to Angela and said, "I don't understand what you're doing."

"You will."

"When?"

Angela grinned, "Soon."

Erin asked, "Angela, have you been up there in the belfry?"

"Of course. Had to scout the place out. But no way could I climb a ladder."

"I meant the artwork."

"Sure, I've seen it, just more of Friar Tuck's rage getting vent."

"I keep stumbling over his artwork in strange places."

"Our local monastic mystic has his visions all over. Just last week a sewage worker told me he went into the — as he called it — fetid tombs to repair a broken electrical circuit. When he opened the electrical panel he was startled to see a tiny drawing of Donald Trump."

"Just that? An image of the president."

"No. Behind him was Putin holding a puppet master's strings attached to Trump's shoulders."

"Why place artwork where almost no one will see it?"

"Jesus did speak to the multitudes, but He also met with the few. I think it's Friar Tuck's way of emulating Christ."

Chapter 32

The Priests of Saint Jude's

Erin entered the saloon. Father Mario was sitting in the rear booth counseling a policeman. The other four priests were not there.

She wondered, *how much do I really know about the priests of Saint Jude's Parish?*

Her personal observations were limited to seeing them in the Triple M. She hadn't been a regular at church since before her divorce. Even when married, she wasn't a Sunday regular. Being beaten by a drunken cop/husband, and then told by some religiously rigid priest that she took a marriage vow so learn to live with the brutality, was not conducive to faithful observations to one's religion. But she did like the maverick priests who ran the smallest parish in The City.

Why the parish had such small attendance was the nearby Saint Ignatius Church and the University of San Francisco, only five blocks up the hill.

Saint Ignatius had a large number of Jesuits; all who needed to fulfill their priestly obligations, which meant non-stop access for sinners to Masses, confessions and anything else a believer needed.

Saint Jude's, on the other hand, with its five priests tending to essentially 105 old ladies and six equally old men, whose varicose-laden legs didn't allow them to hump up the few blocks to the competition, should have had an equal quality of religious services.

The problem was 111 parishioners can be handled easily by one priest. And the one who enjoyed doing it the most was Monsignor Mulheye. Four of the five priests had nothing to do.

They took turns every Sunday morning performing the only Mass at 9:15, the rest did their religious obligations, like reading the breviary, in the privacy of their rooms.

It had been a decade since the Baptismal Fount was used in a ceremony. There hadn't been a marriage performed in five years.

Erin knew baptisms and marriages were a source of revenue for parish priests. She had learned by observation how each priest at Saint Jude's subsidized his income.

Friar Tuck did not need financial subsistence. He spent most of his time down at Saint Anthony's soup kitchen helping Franciscans feed the hungry. If the monk could be labeled as having one of the seven deadly sins, it was sloth in regards to his religious obligations. He refused to perform any priestly function beyond the bare essentials required by the Canons.

Fathers Lewis and Hillman had an LLC partnership that took them to the Financial District every working day. Their sin was greed.

Monsignor Mulheye actually tried each week to visit ten or twelve of his ancient and crotchety old women who constituted the bulk of his flock. He also led the family rosary every Friday night, the "family" being a couple dozen old ladies and one old gentleman.

Mulheye didn't golf, rarely drank and didn't gamble. His sin was envy. When he was young he had envisioned a career taking him as high as cardinal, but now languished as monsignor.

Father Mario conducted outdoor marriages in Golden Gate Park between divorced Catholics. His sin was wrath towards the hierarchy.

None were overweight, so no gluttony.

All five priests did share the sin of pride, thinking their interpretation of the rules was correct and the Church's wrong.

But not lust, Erin thought, *or at least outward lust. Who knew what really went on in another person's mind?*

Puzzling, she thought. All five men were good-looking in their own individual way. Mario had Italian, olive-oil, unblemished skin. He was not the best-looking of the lot; Father Lewis was, and after him Hillman. Mulheye looked like a poster for a kindly grandfather. Friar Tuck looked like Grigon Efimovich Rasputin.

She noticed that Father Mario and the cop he was counseling were headed for the door. The policeman left; Mario took his usual bar stool in the corner.

Erin's Android vibrated. She listened, then disconnected and joined Father Mario. "Just learned a bicyclist came to Park Station," she said. "He'd read what happened in the paper. He said he saw the kid about a quarter to midnight. He asked the kid if he needed help and gets a 'Fuck you,' for his troubles."

Father Mario said, "Then the kid runs into a priest, says the same thing and that's supposed to drive a man of the cloth to homicide? If that was all it took, the world would have a lot fewer people."

Chapter 33

Padre Pio's Blackout Lifts

During the past hour snatches from the night before had started to flash like lightning bolts through Padre Pio's mind as he remembered: a strange pulsating glow in the darkened tunnel; the kid trying to borrow five bucks; the kid telling him to go fuck yourself; the kid accusing him of touching his pee pee.

He entered the Triple M Saloon and watched as Max changed TV stations and *A Christmas Carol*, starring Alistair Sim, started.

The barkeep said, "I love this movie."

Erin asked, "Have you seen the Netflix one starring Guy Pierce?"

"No," Max answered.

"Totally different take on Scrooge."

Max searched and the movie began.

After the scene where Scrooge's sister Fran comes to take her brother away from school ends, Max said, "Dear Lord, talk about dark, bleak and upsetting."

Padre Pio finished his drink, left the bar and went to Alvord Lake. He sat at the picnic table and stared at the rippling water.

I have to get that Goddamn, rotten scene I just watched out of my head. How could they change Dickens' story from Fran telling him their father had changed to Fran telling the schoolmaster she knows what he has been up to when alone with Scrooge at Christmas time?

That bastard teacher was molesting Scrooge.

I managed to dodge that bullet, but not by much. Ten years old and that fucking janitor asks me for help and then locks me in his office.

Never seen porn before. Never seen it since. I blindsided that fucker with his typewriter. Cold cocked him, then kicked him as hard as I could in his genitals. Threw up in his wastebasket, took his keys and left.

Waited four years before I told anyone and then pick Christmas day to tell my grandmother. I have never seen anyone cry so hard.

She embraced me and said, "We have to tell the authorities."

"He died last summer. Should I tell Mom? Or Dad?"

The look on her face was terror. "With their tempers? The janitor's dead; there's no reason."

Padre Pio chuckled. *Years later I did find his grave. I was drunk. angry, sad, but felt better after I pissed on his headstone.*

He slammed both fists on the picnic table and muttered, "Why did that fucking kid shout I was touching his pee pee?"

I never intended to hurt that kid, just tried to get him to shut up. God, I should never have shoved him. So much blood.

But it was an accident. The cops will claim manslaughter and probably voluntary manslaughter because I had my hand around his throat.

I was drunk, depressed.

Pretty lame mitigating and extenuating circumstances when balanced with a dead kid.

Except I did that foul-mouthed shit a favor. If he had grown to manhood he was destined for eternal hellfire.

Chapter 34

The Bank of Justice

"Father Mario," Erin asked, "have you ever been in the backroom poker parlor?"

"The buy-in's way out of my league."

"Something is bothering Lewis and Hillman. Need to learn as much about all you priests as I can."

"Can't help you," the priest said.

"I can," Max said. "There's no one back there right now." He handed her a card. On it was written: 666. He explained, "It's a key code."

"Six, six, six," Mario said, "is very symbolic as it's the devil's number. And what goes on in that poker room is certainly devilish."

Max led Erin to the rear, swiped the card, punched in the code and the door swung open. Lights automatically came on. There was a short hallway and another door.

Erin said, "Obviously Friar Tuck's been in this hallway."

On the left wall was a full pastel portrayal of a military parade, complete with soldiers goose-stepping, gigantic rockets on massive trucks rolling and large tanks with cannons lifted high in salute. On the right wall were the image of three sites easily identified as the Kremlin, the White House and the Vatican. On the balconies of two of those famous locations were images of Stalin and Mussolini. In front of the White House was Donald Trump, dressed in a diaper and holding a lollypop. Above him were the words, "Where's my parade?"

Max said, "A few of the poker players wanted me to repaint the hallway." He paused, grinned, and then added, "I lacquered over the art to preserve it." The bookie waved, "I'll leave you to it," and left.

She opened the second door.

The room was in the shape of an octagon. Dead center was an eight-sided green-felt poker table; above was a crystal chandelier. There were eight chairs, each made out of a different kind of wood. She recognized rosewood, teak and walnut, but some of the other variations were foreign to her.

The walls held five-foot high wainscoting made out of cherry wood. In addition to the entry there were three other doors.

Erin went to the door on her right and opened it. It was a bathroom. The floor's marble was from Carrara, Tuscany, the vanity countertops Cote de Paris granite.

The long cabinet holding the sinks was Fairmont in design and made out of Asian hardwoods. There were four washbasins, and each had a brass plate with a number on it running from one to four. Each Moen faucet had metal lever handles.

The metal was gold and Erin had no doubt that it was not plated gold.

There were no urinals, but there were four privacy stalls. She pushed open one of the doors; the toilet was freestanding. There was a small flat screen television on a side wall.

The bathroom was oddly shaped. She realized that the original space, before the poker room was built, had been a square. Creating an octagon poker room left spaces that had been filled leaving odd-shaped walls.

She left the bathroom and went to the next door. Inside were eight oak lockers. Each had a plate with a number on it.

There were no locks.

Search warrant? I'm alone. A kid died. Some rules I ought to be able to do an end-run. Why not just open each? Who'd know?

I'd know.

She turned, saw Max and said, "Didn't hear you come in."

"Wearing moccasins. Anyway, bravo. I know you were tempted to open the lockers. I'll do it; I do own them. The poker players decided the numbering should be by greatest wealth. Hillman's number one, Lewis number two."

She opened both lockers. Empty.

She arched an eyebrow at him.

"The gentlemen use these to hang up coats or raingear." Max pointed at a far wall. "However, behind that painting is a storage shelf."

He touched a light switch on and off rapidly and the painting slid open.

He thought, *Max revealed what was behind the painting, not me. No need for a warrant. Still can't touch anything.*

Max reached in and removed a map. It was a layout of the San Francisco Zoo.

"The *zoo*?" a puzzled Erin said.

"I've been overhearing a lot involving our city's animal haven and its involvement with the firm of H & L Enterprises LLC."

"I don't understand."

"Neither do I. Just that the zoo's map seems lately to hold more interest than a deck of cards."

"Who are the card players?"

"Eight men approached me a few years ago and asked me to convert this room, which was once a large stockroom, into what you see today."

Erin motioned, "What behind the fourth door?"

"Another bathroom, exactly like the other one."

"All this looks expensive."

"The eight men paid for the remodeling, and they pay a monthly rental—one thousand each. Ninety-six thousand a year to guarantee this room is exclusively theirs. These men are all lawyers: one's a tax attorney, another class action, banking, real estate, securities, torts, corporate law and criminal defense. Of course, all are involved in a wide variety of investments."

"Strange, but not illegal. But no prosecutor?"

"No money in it. Prosecutors are city employees. There is a vast amount of money involved with the men using this room every weekday late afternoon and early evening. And these guys overlap, getting involved in what another specializes in helping each other out. For instance, the tax attorney's top clients are the other seven guys. Or, say hypothetically, Hillman was guilty of the kid's death. He would write a check for a million and retain the criminal defense attorney."

"Birds of a feather flock together. Getting a feel for Hillman and Lewis."

"Those guys stay under the radar as far as the media. But as far as legal brainpower think billionaire lawyers like Joe Jamail Jr. and Richard Scruggs."

"When news came out about the tiger killing the teenager I heard Hillman use the word 'disastrous.'"

"That must refer to an investment. The tiger's killing of the kid adversely affected whatever those guys are up to involving the zoo."

She pointed at a business card stapled to the zoo's map. The card read: "The B of J." There was no email address, no phone, no person's name and no physical address.

Erin said, "A business card with no information? What's the point?"

"Not needed. If any person high in finance was handed that card he would know that the person delivering it was connected to the very apex of the law and wealth."

Erin asked, "Know what 'B of J' stands for?"

"Bank of Justice."

Chapter 35

An Avenging Angel

Erin turned on her Android, ran a search on the Bank of Justice and found nothing.Max said, "Not surprised. I accidentally found out it's a privately held entity, an investment bank, with a limited clientele."

"Eight lawyers, I'd bet."

"No bet."

Erin ran her hand over the wood of the poker table. There were slots on all eight sides of the table to hold a drink. There were also long slots to hold poker chips.

She said, "Fabulous looking."

"African hardwood from Mozambique. The legs are Blackwood from Panga Panga. The green felt is changed every month."

On the opposite wall from the entry door was a huge picture. It was obvious the scene involved the foot of the cross as the bottom of Jesus' feet were seen with a huge spike in them. Below were Roman soldiers casting dice on a red robe.

On the walls on ether side of the painting were enormous flat-screen televisions. Flanking the opposite walls were two more television screens.

Erin asked, "Why TV in a poker parlor?"

"When the men are here one is constantly turned on to whatever case is being aired on networks like Court TV. The others display tickertapes from New York, Tokyo and London. The men who exclusively use this room may all be attorneys, but they are also investors and venture capitalists."

"It's like a chapel in here."

"The chapel of the Midas Touch."

The Midas Touch, she thought, *how depressing. And depression can lead to anger and anger can lead to violence. All those emotions intensify if one is drunk. All five priests were drunk last night. Now it appears that Hillman and Lewis took some sort of massive financial hit involving the zoo.*

I also have find out why Mulheye and Friar Tuck were crying.

Erin returned to the bar. She asked Max for a warm-up on her coffee. Her Android vibrated. She had an email with contact information stating: CALLER I.D. BLOCKED. She opened the email and read: "Bitch. Drop out of the kid investigation and resign homicide or you're a dead cop. Hell awaits you. — An Avenging Angel"

Prank or real threat? And why?

More important, who?

Forget it. I used to get threats when I worked undercover in vice — mostly angry pimps pissed because I nailed them. Just angry vents.

People who want you dead rarely warn you in advance.

Chapter 36

Hate for the Blessed Mother

Erin asked, "Paddy, where did Friar Tuck go?"

"Just left," her brother said, "headed for the church."

Erin jogged up Haight Street and caught the monk at the church steps. She asked him to sit with her on a bench facing a life-sized Nativity scene. For a long five minutes she did not speak.

She knew she could only ask the religious yes or no questions. It was too much to expect an actual dialogue.

She asked, "I noticed last night, that when you were sitting in the rear booth with Monsignor Mulheye, you were crying. Are you all right?"

Friar Tuck nodded.

"Is the monsignor all right?"

He sobbed a soft, gentle sob.

"Are you depressed?"

Another nod.

"Are you angry?"

The monk pointed at the Nativity scene, shook his head and walked away.

Someone had drawn clown lips on the statue of the Blessed Mother — huge red slashes that turned down at the ends.

Taking tissue from her purse, she wiped away the angry scarlet statement.

Why desecrate someone so beloved by so many? Of course it was hate, but why against the mother of Jesus? Hate the church? Sure, many did. But hate an innocent mom guilty of nothing but loving her son and having to suffer with Him while watching His crucifixion?

Chapter 37

A Headless Rooster

Erin used her Android and called the archdiocese. She set up an appointment with Archbishop Dooley for the following morning.

She walked back to the Triple M Saloon and joined Paddy and Mario.

Father Mario was reading the newspaper. "Look at this ad for underwear. A good-looking gal in bra and panties. Teenage boys don't have a chance to remain chaste. I remember how sexually tormented I was just from watching the girls in their below-the-knee modest parochial school outfits. Now they might as well wear bikinis to school."

Erin asked, "Have you listened to some of the lyrics on MTV? Nothing left to the imagination."

"Paddy," Father Mario said, "your name's in the paper; retired cop finds dead kid. You've been complaining lately about not having anything to do. You should make solving this crime your mission."

Paddy said, "I'll do it."

"No you won't," Erin said. "My case, butt out." She looked at her watch, said, "Autopsy time," and walked out onto Stanyan Street. She saw Captain Fitzgerald by his car surrounded by the press and TV cameras.

The head of homicide looked like a cornered rabbit as a newspaper reporter shouted, "How did the tiger get out?"

Captain Fitzgerald said, "Tiger's dead, what difference does it make?"

"A teenager died," yelled another reporter. "How the tiger manage to escape makes all the difference. Whose fault? The zoo's or the American Zoological Society for rating the cage safe?"

"This is an ongoing investigation. It's premature to make any definitive statement at this time."

Captain Fitzgerald signaled Erin to get into his car.

Erin said, "So much for the tiger being an easy case."

"Fuck you. They smell blood. Someone screwed up, but who? Why would a tiger, after being in the same cage for years, pick that moment to escape?"

She said, "I was planning on taking my own car."

He let her out at her home.

Her front right tire was slashed. Angrily, she opened her trunk and instantly jumped back. There, on top of the spare tire, was a headless chicken. Blood was spattered about. She slammed the trunk lid and then noticed a dripping red cross on her rear window. On one side of the cross was the word "Hell"; on the other "Erin."

She removed her Android and took photos of the graffiti. She reopened her trunk and peered closer at the dead fowl. She realized it was not a hen, as she first thought, but a rooster. She took more photos.

After she fixed the flat, she threaded her way through the streets of San Francisco. She wondered if she should talk to Fitzgerald about the threats.

Motive seems clear, she thought. *Whoever did this wants me to quit the case. And if I don't quit it, the secondary motive is to get my mind cluttered with the threats instead of the investigation.*

And if that was true, then in all probability whoever did this was the person who killed the boy. And that could mean that the email, the bloody cross and the dead rooster might help solve the case.

Chapter 38

Getting Parts for Frankenstein

Erin entered the Hall of Justice. This monument to law and order held the courts, district attorney's offices, Southern Police Station and county jail. The gray concrete structure was never mistaken for a commercial building. It was stark — nondescript in the daytime, ominous and foreboding at night.

She met Captain Fitzgerald in the basement.

He said, "You're late."

"Flat tire." She explained what had happened.

"Turn the evidence over to the lab," he ordered. "Whoever did this might have gotten careless. But threats kind of go with the job, especially in homicide."

"How could someone get into my trunk?"

Captain Fitzgerald opened his briefcase and held up a burglar's kit. "With these I can get into your trunk, your front door, your locker."

"Who's doing the autopsy?"

"A mortician known for meticulousness."

They entered the morgue and were greeted by a small, rotund, balding, obviously Korean man wearing a white smock.

Stainless steel sinks lined one wall. Machines and equipment were scattered about. The doctor opened a drawer and removed surgical instruments. He asked, "Erin, have you been to an autopsy?"

"I went to one while at the police academy — a drive-by shooting. I didn't handle it too well."

"Understandable," Captain Fitzgerald said. "Erin lost her father to violence, a terrible image to carry through life."

The doctor said, "The captain here told me this is your first homicide case. The first few homicide autopsies are difficult. One has to keep a sense of perspective on this job or you go crazy."

"I'll be all right."

Captain Fitzgerald added, "I'm just here to observe."

The doctor pulled down an overhead armature and said, "I have to talk into this as I do the autopsy." He removed a white sheet, exposing the young, naked corpse. He did a minute examination of the skull. "Unidentified male, around ten. There is blunt trauma to the back of the skull. I am removing a sample of the hair."

The doctor removed a lock of the youngster's hair and placed it in a glass jar, writing the case number on the label. "There is a small cut on the lip, irregular abrasions and half-moon scratches on the cheek. These indicate the boy may have been throttled with one hand, the right, and..."

The doctor's face was only inches from the neck. "Yes, the right hand was used for compression. No sign of violence on the torso."

The doctor removed an instrument and cut through the skin at the boy's neck. "The hyoid bone is not fractured. Strangulation was not successful. The boy died by bleeding to death."

The doctor started cutting off blocks of skin in one-inch squares.

Erin asked, "What are you doing?"

"Samples as evidence. I am now going to remove the tongue *en bloc*."

"Captain Fitzgerald," she said, "this is bull. We know how the boy died. Why desecrate the body?"

"It's better not to have any autopsy than an incomplete one. An incomplete autopsy leaves the door open for all sorts of speculation by a savvy defense attorney."

The doctor said, "I am now removing the larynx." He picked up a tiny buzz saw. "I am removing the brain to search for evidence of disease or injury."

Erin growled out, "You're like a ghoul getting parts for Doctor Frankenstein."

Captain Fitzgerald said, "Wait for us in the doctor's office."

"I want—"

The captain ordered, "Go."

Erin left.

Fitzgerald said, "Doc, cut the bullshit. I don't care what the kid ate, or the state of his teeth, get to the heart of this."

"I have a certain order that I do things and—"

"First. Was there a transfer of evidence? Did the kid fight back and have DNA material under his fingernails?"

"No."

"Second. Was there evidence of sexual contact? Last thing I or this city needs is a murdering pedophile priest on the loose. Look what happened in Pennsylvania and the hundreds of priests and thousands of children raped."

"I did that exam first, before you and Erin arrived."

"And?"

"No signs of sexual involvement."

Chapter 39

Clouding the *Corpus Delicti*

An hour later, the medical examiner and Fitzgerald returned to the doctor's office.

The doctor said, "Erin, after you left I removed the heart and lungs and examined them, also the interior of the chest cavity. Next, I removed the intestinal tract. Then the liver, the spleen, the pancreas, and the kidneys from the abdominal cavity, and examined them. I took a sample of blood for analysis. I'll have the report for you as soon as possible. We'll then know the blood group and type and whether there was alcohol, drugs or poison present. I examined the genitals and pelvic. I also drew some urine from the bladder. I will have the results from those tests early tomorrow morning."

Captain Fitzgerald said, "I want them by five this afternoon."

Erin asked, "Was there a transfer of evidence?"

The doctor answered. "Unfortunately, the body, having been in water, removed any possible evidence. No hair or fibers were found, unusual except for the submersion in water for hours."

"Why unusual?" Erin asked.

"Between violent incidents such as murder, rape, fist fight, hit-and-run, there is usually a tremendous amount of transference between things."

Captain Fitzgerald asked, "What's your estimated time of death?"

"Because the body was in cold water for an undetermined length of time, a temperature test is useless."

"Cut the bull, what's your estimate?"

"I'd say sometime between eight and an hour after midnight."

"That doesn't narrow it much," Captain Fitzgerald said.

Erin said, "Got a call from Park Station." She explained about the bicyclist getting a "fuck you" from the boy about a quarter to midnight.

"Important information," Captain Fitzgerald said, "when were you planning on sharing?"

"I forgot. I guess because I was distracted by the headless rooster."

The medical examiner said, "I can make a definite statement regarding *cause* of death. The gash to the back of the head caused massive bleeding. Now you have a *corpus delicti.*"

Erin said, "I could have told you all that a moment after I arrived at the crime scene."

"*Corpus delicti* does not refer to the dead victim," Fitzgerald explained. "It is the fact that a person died from illegal violence."

The doctor added, "There must be no question the victim died of something other than the act of violence, which is why such a thorough autopsy is a must. An aneurysm discovered in the boy's brain, for instance, could cloud the *corpus delicti.*"

"I apologize for getting angry," Erin said. "It was unprofessional."

"Not really," Captain Fitzgerald said. "I know how you feel. I hate investigating a kid's death. I always wonder if somebody hadn't slaughtered a potential Mozart. Of course, the killer also might have taken out a Bundy or fuckin' Dahmer."

Chapter 40

Un-priestly Finances

After dropping off the Avenging Angel note, the headless rooster and the photos to the lab, Erin went to her office. She had only been assigned a new space the previous week, so it was still sparse of things to call her own. There was a picture of her mom and dad on the desk, both in uniform.

On top of a file cabinet was a picture of Paddy on his horse. He was next to the photo of a statue of a white Sphinx in front of the de Young Museum. On top of the Sphinx's back was a girl, seven or eight, waving. She was wearing Paddy's police cap and her right hand held a pair of handcuffs. The picture was one of Erin's favorites.

She checked her computer. She had asked the archbishop to send her PDFs with background information and financials on all five priests.

The file had come in with last year's tax returns and current balances in savings, checking and investments.

File on Friar Tuck: No checking account, no savings account. Monthly allowance paid by the firm of Lewis and Hillman LLC, of $1,500 sent directly to Saint Anthony soup kitchen.

She opened Father Mario's file. Checking account: $1,201.23; savings account: $23,404.74. Other assets: zero. Pay from the archdiocese $18,000 a year. $95,000 a year as police chaplain. Another $44,000 as one of the four chaplains at San Quentin, plus a stipend of $100,000 a year from a family trust fund.

Over a quarter of a million a year, she totaled. *And he's almost broke. Why?*

She knew from the few years she worked in vice that certain weaknesses were expensive. Was Mario hiding a terrible secret?

She opened Monsignor Mulheye's file: Checking: $1,908.44; savings: $48,326.31; other assets: zero. Allowance a year from the archdiocese $20,000. His tax return revealed no other sources of income.

Father Hillman: One sheet: Confidential information protected by law. See attorney Father Lewis for possible legal access to information.

She knew before opening Father Lewis's folder that there would be a single sheet with nearly identical information.

Tweedledee and Tweedledum, except not dumb at all.

She opened Mario's personal file.

Born April 15, 1970, S.F. Children's Hospital.

Education: Saint Brendan's Grammar School, Bishop Riordan High School University of San Francisco, BA. University of Santa Clara: Theology and Psychiatry — then ordained from Saint Patrick's Major Seminary. Parents born in Italy, immigrating to America in their young twenties. Father owned a string of restaurants, mother a doctor. Both dead from natural causes.

Trust fund set up on the day of Mario's ordination.

She read: One younger sister: murdered during carjacking age twenty-six.

She closed Mario's file and opened a combination of both Lewis and Hillman personal files. They had taken similar paths to ordination, both being Jesuit-trained: Lewis Notre Dame, Hillman Holy Cross. They met at Saint Patrick's, a major seminary south of San Francisco. They were ordained together and attended law school together — first at Golden Gate University, then at Boalt Hall School of Law, University of California Berkeley.

Both had PhD's in psychology and theology giving them, uncanny insights into human nature. They had a dead-on perception about jury selection and the verbal manipulation of same if selected. Besides consultation, they also specialized in civil and corporate litigation.

Their recreational time was spent playing Texas Hold 'Em in the Triple M's backroom or golfing at many of the private country clubs that dotted the Bay Area.

Their friendship led to mutual investments ranging from commercial buildings to various business ops. People who drank coffee at certain Starbucks or ate hamburgers at certain McDonalds would have been surprised that a portion of their bill ended up in the account of Hillman & Lewis Enterprises LLC.

Erin knew her case involving the kid that money appeared not to be a motive. But if the motive came from depression leading to anger fueled by liquor and an accidental meeting with a child who liked to tell people to go fuck themselves, then they were both suspects.

She had to find out what happen with the zoo and their wallets.

She opened the file on Friar Tuck. After his military discharge and entering the Trappist New Clairvaux Monastery near Vina, California, he ended up at Saint Jude's. Born on January 25, 1961. Parents worked in the outback of Australia dealing exclusively with the Aborigines until killed in auto accident — truck crashing into a ditch halfway between Kalgoorlie Boulder and Broome.

Erin opened Monsignor Mulheye's file and read: Father once the U.S. Ambassador to Mongolia. Mother, an archeologist, worked on a dig near Darkhat, in the northeastern region of Mongolia. She was murdered by a nomad who claimed she had defiled a megalith created in the thirteenth century in honor of Genghis Kahn.

Strange, Erin thought. *I now know three of the priests had relatives who died tragically: Mario's sister, Mulheye's mother, and Friar Tuck's parents. I must remember to ask Sarah, the police psychiatrist, if she knows anything about Lewis and Hillman family history.*

She called the saloon and learned from Max that all five priests were there trying to figure out if they should have a Requiem Mass for a kid no one was able to identify.

She wondered, *why haven't the parents reported their child missing?*

Chapter 41

Love, Hate, Close Emotions

Erin received a call from the police lab. Results: Blood on car's rear window came from the rooster. No fingerprints on the window of her car, writing came from someone wearing gloves.

She retrieved her car from the lab and drove home.

As she parked outside her flat she saw Angela on the stoop. The old lady's entryway had small statues of the Blessed Mother and of Jesus, complete with votive candles on each ledge.

On the inside hallway were pictures of the Sacred Heart of Jesus and all twelve apostles. Lining the entryway were small plaques replicating the fourteen Stations of the Cross. On the wall to left upon entering was a Holy Water font. There was a Holy Water font inside the bathroom, another upon entering the bedroom, another by the light switch for the kitchen.

Erin took the old lady by the arm and asked, "Headed for the saloon?"

Angela nodded.

"I'll walk with you."

Erin stopped at the mailbox. She removed an envelope and caught her breath. It was from the Ukrainian Adoption Center.

My last chance, she thought.

Now she was afraid to open the envelope from the adoption agency.

From Erin's flat there were two routes to the saloon: either up Stanyan, or through the parking lot behind Park Station on a path to Alvord Lake.

Angela and Erin linked arms and strolled the path towards the lake.

Erin wondered, *what's it like — no matter how healthy you are — to know you only have, at best, a few years left to live?*

Angela didn't act as if it bothered her at all that she was ninety-six.

They entered the park and saw a young couple holding hands. Angela said, "I was married for sixty-seven years."

"You must have been deeply in love."

"Matchmaker arranged marriage, met him when I headed for the altar."

"You told me you caught his eye while sashaying and flashing allurement."

"In my dreams; in real life it was at the altar."

Erin said, "I thought I was hopelessly in love with my ex, but soon found out he was hopelessly in love with sexual romps with other women."

"I never cheated."

"Me neither."

"I really didn't like my guy for the first twenty or so years, but then he kind of grew on me."

"I started hating my guy about a year after I swore to love him forever."

"Love, hate, close emotions."

Chapter 42

I Hate Liars

The two women entered the grove of trees surrounding Alvord Lake. There was a huge placard nailed to a tree. One was written: Two weeks ago POTUS aka PATASS said the people would *revolt* if Dems started impeachment. I think he means *rejoice*."

Erin said, "Why would Friar Tuck stick something political next to a murder scene?"

"Maybe to get their minds off of the tragedy that happened here."

"Would you rejoice if Trump were impeached?"

Angela said, "I probably would just say a prayer of thanks and a prayer for him. He's going to need as many as he can get."

"I actually voted for Trump," Erin said, "But I agree with Friar Tuck, that Tax Reform Bill and so-called Jobs Act is the biggest rip-off of the masses in the history of the world."

"Not if you're a one percenter, like Hillman and Lewis."

Erin asked, "Do you know why Friar Tuck's so angry with the president?"

"John McCain," the old lady recited in a singsong voice, "Bone Spurs. Gold Star parents. Draft dodger. Military service. Friar Tuck has a wounded warrior's heart. Pretty obvious where the rage against Trump comes from. And one more reason. I actually asked him so I know the answer."

"Friar Tuck spoke to you?"

"In a way. I asked why he loathed Trump. We were standing in the old abandoned playground next to the rectory. He pulled out a can of spray paint and in huge black letters painted, "I hate liars!"

"Wow," Erin said, "the prophet of Saint Jude's makes his stand in defiance on the exterior wall of his home against the lies of the president of the United States."

"The words are still there, unfortunately where no one walks by to see even on the way to Mass." The old lady glanced at Erin, "I never see you at Mass."

Erin countered, "How often do *you* go to Mass?"

"Every morning, I always go to the six-thirty. I love the way Monsignor Mulheye gives a short two-minute sermon. Nowhere else does anyone give a sermon except on Sunday."

"What does he talk about?"

"Love, salvation, charity, forgiveness."

Forgiveness, Erin thought. *I hated myself after Dad died. I allowed Fitz to shatter the law. I hate liars and I was one.*

They stopped by the lake. Angela made the sign of the cross and said, "So young. What a waste."

Erin nodded. Monsignor Mulheye saved me. *I confessed, not the specifics, but that I had broken the law and my oath as a policewoman. I was an accomplice to the cover-up of a serious crime.*

She asked Angela what she thought of the priests stationed at Saint Jude's.

"Lewis and Hillman are never there. The only time I see them anywhere besides entering or leaving Max's poker room is on the big days, like Christmas, when they help with High Mass. I like Friar Tuck. Sometimes he sits with me on the bench in front of the church. We don't talk, but he holds my hand and fingers his rosary. Monsignor Mulheye is always kind to me too."

The monsignor was kind to me too.

He asked me, "Will it help anyone if you tell the truth now?"

"No, it would only hurt people."

"Do you consider yourself a truthful person?"

Erin thought of her upbringing and her parents constantly hammering her with the truth was always better than a lie.

"I do, monsignor. I have tried to live my life honestly. The situation that happened was so sudden, so impactful I had no time to think, only follow another's lead."

"Stop condemning yourself. I absolve you. Your penance: try never to lie again."

I have tried.

Angela said, "But Father Mario? What a disgrace."

"What? What? Sorry, I don't follow."

"You asked me about the clerics at Saint Jude's. I said Mario is a disgrace."

"Why?"

"I went to confession once thinking Monsignor Mulheye was in the confessional, but it was Mario. My penance was to go to Max's place and have a glass of Campari."

"You think Father Mario's a bad priest?"

"I didn't say that; I said he was a disgrace: marrying divorced people, giving weird penances, spending all day in the Triple M. But I like his Monday service here in the park."

"*Monday* service?"

"Every Monday at ten Mario sets up a table by this lake, complete with altar cloth, and says Mass. Lots of people attend: cops, fireman, a few park bums, a couple of prostitutes, your Captain Fitzgerald, and, of course, me. Mario gives a general absolution and a penance that is always the same, 'Everyone must take Communion.'"

"Today's Monday."

"Obviously, Mario decided to cancel, what with the crime scene."

"Maybe one day I'll go to Mass here with you."

"Great," Angela said. "How's the investigation? Any clues?"

Just a Roman collar.

Chapter 43

Deadly Sins

Standing by Alvord Lake, Erin saw Father Mario strolling towards her. She told Angela she would join her shortly in the saloon.

Father Mario met her and they sat at the picnic table.

She pointed a finger at the placard nailed to a tree. "Have you read Friar Tuck's latest?"

"Yes, but you want to talk about something else, so fire away."

She ascertained he had no alibi and couldn't provide even a hint of a timeframe to help with the other four men he lived with under the same roof.

She said, "I researched your education. Impressive. You could have risen high in the Church."

"I never became a priest to rise high in the Church. I became one because I was flawed and thought I might lead a purposeful life by becoming a priest."

"Flawed?"

"Name a deadly sin and you can pin my name next to it, which is why I always liked the life of Saint Francis of Assisi. He was a wastrel, a womanizer, a gambler, a soldier, a drunkard. Yet he managed to found the Franciscan Order. He came to realize doing something with his life beyond just attending to his own pleasures meant something. My life during my twenties was similar as far as the wastrel, gambler, womanizer and boozer. I managed to avoid the soldiering part."

"So you founded the outcast order of Saint Jude's, the rebel parish?"

"Something like that. And because I've broken every Commandment."

"I'm calling you on that. I bet you never had false gods before you?"

"I bowed at the sacred altar of women and booze. Cut to the chase, Erin, and ask the question you really want an answer to."

"Have you killed someone?"

"Yes."

She felt stunned.

His eyes were mild, no stress on his face, no tension in his body.

Erin thought, *should I read him his rights?*

"I was an *accomplice* to a killing," he said. "A friend of mine, a dear, sweet, loving woman, made a mistake. She slipped from grace, as we all do, and ended up pregnant. It would have destroyed her marriage, her career, her husband's life and their children's lives. I absolved her in advance, before she had the abortion."

"In *advance*? Can you do that?"

"I'll find out after I die and am judged, but I did it, and more than once for many people, including giving eternal absolution to your brother Paddy."

"Still, you aided and abetted a planned killing in advance."

Interlude One

Secrets

Independence Day, Saturday, July 4, 2020, Early Evening

Wearing N-95 masks, Erin and Father Mario left Saint Jude's and went down Stanyan Street.

Erin said, "Sorry I lost my temper, Mario."

"No problem, everyone who knows you realizes that you go viral when you think you're getting your ox gored."

They passed a group of five teenagers, none wearing masks. One called out, "Hey, old timers, no need for masks."

Erin muttered, "Old timer? I'm forty-six."

"They're young," the priest said, "they think they're immortal."

"I plan on wearing mine until there's a vaccine."

They walked into the alley behind the Triple M Saloon.

The priest tapped in the key-code on the lock and the rear door swung open.

They walked down a corridor, passed the restrooms, and entered the bar proper.

Angela sat on a barstool, Max stood behind the bar.

Max donned a mask, held up a Hammacher Schlemmer hospital grade, no contact, infrared thermometer and said, "Time to check whether either of you has a fever." A few moments later he said, "Both clear, you can remove your masks."

Erin opened her briefcase and tossed the crumpled newspaper on the bar,

Angela picked it up, smoothed it out and said, "I really made a mistake. I'm sorry."

Erin patted her landlady on the back. "Mario told me why."

Mario said, "I'll have glass of chardonnay."

Max poured the wine and said, "I assume, Erin, you have confronted Mario with today's *Chronicle* and what it means."

"I confronted him," Erin said, "and he stonewalled me until he knew Angela had dumped the Friar's ashes off the Golden Gate Bridge."

"I didn't dump then," the old lady said, "Max drove me out to the bridge. He parked on the east side in the overlook. We started walking, me carrying the urn. Wouldn't you know the luck, a Highway Patrolman stopped and asked what we were doing? I told the cop that I wanted to scatter my dead husband's ashes into the Bay."

"Your husband died years ago," Erin said.

"Right," Max chuckled, "and the Chippie wasn't buying the story either until Angela started to weep and stammer that her mate was a fisherman who plied the waters from the Bay to the Farallon Islands for sixty years and his last wish was to spend eternity in these same waters."

Angela nodded, "Except then the cop starts going on about it being illegal to throw anything off the bridge. I stopped crying and started clutching my left arm. I kind of swooned into him when I told him I wanted to join my mate when I die and have my ashes tossed off the exact same spot. Took five minutes but then I had his eating out of my hand. I love playing the little-old-lady-in-distress bit."

Max added, "He took the urn and, holding the rail, dumped the Friar's ashes. The wind took the remains and blew them in a wide arc as the ashes drifted down to the waiting water."

"Angela," Erin said, "you got that patrolman to break the law."

"So what? I thanked him with a big hug and kiss on the cheek and told him his mother must be proud of him." The old lady stood, "Speaking of thanking people, Max, forgot to tell you, a few weeks ago I made something for you."

The old lady went to her shopping cart and returned with a large rolled up paper. She said, "You're going to have to frame it, but I hope you like this." She spread the drawing out on the bar top.

"I love this," Max said. "Who's A-ninety-six?"

"Me," Angela said, "I'm ninety-six. About the art, Friar Tuck was teaching me. I thought it would look nice alongside the colorful one you have hanging above the God's Bookie Board."

Max said, "This isn't a drawing, this is a photograph."

"Yes, it is," Angela said, "Friar Tuck suggested it would help if I chose art images from sources like Picmonkey or Shuttlecock then recreate it as a drawing."

"Have you?" Max asked.

"I tried, it's not easy. I keep messing up."

Erin said, "Angela, I need to talk to Father Mario... alone."

The priest joined her in the rear booth.

She said, "You're right about me having a devastating secret bigger than the Friar living six months more after being declared dead. Mine is an enormous secret I need protected. But all hell is going to break loose over that drawing of Trump showing he favors money over human life."

"Why?"

"The media is already howling over this. A shit storm of questions: 'Is the Friar alive?' and, 'Where has he been hiding?' and 'Who's been harboring him?' On and on and relentlessly on."

"Only you know," Mario said.

"Bullshit. Angela knows, Fitz knows, Hillman and Lewis know, Max knows, I assume Monsignor Mulheye knows. It is hard enough to keep a secret when only two people know, but a mob?"

"All of us have kept the secrets since Christmas and not talked."

"I can keep a secret," Erin said, "for instance, I've known for months about your approved blessing of an abortion before the fact and haven't done squat."

Chapter 44

A Desperate Parish

Monday, December 23, 2019, Triple M Saloon

"Father Mario," Erin said, "you just said you gave your blessing to a planned abortion in advance. Isn't that a sin?"

The priest said, "I'll find out when I die. I'm actually against abortion, the death penalty and euthanasia. But that one time, while consoling that marvelous friend, I felt I had no choice. Yet I know what I did was a mortal sin."

I had an abortion, a mortal sin, and no one absolved me in advance, Erin thought and asked, "You know the four other priests at Saint Jude's better than anyone. Is it possible a priest killed the child?"

"I have lived long enough to realize just about anything's possible when it comes to the actions of humans. Sure, one of us could have killed the kid. Do I think it likely? No. We screw up, but only in the eyes of the church and Dooley, not in our own eyes."

Erin nodded.

The priest continued, "There is nothing intrinsically wrong with the firm of Hillman and Lewis LLC. They actually seek justice and the fact they're getting rich doing it doesn't detract from their actions."

"But shouldn't they be using some of that money to help others?"

"What makes you jump to the conclusion they're not? For instance, I know those two priests are donating enormous sums, millions and millions, creating a huge halfway house, which is more like a gigantic opulent hotel, for released felons. Not some shabby room in a slum. I've seen the blueprints: a library, classrooms, individual private bedrooms, even a basketball court. Hillman and Lewis are spending the money that comes from their work and investments by taking care of the downtrodden. Besides, secular priests take no vow of poverty like monks and nuns."

"Friar Tuck gets a paycheck."

"The monk gives it all to charity, keeping his vow. He *is* a mystic.

He goes where he thinks good is and he goes where he thinks evil is, same as Jesus Christ."

"The monsignor?"

"Mulheye is actually one of the most sensitive persons I have ever met. If anything, he is dramatically opposite from me."

"Meaning you're insensitive."

"I never claimed to be sensitive. I fight things in my religion that have nothing to do with the teachings of Christ."

"Do you think any of the other priests will help me by cooperating?"

"Hillman and Lewis will not cooperate at all."

"How do you know?"

He withdrew two pieces of paper from his pocket and gave them to her.

One read: "I am legal representation for Father Hillman. Unless he is charged with a crime, he refuses to talk to you. Signed: Father Lewis, attorney-at-law."

The other paper was identical except the two names reversed.

She placed the letters in her briefcase.

Father Mario said, "I don't think their position is indicative of anything, just their stubborn way of insisting on their rights."

"I assume Friar Tuck will be as equally tight-mouthed?"

"Because he *is* tight-mouthed."

"Mulheye?"

"He's busting to talk. He feels this has cast an even darker pall than normal over our parish. He said to me that it's one thing for us to be labeled rebels, but a possible murderer?"

"What do you think he can contribute?"

"Nothing. There's no smoking gun that I'm aware of. Like the missing tennis shoe."

"How do you know about the missing... Of course, Paddy."

"Who else?" the priest said. "Maybe the collar was stolen and sold."

"Sold?"

"It's surprising how many laypeople fantasize and act out being a priest or a nun. Ask a costume rental shop."

"But this one had Saint Jude's stamp on the inside—"

"I didn't say it came from a rental, some people would rather buy a piece of equipment clandestinely than risk being seen buying or renting the same thing."

"Tomorrow's Christmas Eve," Erin said. "What are you up to?"

"I have to go to San Quentin. Correctional officer killed a prisoner who assaulted him. More counseling."

"How long have you been the prison's chaplain?"

"Three years. There are four of us: me, a Baptist, a Muslim and a Rabbi. Four to tend more than seven hundred prisoners on death row, plus the rest of the con population and guards. That's one huge and desperate parish."

Chapter 45

Friar Tuck's Sistine Chapel

Father Mario pointed. "Erin, have you ever walked through that tunnel."

"Sure."

"Ever brought a flashlight and seen what's on the ceiling of that dark place?"

"No. Why would I?"

He reached in his robes and handed her a flashlight.

She entered the tunnel. The construction was a half arch and made of stone. She turned on the light on the ceiling and saw the words:

"Dante's Circle of Hell"

First level:

Limbo = Being caught between two stages

Trump's growth since becoming an adult

Humility = zero — Arrogance = 100%

Gives Loyalty = 0% — Demands Loyalty = 100%

Empathy = zero — Insensitivity = 100%

Forgiveness = zero — Vengeance = 100%

Truth = Number Unknown — Lies = First 3 year — 16,241

She shown the light over the next panel:

"Second level: Lust." Below was the image of Stormy Daniels stating, "Worst lover I ever had paid me 130 grand to keep silent."

Third level: Gluttony. Image: Trump, stomach bloated to an enormous size, lying on a divan surrounded by discarded boxes from McDonalds and Coca Cola cans piled up like pyramids.

Fourth level: Greed. Disney's Scrooge McDuck and Donald Trump playing in the cartoon character's vault, tossing gold coins in the air. Scrooge says, "There's never enough." Trump says, "One can only try."

Erin muttered, "The monk almost never uses color. Maybe because this is in a tunnel and rather dark."

She removed her Android, got close to Dante's Fifth Level of Hell, and took a photo.

Sixth level: Heresy. Trump, using a flamethrower, setting fire to a huge pile of law books. Above his head: "Screw the rule of law."

Seventh level: Violence. A ghostly image of the journalist Khashoggi's face with Trump shrugging, "Can't do anything, Saudi's buy too much of my stuff."

Eighth level: Fraud. A head shot of a man, surrounded by piles of tax returns. Above his head a sign reading: "Where to begin?"

Ninth level: Treachery. Trump standing between Cain (with his dead brother Abel at his feet) and Judas Iscariot (with the vague outline of three crosses behind him.) Above: POTUS, "I love BLINDSIDING people!"

At the end of the tunnel was one final quote: "Mr. President, your time in Dante's Inferno will come."

Chapter 46

A Death Bed Promise

Erin left the tunnel and rejoined Father Mario. She said, "Friar Tuck sure hates President Trump."

"No, he doesn't. He *is* enraged at Trump's draft dodging and speaking as a shrink I know that anger comes from the horrors the monk saw in war. Friar Tuck does hate what Trump *does*. He wants people to clearly see those actions. But the monk doesn't hate anyone."

"He wrote Trump has zero loyalty. He's loyal to his family."

"The Friar is attacking the president's public life, not his private." The priest glanced at his watch. "Five o'clock, quitting time."

Erin said, "Meaning martini time."

"Exactly."

"I am off on my run. Missed it this morning because of the crime."

"Where to?"

"Fort Point."

"Back to *the* bench?" Mario asked.

"Yes, a bench with such sorrowful memories."

The priest headed across Stanyan Street toward the Triple M.

Erin headed toward Fort Point.

She ran faster that her normal six-minute-a-mile pace.

She entered the Presidio and swept past the graves of those who died in the Great War.

Her pace got slower and slower as she neared Fort Point.

She was walking slowly when she saw the bench.

The area was empty.

She said softly, "Mom, once again I've kept my promise to return each year at Christmas time."

The memories from years earlier swirled in her mind.

She bent forward, cupped her head in her hands and closed her eyes.

Erin saw herself pushing the wheelchair closer and closer towards the bench.

She watched herself place her mom's frail body on the bench.

Her mom said, "I love this spot. I wanted to visit one more time, to remember and cherish the memories before I die."

The vista included the Golden Gate Bridge, Alcatraz Island and the Marin County headlands. The Bay's blue waters were sprinkled with the white sails of boats. The fog wasn't coming in on "little cat feet," as the poet Carl Sandburg once wrote. It was dancing like a ghostly dervish around the giant columns that support the bridge.

Erin noticed a girl, around fourteen, with long, curly red hair. She wore a bright purple, hand-weaved smock. She was walking between two Great Danes. The dogs had black markings dotting their white bodies and looked like slightly smaller versions of Holstein cows.

The girl went to the water's edge. The two huge dogs, on either side of her, rested on their haunches. All three stared up at the bridge.

Her mom said, "That's a lovely picture, did you bring your camera?"

Erin removed her camera and sidled around until the girl and dogs' backsides were in the foreground, the golden bridge's columns and swirling fog in the background. She snapped a photo just as a freighter, its rust stained bow peeking out of the misty gray bank, came churning into view.

"Mom, a lucky shot," she said.

"This spot's always been lucky for me. Your Dad proposed to me here." Her mom let out a gentle chuckle. "Then we went back to his car and consummated the deal."

"And nine months later Paddy appeared."

"Everyone needs a big brother. And I need you to promise me a few things." And emaciated arm, consumed by cancer, swept out at the bay. "Return here every year near Christmas, remember me and say a prayer for my soul."

Erin started to weep. "Mom, I don't want to remember you like this. I want the image of my Mom, the hardnosed, pistol-packing cop, getting her reward for valor above and beyond."

"I shot and killed a guy, Erin," she said as she pointed a few feet away, "right there. Not exactly my favorite memory. And because I did kill a guy is why I want that yearly prayer said right here, on this bench. Promise."

"I promise."

"You need to try and adopt a child."

"My husband is adamantly against it, the loveless asshole. I am going to divorce the prick."

Her mother held her hand. "How many times have I told you that swearing is the act of a lazy person? Your husband is abusive, downright nasty, but—"

"That's a definition of what an asshole is."

Erin started a low keening sound that wrenched itself from deep within.

"I know you're sad," her mom said. "But dying is inevitable. Ask not for whom the bell tolls, it tolls for thee."

"Fuck John Dunne."

"I want you to promise me you'll stop swearing."

"How can I refuse with my dying mom's pleading eyes drilling into my heart? I'll try."

"Promise you won't drink if you're mad or sad."

"I promise."

"I know you were raised to tell the truth. You will try to adopt, even if divorced. You will try to stop swearing, and you will not drink if mad or sad. Promise me and promise God."

"I promise."

I promised, Erin thought as the fog swirled around her. *I did manage to get Mom to agree mental swearing wasn't the same as verbal. But I've smashed those three promises to shreds.*

Erin stood, looked up at the sky, and said, "And then every year I come here and make the same promises all over again."

Chapter 47

How the Mind uses Dissociation

Doctor Sarah walked in the Triple M Saloon. She was in full dress black leather motorcycle gear, including chaps. On the back of her jacket was a patch that read: "Land of the Free because of the Brave." Below these words was a woman on a motorcycle, long hair flowing out behind her with the words: "Therapy is expensive — the Wind is Free."

Wolf whistles came from male customers with a few cries of, "Lookin' good," or, "Blistering hot, Sarah."

She gave two thumbs up to the crowd.

Erin and Sarah went to the rear booth.

Sarah said, "I expected your call once I learned you caught the kid killing. Terrible, and tragic what the ramifications of that Roman collar might mean."

"Who told you about the Roman collar?"

"Your brother."

Fucking Paddy and his loose lips, Erin thought and said, "I need you to do some background research on Hillman and Lewis. Is that okay?"

"Neither is or has been a patient, so no conflict. Besides being a doctor, I am a policewoman. Will get the info to you by tomorrow afternoon."

"Thanks. I also need your opinion on whether or not this killing could be a motiveless crime."

"Motiveless killings are rare, but do happen."

"I have five strong suspects. I know all five of those priests were drunk last night; they were all upset about the tiger mauling, except for different reasons."

"You want to know could one have blacked out and done the murder."

"We're thinking manslaughter," Erin said, "not sure whether voluntary or involuntary. And yes, that's one of my questions."

"The answer is yes. And depending on how drunk the person was, the memory of what happened might come back only in small flashbacks. A blackout is not the same as passing out."

"Just remembered," Erin said, "we had this same discussion during the Kavanaugh Supreme Court hearings."

"And I told you I thought the latest member of the highest court in the land was full of bullshit. Those who blackout can still seem fine to those around."

"Depression could lead one of the priests—"

"Sure, depression can lead to anger and violence, especially if exacerbated by alcohol. But I'm talking about the distancing the mind is capable of protecting itself. Meaning disassociation."

Chapter 48

A Primordial Trigger

Father Mario walked over. "Private party or can anyone join in?"

Sarah motioned, "Handsome men, especially priests, always welcome."

Father Mario sat and said, "I have a hunch what this discussion is about: Erin wants to know if booze and rage can lead to murder?"

Sarah said, "Father Mario, you're a psychiatrist. You know the answer, both short and long. Erin, the short answer is yes. A longer answer is that rage can trigger a primordial response instead of a rational one. But something has to act as a trigger."

"It can be as simple as an overt act," Mario agreed, "like swearing or taunting. Even a gesture can fire off a signal to the brain to do something irrational."

Erin said, "The boy who was killed told a bicyclist to go fuck himself."

"If he said that," Sarah said, "to a drunken, depressed, enraged person, it could act as a trigger to violence."

Erin asked, "A normal person can kill if provoked?"

"We all have a breaking point," Sarah said. "Most of us never get even remotely close to that tipping moment, but the perfect storm can and does happen — a convergence of events — that sets off an H-bomb inside a person's brain."

"And being a priest does not anoint one to be above this," Father Mario added. "We can go off the deep end like anyone else."

"Ever go off the deep end regarding chastity?" Sarah asked as she batted her long black eyelashes and gently patted the priest's arm.

"All the time," Mario grinned, "except in dreams where the Ethiopian slash Jamaican goddess named Sarah stars."

"Now I know who I will be thinking of next time I shag a guy."

"Next time you shag a guy." Erin said. "Whatever happened to what's his name?"

"What's his name has been given his walking papers."

"You seem to break up every three months," Erin said.

Mario said, "Not in my dreams."

"I'm glad I'm faithful someplace," Sarah said. "Guys, ever notice I only date attorneys? And only corporate, financial types."

"Haven't kept track," Erin said.

"Well I do because I don't want to get serious. Which is not hard to do when all the fellow talks about is money. But I just turned thirty. I may settle down, I do want a child or children. But with someone who understand loyalty, decency, ethics, morality, understanding and—"

"Like Max," Mario said and looked at Erin.

"He's forty-eight, way closer to Erin's age than mine." Sarah glanced at her watch. "Have to scoot."

Erin said, "I'll walk you out."

Sarah received another volley of wolf whistles which she returned with a split-fingered salute which can symbolize either peace or victory.

Outside, Sarah climbed on a Harley Davidson. Known as the XR750, her type bike was also Evel Knieval's favorite and the model with the most wins in AMA's racing history.

There were saddlebags over the modified rear tire guard. On one was a patch that read: "Only bikers understand why dogs like to stick their heads out of windows." On the other saddlebag: "Never ride faster than your angel can fly."

Sarah gave Erin a casual salute, fired her hog, and roared off.

The Triple M's night bartender, Charlie, walked up, pointed at the disappearing Sarah, and said, "Damn, I just missed her."

"She'll be back tomorrow; helping me with a case."

They entered the bar.

Charlie relieved Max.

The night bartender always wore a white shirt and tie, a vest complete with watch fob and a butcher apron. .

Erin asked, "Charlie, last night you were on duty. After I left, did the priests act out of character?"

"I've seen Mario a little drunk and the monsignor tipsy only once. I've never seen Friar Tuck, Hillman or Lewis even slightly intoxicated. But last night they were all flat-out shit-faced."

"What were they doing?"

"Arguing. And loudly. I told them a few times to knock it off but they ignored me. Besides, I let is pass because late last night there was only one other person in here, your brother, the priests weren't bothering him."

"What were they arguing about?"

"Hard to tell. They switched from English to Latin. But it sure sounded like they were angry."

"Anything else you remember?"

"Mario ordered a stinger and they all switched to drinking them. Those things are brutal. Goes down like honey and then hits the brain like a sledgehammer."

She rejoined Father Mario and asked, "Did you blackout last night?"

"Don't remember getting to the rectory or going to bed. I usually pace myself. I don't get that drunk often. Dangerous."

"Because?"

"I had a small stroke a few years ago. I'm on blood thinners. If I fell down and hit my head I could bleed to death. What's next on your schedule?"

"Going home to eat dinner."

"If you get bored come back."

"You'll be here?"

"Where else?"

Chapter 49

A Tough and Depressing Day

Erin went home, ate dinner and fed her parrot De De. She muttered, "A priest, a priest. Who better to sign off as An Avenging Angel?"

She opened a closet and took out her cello. She had learned to play when young. One of the pictures on her bedroom wall was a three-generation photo with herself, her mother and her grandmother all holding a cello.

She removed a folding chair from her hall closet, sat down in the living room and said, "De De, what to play? I'm no Yo Yo Ma, but playing helps me clear my head."

She played the prelude from Bach's Cello Suite No. 1.

She found it hard to concentrate. The image of the dead boy kept interfering. She put the cello back in its case.

Erin changed to a jogging outfit. At her front door she ran into Angela who said, "Dark out, funny time to be running."

"Need to clear my head. Need a short, fast run."

Erin cruised through the park at her fastest pace: five-and-a-half-minute miles. Then jogged back to the saloon. She found Father Mario on the corner stool reading his Breviary.

The priest said, "Just finished this obligation." He ordered a bottle of Cakebread Cellars Chardonnay.

Charlie, the night bartender, opened the bottle and poured two glasses.

Erin said, "Mario, I thought you were a vodka drinker."

"After last night I thought I'd slow down on the hard stuff. Figured just one martini after work and then switch to something softer."

Erin asked, "Have you seen Paddy?"

"Left ten minutes ago, pretty drunk."

"How old were you when you become a priest?"

"I became a priest at thirty," Father Mario answered, "but I didn't spend the usual six years at Saint Joseph's minor seminary, or six at Saint Patrick's major seminary. I didn't start my vocation until I was twenty-eight. I, like our leader Dooley, only needed two years to finish at Saint Pat's and become ordained."

She wondered, *how does he know Dooley only needed two years? Maybe Mario has a book on the archbishop as thick as Captain Fitz's?*

The priest continued. "Between around sixteen and twenty-eight, I managed to debauch at a level set as high as our dear patron saint of San Francisco."

"What knocked you off your debauching horse?"

"Two things," he replied. "My sister was murdered. That brought things in my life under huge examination."

"The second thing?"

"I learned Mother Teresa, the saintly woman of India, had doubts about the existence of God her whole life."

"I read about that."

"She had doubts yet still served the poor and the sick. That was my epiphany. By that time in my young life I had already tired of a seemingly endless parade of sexual encounters. Women, women, women were my primary devotion."

Erin sipped her wine and said, "Your family's rich. I did a background check on you and the other priests. You're not rich, yet you earn more than a quarter of a million a year."

"Most of which goes to Max."

"You're a gambler?"

"No. Someday I'll tell you where the money goes."

At the other end of the bar, Charlie held up the phone, "For you, Erin."

She listened, and then rejoined Father Mario.

The priest asked, "Something important?"

"Parents of the dead boy from last night have been found. Apparently they had a family dinner. Aunts, uncles and cousins type of thing. The kid's parents are divorced, but get along. Their kid told his mother he was going home with his father. Then, after she left the dinner, he immediately told his father he was going home with his mother. Then he left."

"Ten's young to be a runaway."

"Whatever. Both parents have solid alibis, left the party with other people."

"Anything else?"

"I know for sure from the bicyclist the kid was alive just before midnight. And according to the coroner to maybe a half-hour later."

"Narrowing the timeframe down has to help."

"Do you know where any of your fellow priests were during that time?"

"No. Don't know where any of them went after we left this place." He glanced at his watch. "Getting late, almost nine. Pooped."

"Give me a minute." Erin told him about the adoption letter.

"Open it, stop torturing yourself."

She thought, *if it's a yes there's no way I'd treat a child like dad treated Paddy. No matter what he did it was never good enough.*

She tore open the envelope. Her heart sagged as she read: "We are sorry to inform you that because of your age, occupation and single status we have determined not to select you for one of our orphaned children."

Father Mario said, "I can tell by your face it's bad."

"Yes."

"Can I buy you something stronger than wine?"

"I never drink if sad or mad. Right now I'm both." She pushed her unfinished drink in front of the priest.

Father Mario glanced at his watch again. "I repeat, tired, time for a nap."

"It's only ten to nine."

"So? Didn't sleep well last night and it has been a depressing day."

Chapter 50

The Fifth Disaster = I Baptize Thee

Padre Pio sat in his bedroom. The images from the night before had become clearer and clearer during the day.

He thought, *that kid really pissed me off when he thrust that offensive finger into the air. That's what my father used to do. I'd say, "I want to become a priest."*

Dad would say, "Fuck you," then give me a mighty one-armed thrust in the air with middle finger extended towards the heavens. He'd say, "You're a pussy. You want to be a priest? All priests are pussies. Be a man. Act strong. Act decisively. If you think something is right, act on it."

The kid last night. I didn't accidentally kill him, I saved him.

That kid was too young to have committed a mortal sin. I sent him to Heaven. He's basking in the Beatific Vision of the Almighty.

Padre Pio left his room. He walked to Children's Playground, located just beyond Little Rec Soccer Field, about 75 yards west of Alvord Lake. He knew that the children who romp and frolic there in the daytime would be gone. Night had fallen. He moved between the swings, slides and teeter-totters and felt the goodness of those who used them.

From the filth I listen to from those confessing I know once a person reaches puberty, once they're no longer pure, they're doomed. There's only one possible fate awaiting them and that is to grow up, sin, die, then plunge into Hellfire.

The Lord said, "What profit a man to gain the whole world and then lose his soul?" That's what all seem to do when grown. They search for pleasure, search for wealth, search for power. They yearn to gain the whole world and, in the process, loss their eternal souls.

Evil is everywhere. The only place it is not is places like this — where the children play. They're not greedy, proud, lustful, envious, wrathful, gluttonous or slothful. These pure of heart are too young to take on the sins that are a scourge and a plague on adults.

The only true path — the holy path that can actually save another — is to free them from this vale of tears and give them Paradise.

Like I did last night; I freed that kid.

He noticed a boy with curly brown hair, round cherub face, sharp almond eyes and a solid body. He was young, about twelve or thirteen.

He's old enough to have gone through puberty, old enough to have sexual awareness, old enough to sin.

The boy hurried through the meadow abutting the playground.

Padre Pio called, "What are you doing out so late?"

The boy approached. "I'm taking a shortcut, Father. I've just been to a Christmas play rehearsal. Then I started talking to friends. I forgot my dad was picking me up in front of the church hall, I was at the back. He must be worried. I have to get home."

"I will walk with you, to see you safely home."

The boy fidgeted. "I don't know. My dad told me not to—"

"How old are you?"

"Fourteen."

"Are you Catholic?"

The boy looked nervously over his shoulder. "I have to go, I'm really late."

"I asked a question."

"No."

"Have you ever been baptized?"

"My dad doesn't believe in that stuff."

His dad didn't believe in the Sacrament that washes away all sin and gives new life, and grace, and makes us children of God?

Padre Pio asked, "Do you know what baptism is?"

The boy moved sideways, looking left and right.

Padre Pio reached out, grabbing the boy and drawing him close. "Baptism removes original sin."

"I've been good, Father, let me go."

"Baptism is necessary for all men's salvation. Unless a man is born again of water and the spirit he cannot enter the Kingdom of God."

The boy whimpered, "Please."

"Would you like to be baptized?"

"Will you let me go then?"

"I will *free* you then."

They walked to a nearby water fountain. Clear liquid cascaded across the boy's face, forehead and hair, making it soaking wet.

Padre Pio said, "I baptize thee in the name of the Father, the Son and the Holy Spirit."

The boy's soul is now purged of original sin. He is as pure as Mary, the Blessed Mother of Jesus, and her Immaculate Conception.

His hands closed around the neck. The boy fought, thrashing and clawing, pulling both himself and his attacker into the surrounding bushes.

The boy grabbed Padre Pio's hair and dug his fingernails in deeply. He was wearing a ring. When the boy let go of the hair his ring raked across the scalp.

Blood dripped down Padre Pio's face as he thought, *the coarse shell of this boy's mortal body battles to remain alive, to grow and to sin, to mock the word of God in thought and deed. His efforts now weaken as his immortal soul approaches sanctity and immortality.*

The boy grew limp.

He is no longer of this world; he is in the eternal reward of the everlasting sight of the Beatific Vision. He is with God now.

Padre Pio closed his eyes as a panic crashed through his mind. *What have I done?* He reached down to feel for a pulse and thought, *there's a faint one. He's alive.*

There was a flash of blinding white light.

What was that? Was that the Lord showing me a glimpse of the Beatific Vision?

Completely confused, he stumbled away.

Chapter 51

Homicide Inspector Carl

Erin's Android vibrated. She listened as Captain Fitzgerald said, "Another young boy's been found dead in the bushes between Children's Playground and the bowling green; head immediately to the crime scene."

Erin disconnected and said, "Shit, shit, shit."

It wasn't until the third verbalized shit that she realized she was speaking aloud. Not just speaking, but yelling.

She said, "Sorry Mom, sorry God" and thought, *I will never stop swearing no matter what I promised. Going to be saying 'Sorry, Mom,' and "Sorry, God," the rest of my life.*

Erin entered the park via Alvord Lake. She trotted through the pedestrian tunnel under Kezar Drive and soon Sharon Meadow, a few yards north of children's Playground, came into view.

There were people all over the grass, held back by police and wooden barriers. She saw a mass of cars, television trucks and an ambulance. The area was flooded with false suns from TV spotlights, flashing out from behind barriers, probing their beams here and there through the trees.

She hurried to Captain Fitzgerald. He said, "Carl's the inspector in charge. He called me because of the similarities with your case."

Carl was 35, African-American and beginning to bald, with deep-set eyes and a forehead that would have made Dr. Frankenstein salivate. He was completely nonchalant about his attire, shirttail hanging out, hair unkempt.

In her approach to on-duty dress Erin chose a conservative look. Usually business suits that made her look like so many of the women walking around the Financial District. Professional, not provocative. And always makeup toned way, way down. On her days off she dressed in either jogging gear or tattered jeans, with over-sized Pendleton shirts, sandals or tennis shoes.

She thought, *this makes two crime scenes in one day where I show up in a jogging outfit and looking sloppier than my brother.*

Carl led Captain Fitzgerald and Erin away from the other people. Standing by a towering weeping willow, he said with a larynx sounding like it had been sandpapered, "Some bum found the body. He went to Park Station and told the officer in charge. They called homicide and the dispatcher's radio call was picked up by one of the newspapers. The press is going crazy. Fortunately, I managed to get enough men to seal the scene before the horde arrived."

Captain Fitzgerald said, "I hate the media as much as Donald Trump does."

Carl said. "People are getting angry. The call went out just after nine and the TV guys are trying to make the eleven o'clock news. They're pissed because I won't release anything. I'm also getting shit from the newspaper reporters who want to make the early edition."

Captain Fitzgerald asked, "Any ID on the deceased yet?"

"The father got here same time as the reporters. Guy's devastated."

"What happened?" Erin asked.

"The father called Park Station about nine o'clock. His son should have been home. He'd been to a Christmas play practice at his school. The station keeper writes it down in his report. When the bum reports the murder, the dispatcher calls the father."

Captain Fitzgerald asked, "What did you do?"

"What *could* I do? I had to let him see if it was his kid. I couldn't exactly keep this guy, who's a widower, away with half the City's reporters milling about. They'd have crucified me. I still turn out looking like crap because I had to restrain the dad from throwing himself on the body and ruining evidence."

Carl shook his head and continued, "It's been a circus. Those assholes have been trying to sneak through the barriers to get a picture of the body. They want their usual on-the-scene bullshit photos. It's been a battle trying to keep those pricks from trampling all over everything."

Captain Fitzgerald borrowed a bullhorn from one of the patrol officers and went to the barricade. "You all know me. The next asshole who tries to sneak in will be arrested for interfering with an investigation. You will spend the night on the seventh floor of the Hall of Justice in a cold, damp cell. Feel free to put that on the news along with the asshole part. Or maybe I should change that to *fuckin'* asshole?"

Erin asked, "Carl, did you preserve anything?"

"Of course, it's just battling those pricks instead of doing my job that pisses me off. The killing took place in some bushes. The ground was soft and moist because the sprinkler system was on between eight and eight-thirty. There's one good impression of the right-shoe print. They're taking a casting as we speak. I've finished the crime sketch. The photographer's finished except for shots of the casting. And the lab crew's done."

"Did the lab find anything?"

"There was transfer of evidence. They found blood and hair under the boy's fingernails. Also, blood, fiber and hair on some of his clothes. At least this time everything wasn't screwed up by being under water."

Captain Fitzgerald asked, "Have you talked to Brendan?"

"When I saw what this looked like I called the deputy police chief. Brendan wants to see all three of us, at his home, when I'm through here. I haven't interviewed the bum yet. Want to sit in?"

"Whatever you want."

"I want help, Captain, you're senior officer."

"Captain Fitzgerald," Erin said, "the odds these two murders were done by the same person are astronomically favorable. Locations only a few hundred yards apart, age of victims almost identical,"

"Maybe," Captain Fitzgerald said. "Too soon to call."

Carl said, "Let's go to the stationhouse. The bum awaits."

Chapter 52

A Walk to a Beach

Padre Pio walked through Golden Gate Park to the ocean. From Sharon Meadow it was less than three miles to the beach. He took his time strolling down Kennedy Drive, richly lined with an enormous variety of trees. He could smell the aroma of sea air being carried inland from the Pacific by a sharp breeze. Overhead, the sky was dotted with stars.

He crossed The Great Highway and stood on the concrete parapet dividing sand and water from the road. Waves broke with ferocity, spaying white drops of surf. Over the ocean, in the distance, the clouds, illuminated faintly by the moon, were ominous, promising rain.

I didn't kill that kid. He was still breathing when I left.

He took off his shoes and walked in the surf. He watched the eternal power of moon and tide.

Thank you, God. Last night was an accident — if the boy tonight had died it would have been murder.

His mind filled with the music of Beethoven's *Moonlight Sonata.* He felt tranquil, in sharp contrast to the fury of the waves in front of him.

He hailed a cab.

The driver asked, "Been in a fight, Father?"

Padre Pio asked the driver to drop him off at a gas station five blocks from Saint Jude's. He hurried into the restroom and looked in the mirror. Blood was caked against his nostrils, on his lips, in his hair. The boy had managed to dig his ring deep into the scalp, causing Padre Pio to bleed. The wound itself was hidden by hair.

He looked ghastly.

Meticulously, he cleaned himself as he wondered, *What was that flash of light? Much brighter than the glowing ember in the tunnel last night.*

Whatever it was it stopped me from strangling that kid..

Chapter 53

Smokey

In the Park Police Station, Carl stood by Captain Fitzgerald and Erin. He said, "I've been going over it in my head and the killing had to take place right before the bum found the kid. I took the victim's temperature when I first arrived and it was still ninety-eight degrees. It didn't start to drop until about thirty minutes later. It would have taken the derelict at least five minutes to get to this stationhouse and report what he'd found. It took at least five minutes for me to respond and another five to take the reading. That's the whole forty-five minutes."

Erin asked, "What 'whole forty-five minutes?'"

"It takes about forty-five minutes for the temperature to start to drop after a person's expired. That puts the bum there almost at the time of death — which had to be almost exactly nine o'clock."

Captain Fitzgerald said, "Let's hope he hasn't completely fried his brain and remembers something."

Erin and Captain Fitzgerald entered a room with a two-way mirror adjacent to the interview room.

Park Station was old. Most police stations had upgraded to using closed-circuit televisions that could record what happened during the interview or interrogation. For someone unable to attend the original interview, they at least had access to a visual and audio record that was much more accurate than a dry transcript or tape recorder.

A disheveled man, dressed in rags, was led in. He sat at the table. His face was leathered a nicotine brown. Head bald, face covered with a raggedy, filthy enormous beard.

Carl entered, placed a tape recorder on the table, and said, "Well, old-timer, what happened tonight?"

The man peered at Carl through bloodshot eyes. "I ain't a goin' tell you."

"Why not?"

The wrinkled face took on a conspirator's look. He winked his left eye and placed a finger to his lips.

"Look, grandfather," Carl said, "I'm not trying to do anything to you. Just tell me what happened when you found the boy."

The old man crossed his arms. Spittle ran from the corner of his mouth, wetting his tangled beard.

"At least tell me your name. There's nothing wrong with telling me your name is there?"

"What do you want to know for?"

"Because you look like you have an unusual name. I'm interested in unusual names, a hobby with me, like collecting stamps."

The old man grinned, revealing blackened teeth. "Smokey."

"Smokey, what time did you get to the park tonight?"

The homeless man squinted at the overhead light. "I haven't been in one of these rooms in awhile."

"What did they get you for the last time?" Carl asked.

Another river of saliva oozed out of Smokey's mouth. "I'm no fink."

"I'm not asking you to fink, Smokey. I asked you what you were busted for. You can't fink on *yourself.*"

"You're right, I've been busted for a lot of things."

"Like what?"

"Common drunk. Vagrancy. Shoplifting."

"Where'd you do time?"

"The county."

"Great place, good chow and easy time, green lawns and no work. I've thought about pulling something so I could take a vacation there myself."

Smokey burst into a cackle, spraying saliva like raindrops, causing Carl to duck. "I get myself sentenced there every winter when the park gets too cold."

"You're one of those legendary guys who live in the park. Smokey, you're famous. Living outdoors, sleeping under the stars. Much more dignified than the bums who sleep under bridges, those hobos and their cardboard boxes. No class. You park bums, now that's class."

Smokey grinned.

"And to think you're smart enough to let the county take care of you when it gets cold. It's December, Smokey, so why aren't you in the slammer?"

"I was. The pricks let me out and I haven't been able to get back in."

"If you help me out on what happened tonight I'll make sure you get, say, ninety days on the farm. That will get you out near the end of March when the weather starts warming up again."

Smokey put a hand to his chin and stroked his beard. "I ain't a goin' tell you."

Carl jumped out of his chair and yelled, "Listen, you old fart! If you don't tell me, I'm going to talk to every judge on the bench. I'll see that you never get sent to the farm again. You'll freeze your ass off. This winter they'll find your frozen body."

Smokey mumbled, "You'd do that to an old man?"

"You bet your wrinkled, ugly, smelly ass I will. I'll run you out of the park too. I'll talk to every cop on the mounted patrol. They let you old shits get away with living there because they feel sorry for you, but when I tell them what an asshole you are, they'll run your butt out. You'll end up under a bridge sleeping in a cardboard box with those other lowlife pricks."

"Don't do that to me, officer, *please*."

"What's it going to be, Smokey? Ninety days in a warm cell or freezing to death under a bridge?"

Smokey put his head down in his arms remaining motionless for almost two minutes. Then he lifted his head. "What did you ask me?"

"What happened in the park tonight?"

Smokey's face cleared. "I ain't a goin' tell you."

Carl's shoulders sagged. He told Smokey to stay put and entered the adjoining room. "I thought I had him."

Fitzgerald said, "He's been drinking so long anything he told you is suspect. We ought to be thankful he didn't forget the boy somewhere between the crime scene and the police station."

Chapter 54

A Long Black Dress

Through the two-way mirror Erin studied the forlorn figure. Smokey had his head cupped in his hands. She said, "He was there so soon, he just may have seen something."

Carl said, "I gave it my best shot."

"Let me try," Erin said, "using a different approach."

She went outside, found a water faucet, pulled her windbreaker's sleeves above her elbows, wet her hands, rubbed them in the dirt and spread the mud on her forearms and face. Then she rubbed mud on her sweatpants.

She paused, and then rubbed mud into her hair.

She turned on her Android's recorder, slipped it into her windbreaker, entered the interrogation room and sat across the table from Smokey.

She said nothing.

The old man started to act nervous, fidgeting and squirming. He kept looking at Erin and then looking away. Two minutes passed.

Smokey asked, "What are you doin'?"

"I ain't a goin' tell you."

"Why not?"

"Because I ain't no fink." His watery eyes stared at her. "Are you a cop?"

"I ain't a goin' tell you."

"Did you get arrested?"

She rasped, "You one of those undercover cops tryin' to get me to fink?"

"I ain't no cop. What makes you think I'm a cop?"

A sly look came over Erin's face. "I know how they put cops in with guys to shoot the shit. To get them to talk when they don't realize they're talkin' to a cop. I ain't a goin' fall for that shit."

"I ain't no cop."

"I ain't goin' take no chances. They brought me in here because something happened in the park tonight and I ain't a goin' tell them diddlysquat."

"What'd you see?" Smokey asked.

Erin said in a disgusted voice, "You're tryin' to get me to fink."

"I ain't. I'm in here just like you."

"You can't tell me because you didn't see crap."

"God damn," Smokey roared, "I found a kid tonight, under some bushes. I was a lookin' for leftovers from picnickers. They sometimes throw stuff in the bushes and I get a lot of good meals that way."

"What about the other guy?"

"What other guy?"

"Guy backin' out of the bushes."

"Oh, *that* guy."

"Yeah, that guy. You're just trying to steal the credit from him."

"What credit?"

"The reward he'll get for discovering the body."

Smokey's jaw jutted. "He didn't discover the body, I did."

Erin dropped her voice to a whisper. "The cops know I saw what happened. They want me to identify who first saw the body. I didn't get a good look at the other guy, but I'll tell them it was you instead of him. You'll get the reward. I'll meet you somewhere after we get out of here and we split the money. Fifty-fifty."

Erin started glancing nervously around the room.

Smokey asked, "What's wrong?"

"I didn't get a good look at the other guy. How can I tell them you were first if I can't describe the other guy? They'll know I'm lyin' and we won't get shit."

"I'll tell you what he looked like."

"And?"

"He was kinda big."

"Big deal. Lots of people are kinda big. What else?"

"It was dark. I couldn't see too well, I was on my hands and knees lookin' for food in some shrubs. I saw him back out of the bushes. I was scared."

"Did he see you?"

"No. What scared me was this huge flash of light that came from the bushes. It was like a sunburst."

"What did you do?"

"I said I was scared. I waited until the guy disappeared, kind of hid for a minute, then I went lookin' hoping that he threw away some food."

"You had to see more than he was just big. Was he thin? Fat? Did he have hair or was he bald?"

"That's all I saw, really. He walked away from me, so I only saw his back."

"How was he dressed?"

"He had on a dress. I thought he was a fag, which is another reason I hid until he was gone."

"What kind of a dress? Short? Long?"

"Black. Down to his ankles."

"Do you know what a cassock is?"

"Some kind of Russian?"

"Not Cossack, cassock."

"No."

"Do you remember anything else?"

Smokey's head bobbed down and rested on his chest. Two minutes later he looked up and said, "I ain't a gonna tell you."

Captain Fitzgerald knocked on the glass. Erin entered the adjoining room. He said, "Great interview. Too bad he didn't get a better look at him. Sunburst bit is puzzling."

"Smokey's been drunk for years, " Carl said. "Who knows what sort of flashes go off in his mind?"

"Forget it," Captain Fitzgerald added, "the black dress is what counts."

Erin said, "Which makes it almost absolutely sure the two cases are related."

Captain Fitzgerald nodded.

"I'll go to the Hall of Justice," Carl said. "The lab and the coroner guys are doing a rush job. Once they're finished, I'll meet you at the deputy chief's home."

"Tell the lab," Captain Fitzgerald said, "I want the DNA done ASAP, no more bullshit delays."

Erin asked, "What about Smokey?"

"What the hell," Captain Fitzgerald said, "arrest him for vagrancy. I'll make sure he gets ninety days at the farm." He studied her. "You look like a bum. Go home. Shower. Put on something nice. Then get over to Brendan's house. I will ask the deputy police chief to form a taskforce."

Erin walked to her car. This time she was cautious and inspected all four tires to make sure none had been slashed. She unlocked the driver-side door and slid in. On the passenger seat was a small, brown envelope.

She realized she had left the passenger window down about a half an inch. She opened her briefcase and put on surgical gloves. Using a small pair of scissors, she opened the envelope and slid out the note.

She read:

> *You must be a really dumb, dumb, dumb fuckin' bitch if you think I won't follow through on my threat. Another child killed and on your watch! The pit of Hell awaits you if you don't quit homicide.*
>
> An Avenging Angel

Chapter 55

Reign of Terror

Paddy entered the Triple M Saloon. It was fifteen minutes after midnight. Father Mario was in the corner.

Paddy waded through the mob, stood next to the priest and pointed at the cup and asked, "Coffee? It's midnight."

"Backing off after last night's drinking bout. Paddy, where you been?"

"Across the street investigating, I figured someone might have seen something last night."

"Did you find anything?"

"I think the murder took place around midnight."

"How do you know?"

"This morning Erin told me the time of death was between eight and just after midnight. I've been at the lake talking to people."

"And you learned?"

"I only ran into a few people: a couple of women jogging, a man walking his dog, and a night chef on his way home. None of them saw a thing. But then, about midnight, I decided to call it quits, mainly because my thermos that was filled with vodka was empty and the Triple M's neon light was driving me crazy. I saw a small circular fire gleaming in the darkness of the tunnel, a pinpoint of light, fading and glowing. Then a guy came out of the tunnel smoking a cigar."

"Do I need details like he was smoking a cigar?"

"I introduced myself and told him why I was there. He sat down with me at the picnic table. The man's breath was a tar pit of cheap tobacco. I turned my head away and gasped, 'Were you here last night?' He told me he was here just about every night. For years now, after the eleven o'clock news he says he goes for a stroll in the park and has a cigar."

"And all this means what?" the priest asked.

"I felt like I was drowning under an onslaught of disgusting smells. Trying not to inhale, I asked about last night. He answered that he was there. He was in the tunnel finishing off the last of his cigar, and heard something. He turned and saw two people across the lake."

"Two figures?"

"He said they stood close together. One looked like he was staring at him in the tunnel. He was spooky, dressed completely in black and much taller than the other."

"What happened next?"

"His cigar was finished," Paddy said, "he went home."

Father Mario asked, "Did you get the name and address of the witness?"

"I forgot."

"But you were in the park at nine?"

"Yes, why?"

"First off," Father Mario said, "your sister already has a witness that places the kid at the scene and alive last night a few minutes before midnight. Second, awhile ago I was across the street watching the wrap-up of a police investigation, an investigation involving another kid's murder."

"What?"

"I ran into Carl. Don't think you know him. He's a homicide cop. He told me a bum said he saw the killer and he was wearing a black dress."

"A black dress? A transvestite?"

"A cassock," the priest said. "A Roman collar at the first murder, now a cassock. *Dumexcrementum volare incipit, monumenta cascadere ad tuum expectandum est.*"

"What?" Paddy asked.

"Translation: When crap starts flying, expect a pile to cascade upon you."

"Like shit hitting the fan?"

"Exactly. The press is going to find out about that collar and cassock, tie the murders together, and five priests are going to be on the news every hour."

"Why?"

"Friar Tuck is off the deep end. He's across the street casting Holy Water, trying to consecrate the ground where the second kid was just murdered. He's getting his picture taken by a bunch of paparazzi and TV news crews. The monk's over there giving one spectacular show, the kind of show those bloodsuckers love."

"Where's Mulheye?" Paddy asked.

"He's up at the church kneeling in front of the altar asking God 'Why?' I don't know where Lewis and Hillman are."

"I don't see what you're so upset about. None of you guys could have done it. Murder, no way. You must all have alibis. "

"The second murder happened at nine. None of us were here then. I have no idea where the other four were."

"Bad luck," Paddy said and sipped his cocktail. "It will all blow over once they find who actually killed those kids."

"In the meantime? The longer this takes the worse it will be for me and my four brother priests. For instance, in my case the press usually overlooks stuff I've been doing, like marrying divorced people and stirring up problems for the archbishop. But now they'll become a howling pack of wolverines, searching for anything that can make a headline, add a paragraph, and embarrass whomever. Anything to sell a newspaper or add one person to the TV viewing audience."`

"What did the cops find?"

"The kid fought back," Father Mario said. "They know that, so there should be a transfer of evidence. What's the motive? Who randomly kills kids? This wasn't a Jonestown massacre; these kids were *selected*, and then dispatched. The press feeding frenzy is just beginning.

"I just overheard one TV guy calling it The Reign of Terror."

Chapter 56

Incoming from AAA

Erin went home, took a shower and scrubbed caked mud off her arms, hair and face. She opened her bedroom closet door, studied the contents.

She decided on an Evan-Picone almond Shadowstripe pants suit.

Erin arrived at Deputy Police Chief Brendan's home. Located in the prestigious Forest Hill neighborhood, the house was on a large lot with well-maintained landscaping.

The foyer led to a living room off to the left, dining room to the right, and central staircase straight ahead. She was shown into the living room. Fitzgerald was sitting on the sofa.

Brendan said, "We're still waiting on Carl to arrive. I'll rustle up some sandwiches." He left.

Captain Fitzgerald said, "Erin, results from the park's bench have come in. Earlier today at the saloon, I managed to lift glasses or coffee mugs used by all five priests — getting their fingerprints. Results: No match on any of the priests."

Erin told Captain Fitzgerald about the note found on her car seat and how she had protected the evidence.

The head of homicide said, "Turn it over to the lab tomorrow."

"Where can one buy a live rooster?"

"Chinatown or the Mission. If it came from the Mission then it was a fighting cock. Those critters are expensive so I doubt one would be killed, even to intimidate or threaten. If it was a fighting cock no one will talk."

She said, "Chinatown?"

"Those folks never talk to cops."

Erin nodded.

"What have you been up to?" he asked.

"The archdiocese's central purchasing revealed two-dozen Roman collars were delivered to Saint Jude's just after Thanksgiving. There were fourteen left in inventory. The priests signed for eight. Two are missing; no priest admits to losing one."

"So a priest lost his collar and is not confessing he lost it."

"It *appears* one of them is lying. Maybe someone else had access to the supply room at Saint Jude's. I have to check to see if that room is locked."

Captain Fitzgerald's cell phone chimed. He answered, listened, then roared, "The police chief told you *not* to release your investigation findings at the zoo? Who the fuck does she think she is? Didn't you tell me *no* forensic evidence was found in the tiger's cage?" He slapped his cell phone shut.

Erin asked, "Problem?"

"Yeah, the usual — political maneuvering. Been thinking about writing a book called *Politics: How it Screws Cops.*"

Captain Fitzgerald had written numerous books and Erin had read them all. The first one she read her dad gave her. It was called *The Mind of a Cop.* After that she read *The Art of Interrogation,* then *Don't Become One of Them.*

Some had astonished her. *Be Prepared for Guilt if You Lie* was basically a treatise on perjury and justification of same. Other books were *How to Deal with a Cop Involved Fatal Shooting, The Art of Interrogation Room Deception; Bad Cop/Bad Cop;* and the sequel *Good Cop/Dead Cop.*

Erin's Smartphone vibrated. She turned on her Android and went online. She had an email from an unknown source. It came with the handle *AAA Homicide Investigations.* The message read: "Attachment contains vital information involving your murder investigation."

Erin wondered, *why would anyone send me an attachment with vital information using my email address? Wouldn't they either phone me or contact the police department?*

AAA is suspiciously close to An Avenging Angel.

She knew because of a constant barrage of all-consuming viruses attacking hard drives, the P.D. had decided not to throw away computers being replaced by more modern models. Instead they sent them to storage. If a detective felt there was a virus threat from an attachment, they could use a discarded computer to open the attachment.

I'll download this tomorrow.

Chapter 57

Fitz as Suspect

Captain Fitzgerald's eyes were closed, his hands folded in front of him. Brendan was in the kitchen making sandwiches.

Erin thought, *anyone can buy a cassock.*

What if Fitz is the killer?

Time to do some research.

She went online and learned Fitzgerald had never married. He supported the Police Athletic League. He was a patron of Cops for Kids and Cops for Christ. He was the only son of Irish parents. He had sponsored, through Christian Children's Fund, over 20 impoverished youths from far away places like Vietnam and Ethiopia and Brazil. He also sponsored three Little League baseball clubs.

Always involved with kids.

Where was he Monday at midnight? Where was he tonight at nine? He lives alone. I can't just point blank ask him.

She dug farther back. College. Lots of pictures: debate club, chess club, political action clubs; never with a woman.

She accessed Fitzgerald's police records.

Not one complaint on file? Impossible. Every cop on the force for awhile had complaints filed, usually based on fictitious smoke and malicious motive.

But Fitz?

None?

He's had them expunged.

Why?

And why did he give the first kid-case to me? The biggest hog of sensational cases drops this monster in my lap, the lap of a rookie homicide cop? Something stinks.

She tried to dredge up when she had actually seen the Roman collar under the bench by Alvord Lake. Not when she first arrived, she was too upset with Paddy for calling her instead of 911. And she couldn't recall seeing it over the next few minutes while she was busy supervising uniforms in securing the area. Then Fitzgerald arrived and pointed out there was a Roman collar under the bench.

A plant? By Fitz?

One problem with suspecting him is Smokey said the guy wearing the black dress was "kinda big." No way would anyone describe Fitz as big. Of course, size is a matter of perspective. If Smokey crawled into the bushes on his knees, searching for whatever the stranger had thrown away, his view looking up would make a small person seem much larger.

She studied her Android's screen.

Fitz, or anyone, could buy a cassock at a rental store, but where else besides Saint Jude's could they get a Roman collar with the archdiocese's stamp on it?

I have to find out how religious Fitz is. Start with his hatred of Dooley.

Chapter 58

What Day Really is the Sabbath?

Deputy Chief Brendan came out of the kitchen. His eyes were as blue as any lake in Ireland. Like many large men he did not plod; he was graceful on his feet.

He asked Erin if she wanted a drink.

"I never drink when I'm upset. And right now I'm mad at the useless deaths of two kids."

He said, "Aren't you married to a cop? Might want to talk this over with him, get it out, helps to verbalize."

"Been divorced six years."

"Sorry, didn't know. Plenty of good men on the force."

"After being married to a cop for sixteen years, I refuse to date a policeman."

The deputy chief returned to his kitchen.

Captain Fitzgerald said, "Great when one gets in a nap, refreshing."

Erin said, "I have to meet with the archbishop again tomorrow. Follow up stuff. But need more background. Besides being an illegal immigrant, why do you dislike Dooley?"

"The phony Eminence. He's as tight as a Muslim at a Knights of Columbus fundraiser. Only reason he wastes time saying Mass is because he has to."

"I assume you never go to Mass."

"I go every Monday."

"Monday?"

"A Commandment states Keep Holy the Sabbath. In the nineteenth century the difference between old Pope Gregory's calendar and the Julian Calendar was discovered to be twelve days. I like Julius Caesar. His calendar was created in before Christ was born. No one really knows what day of the week is actually the Sabbath, so why not Monday?"

"I assume you never go to confession, how can you—"

"Twice a year I go to confession. I go to Mario. This tradition started nineteen years ago when Mario was first ensconced at Saint Jude's. I made a normal confession just before Christmas. A few months later, when Easter rolled around, I was in the Triple M Saloon. I cornered Mario, told him to put on his purple stole, and said, 'Bless me, Father, for I have sinned. Ditto.' I remember Mario grinning as he said, 'I absolve you and ditto on your penance.' Twice a year thereafter the same thing has happened."

"Father Mario is one weird priest."

"A *realistic* priest. He told me a few years ago, when I asked him if I should go back to making a normal confession, 'There's truth in your confessions. It emulates every confession I hear. People promising to go and sin no more and then coming back in a week or two with the exact same sins. All you're doing is getting down to what it actually is: Man's flawed and no matter how hard he tries, usually falls right back into the same rut.'"

Chapter 59

Forming a Task Force

The doorbell rang. Brendan let Carl in. The four cops sat at the dining room table.

Without preamble, Carl handed each of the police officers a copy of the autopsy report and opened his notebook. "The boy had lacerations and abrasions on his neck indicating throttled from the front with both hands. Appears the attacker pushed the boy into the bushes, forced him to the ground and then tried to strangle him. What's curious is the bruises on the neck apparently did not break the hyoid. It seems something other than hands was used to violently crush that vital point. The medical examiner thinks it was something solid, like a rock or a weapon."

"Did the boy draw blood?" Erin asked.

"There was blood and hair under the fingernails, indicating the boy scratched his attacker. There was also blood on the kid's ring. The kid may have cut into his attacker's scalp. We also have a good impression of the murderer's right shoeprint. One impression, the others were disturbed during the struggle. The impression did not match the right shoe of the bum who found the kid."

Captain Fitzgerald said, "There's something about Smokey's interview that's bothering me. When Erin asked, 'How did he walk?' the bum answered, 'He just walked away.' No sign of flight. I find this interesting."

"Why interesting?" Brendan asked. "We know the guy's psycho."

"I'm assuming we're going to start a personality profile. This information should be turned over to whoever is assigned as police psychiatrist, like Sarah."

Erin studied the autopsy report. "This states the boy's hair was wet."

Carl nodded. "Sopping wet when I arrived at the scene."

"The ground was wet," she said. "But the sprinklers were only on from eight to eight-thirty. The boy died at nine. He didn't leave the Christmas play until a quarter to nine. Even if he fell to the ground when attacked not all his hair would have ended up wet. Why was the hair sopping?"

Brendan said, "When we catch the bastard I'll ask him. Any doubt the cases aren't related?"

The three cops shook their heads.

"A few hours ago," Brendan said, "I talked to the chief. I figured we had a repeater on our hands. Fitzgerald asked for and the chief agrees — a taskforce will be set up immediately." He handed Fitzgerald a sheet of paper. "Set up a command post in your office. Erin and Carl will act as liaisons between you and the rest of the taskforce. To start with you'll get six fulltime investigators and four patrolmen from Park Station. Plus you three, of course. I'm going to make an announcement to the press this morning detailing what the department's done in response to this situation. Any questions?"

Captain Fitzgerald said, "I want to saturate the eastern end of the park tomorrow night."

"You'll be falling over undercover cops."

"I will divide the six investigators into three teams. One team to check out the parents, the kids classmates and teachers. A second team will interview the bus drivers who pass that end of the park and examine all local taxi trip tickets. Third team will canvas the neighborhood."

Carl asked, "Erin? Me?"

"Special assignments, let you know in the morning."

"What else?" Brendan asked.

"Some luck."

Chapter 60

Who Needs a Search Warrant?

Brendan asked, "Conclusions, people?"

Captain Fitzgerald said. "There's something I'm working on, it might pan out or it might not. I'll know soon."

"What does it involve?"

"Speculative, but worth pursuing."

"Anything else you need to discuss?"

Captain Fitzgerald said, "This latest murder gives us a sample of the killer's blood, hair and skin fragments found under the boy's fingernails. Carl, when will the lab have the DNA work finished?"

"Bad news. All but one technician is off for the holiday week. And there's a rush job in front of us. One of the supervisors has been accused of sexual harassment and rape. He's Priority One — top of the mayor's list."

"Priority One?" Captain Fitzgerald said. "What's more important than stopping a kid-killer?"

"Politics."

"When will they have *our* analysis completed?"

"Who knows? It's just after midnight, now Christmas Eve."

"Chief Brendan," Captain Fitzgerald said, "once the DNA workup's completed, if I can get into the rectory for ten minutes I could get samples of all five priests' hair off of their combs or razors. We'd learn one of two things: Which one did it or none of them did it. Either way it'd save a huge amount of time."

Erin asked, "How are you going to get a search warrant with Hillman and Lewis standing legal guard over the rectory?"

"Who said anything about a search warrant?"

Brendan said, "Fitz, don't want to hear about it, but do what you have to. Anything else?"

"Remove me as lead in the tiger case," Captain Fitzgerald said. "Replace with someone who's politically sensitive."

"What's going on?"

"Someone obviously hired a spin doctor to turn the public against the tiger's victims. Did a wonderful, if not monstrous, job with the slingshots. Polls now have ninety-nine percent of the public hating the victims."

Brendan said, "A case to strengthen the liability defense?"

"So it appears. Also orders are coming from sources on high for the investigation to drag its feet."

"Why?"

"I assume to keep the investigation's findings away from the lawyers representing the tiger's victims. Results don't have to be turned over to the attorneys until the investigation is officially closed."

"You want me get involved?"

"No," Captain Fitzgerald said, "a waste of time now that politics has arrived. I do think I know why the tiger was able to get out. When the Big Cat Grotto was built so many decades ago, it observed the standard height for the moat to keep an animal from escaping. Then a few years after it was built, a new director didn't like the tigers having to walk on concrete when they were at the bottom of the moat. He added a half-foot of soil and planted grass. When a new director took over, he found the dirt was fouling the drainage system, causing a mess. Instead of removing what was there, he added about a half foot of concrete on top and installed new drainage. Then—"

Brendan held up a hand, "I get the idea."

Erin said, "That explains how the tiger got out, not why it picked that moment to escape."

"That," Captain Fitzgerald said, "we may never know."

Brendan glanced at his watch. "Go home, people, get some rest, none of us are taking today off."

Captain Fitzgerald added, "And none of us will be taking off Christmas."

Chapter 61

A Cathartic Cleansing

In his sparse room, Padre Pio's alarm went off: 5:30 a.m. He turned on his computer and printer. He removed a journal, some paper and a three-hole-punch from his closet.

He clicked on the television. The TV commentator stated, "A taskforce has been created to investigate the brutal slaying of two young children, both murdered in Golden Gate Park."

What? Two children? That second kid was alive when I left him.

The TV commentator continued, "Those vicious, wanton attacks on the defenseless make the heart cry out for revenge. I know there are fringe groups, unsympathetic to the needs of society as a whole, who will, even with the provocation of these bestial crimes, oppose the use of the ultimate weapon at the disposal of the state to inflict. Yet some crimes *deserve* the death penalty."

My God, I've killed two children. Both in the park. Prosecutors will claim I was lying in wait. Special circumstances. Death penalty.

Think, think, think. Is there a defense? A solution? A shield?

He sat at a small table. In front of him was an old computer. He slowly, carefully typed: *Scribo in lingua latina. Cur non? Latina est apta ad essentiam verbi isti quia est lingua sacerdotorum atque juris periti.*

He paused, then continued to type: No, writing this journal in Latin will not protect me. The Church, for centuries — never teaching those they served — hid behind an ancient language few understood. Instead, they dished up pageantry and rituals and threats of eternal hellfire.

I know what I write in this journal will eventually be used to condemn me. I will not use Latin and save some priest time in having to translate into English.

When before the tribunal, Christ Himself used words in His self-defense. He justified His actions. Then He condemned Himself when asked the question, "Are you the son of God?" by answering, "Thou hath said it."

Like Him, writing these words, I condemn myself but with an explanation justifying my actions. I condemn myself not by acknowledging guilt, but by admitting I committed the deeds. There can be no guilt if an act is done out of love. Explaining my actions is the reason behind writing this journal.

Why? I feel those who hunt me are closing in.

I'm not writing in pen. I use a computer as my handwriting is atrocious and I want my words clearly understood, at least by a fellow priest.

It's therapeutic, these mindless tasks: feeding a piece of paper into the printer, using the three-hole punch, and inserting the page into the loose-leaf binder.

Then forcing myself to remember the events over the past few days and what I've done. The media is calling it The Reign of Terror. If they only knew the truth they would change that to The Age of Innocence.

A new page and another break from the chaos of memories rampaging in my mind. As I finish each page I use a white handkerchief and wipe the sheet as a cathartic cleansing of what is written there. These small acts, done with such precision, keep memories of my larger acts at bay.

What catalyzed me into action?

How can I try to explain the moral logic of my actions?

The media frenzy calling for bloodlust can't be cooled by logic; it can't be soothed by anything less than my death in exchange for the children I saved.

My mind is fighting itself; first guilt, then mental justifications. Was this Christ's way of telling me He was also persecuted for His attempts to save souls?

Christ was crucified on a cross because of His love of mankind and His desire to give salvation.

Will I be crucified? Strapped to a chair? Needles shoved in my arms? Deadly fluids forced into my veins? Will my body jerk and twitch in the last moments of life?

Am I brave enough, courageous enough, to face this reality? Or will I kill myself first and leave life committing one more monumental mortal sin?

Padre Pio printed out what he had written and turned off the computer. He carefully wiped each page and then did the same to the journal.

He whispered, "I just might pull this off."

Chapter 62

God's Bookie Blackboard

Christmas Eve morning Erin slept in late and missed her usual run.

Her parrot screeching, "De, de, de, de, de, de," woke her up. She added fresh water to the bird's drinking dish and fresh seed to its feeding bowl.

She donned a business suit and drove to the Triple M Saloon.

She entered the bar. Her brother was talking to Father Mario. She stood behind them, unnoticed.

The priest said, "Maybe you did strike out last night, but that doesn't mean you should quit trying."

Erin asked what Father Mario meant about Paddy striking out and he explained what her brother had done the night before.

Paddy said, "It was all a waste of time. You already knew that the murder happened around midnight."

"But you tried," she said. "That's what counts."

Father Mario said, "The newspaper states the cops arrested some bum who found the second kid."

"Yes," Erin said, "except he's not guilty. Name's Smokey."

Paddy said, "I know a bum called Smokey."

"Then that's something you could do," Father Mario said. "Talk to Smokey — if you can find him. You have an affinity with his kind, a soul-brother relationship cemented by alcohol. You might discover something he didn't tell the police."

"Good idea," Erin said. "Do that, Paddy."

Max came out of the storeroom with the stepladder. On God's Bookie Blackboard he changed the odds: Monsignor Mulheye 15-1; Father Mario 1-1; Father Hillman 8-1; Father Lewis 8-1; Friar Tuck 1-1. Total pot: $4,235.

Mario said, "I'm getting annoyed. People actually think *I* killed those kids."

Max said, "Do I have to remind you every day that the pool is on who *lost* a collar, not who killed a kid?"

Chapter 63

Round Two with Dooley

Erin's appointment with the archbishop was for nine-thirty.

She arrived at the Chancery Office. A cleric led her to the archbishop's opulent dining room. She stood at the end of the table and watched Dooley spoon in a soft boiled egg.

She said, "I have learned that—"

"What's this business of a guy in a long black dress?" Dooley asked. "That is hardly evidence that a person is a priest. It could have been a black raincoat. And why listen to anything a derelict says?"

"I understand. However, I am here inquiring about the health of your priests at Saint Jude's."

"Why?"

"Sarah, the police physiatrist, told me certain illnesses can cause erratic behavior."

"Friar Tuck's dying," Dooley said. "We thought his cancer was in a state of remission, but last week we learned his brain tumor was back — and back as virulent as one can imagine. He'll be lucky to last a week."

"I am sorry to hear this."

"I talked to his physician; she's at Mercy Hospital. She said the monk was at first shocked. He thought he'd received a reprieve. He was deeply shaken, but is now resigned to the point of actually being in good spirits."

"Does the diocese offer psychiatric help on situations like this?"

"What are you getting at?"

"Alcohol can intensify emotions. I have noticed Friar Tuck is drinking far more heavily than usual."

Dooley's chin jutted out. "And you wouldn't be drinking a tad more heavily if you'd just learned you have about a week or so to live?"

"Good point." She paused for a one second beat, then, "Have you heard of The Bank of Justice?"

The archbishop looked startled, then said, "No."

He's lying. "It's an investment fund started by Fathers Lewis and Hillman."

"Nothing illegal in that."

"Are you part of The Bank of Justice?"

"No," he said staring straight at her.

That's sincere. "Is the archdiocese an investor?"

"No."

That's a lie.

She asked, "As all five priests at Saint Jude's are suspects, there are a few questions I need to ask about your relationship with them."

His eyelids glided to a grim half mast.

She said, "Saint Jude's Parish has a hair over a hundred parishioners. After seeing how cost effective your methods are through central purchasing I am having a hard time understanding why you waste money on that parish at all. Shouldn't it be closed?"

He barked out a grunt that passed as a laugh. "That parish costs me nothing."

"How's that possible?"

"A few years ago I *was* going to shut Saint Jude's down — Hillman and Lewis like that part of town: weather's good, relatively safe, and walking distance to their private poker parlor. So they came to me and offered if I sold the land and buildings to them, they'd cover all costs: maintenance, utilities, and wages."

Erin said, "Hillman and Lewis have created their own private mini-diocese."

"Saint Jude's is the only parish that never passes a collection plate."

Erin thanked the archbishop for his time and left.

She thought, *now I know why Dooley let's those mavericks get away with what they get away with. No overhead.*

Chapter 64

The Face of Satan

Erin had parked across the street from Mission Delores, one of the many missions established by Father Junipero Serra along the Pacific Coast. She noticed a photo op, took out her Android and clicked a snapshot. The digital photo had the mission in the background, three priests chatting in the forefront, and a homeless woman sitting with her back against the mission's wall.

Erin walked across the street, circled the three clerics and dropped a twenty onto the old lady's lap. She wished her a "Merry Christmas" and went to her car.

She drove to the Hall of Justice, went to the basement storage area and asked access to an old computer.

She was led to a desk, sat down and went online. She accessed her email account and downloaded the attachment sent from AAA Homicide Investigations.

Instantly the face of Satan appeared on the monitor, complete with fire belching out of his head. He growled in a guttural voice, "You're fucked, fucked, fucked. Say goodbye to your files, you slut. I am Lucifer, the prince of Avenging Angels."

The screen turned to black.

Erin left the Hall of Justice and headed for the Triple M Saloon.

She thought, *what do I know about brain tumors? Do they change a person's personality?*

Friar Tuck, with the exception of Monday night, doesn't seem to have changed even with the knowledge that he is basically a dead man walking.

Chapter 65

The Value of a Life

The Triple M Saloon held quite a crowd for an hour before noon: twelve off-duty cops who had nowhere to go to celebrate Christmas Eve, all five Saint Jude's priests, Angela, Paddy, and his sister Erin.

Angela said, "The tiger lawsuit case is sure to cost someone a fortune."

"No," Father Hillman said. "The boy the tiger killed was only seventeen."

"Lived at home," Father Lewis added, "still in school, no income, no dependants. Life not worth much."

Father Mario said, "That doesn't seem right. I thought the law was conceived to serve justice?"

"Are you really that naïve?" Father Lewis said. "Now if Hillman or I were the one mauled to death, both in our young fifties and making a huge fortune every year, even though we have no dependants the settlement would be astronomical."

Erin said, "So it's based on earnings *potential* instead of the loss on the *possibility* of what a life could achieve?"

"Yes."

"The tiger case is finished," Erin said. "But these kid killings — I can't get a handle on them."

Paddy said, "It's always the one you least suspect."

"What?"

"In Agatha Christie or Rex Stout novels, it's always someone you'd never suspect."

"I've been suspecting *everybody*."

"Think motive," Father Mario said. "What I've noticed in my life is that the most prevalent sin is greed, and right behind it is lust and hypocrisy. Except in Paddy's case, and then it'd be alcoholic gluttony."

Paddy went to the men's room.

Erin asked Father Mario, "Why do you rag my brother so much?"

"I rag him about his drinking, being overweight and purposeless life in an attempt to get him to change."

"Good luck."

Angela took Erin's hand and said, "Come with me."

"I have to—"

"Come with me."

The two women walked towards Saint Jude's and stopped a block away.

Angela checked her watch and said, "Any second now."

The church's belfry rang with the chimes for the noon Angelus prayer. Twelve gongs peeled. After the last bell sounded Angela pushed a button on the device she was carrying and a thirteenth gong rang.

Angela said, "I'd love to see the look on the faces of the little old ladies in the church."

Erin asked, "How did you make this happen?"

"First I made a tape of the church's gongs. What you put outside the belfry vent was the antenna. The chimes and gongs from the church are pre-recorded and automatically played on speakers. All you did was attach my device to the existing system."

The two women headed back toward the saloon. Angela borrowed Erin's Smartphone, called the *Chronicle* and asked for the news desk. She explained that something had happened at the church, a mysterious thirteenth toll. The old lady disconnected and gave Erin back her phone.

Erin said, "Won't one of priests discover—"

"You think any of those guys are going to hump up two hundred steps? Mulheye will tell the press he has no idea where the thirteenth gong came from. Plus you placed everything in the shadows, on beams, so even if one of the priests climbs the stairs, there's no way they'd tote a ladder up there as you did. They won't see anything."

"What's this practical joke supposed to accomplish?"

"It will get more people to church tomorrow, Christmas day."

Chapter 66

An Economic Implosion

Erin drove to the zoo. She went to the director's office and was shown in immediately. The zoo's head was a jovial, diminutive Hispanic man, with an infectious smile and a warm greeting. The smile vanished when Erin brought up the tiger escaping.

"Tragic," the director said, "unbelievably tragic."

"I understand lawsuits have started."

"The zoo's getting sued; the owners of the tiger are getting sued. The Zoological Society is getting sued."

"Doesn't the zoo own the tiger?"

"No, many of the animals are sponsored by patrons."

"Like the Bank of Justice?"

"That bank's a lifesaver. The zoo is costing a fortune every year."

"Meaning?"

"The mayor's going selling the zoo's land to the Bank of Justice. The government can't sell its property without first offering it at fair-market value to other government agencies. That legality has been taken care of by Hillman and Lewis — no takers matched what those two priests offered."

"What about the animals?"

"The zoo doesn't own the animals. They're owned by the city's rich and famous. Bragging rights like, 'I loaned the zoo a baboon, great tax deduction.'"

"What about the animals' home?"

"The Bank of Justice has a lease with an option to buy on twenty-thousand acres of ranchland between San Jose and Modesto. They plan on developing it into a safari park. Visitors will be able to view the animals in a much more natural setting. The weather there is similar to Africa. Where they are now the fog rolls in all the time. Horrible dampness for the animals."

"What will happen to the zoo?"

"The Bank of Justice plans on using the zoo's hundred or so acres as a site for forty mansions. The facility is already gated and sewers, water, electrical are already in place. Even the existing roads will be used."

"Forty multi-million dollar mansions? Who—?"

"All forty were snapped up on options. Lots of those people are members of the Olympic Club; the golf course is just a stone's throw down the road."

"How could the City even consider doing this?"

"The carrot on the other end is the new property tax revenues. Forty private estates on acreage with each worth twenty million, or more, adds up to a lot of new property tax revenue. Not to mention getting rid of the drain this existing white elephant is siphoning off."

"I assume the stockholders in The Bank of Justice are Hillman and Lewis."

"You assume correctly. The Bank of Justice gets a payday on both ends. Our friends the priests negotiated a sensational lease-option to buy on the proposed safari land from a rancher. The financial numbers are astronomical. They get two percent of the construction costs of the mansions — a side deal cooked up with a local hotshot architect/builder/lawyer. They are buying the zoo for peanuts — about fifty million. Forty estates just for the raw land sale — a couple of acres apiece — of around five million per is two hundred million. On the other end they plan on selling the safari zoo when finished for ten grand an acre."

"To whom?"

"All the Bay Area municipalities, plus Central Valley cities like Fresno, Modesto, Sacramento. They're calling it The Northern California Zoo For All."

"The safari land. How many acres again?"

"Over twenty-thousand. At ten thousand per around two-hundred million dollars. None of the cities are doing that well economically, so the payoff is in getting rid of their own zoos and not having to front any money. The loans will be made by The Bank of Justice — at six percent of course. And the bank is in negotiations to buy the existing zoos from various cities like Sacramento, Stockton, Fresno, Oakland and sell the land for residential mansions to the rich in each community."

"A twenty-thousand-acre zoo? More than thirty square miles."

"By covenant, five-thousand acres were slated to be set aside as a hunting preserve, like they have in Texas. Rich guys pay small fortunes to kill things like a gazelle or a lion."

"Dear Lord, I assume the animals that will be offered for the hunt are the ones that will be soon put down anyway?"

"You assume correctly."

"Thereby saving the cost of a vet euthanizing the animals. Hillman and Lewis can see a profit on both ends on everything. Do they also have a taxidermist on standby to make a profit on the hunted animals?"

"I wouldn't be surprised," the zoo director said.

"The tiger getting out could queer the whole deal?"

"Precisely."

"Were they the ones who leaked the bit about the ball bearings?"

"No. They hired a spin doctor. He did. They wanted to divert people's attention from this zoo. Big miscalculation. What it really did was bring into focus the question of how the tiger managed to get out in the first place. And that's the last thing the priests wanted."

"Because it'd question the safety of the whole project, like how safe could a safari zoo be?"

"Exactly."

She asked, "What's the plan now?"

"Use the tiger's escape to show the zoo should be shut down. Not safe."

"And how's that working out?"

"Not good, too much public focus on the zoo now. I plan to make the wild cat grottos super-safe next week — huge Plexiglas viewing windows. No way will an animal be able to get out in a week, or a person fall in."

"I'm relieved to hear this."

"People love this zoo. Attendance has soared since the tiger escaped. You'd think it would have created bad publicity, but a lot of folks are curious; they want to see the grotto. The initial PR disaster has become a PR bonanza."

"The Bank of Justice deal is—"

"Dead. Received a letter this morning from them informing me of such."

Erin thanked the director and drove home. She changed into a jogging outfit and drove back to the Hall of Justice and headed for the shrink Sarah's office.

Could losing a fortune cause either Hillman or Lewis to become so depressed they could kill?

Chapter 67

Twisted Justification

In Sarah's office were pictures of some of the most famous killers in San Francisco history: Dan White, M-13's Edwin Ramos, Charlie "the Cheetah" Ng and his partner Leonard Lake. Also on her wall were wanted posters related to the Zebra and Zodiac murders.

The police psychiatrist was dressed in a New York & Company's 5th Avenue jacket and pants, with white blouse buttoned almost to the top allowing a single strand of white pearls to peek out.

"What's up?" Sarah asked.

Erin said, "What's up with you? You're usually casual Friday every day."

"Just finished a court appearance. Can't go into court wearing roller skates or riding a Harley."

"I assume you've heard the news of the second murder?"

"Fitz sent down copies of the investigation involving both. This changes everything. Monday night could have been triggered by depression leading to dissociation, but last night? That was planned. That kid was stalked."

"Which means?"

"There's no disassociation with the second kid. Plus in the second murder, like the first, there was no apparent need to hide the act. The murderer was unaware that a hobo was near him. That means he didn't check the area before throttling the child. Smokey said the man just walked away. No flight. No flight might mean no fear. And no fear might mean no guilt. Odd, isn't it?"

"To say the least."

"I don't understand is the autopsy report. The second kid's *almost* strangled, then dies of a blunt smash to his hyoid bone? Why? Why not just keep strangling the kid until he died?"

"If this *is* a serial killer how soon can we expect the next one?"

"He waited less than a day before killing a second time. That alone is rare. There is usually an extended period of time between the first and second. Then the time between murders starts to drop. I am afraid the next one can happen anytime."

Erin nodded.

Sarah continued, "No evidence of sexual molestation in the autopsy report. Has the department informed the FBI's Behavioral Science Unit?"

"Not my call," Erin answered.

"There was transference of evidence in the second killing. Has the DNA been sent to CAL-DNA?"

"Not my call."

"Then whose call is it?"

"Fitz's."

"Why is he sitting on all this?"

"I can only guess. Fitz hasn't mentioned using the DNA — other than trying to eliminate or discover which priest did it. And bringing in the FBI would shove Fitz to the sidelines."

"Figures," Sarah nodded. "But not to use CAL-DNA is sloppy. They have DNA for nearly two million people in their data bank. Why wouldn't Fitz use such a great resource?"

"I haven't a clue."

"If I were to do a profile, the first thing I'd note is the acts were extremely disorganized. It appears that both children were just stumbled upon."

"I've been thinking about that. It was unlucky for the second boy to have been where he was when he was. I sometimes jog at night, just to unwind. I've been through the Children's Playground area a hundred times and have seen only a few kids wandering around."

"Something you might want to keep an eye out for is a change in behavior."

"You mean the priests' Monday night drinking bout?"

"No, I mean now. Even if Monday night's murder was performed in an alcoholic blackout, snips and pieces should be coming back to the murderer. Then he kills again. Maybe some sort of *twisted* justification. But still, unless the person is psychotic, he should be feeling remorse. Keep an eye out for that with all five priests."

"Haven't seen remorse from anyone."

Sarah said, "Also, there's no apparent necessity to disguise himself, he was dressed in his cassock."

"Strange."

"We must keep in mind that the killer might not be a priest, rather someone who dressed as one."

Erin thought, *just what I wondered about last night when I considered Fitz as a possibility.*

Sarah said, "Here is the information you wanted on Hillman and Lewis."

Erin took the files, thanked Sarah and went to her office.

The first file was on Father Lewis. He was born in Argentina, in Buenos Aries. His father was a banker, his mother a lawyer. Lewis was born November 1, 1960 — the Day of the Dead for Hispanics. His father was English, his mother Brazilian. His mother died of a stroke when he was nineteen while he was attending Notre Dame. A few months later his father committed suicide.

Erin thought, *just like my dad.*

Lewis inherited $27 million.

He had an aunt living in San Francisco. She was a member of the Blue Army — an international group devoted to the Blessed Mother. She convinced him he had a vocation.

Erin opened the file on Hillman. Born on July 12, 1962 in Maseru, capital of The Kingdom of Lesotho, Southern Africa — the southern-most landlocked country in the world. His parents were heavy investors in the garment district — supplying such giant retailers as Wal-Mart, J.C. Penny, Foot Locker, Levi Strauss and Saks. They employed over ten thousand females, paying them $1.25 a day. They were also heavy investors in the diamond mines near Letseng, Mothae, Liqhobong, and Kao.

The family moved to Boston when Hillman was fourteen. Eight years later, while attending Holy Cross, his father was murdered by the outraged son of one of the garment workers who had died of a stroke while she worked the assembly line.

Hillman's mother moved to San Francisco to be near the Levi Strauss headquarters. She died 22 years later, leaving her vast fortune to her only son.

Strange, Erin thought, *all five priests lost someone to violence. Can that cause a tendency towards violence in the survivor? Have to ask Sarah about the possibility of deep, repressed thoughts regarding murder on the mind.*

After all, I lost my father to violence. And I have had violent thoughts, particularly involving my ex husband.

She phoned and asked. Sarah explained that, of course, violence can breed violence.

Chapter 68

More Confessions

Erin walked into the Triple M Saloon. At five in the afternoon Christmas Eve the place was nearly empty; just Paddy and Mario. Charlie was tending bar.

Erin ordered an ice tea with a lemon twist.

Father Mario held up the newspaper. "Missing children reports on the rise."

"More murders?" Charlie asked.

"Just people starting to worry about their children when they're five minutes late getting home."

Erin said, "I learned from Dooley how the finances of Saint Jude's works."

"Hillman and Lewis," Father Mario said.

"They've purchased the rectory," Erin said. "They could have built their poker parlor in the rectory's conference room. Why didn't they?"

"Might have thought it a tad sacrilegious — and because Hillman and Lewis know what Max does with the money generated from the backroom rents."

"What does Max do with the money?"

"Not my story to tell."

Erin turned and faced Paddy. "Are you going to look for Smokey?"

"Yes, now." Paddy downed his drink and left the pub, holding the door open so that Angela could enter.

Late each afternoon the old lady went shopping for her dinner. She had her own cart, which she "appropriated" from an Italian market down the block and, unbeknownst to her, Max had paid for.

Angela usually had a Campari on the rocks and ask Max to play something Italian on the jukebox. He always obliged with romantic tunes like *Giorgia — Goccce Di Memoria* or *"Loredana Berte — Sei Bellissima."*

Because today was Christmas Eve Angela *had* to go to confession. She cornered Father Mario, they went to the back booth, and she related her sins. When they returned to the bar, Angela ordered a drink and sat by Erin.

Angela said, "Paddy just left. Aren't you supposed to stay with him? It's Christmas Eve."

"He has something purposeful to do, better than sitting at my flat watching me cooking dinner."

"Your Dad's death sure had an impact on both of you." The old lady paused, then asked, "At least you have the kid case to work on? What's next?"

"Discovering what I can about the priests of Saint Jude's."

"You can learn a lot by the way a priest hears confession, even an old gal's."

"What do you mean?"

"Take Mulheye. Sometimes in the confessional I lower my voice so he can't hear me. I whisper away, basically talking nonsense. He never embarrasses me by saying he can't hear or understand what I'm repenting."

Erin nodded, "Considerate."

"Now take Hillman or Lewis. Probe, probe, probe. Lawyers to the nth degree while cross-examining the pettiest of sins."

"Father Mario?"

She waved her drink at the priest. "The Italian's the best, always tells me what I think are sins aren't really sins because I don't act on them. Always gives me a penance of having a cocktail every day for a week, which is why I stopped going to Mulheye and started going to Mario."

The jukebox started to play, "Luck be a lady tonight."

Erin asked, "Why does Max have so many tunes from *Guys and Dolls* on the jukebox?"

Father Mario answered, "Because the first time he ever saw his wife was at a high school play of *Guys and Dolls*. Her role was Sister Sarah. Max told me he sat transfixed in the darkened auditorium and knew this was the woman he wanted to spend the rest of his life with."

"Love at first sight. What happened to her?"

"Ovarian cancer. She basically just wasted away, but never lost her courage, never became angry, never raged against her fate. I heard her last confession. Brought tears to my eyes. She was an amazing woman. It's taken years, but Max is finally starting to heal."

Chapter 69

A Perpetual State of Grace

Paddy wandered into the bar. He gave Charlie a thermos and asked him to fill it with vodka. He looked at Mario and said, "I found Smokey, but he won't talk to me unless I bring him and his pals some wine."

"Why the vodka?"

"The vodka's for me; you don't think I'd share this with a bunch of bums, do you? I'll grab some cheap wine at the store for those guys."

"Are you going to Mass tomorrow?" Mario asked.

"I have trouble with the whole transubstantiation thing, the changing of water and wine into Christ's blood and flesh. If God is everywhere in all places and in all things, then what you priests do on the altar is mere ritual and you could find the living Christ in a glass of vodka or a piece of burnt toast."

"Thank God you dropped out of the seminary," Father Mario said, "also thank God and me you are always in the State of Grace."

Erin asked, "Why is Paddy always in the State of Grace?"

"A decade ago I was getting tired of listening to the same old sins from him. So I absolve him for any of the sins he might commit in the future."

"Can you do that?"

Father Mario said, "I'll find out after I die."

Erin asked, "Paddy, how well do you know Smokey?"

"Over the years I have shared many a belt with him. Served in Vietnam, where he lost part of his mind. The rest of his brains have drowned in booze."

"Do I know him?" Father Mario asked.

"Smokey never misses your Monday Mass. Shy, stands behind everyone else. When he's lucid, he talks about how he wishes he had achieved something in his life besides slaughtering Vietnamese."

Chapter 70

Paddy Arrested

Erin arrived at the Park Police Station.

The night was gloomy, with dense fog enveloping the area. There was a crisp, chilly breeze floating through the trees causing the mist to swirl.

Captain Fitzgerald was in the commander's office studying a map. Various red X's dotted the east end of Golden Gate Park.

The head of homicide showed her where he had positioned the surveillance teams. "Some uniforms volunteered, even though off duty. We have fifteen men and three women in plainclothes scattered about."

"What do we do *now*?"

"We stand by communications here and wait."

"Praying might help," she said.

"My prayers aren't worth fuck-all, but maybe you're still young enough that God listens to you."

Hidden in some bushes in Golden Gate Park were two police officers. It was dark, quiet; only the faint rustle of wind through the leaves made any sound.

They heard a faint moan.

One policeman whispered, "What's that?"

"How should I know?"

Another moan filled the night air. Twenty yards away, a shape, distorted by the darkness, rose from the ground.

"Stop! This is the police."

The shape froze.

"Who are you?" yelled one cop.

"I, ah, I..."

"What are you hiding in the park?" yelled the other cop.

"I, ah, I..."

"What's your name?"

After a pause, "Paddy."

"Hands in the air."

Suddenly, two more men appeared. They talked quietly with the two police officers. Then they searched Paddy and found his service revolver. They handcuffed him and led him to the Park Police Station. Outside a group of reporters and a few onlookers had gathered.

Someone called, "Is this the man that killed the kids?"

Abuse was hurled. A woman, face red with anger, spat on Paddy. Hands cuffed behind his back, he was unable to wipe the spittle away. It trickled down his face.

He was led to an interrogation room.

Through a two-way mirror, Captain Fitzgerald and Erin watched Paddy, now un-cuffed. He sat at a table, head bent forward, hands on face.

Erin said, "I'll handle this."

She entered the room and sat across from Paddy. "Why were you hiding in the park tonight?"

"I wasn't hiding, I passed out. Earlier I was talking to some people and drinking. The booze hit me, mainly because I'd been drinking since early this morning and never took my nap. My head's killing me. Then cops arrested me."

"You might have scared off the killer, what with the commotion caused when you were led here. I want you to tell me exactly what you did tonight."

"I found two bums in Sharon Meadow sitting on a bench. I told them I was looking for Smokey."

"Did you find Smokey?"

"Yes. But he refused to talk unless I bought some booze. Which I did."

"What did you find out?"

"Smokey was pissed. He said he was promised ninety days on the farm, but the cops reneged. I kept asking him if he remembered anything else from last night. But all he could remember was a black dress and some brilliant flash of light. After the booze was gone, the bums left. I was alone."

Captain Fitzgerald entered the room. "Go home, Paddy. And I mean your dump of a studio apartment, not the Triple M Saloon. If you go anywhere beside your place, I will have the two guys who just arrested you re-arrest you. Do you understand?"

"How long do I have to stay in my apartment?"

"I wish I could say forever, but at least until six tomorrow morning."

Paddy left.

Erin asked, "Captain, why were four guys at that location?"

"I assigned two guys to tail your brother."

"Are you still beating that drum?"

"Just a precaution, it's really for your protection. I felt if another killing happened and we knew exactly where your brother was at the time, we could cross him off the list. A lot of murder investigating is eliminating as many people as possible — saves manpower in the long run."

"Why aren't you having the five priests tailed?"

"I am."

Chapter 71

A Shortcut to Death

Padre Pio turned on his computer and typed:

Tonight was frightening. I headed toward the park. I thought about entering via Alvord Lake but decided to head over to Kezar Stadium.

That's when I saw Paddy, handcuffed and between two men, led toward Park Station. I stood at the rear of the mob. I watched a woman spit on him. People hurled curses and threats.

All this anger's really directed towards me.

I feel the spittle on my own face.

They don't understand. No one did. They don't realize that it's because I *love* children that they had to die. Without me they'd end up in everlasting fire.

What would happen if I were caught? What if the police discovered me in the act of taking a life? I'd be bound, the crowd shouting their angry oaths, police beating me — a judge sentencing me — the state executing me. If I'm executed, what will I see?

Either nothingness or eternal suffering.

They have too much evidence from the second boy. Sooner or later the DNA lab work will be finished. Soon they will get some sample of my DNA — a hair, a drop of saliva, something.

After leaving Park Station I decided to walk.

In front of Saint Jude's is a life-sized Nativity scene. What happened was too intense for third person. I am switching to first person.

I study the figures. A shepherd, frozen in wooden immobility, lies prostrate. The three wise men are by the manger, holding gifts as if waiting their turn.

The Blessed Mother stands.

Stands!

My heart felt as if it stopped, then raced ahead chaotically. I watch as the other statues stir, the shepherd kneels; the three kings deliver their gifts.

"I bring gold."

"Frankincense."

"Myrrh."

Joseph hovers protectively beside his wife. Mary, queen of the universe, stands by the manger. The baby's eyes are closed. His face relaxed. His fragile hands rest against the swaddling cloth enfolding Him.

Never have I known such joy. My own hands are empty. I have nothing to give the King of Kings.

The Christ child's eyes open and stare directly at me. His eyes fill with loathing and disgust. The baby Jesus writhes. Tiny hands clench, then violently beat the air, the anger palpable.

My body quivers from a cold deep within. A distant siren blends with the wail of the child.

The Nativity scene became immobile. Each character from a play 2,000 years old is, again, frozen.

Am I having the DTs? I know I am drinking too much.

My dreams are now nightmares.

Chapter 72

The Sixth Disaster = Another One

Erin sat in the commander's office at Park Station. It was 9:10 p.m., Christmas Eve. So far they had rounded up four people, all wash-outs.

Captain Fitzgerald said, "A lot of times in a case like this you arrest someone and later it turns out it wasn't him."

Erin said, "So?"

"But what happens in the meantime? When the press announces some poor sod's been caught, the real asshole decides he's had enough fun and quits. So it stops. That's all that counts right now, it stops. You can't have every cop in the City looking for one prick. What happened to Smokey?"

"Released."

"Hmmm, that has possibilities. If I tell the press we have a suspect and they plaster it all over the front—"

"And the real killer quits? Then we never catch him."

"If we do catch him no jury in this town is going to give the fucker first-degree and the death penalty. The defense will have shrinks lined up testifying no one in their right mind could do such a thing. The bastard gets ten years in a loony bin as a ward of the state. Fuck him. The point is to have it stop."

The command post's phone rang. Captain Fitzgerald answered, listened, and then hung up. "There's been another one, in the alley behind Saint Jude's, next to the playground. Uniforms have already been dispatched to seal the area. Let's go."

Erin and Captain Fitzgerald were at Saint Jude's in less than five minutes.

She walked down the alley. To her right the parish house and a no longer used playground were supported by a retaining wall eight feet high. To her left was the church's parking lot and Saint Jude's. That wall was only two feet high.

The body was against the playground wall. There was no lamppost in the alley; the body was hard to see unless one was only a few yards away.

Erin studied the corpse — older boy, around eighteen. Nose looked broken. There was dried blood caked all over the cheeks and throat and matted hair. Face looks crushed. Unrecognizable.

Deputy Chief Brendan said, "The body was found by Monsignor Mulheye. I told him to wait at the rectory; we want to talk to him."

"Any I.D. on the victim?"

"No. The photo and lab teams are just starting to unpack their gear."

"I see policemen at each end of the alley," Erin motioned, "but what about the playground?"

"That area's also being protected," Captain Fitzgerald said. "The victim's neck looks broken. He could have been thrown over the short fence guarding the playground."

Erin remembered something. She shown her flashlight up against the rectory wall facing the playground and saw the words, "I hate liars."

Captain Fitzgerald said, "You knew that was there. What's it mean?"

"Just another statement by Friar Tuck about Trump."

The coroner took a body temperature reading. "Ninety-eight, happened less than forty-five minutes ago."

Captain Fitzgerald told Erin to interview Mulheye.

She went to the rectory, found him in the sitting room and asked, "Can you think of anything that might help?"

"No." He stared straight ahead. His hands, folded on his lap, held a rosary. Directly in front of him, on the wall, was a small crucifix.

She asked, "Why were you in the alley?"

"I lock the church every night at nine, and then use the alley to get back to the rectory. I like the night air."

She thanked him and walked back down the alley. She said, "Captain Fitzgerald, nothing from Mulheye; he's in shock."

"The teenager put up a struggle, left hand looks broken. He's in good shape, tough, lean muscles. The killer must have surprised him; otherwise I think he could have done some real damage, especially as he had a switchblade in his back pocket."

"Cause of death?"

"Broken neck."

"Any blood from the perpetrator?"

"If the teen managed to get a good hit in, and the broken hand indicates he might, maybe some of the bloodstains on his shirt aren't his. Especially if the killer bent over him and was bleeding."

"Any estimate on when this happened?"

"The temp's dropped. He died about nine-fifteen to nine thirty." He pointed; coming down the alley was Friar Tuck, sprinkling Holy Water. Fitzgerald ordered a uniform to keep the monk away from the crime scene.

Erin asked a lab tech, "What did you find?"

"Not much. The alley's been searched, nothing."

"Not exactly the same M.O. — what with the age and method being different."

"There's a lump on the kid's noggin, backside. Hit from behind, whirls, hit hard in the face, goes down, and then maybe starts to fight back. But already the bad guy has the high ground and advantage. If this kid broke his hand when he went down, instead of from punching the perp, then he didn't fight back. If he went down heavy and the hand was at a bad angle, that could've happened. Or it could've happened when he landed down here."

She asked, "Has the church playground been searched?"

"We're bringing in spotlights. Dark as a pit up there, can't see fuck-all without a flashlight. A patrolman up there said there's a hole in the fence on the opposite side of the playground."

"Why wasn't it fixed?"

"Playground's not used," Captain Fitzgerald said. "The school's been closed for years; not enough attendance. Most of Saint Jude's parishioners are elderly." He pointed at the staircase leading to the playground and said, "The teenager probably used the hole in the fence and headed towards the staircase. A shortcut."

Yeah, Erin thought, *a shortcut to death.*

Chapter 73

Does God Care About *Anything?*

Wednesday, December 25, 2019, Christmas Day, Midnight

Padre Pio turned on his computer and printer and typed:

I've been able to clean the blood off my hands and face. The teenager I killed tonight bled and bled, with a lot of it getting on me.

Inside, my wounds run deep. Like an ax cleaved to my skull. In the chaotic fibrous mass of my brain suns explode, flashing into brilliant novas, then tapering into dying, dead stars, immediately replaced by other burning suns, other dying galaxies.

I went to Saint Ignatius Church tonight. I stood at the rear of that magnificent edifice. There was only one confessional with a light on, signifying a priest was available. A teenager walked in. I know him, he's only eighteen. Bad seed. He entered the confessional.

The confession takes a long time. How many sins can a teenager his age commit? How soon before he's back to committing the same sins over and over?

I had to do what I did. It was his only chance at salvation after leaving the church cleansed, a finite few minutes before more temptation arrived, for everlasting salvation.

I followed him. He snuck through a break in the playground fence. I picked up a rock and bashed him on the back of the head. His blood splattered all over my face as he whirled and went down hard. I used the rock and smashed his face, giving him Paradise, and then tossed his body over the fence into the alley.

I meandered down a path until I stood by the park.

More than 2,000 years ago a baby is born and changes history. Science states there are billions of Milky Ways, trillions of stars, gazillions of planets.

Did God really care about the teenager mauled to death at the zoo in this solar system out on the rim of a galaxy lost among so many other galaxies?

Did God really care a tiger was executed for doing nothing more than what it was created for?

Did God care about the three boys I've killed?

Did God care about *anything*?

He either did or He didn't.

If He did, everything we do is seen by His eyes. If He didn't, then nothing means anything. How does this fit into the equation of unexpected death?

If God cares and loves with a divine love, then most likely the tiger's victim, even if in mortal sin, was exonerated and in Heaven.

Did God whisper to the teenager as the claws lashed out to rip his young throat, "Tonight you shall be with Me in Paradise?" Or, if God was uncaring and away tending to other universes, was the boy's death meaningless?

From what I've seen of the human condition, either way the mauled boy's better off. And so are the three I saved.

This last killing was different than the others. I am not restricted to saving only the young. I hold redemption for any person who is repentant. To find the moment when a sinner feels remorse and feels, even if only momentarily, amends, that was the time to strike.

That moment is after confessing. As a priest, I know every time when the moment arrives.

I daydream of the multitudes I can save: young and old, men and women, each generously brought by me to the face of the Almighty.

Chapter 74

Another Senseless Death

Erin arrived home, tossed her keys on the kitchen counter and froze. In gigantic red letters across all four of her Monet paintings were the words: "*Fuck you!!!*"

On the opposite wall, her own photos of the four seasons were savaged by the lettering: "*Die, you fuckin' whore!!!*"

She saw a red spray can under her radiator. She took an evidence bag out of her briefcase, took photos of the violations on the Monet's and her photographs and then bagged the spray can.

She realized that if it had been chilly, instead of balmy, that spray can could have overheated and exploded.

She went back to the kitchen and opened the refrigerator. Inside was her parrot De De — missing his head. Next to the mutilated body was a brown envelope. Once again she used her camera and took photos. Then she carefully opened the note and read:

> *Last warning, bitch.*
> *Children have died.*
> *Quit homicide or I will kill you.*
> *I can feel my hands closing around your fuckin' neck.*
> *I can feel the joy in my heart as I watch the life dissipate*
> *out of your eyes.*
> *You will burn for all eternity.*
>
> An Avenging Angel

She took a photo of the letter then placed all the evidence in a plastic bag. She thought about driving back to the Hall of Justice to turn in the evidence, but she knew she was too tired. Instead, she stored the bag in the refrigerator.

Erin felt the tears coming and tried to fight them off. She had bought De De a few months after her divorce was finalized. Over the years she had become fond of the pet and its antics.

Who'd kill such an innocent creature? What a senseless death.

She went to her bathroom and opened the door. Once again she froze. A huge cross, with dripping red blood, covered her vanity mirror. Underneath the cross were the words *Hell* and *Erin.*

She found De De's head in her shower. She reverently brought it to her refrigerator and placed it with the other evidence.

She choked back a sob.

Erin examined her front door for evidence of tampering. She found none. She went to her bedroom window, which gave access to a fire escape. The window was unlocked.

Did I leave it unlocked or did someone jimmy it?

She found her butcher knife in the clothes hamper. The blade was covered with blood. She put this with the other evidence.

Just as she was falling asleep there was a loud knock on her front door. She opened it and Angela staggered in. She was holding the small statues of the Blessed Mother and Jesus that she kept outside on her stoop. Both heads were missing, the necks covered in blood.

Angela sat on the sofa and sputtered out, "Who did this? And *why*?"

Erin went into her bedroom, picked up a pillow, returned and placed it on the armrest of the sofa. She patted the pillow and the old lady lay down.

"Close your eyes and try to relax," Erin said and picked up her cello. She inserted a DVD into her stereo. The piano part of Mozart's Seven Variations for cello and piano in E flat major began. From the stereo came four metronome taps and then the music began. She played along while carefully watching Angela.

Erin thought, *whoever did this entered through the bedroom window. Then went downstairs, picked up the two statues, came back upstairs, killed*

De De and soaked the blood on the statues. Then marked the bathroom mirror with...

That's not what happened, it would take too long and been dangerous. Angela might have heard him on the stairs and, thinking it was me, saw him.

By the fourth variation she heard a faint snore. She turned off the stereo, took the comforter from her bed and tucked it around her friend.

She examined the statues. She held one up to her nose and sniffed. The red wasn't blood — *it was dried paint.*

Whoever did this entered via the window, spray-painted the walls, killed De De, used the bird's blood on my vanity mirror, left by the fire escape, went around the building, retrieved another spray can, snapped the heads off the statues, sprayed the red paint, then left with the two heads.

This has gone beyond me. Why hurt an old woman?

Chapter 75

A Whore and a Hag

Padre Pio sat in front of his computer. He went online, researched and then typed as quickly as he could.

He printed out his latest entry, used the three-hole punch, and inserted it into the journal.

He reread what he had written about a dream involving a woman: There's a noise in my head, a buzz of angry bees fighting someplace behind my left ear. Bees seem to flash by the thin curtain of my eyes. It feels as if they're spreading layer after layer of honey in the already diminishing space left in my skull.

I imagine the lake and the fiery, pulsating glow; the boy's face filled with hate. I still feel the texture of the boy's neck against the pressure of my hand.

The voices from hearing confessions swirl in my mind; a snatch here, a bit there. They taunt me. Yes, we've sinned, we've fallen to temptation, but not to the depths you have.

I feel sleep coming.

I'm in a daze, moving without seeming to move — one moment in the rectory, the next outside. I wander. My senseless lack of direction seems to sooth me. Soon I am in an area with gaudy lights and bustling crowds.

I ask a woman if she can help me get home.

"If you have the price, I have the help."

A streetwalker. I feel no revulsion; I am far lower on the ladder of sin than she. I say, "I'm a priest."

"Then you need help more than most." She grins, white ivory surrounded by red rouge. She takes me by the arm and steers me down a hallway that seems to stretch on forever.

The woman opens a door and pushes me inside. The room is white, except for one wall covered by a black curtain. The harlot disappears.

On a bed in front of the curtain is a young and beautiful woman with luxurious black hair cascading over her shoulders. She wears a yellow blouse; a tan skirt barely covers her knees. Her eyes are closed. A wisp of hair falls carelessly across her forehead. Her lips are partially open, revealing a luminous gleam of teeth.

My mouth is dry, lips taste of salt.

Music explodes in my brain. The lyrics of the group Nine Inch Nails reverberates its monstrous thunder in my head: "*Let me violate you, let me desecrate you.*"

A disembodied voice says, "*Sing along.*"

"I've got no soul to sell," I sing.

The young woman smells like lilacs.

I want to touch her. I clench my hands by my sides.

Somewhere overhead a disembodied female voice commands, "*Touch her cheek.*"

My hand rises involuntarily, moving to another's will. My fingers brush her skin, an electric spark sizzles through my body. I caress her hair.

"You can have my isolation. You can have the hate it brings."

I implore my mind to think of God, to think of Jesus, to think of anything else besides the words oozing from behind the curtain and into my brain.

"*Touch her neck.*"

I mumble, "Oh my God, I am heartily sorry..."

"*Kiss her.*"

I feel the soft pressure as she returns my kiss, feel the soft air as she exhales.

"*Unbutton her blouse.*"

Quivering, my hand unloosens the top button. The blouse falls partially open. Her skin is unblemished. I quickly unfastened the remaining three buttons. Her breasts shallow rise and fall is in a counter tempo to my own wildly beating heart. Her waist is tiny, with two shallow troughs between pelvic bone and stomach.

"*Touch her ribs.*"

My hands jump to obey. Her body feels warm. Her tongue wets her lips.

"*Move your hands away.*"

I fight this order. This delicious feeling must continue forever. With sheer force of will I keep my hand upon her body. I cup one of her breasts.

Incredible joy.

"*I command you, move away.*"

I refuse. My resolve is fueled by my continuing contact with her flesh.

She takes my hand and as one we explore her body.

"*Fornicator!*" roars from the curtain. "*You are condemned.*"

"No," I mumble. Her skin is moist, glistening with sweat. My hand moves inside her thigh.

I reverberate with passion. Blindly mounting her, we seem as two beings merged into one. My mind blackens, my hips grind, my back arches. All strength rushes from me. I slump to the floor, drenched in perspiration.

A screeching cackle filled with hate comes from the curtain. "*Look at her!*"

The woman's face is now that of a hag; her body sagging, wrinkled and coarse.

Triumphant words ring out, "*For this you are damned, for this you will burn, burn, burn.*"

I beat the hag with my fists, my hands find their way to her throat, her eyes fill with agony, not repentance. I squeeze harder. I will teach her to atone for her sins. I will save her from herself. Her body thrashes from inner confusions.

The life in her eyes vanishes.

Chapter 76

Who Murdered De De?

Erin woke up just before seven. She was bone-tired and decided to skip jogging. Outside it was foggy, with a faint drizzle.

She put on a faded pair of Levi's tucked into calf-high boots, a black, long sleeved blouse and a leopard-print cashmere shawl that she had bought last Christmas when she splurged at Neiman Marcus.

She drove to the saloon. Charlie was tending bar. She saw Paddy sitting in his usual spot near the far corner. She joined him and asked the bartender, "Back-to-back shifts? Where's Max?"

"Don't know. He asked me to fill in this morning until he gets here."

Father Mario entered. "Just finished saying the six-thirty Christmas Mass. The old ladies are in shock about this third murder. So am I."

The bar's phone rang. Charlie gave it to Father Mario who listened for a few seconds then said, "No can do."

Erin asked, "Who was that?"

"Archbishop Dooley. I should be ashamed that my heart soars when he phones and makes useless threats. But it doesn't. Just ordered me to tell Hillman and Lewis no Latin at this morning's High Mass."

"Aren't you afraid of his wrath?"

"Dooley will never move on me because he knows if he does, my next phone call is to the INS. The federal government will never deport that Irish wetback; too much political flack. But Dooley understands that if it ever came out he's an illegal, he'd end up a laughing stock — the butt of jokes from here to Dublin."

Erin nodded.

Father Mario eyed her. "This case with the kids has to be depressing for you; why don't you go out to dinner with Max? Might cheer you up."

"What?"

"I think you two would make a great pair."

"I told you, he's lucky I'm in homicide, not vice."

"When you *were* in vice you never did anything about his bookie business. Why is that?"

"Too many cops use his services."

"You overlooked it then and you overlook it now. So why not go out with him? Trust me, you need someone."

Erin thought, *Max is a rough-edge, good-looking guy, wife dead, and, as far as I know, no girlfriends. He was also age appropriate. Of course, the downside was being a bookie. Upside a bookie's better than dating a cop.*

A couple of times in the past year she had sent out a few mild feelers. Things like, "Max, you always eat delivery or takeout food, like pizzas or fried chicken. Don't you ever hanker for a home-cooked meal?"

"I'm kind of set in my ways."

She never built up enough nerve to just out-and-out ask him to her place for a meal. She was out of practice with small talk, plus any emotional or physical feelings, all of which seemed to have died during her vitriolic divorce.

Max walked in and bought a round: screwdrivers for Paddy and Charlie, coffee for Father Mario and Erin.

Paddy asked, "Where have you been?"

"Reno."

"You don't get enough gambling in your life here?"

"Wasn't gambling. Super Bowl's coming up. I set up a deal to layoff action if too much comes down on one side." He asked Charlie if any bets had come in on the latest God Pool.

Charlie handed over a huge wad of betting slips and said, "I'm bushed, ended up sleeping in the rear booth last night. Are you taking over?"

Max relieved his bartender. He went to the blackboard and changed the odds. All three shifts at Park Police Station had gone through their rotations over the past three days, all the cops had heard of the pool.

Using chalk, Max wrote: "Monsignor Mulheye 13-1; Father Mario 1-1; Father Hillman 5-1; Father Lewis 5-1; Friar Tuck 1-1. Pool total: $8,965.00."

Erin asked, "How does this work? What if the collar belongs to Friar Tuck?"

"Same as a horserace, odds fluctuate with the bets. In the last pool there could only be one winner. This time there will be multiple winners and the more money on one person, the bigger the payoff on the others. Right now, if you bet a dollar on Friar Tuck you'd get back two. If you bet a dollar on the monsignor you'd get back fourteen; your original dollar plus thirteen."

"That foundation's going to get a large contribution."

Angela came in with the morning paper. She sat next to Erin and said, "Nothing, no report of a noon miracle at Saint Jude's involving a thirteenth bell. I can't believe it, there were at least a half-dozen women in the church. Can't they count?"

"Someone from the press will show up to investigate. Were you planning on doing the same thing at noon today?"

"No, I'm disgusted. All that work for nothing. Drive me home."

Erin left the saloon, dropped Angela off at her flat, and drove to the Hall of Justice. Carrying the plastic bag holding the evidence of De De's murder, she went to the lab. She asked the technician to dust the handle of the butcher knife for prints. He did and found some. She asked him to compare them to her own. They matched.

As she walked to her office, a crimson image flowed through her mind: an image of her using the butcher knife to behead whoever had murdered her beloved pet.

Chapter 77

Proper Seduction as an Art Takes Time

E rin left the Hall of Justice and drove home. She knew she had to do something to perk herself up. She wondered, *should I immediately buy another parrot, or should I just donate the empty birdcage to the SPCA?*

She stood in front of her bathroom mirror. She had cleaned away the bloody cross the night before, to ensure that Angela would not see the awful thing.

She picked up a lipstick. *Maybe I should start thinking about finding a man instead of a pet. Trouble with makeup is it doesn't work for the athletic type. And if I have to choose between running or dabbing on a bunch of different color touches that are supposed to make my face look healthy, think I'll opt for just making my face look healthy by having it actually be healthy.*

That's one of the most ridiculously convoluted conversations I've ever had with myself.

She opened her bedroom closet: a dozen business suits, a dozen jogging outfits and one black cocktail dress. She went to her hall closet: skirts, blouses, and sweaters — none of which she had worn in ages.

She wasn't sure what to do. Dress for success or seduction?

Maybe middle ground.

She chose a chartreuse-green, below-the-knees skirt and a white blouse. Her favorite sweater was a raspberry-colored, cashmere turtleneck.

She put the sweater on and thought, *I know these really clash, but I'm so rusty at this I need help.* She phoned downstairs and a minute later Angela toddled in.

The old Italian looked at her, a stare that took an excruciatingly long time to go from bare feet to hair, then said, "Are you using drugs?"

"No, just lost the touch on makeup and dress. Are you feeling better?"

"Yeah, I'll just buy new Blessed Mother and Jesus statues. But if I find out who did this I will nail him with my wasp spray right in the eyes, full can load. I'll blind the son of a bitch."

"I really *have* lost the touch with dress and makeup."

"When you have sapphiress for eyes you don't need help in that area. You have lovely eyebrows, so forget eyeliner. You have a honeymooner's dream of a crimson sunset for hair, so don't need help there. But your hair is a jumbled mess. Ever heard of rollers?"

"Takes time, easier to just comb."

"Seduction takes time. Who's your target?"

"Beg your pardon?"

"You need a different approach depending on your target. If, for instance, you're going after Mario—"

"Father Mario? He's a priest."

"Dear, I was in the saloon one night when you were both tipsy, huddled up in the corner oblivious to anyone else in the place. You were all over the poor guy. I became so embarrassed I left, and after only one Campari."

"Father Mario's not the target."

"Then who?"

"I think me. Meaning I have to make *myself* feel better just by being better before I go trolling."

Angela nodded. "Let me know when you figure out who you want to allure. Each man takes a different approach. You don't go fishing for a whale with a hairpin, anymore than you use a blunderbuss on an insect."

"Give an example."

"If you really wanted to win Mario, I wouldn't try it in the Triple M. That's his stomping grounds. His kind needs the outdoors. You have to become the mother hen with the broken wing; the helpless, wounded look of the injured that turns to the adoring shine of the healed when he pays attention to you."

"And just how am I supposed to accomplish this, assuming for a moment that I actually *want* to?"

"When you actually want to, let me know."

"What if the target was Max?"

"Max? Easy, slow, slow, slow. Two steps forward and four steps backwards."

"That will never lead anywhere."

"Two steps forward, four steps backward can lead to him taking two steps backwards and four steps forward. Max wants to open doors, take his hat off in elevators, pull your chair out, stand when you enter a room, kiss your hand. He wants a woman on a pedestal so he can adore her."

"I don't want adoration; I want a partner," Erin said as she changed back into jeans, blouse and shawl.

"Ever tried being adored? I was, before my man went crazy. Don't knock it if you haven't had it. Flowers, poems, a kiss when you first wake up, aren't the worst way to live with a mate. Don't get me wrong, I think Max also wants a partner and needs a partner, not a goddess. But he also cherishes what goes on between a man and a woman."

"Sometimes you just can't compete with a ghost."

"It's the ghost who can't compete. You've assets a ghost hasn't: flesh and blood."

Chapter 78

I Expect the Truth

Erin and Angela sat at the kitchen counter. The old lady said, "If you're not going to try and spark Mario, maybe you should just talk to him."

"Why?"

"He gives great advice. Maybe go to his next outdoor service. I love his Monday morning Mass. I get tired of all the old ladies at Saint Jude's. Out in the park the sun's rays penetrate through the trees. After Mass Father Mario plays the French horn, and the man who owns our favorite den of iniquity, Max, he's always there playing the violin."

"Max plays the violin?"

"He plays lovely. Your brother comes too, with his clarinet. During Mass they play things like *What a Friend We Have in Jesus* — which I don't approve of as it's Protestant. But they play it so beautifully. After Mass they play snappy tunes. Once in a while Lewis and Hillman show up and sing. Those lawyerly mouthpieces have unbelievable, sensational voices."

Erin said, "Paddy quit playing clarinet and cello duets with me years ago, but now I find out he's part of a trio with Max and Mario? What else about Paddy's life has he left me out of?"

"Who knows why Paddy does anything? Or anyone else, for that matter."

"Angela, if you think of anything involving those five priests will you tell me immediately?"

"Of course," the old lady grinned, "unless you want to debate about your love life first. You shouldn't be spending a beautiful Christmas day with an old crone like me. You should be sparking some fellow. Lowering the eyes and fluttering the eyelashes."

"Doesn't work that way anymore."

"You think I don't watch television or movies? All these women giving it away? No seduction dance, no sashaying, no coquettishness, no mystery. Just hop in bed and break the springs. Stupid."

"Times have changed."

"Times between men and women have *never* changed and never will. What's changed is the way women and men act. But it will all cycle back, you'll see. It's already started. I'd hate to thank a scourge like AIDS, but it has cooled down the, 'Hi, how are you, let's get in the back of my Chevy,' stuff. But you need to make a change in your life. Open up, make a move."

"My life is rigid. Work primary, then health. If my brother is the king of booze, then I'm the queen of moderation."

"Not real healthy to have a non-existent sex life," the old lady said. Adding, "Men must ask you out; you're still a looker."

"I get approached by men all the time at work, but after my ex I will never get involved with a cop again."

"When is the last time you dated?"

"Two years ago, while racing through the park, a runner suddenly appeared by my side. Good-looking, about my age, excellent shape. I was doing six-minute miles and he kept pace and talking to me without gasping for air."

"Ah, the seduction dance begins."

"By the time we reached the ocean I knew his name, his occupation, his education and marital status was single."

"Some enchanted evening, you will date a stranger."

"Not quite. It took three more encounters while running before I said yes to dinner. He took me to a lovely, romantic French restaurant in the Marina. Copper pots hung from a beamed ceiling, a stone fireplace in the corner, and waiters with hushed voices. The more I learned the more I was tempted."

"Completely natural… and healthy."

"The next Monday, however, I went to work and found out through Internet research that everything he had told me was a lie. The biggest lie — married."

"Bastard. Let's head for the Triple M, I'll buy you a Christmas drink."

"In a minute. I was stalked by an immoral predator. I had allowed it out of hope, otherwise I would have Googled him before ever going out in the first place."

"What happened when you confronted him?"

"He laughed and said, 'What did you expect? The truth?' And Angela, I told him, 'Yes, I expect the truth and I will settle for nothing less.' No more lying husbands, no more lying dates."

"I'm sorry."

"I know my social life is near nil. Besides the shrink Sarah, who I love like a sister, a friend, a fellow runner, and a fellow police officer, my closest and dearest pal is you, Angela."

"I am flattered."

"I consider you my grandmother."

"I wish I was."

Chapter 79

Big Brother — Big Sisters

When Erin and Angela arrived at the saloon it was nearly empty — just Max and Father Mario. The women asked what the men were talking about.

Max said, "Sin, and why some things considered sins are ridiculous."

Erin asked, "Like what?"

"No sex outside of marriage," Father Mario said. "Look at you, Erin, a gorgeous example of the female. All the alluring things: flaming red hair like a lava waterfall, body like Venus de Milo. Looking at you, even though a priest, I'm not supposed to feel lust?"

Angela said, "I'm ninety-six and still feel lust, and it's no one's fault but God's. He could have just as easily have made conception a non-contact activity, like the love life of salmon. Lady lays eggs; later man casts seed."

Father Mario said, "Sounds boring. How many kids have you had, Angela?"

"Sadly, none, but not for lack of trying. Each month I prayed, hoping I was with child, but each month nothing. Pleasure, yes; pregnancy, no."

Erin thought, *I made one mistake when I was sixteen, became pregnant and the shit who impregnated me talked me into an abortion. Something went wrong during the operation. Something terrible.*

Angela said, "I have been a Big Sister a few times over the years. Now too old to continue, but it was fun while it lasted. Now I'm just a surrogate grandmother to this one." She patted Erin on the back. "Big Brothers Big Sisters have an office right here in town, down by Union Square. Do you good to have some one to be responsible for."

Father Mario said, "Max is a Big Brother."

Max said, "Mario, I have asked you never to discuss my private life."

Chapter 80

A Search Warrant

Erin asked for coffee, moved to the rear booth and opened her briefcase. For the next two hours she reviewed all the video and audio she had accumulated over the past few days.

Captain Fitzgerald came into the Triple M and told her he wanted her to accompany him to the rectory. He had managed to get a judge to sign a search warrant. "Sadly, he said, "I could only convince him to give access to Friar Tuck's room. I got the monk to sign a release. "

The two police officers went to the parish house.

Father Lewis answered the door.

Captain Fitzgerald said, "I need to look about the rectory."

"Have a search warrant?"

The head of homicide handed over the document.

Father Lewis peered at it and said, "This allows the monk's room, nowhere else. Hillman and I are saying this morning's ten-thirty High Mass. I have to join him soon; we have to make this quick."

The two cops followed the priest up a flight of stairs and down the hall to an open door.

Captain Fitzgerald started to open a door and Lewis said, "That's *my* room. The one across the hall is the monk's."

"Why's his door open?"

"I assume he left it ajar when he went out this morning."

The room was sparse, a single bed, neatly made.

Captain Fitzgerald glanced about the quarters. "No radio? No television?"

"None of us priests have a radio or a television in our bedrooms. There's a TV in the living room downstairs, and also a computer and printer."

A small table had nothing on it except a copy of *The Imitation of Christ*, a Bible and a whip.

Captain Fitzgerald arched an eyebrow at Father Lewis.

The priest said, "The monk believed in self- flagellation, to purge the body, mind and soul of evil."

Erin stared at the Bible and wondered, *why is that ringing a bell? That Bible, or any Bible, is hooked to something else in this case. But what?*

Captain Fitzgerald opened a closet door and knelt. He put on plastic gloves and carefully handed Erin a black right shoe and the whip. "Bag and tag these."

Father Lewis said, "I want a receipt."

Captain Fitzgerald wrote out a receipt for the two items, thanked Lewis for his time, wished him a Merry Christmas and went back into the hall. He started to open another door.

Father Lewis stopped him with, "That's Father Mario's room."

Captain Fitzgerald said, "Just looking for a bathroom."

"If you need a bathroom use the one downstairs."

Captain Fitzgerald led Erin out of the parish house.

She asked, "Don't you have to use the restroom?"

He tossed the bag with the shoe and whip into his trunk. "Just getting the bedroom layout fixed. The one at the end of hallway must be the monsignor's."

"Planning a raid?"

"You never know. It'd make things easier if Lewis wasn't guarding the Bill of Rights so fanatically. He should be president of the fuckin' ACLU. If we could get DNA samples from all those guys, it'd save time."

Captain Fitzgerald parked in front of the saloon. He said, "Going to try and get my hands on Mario's biretta. He leaves it on the bar when he goes to the back booth or the restroom. I'll try to lift a couple of hairs and—"

"Oh, for Pete's sake, wait here while I run inside." She entered, was gone about a minute then reappeared. "I figured Father Mario didn't fall from the same legal tree as Lewis and Hillman. I told him the lab had finally finished doing the DNA work on the transfer of evidence from the second murder. I asked him straight out for a sample of his hair. He yanked out a couple."

Captain Fitzgerald said, "Never thought of the direct approach."

"I'll take the evidence to the lab," Erin said.

"I'm calling the archbishop and get some leverage on Lewis."

She drove off.

Captain Fitzgerald entered the saloon. He used his cell phone and called Brendan. He asked him to come to The Triple M, and then ordered a coffee and brandy.

Mario asked, "Fitz, you rarely drink. Plus, aren't you on duty?"

"Going to need this for what I think is coming next."

Chapter 81

A Fuckin' Tunnel

Erin dropped Father Mario's DNA sample off at the lab and drove back to the Triple M Saloon.

Paddy wasn't there. Captain Fitzgerald was sitting with Mario. She wished them a Merry Christmas.

"What a mess," Father Mario said. "If one of us priests did it and you prove it, then a trial, appeals, on and on. This case will linger and linger and linger smearing the Church... and also you guys."

"Us?" Captain Fitzgerald asked. "How do you figure that?"

"You've had the Roman collar from day one. You hid the fact. You should have had a tail on all five of us from the moment you found the thing. Or if not Day One, absolutely after the second kid died."

"I did," Captain Fitzgerald replied.

"What?"

"Didn't do any good."

Father Mario asked, "Where did you place them?"

"Two parked across the street from the rectory on Hayes, watching the front door, and two on Clayton for the side exit. From seven last night until the third victim was found. I'm going to discipline those cops. No entries. But a teenager died right around the corner from where they were keeping surveillance."

"Your guys watched the rectory," Father Mario said, "not the church?"

"Why should I place anyone at the church?"

"Any one of us could have left the rectory," the priest said, "killed the third kid by the playground, and gone back to our room without your men seeing us."

"How?"

"Via the tunnel."

"There's a fuckin' tunnel?"

"A lot of parishes have a tunnel connecting the church to the rectory, running basement-to-basement. Really depressing place, reminds me of the Catacombs. But it's a great shortcut if it's raining, or to get to Max's place. Use the tunnel, then go out the side door of the church and you save having to walk around the block."

"Then why was Monsignor Mulheye using the alley?" Erin asked.

"He goes every night at nine to the church, getting there via the tunnel. At the church he locks the doors — which have to be done from the outside. Then he walks back to the rectory using the alley."

Deputy Chief Brendan arrived at the saloon, learned about the underground route and said, "I want to see this tunnel."

Captain Fitzgerald asked, "Mario, where's Lewis?"

"Saying High Mass with Hillman and Mulheye. Friar Tuck's down at the soup kitchen."

"Do we need a warrant for you to show us the tunnel?"

The priest shook his head.

"Lead on," Fitzgerald said, "never thought of a fuckin' tunnel."

Chapter 82

The Crypt

Once at the rectory, the three cops followed Mario down a staircase. The walls were made of stone, the stairs creaky wood. When they arrived at the bottom, the floor was large blocks of carved granite. The passageway was wide; they could walk four abreast. There were light bulbs every twenty feet, dangling from cords and encased in cone-shaped shades. The light spilled down, dimly lighting the floor.

"I'm surprised," Captain Fitzgerald said, "it should be musty down here, but the air is surprisingly fresh."

Father Mario said, "The miners who built all this were deep-shaft miners."

Brendan said, "What's that have to do with the air being fresh down here?"

"The five deep shaft miners constructed the airshafts that service this tunnel and the basement below the church. They were good at their jobs."

"If there were wall torches," Erin said, "I'd think I was back in the Dark Ages."

"Before electricity it did have wall torches," Father Mario said.

Erin looked at the walls and said, "My God, a series of murals down here?"

Father Mario said, "Yes, Friar Tuck likes to prove that a picture is worth a thousand words, mainly because he is unwilling to utter a single word."

Erin studied the first panel. On top was: "Thou shalt not have false gods before thee." Below was a picture of Trump. There was money falling out of his pockets, money sticking out of his shoes, money clutched in both hands, money stuck behind both ears.

Erin said, "What's the point? The only people who would see this art are the priests at Saint Jude's."

"Correct," Father Mario said. "The monk never explains any of his work, but I think it was to remind his fellow priests that we have to remember that examples set by those at the top become guidelines for many below. The god of greed is more prevalent in the population now than anytime in my life."

The next drawing was: "Thou shalt not bear false witness." The drawing was a ghostly image of Rudy Giuliani with a cartoon dialogue balloon above containing the words, "The truth is not the truth."

Erin said, "I am fairly sure I can guess what's in the panel involving adultery."

"Coming up," Father Mario cheerfully said, "but please remember: the women were single and were not adulterers — rather fornicators. Trump was married hence an adulterer."

The artwork was of Stormy Daniels on one side of Trump, on the other side of him Heather McDougal. Behind them, standing on a hill bracketed by crosses, was the First Lady holding her infant son Baron.

Brendan said, "Never thought of this before, but who names their kid Baron? Why not Prince? Be interested in hearing a shrink's take on the mindset behind the name. And why not be done with it and name your kid King or Emperor?"

"I am a shrink," Father Mario said, "and the mindset is a continuing example of Trump and his vision of himself as royalty."

Captain Fitzgerald pointed at something hanging from the ceiling. "Mario, is that what I think it is?"

"If you think it's a security camera you're right. This system was put in a couple of years ago. An altar boy snuck in the rectory through the side door, went through the tunnel and stole a bunch of wine out of the sacristy."

"Security system, Mario, more on the security system."

"Simple, motion activated. Not like in banks where the things run all the time. You can store a lot of footage on it before having to replace the disc."

Captain Fitzgerald said, "I want to see that disc."

"Father Lewis has the key to the camera and its supplies."

At the other end of the passageway was a door.

Captain Fitzgerald asked, "This leads where?"

"The basement proper of the church where we store things like our Nativity scene, extra chairs, supplies, the boilers for heating the church, the crypt, plus a staircase leading up behind the altar." Mario opened the door.

They entered the massive basement of the church. Light came from only four bulbs in the center of the immense space. The music coming from the church above filled the underground chamber. "Triumph all ye Cherubim, Sing with us ye Seraphim, Heav'n and earth resound the hymn, Salve, Salve, Salve Regina."

Captain Fitzgerald said, "Mario, who's singing up there? Beautiful."

"Stereo sound system, but not needed once Hillman and Lewis cut loose. Those guys can sing."

An archway gave access to the crypt. There was a massive stone sarcophagus. Chiseled on the side was: "From County Cork to California. From the Mother Lode to San Francisco. From poverty to riches. From life to death. Amen. 1822–1899." On the top of the miner's final resting place was a pickax crossed with a shovel.

There were four other crypts. All had a crossed shovel and pick.

The music coming from the church changed. A female voice sang, "At the cross her station keeping, stood the mournful Mother weeping, close to Jesus to the last."

"That's not Christmas music," Erin said, "that's for Good Friday, when Christ was on His cross."

Father Mario said, "It's a tradition I started ten years ago. Before the Credo's sung, this is played to remind the faithful we may be celebrating the birth of Christ, but shouldn't forget His crucifixion and resurrection."

Music poured over them. "Through her heart, His sorrow sharing, all His bitter anguish bearing, now at length the sword had passed."

Erin felt a shiver run through her as she noticed a life-sized cross dangling between two pillars. A light bulb cast weird and spooky shadows on the tortured and bloody face of Jesus.

Chapter 83

High Mass

"I cannot believe the acoustics down here," Captain Fitzgerald said, "really incredible."

The music soared with, "Christ above in torment hangs; she beneath beholds the pangs, of her dying glorious Son."

Father Mario said, "Next up Lewis and Hillman."

Father Lewis sang, "*Credo in unum Deum, Patrem omnipotentem.*"

Father Hillman sang the translation, "I believe in one God, the Father Almighty."

"*Et in unum Dominum Jesum Christum.*"

"And in one Lord Jesus Christ."

Father Mario said, "Good for Lewis and Hillman. Really angers the archbishop when we slip in Latin. But the old ladies attending love it; reminds them of their youth."

"*Filium Dei unigenitum, et ex Patre natum ante omnia saecula.*"

"The only-begotten Son of God, begotten of the Father before all worlds."

Erin said, "I had no idea those two had such marvelous voices."

Captain Fitzgerald said, "They may have marvelous voices, but you all seem to be missing a key point. We're hearing down here as if we were actually sitting up there."

From above came, "*Dona nobis pacem.*"

Father Mario said, "They're Consecrating the Host."

"Lord," Father Lewis said, "I am not worthy to receive you, but only say the word and my soul shall be healed."

"He didn't sing that," Captain Fitzgerald said, "he spoke that, in a normal, almost hushed voice. And it sounded down here as if he was standing right next to me."

Father Mario shrugged. "Never thought about it, but, yes, the acoustics are incredible. I'd guess something to do with the airshafts."

"Is the basement area as large as the church above?"

"Yes."

Captain Fitzgerald walked between two stone columns. "These pillars match supporting pillars upstairs?"

"I suppose."

"And over here in the corner are the pillars bracketing the two confessionals?"

"Sounds right."

"Why is there a chair there?"

"Never noticed. Not much reason to come in the basement except to hustle through to the tunnel."

"Mario, Erin," Captain Fitzgerald said, "use the tunnel and walk back to the parish house, and then go to the church. Use either of the confessionals and start talking."

"About what?" Erin asked.

"Whatever you want to talk about. Your love life, his, the fuckin' Super Bowl."

The black-haired priest and the red-headed cop left.

A few minutes later Captain Fitzgerald and Brendan heard Father Mario say, "I wish I knew what Fitz's up to."

"So do I," Erin responded.

Captain Fitzgerald said, "Anyone down here can hear what's going on in either of the two confessionals directly above."

"What does it mean?" Brendan asked.

"I think I know exactly what it means. But first I want to review the security camera's tape. I'll need a warrant."

"I'll get one," Brendan said.

"Once you get the compact disc," Captain Fitzgerald said, "go to the saloon. Max has a DVD system in his apartment above the bar. We can view the disc there."

"Why?" Brendan asked. "All we'll see are priests walking back and forth from the rectory to the church."

"Maybe. Maybe not."

Chapter 84

An Angel and a Boar

Padre Pio typed furiously, the words streaming across the monitor's screen.

When he finished his latest effort he reread what he had written:

I have just had another strange dream. I am in an immaculate white room. There are flowers in a vase by a window that allows a vista of green, rolling, tree-covered hills. Next to my bed, hanging on the wall, are a series of television screens with jagged lines marching across each.

Music soars. Metallica sings, "*Angel from below, I wish to sell my soul, Devil take my soul.*"

Tubes run from bottles into my arms. I feel the steady throb of my own heart.

I feel pain. In my brain. In my chest.

Lines on the TV screens become violent peaks and valleys, mountains and chasms.

More music crashes inside my brain. Twisted Sister sings, "*Welcome to the abandoned land, come on in child, take my hand. There's just five words to say, as you go down, down, down, you're gonna burn in hell.*"

The pain is now a fiery lightning scalding its sizzling, blistering message across my tortured body.

My vision dims. The pain ebbs. I know I'm dying.

My essence is slipping away.

Two misty apparitions form on either side of my bed.

On the right, the fog solidifies into a woman. Golden hair falls like a waterfall to her waist. An aura surrounds her, a rainbow of pastels blend with her pure, white flowing robes.

The shape on the left hardens into the head of a gigantic boar; the snout horribly squashed against the brutish pig face. The skin is coarse with oozing open sores. Sunken eyes are two black, endless pits with pinpoint dancing flames in the center.

Both apparitions begin to chant, their words combining in a symphony of exultation and despair.

Her voice, golden tones clear and dulcet, *"Our Father who art in Heaven, hallowed be thy name."*

I feel a foul and putrid breeze waft over my face. The boar's tusks catch the overhead light and shine like flaming torches. The words grunt out, *"Nema, Olama son arebil des menuitat netni sacudni sonn ente."*

The devil's prayer. The grotesque thing is beseeching its master for my soul.

A pink cloud rises from my body.

They pray together now, this angel and demon, words intermingling, strange sounding yet clear.

"Nite oleac ni tucis."

"Forgive us our trespasses, as we forgive those who trespass against us."

"Sileac ni se iuq retson retap."

The pig creature inhales. The pink cloud wafts towards the snout. The woman turns translucent, a look of helplessness upon her forlorn face.

I watch my soul disappear into the ravenous boar, who inhales voraciously while saliva drips from his foul smelling mouth.

The lines on the screens are now straight.

Pain begins, a liquid fire that will burn for all eternity without consuming my flesh.

I hear a gruesome snorting of triumph as the Dark One chortles his victory.

There is no escape, this anguish is mine forever.

The comprehension on what eternity means comes crashing down on me.

Then I awake and bolt upright in my bed. My body taut and sweating a vile perspiration. It takes me a moment to realize where I am, and in relief I slump back onto my bed.

Is this to be my end? This vision to show what will be mine when I am no more? Or was it to show me what I had spared the children from?

It must be thus. Anything preventing that awful end is justified. I will wait. When night falls I will return to the park. I know each soul saved from Hell's harsh destiny is a triumphant victory.

Chapter 85

An Interview with Father Lewis

Captain Fitzgerald called Dooley. The archbishop ordered Fathers Lewis and Hillman to comply with a police interview. The priests told the archbishop he was overstepping his authority and they weren't complying. Dooley told them Fitzgerald promised to release info on the Roman collar to the media — with its arrow aimed at Saint Jude's — if they didn't cooperate.

Their interviews, at the Hall of Justice, were scheduled immediately after they finished saying High Mass.

Captain Fitzgerald told Erin he wanted her to conduct the interviews. "I'm afraid I'm a tad pissed at these two lawyers-slash-clerics. You'd think they'd be volunteering instead of obstructing. I might lose my temper; I'll watch over a closed-circuit television."

She nodded.

Brendan said, "An interview. No Miranda."

She nodded again.

She waited. The interview room was comfortable, different from the stark, bare concrete walls and no windows interrogation rooms had. This room's primary use was for prepping friendly witnesses and interviewing children. The walls were pastel blue, with various colorful paintings of a rainbow, a sunrise and various barnyard animals.

The priests Lewis and Hillman entered. Father Lewis said, "I want it on record that Father Hillman and I were threatened if we did not cooperate."

"Fine."

"I further want it on record that threatening to reveal sensitive evidence withheld so far from the press is one inch short of blackmail."

"Fine."

Father Hillman sat in a chair beside his client. He opened a briefcase, took out a yellow legal pad, a pen, an ashtray, and a pack of cigarettes. He shut the briefcase and stared at her.

"No smoking in a public facility," Erin said, "it's illegal."

Father Hillman lit his cigarette and said, "So is blackmail."

Erin said, "I am surprised an educated man like you smokes."

"I only do so when I know it will irritate someone I want irritated."

"Father Lewis," she said, "last Monday night, the night the first boy was killed, where were you?"

Father Hillman said, "Don't answer that. What are the hours as to the time of death?"

"A bit before midnight to maybe a half hour after."

"That's all the time you can ask my client about."

Erin asked, "Father Lewis, where were you the night the boy died at Alvord Lake between a quarter to midnight to forty-five minutes later?"

"Sometimes I enjoy a late evening stroll."

"Weren't you in the Triple M until almost midnight?"

"Yes."

"Were you drunk?"

"Don't answer that," Father Hillman ordered. "Drunk is a vague and ambiguous term. For one person being intoxicated might mean passed out, for another being inebriated means mental functions impaired, and for another it might only mean a desire for a midnight stroll."

"Do you remember, Father Lewis, where you walked after leaving the Triple M Saloon?"

"Saint Ignatius. I like the historical feel of the old church."

"Did you meet anyone you know?"

"I don't associate with Jesuits."

Father Hillman stifled a laugh and crushed out his cigarette.

Erin took the ashtray, dumped the contents in a wastebasket and asked, "Father Lewis, the next night the second boy was murdered. The time of death for this boy is precise, within a few minutes of nine in the evening. Do you remember where you were?"

"I was in my room."

"Did anyone see you in your room?"

"We priests are careful about not invading each others space. No one goes knocking on doors asking to borrow anything."

"Last night, when the third boy died, where were you?"

"I went to a movie with the monk."

"You mean Friar Tuck."

"I don't like that name. The monk is not some fictional, over-weight character in an ancient story. He is a mystic."

"What time did you and the monk leave the rectory?"

"About six-thirty."

"Do you remember what movie you went to?"

"Of course, it was only last night. I may be getting old, but I'm not senile."

"What movie?"

"The French classic *Wages of Fear,* with the original ending shown to the rest of the world, instead of the watered-down version shown when it first aired in America. Back then, it was deemed too violent for us. Of course, considering the statistics on mayhem in this country, maybe the distributors should have reversed their decision."

Father Hillman chuckled.

"Where was it playing?" Erin asked.

"The Bridge Theatre, on Geary. Started at seven. Around a two-hour film."

"Was it a man or woman who sold you the ticket?"

"Can't remember. Woman I think. I was busy teasing the monk by asking him to buy his own ticket."

"He doesn't have any money."

"That's why I was teasing him."

"Did you meet anyone you knew?"

"Besides the monk, no."

"Was the theater full, half-full, almost empty?"

"We entered as the trailers ended, dark, no idea."

"When the movie ended and the lights came up?"

"We left a few minutes before the ending. The monk became upset when the nitro truck went over the side of a cliff."

"Did you stop anywhere on the way back?"

"We walked directly back to the parish house. When we arrived there the place was in chaos, cops everywhere."

"Did the monk talk to anyone about the movie?"

"I doubt it as the monk does not speak."

"Were there ushers at the theater?"

"I don't remember."

"Did you sit near the back or up front?"

"Last row, on the aisle."

"Did you buy anything at the refreshment stand?"

"No."

Captain Fitzgerald called the front desk and said he wanted a detective at the Bridge Theater ASAP to verify an alibi. He would relay the details to the detective once he got there.

Brendan said, "Why not just have the detective interview Friar Tuck?"

"And learn what? Half the time you ask that monk a question he gets up and leaves the room. I want that alibi checked and it's faster to interview someone who can talk."

"That rich prick Lewis went to a movie?" Brendan said. "What bull shit."

"We'll find out soon enough. And if he's lying I am handling the next chat with high-falutin priest Lewis and it will not be an interview but a ruthless interrogation."

"The blood on the second victim wasn't all his," Erin said. "The foreign blood was type O, your blood type."

"Mine, Father Hillman's and more than a billion of others."

"Will you agree, Father Lewis, to give us a sample of your blood or saliva so we can run a DNA test?"

Father Hillman said, "Absolutely not."

"We ran a check on the supply house for the diocese. The type shoe you both use matches the one which we took a casting of after the second murder."

"Every priest in the city has that type shoe, Archbishop Dooley insists on it. Although when we go to the Financial District we wear expensive shoes. I prefer the Italian maker Testoni. Father Hillman likes The Bally Company of Switzerland's product."

"Father Lewis, can we make an impression of your right shoe that was supplied by the archdiocese?"

"Absolutely not," Father Hillman said.

"Fibers were found under the second victim's fingernails. We ID them as coming from a cassock. They match those sold by the archdiocese's supply house."

"They're selling fibers down there?" Father Hillman said. "Father Lewis and I will have to pick some up next time we go shopping."

Chapter 86

An Uncooperative Interviewee

Captain Fitzgerald and Brennan sat in the deputy chief's office watching the interview on closed-circuit television.

Captain Fitzgerald said, "I can't believe how much I want that arrogant prick Hillman to be guilty."

"Actually," Brendan said, "I think I do believe. And I'm kind of leaning toward hoping they both did it. Two birds with one stone."

"You really mean two arrogant pricks with one arrest."

A uniformed officer entered with a wiry, bald-headed man wearing a cabdriver's cap. He studied the video screen and shook his head. "Can't tell, not for either of 'em. It was really dark in the back of my cab. I saw blood on the man's face in the rearview mirror, but only for a moment. That was out at the beach when he entered my taxi. When he shut the door the overhead light went out. Same thing when I dropped him off at a gas station near the east end of Golden Gate Park. I can't say for sure it's either of those men. I can state that my fare was dressed completely in black and wore a Roman collar."

The cabby was escorted out.

A uniformed officer entered and held up a document. "Search warrant for the security camera."

Erin studied Father Lewis's face, which had remained immobile during the entire interview. She asked, "What can you tell me about The Bank of Justice?"

Fathers Hillman and Lewis remained silent.

Wow, these guys are damned good. Not even a blink as opposed to the archbishop who, when I asked him about the Bank of Justice, looked like I'd stabbed him with a carving knife.

Erin said, "The bank?"

"Don't answer that, Father Lewis," Father Hillman said, "the bank is a privately held investment firm and has nothing to do with this investigation."

Erin said, "The director of the zoo told me—"

"The zoo director is not a member of the board of trusties of the bank. Whatever he knows has nothing to do with the death of the three individuals you are currently investigating. My client will not answer any questions involving The Bank of Justice. Move on."

Erin said, "I'll move on. I went to the autopsy of the first victim. Have you ever attended an autopsy, Father Lewis?"

"Only of the soul."

"Three humans are dead. Two found in the park and the third almost on *your* doorstep."

"The park is home to the people of San Francisco," Father Lewis said, "and the Church is home to the peoples of the world."

"All those people weren't there the past few days."

"Enough were to prevent you from making a precise statement. Otherwise, if you had anything concrete, I'd be downstairs being booked for murder."

"I'm pointing out the weight of the circumstantial evidence."

"In my legal opinion, it doesn't weigh much."

"We have opportunity and we have certain scientific evidence which doesn't eliminate you as a suspect."

Father Hillman said, "What counts is you can't incriminate my client *exclusively.*"

Erin said, "The *why* of this crime has really bothered me. I spoke to a police psychiatrist. She said it might be triggered by sexual repression. I can understand this sort of thing happens when—"

Father Lewis said, "Are you expecting me to cry out, 'You're wrong, I did it for some other reason besides sexual frustration,' and justify my actions?"

"Are you?"

"Dream on."

Erin said, "What do you think the motive might be?"

"Herod had a motive for the slaying of the innocents. Historians place the number in the low forties — a normal week's work for an active abortionist."

"You didn't answer my question."

"Not having committed the crimes, how can I possibly know the motive?"

Erin said, "Depression can lead to anger and that can be exacerbated with alcohol. I know that both of you had reason to be depressed Monday night."

"About what?"

"The deal buying the zoo and creating a safari tour fell through. That cost you guys a bundle."

"Some deals go through," Father Lewis shrugged, "some do not. Father Hillman and I are investors. We know the risks. Win some, lose some. We only lost the option money on the ranch down south. No big dead."

"But you both became intoxicated after hearing the bad news."

Father Hillman said, "I already told you, intoxication is a matter of interpretation."

"So?"

"I don't think Father Lewis or I *were* intoxicated. Tipsy, maybe. Move on."

She asked, "Do you know acute infectious diseases can cause a person to become maniacal and kill for no apparent reason?"

"I'm not suffering from meningitis or pneumonia."

"You left out mental illness brought on by alcohol, drugs and..." She paused, then, "Sexual abnormalities."

"I'm a priest, living the life of a celibate, which *must* mean sexual abnormality, allowing for the possibility of murdering without motive. If that were true, priests would slaughter people all the time. Although considering some of the history of the Church, you might have a point."

Father Hillman stood. "This interview is over. You're on a fishing expedition and wasting our time. If you have something arrest one of us."

"Father Hillman, I need to interview you too."

"I was home alone in my room and did not go out. I have no alibi for any of the crimes."

"Will you surrender a sample for DNA testing?"

Father Lewis said, "He will absolutely not. Not unless you Miranda him and place him under arrest."

The two priests left.

Erin picked up the wastebasket, looked at the closed-circuit camera, and said, "Have the lab immediately run a saliva DNA test on the cigarette Hillman was smoking."

Chapter 87

Mario's DNA

In the viewing room Captain Fitzgerald jumped to his feet, grabbed Brendan's phone and said, "Front desk, there will be two priests leaving the building in a minute or two. I want them both held as material witnesses. They have left an interview before its conclusion."

Brendan said, "Fitz, that won't work for very long."

"I don't need very long," Captain Fitzgerald said and left.

Erin entered Brendan's office. "Guess I will wait for Hillman's DNA results."

"I'll wait," Brendan said. "You to take this search warrant for the security camera's disc and serve it on Lewis. He's being held downstairs. Get the key to the camera and security discs and meet me at The Triple M saloon."

"The priests will want to be released as soon as Lewis turns over the key."

"Tell those two we need to verify Lewis' alibi before they can leave. "

She left.

Brendan's phone rang. He listened, hung up and called Fitzgerald's cell phone. He said, "Mario's DNA taken from the hair samples he gave Erin doesn't match. He's exonerated."

Interlude Two

Friar Tuck's Last Will and Testament

Max poured Angela, Father Mario and Erin another round and said, "I remember, Erin, when you told me Mario's DNA exonerated him."

"So do I," Father Mario said, "and Erin seemed disappointed."

"Not true," Erin said.

"I *was* disappointed," Angela added, "I had fifty bucks on Mario in the God's Bookie Pool."

Hillman and Lewis walked in. Max did a temperature test and the two priests removed their black carbon filtered high-end masks.

"Happy Fourth of July," the old lady said.

She went to her shopping cart and returned with a canvas. She held it up and said, "Selling this to the highest bidder. First offer starts at fifty bucks."

Lewis said, "That's not yours to sell."

"Correct," Hillman said, "I drew up Friar Tuck's will. He left everything to Saint Jude's Parish."

"I have it," Angela said, "possession is nine-tenths of the law." She held up the drawing.

Max said, "I want it."

"The bidding starts at fifty bucks," Angela said.

"I repeat," Lewis said, "it's not yours to sell."

Angela frowned, then brightened, "The Friar gave it to me."

"You lying," Hillman said, "as usual. But forget it, there's not enough money in it to argue over."

Lewis stood at the bar studying the drawing. He said, "Angela, you can have the painting as long as I can take a picture of it and retain the visual rights."

"I have a camera," Erin said.

Angela frowned. "What's the catch?"

"None. You sell to Max, he gets the original and we get the rights to the image."

"All right," the old lady agreed.

Father Lewis said, "There *is* money in this if we mass produced replicas and distributed them."

"How are you going to do that?" Max asked.

"We own a publishing company called H & L Press. We specialize in coffee table books; those things average about sixty pages in length, one page art, facing page narrative, meaning only thirty pages of actual drawings."

"Good idea," Hillman said.

Father Lewis continued, "We could get at least five books out of the one hundred and fifty plus art that's in the crypt. Why stop there? Any of those drawings would make an excellent postcard."

"Right," Hillman said, "our company prints postcards in forty-eight languages and owns gift shops in capitals all over Western and Eastern Europe, from Athens to Zagreb."

"Don't forget Asia," Lewis added, "Oceana, South America."

Father Hillman nodded. "Trump's unpopular almost everywhere. Postcards should sell like hotcakes."

Angela asked, "Why not here in America?"

"We own gift shops in major tourist centers in the U.S," Hillman said.

Max said, "You guys are worth gazillions. Why fool around with Mickey Mouse gift shops?"

Lewis answered, "We own production, our publishing company. We own distribution, our gift shops. No middlemen."

"Of course," Hillman said, "travel is in the tank right now all over the world, thanks to the virus, but it will come back."

Father Mario asked, "You mentioned the monk left a will."

"Yes," Hillman said. "He left everything, which in his case was almost nothing, to Saint Jude's. But his art is worth money."

Lewis said, "Saint Jude's Parish *is* owned by H & L Enterprises LLC, which is where the profits would end up."

"Aren't you guys' rich enough?" Erin asked.

"We would donate all proceeds to soup kitchens around the country in the monk's name," Lewis said.

"Net, not gross," Hillman reminded his partner.

"Is there really big money in postcards?" Max asked.

"You're kidding?" Hillman said.

Lewis said, "Max, I'll give you an example. We own the gift shop in Fisherman's Wharf, right next to where the boat takes people to Alcatraz for a tour of the prison. We sell a few thousand postcards a week there."

"Or used to," Hillman corrected, "before the Coronavirus showed up. We make a dollar a postcard."

"Big deal," Max said. "You guys are billionaires and you're talking about nickel-and-dime stuff."

"Those nickels and dimes add up when you own more than ten thousand gift shops," Father Lewis said, "in premium locations, spread around the world. We used rake in millions a month from those cards."

"And will again," Hillman said, "once a vaccine is created. We can start a nonprofit called The Friar Tuck Foundation."

Hillman and Lewis began arguing about how to structure the foundation.

Max asked, "Isn't a non-profit just that, a non-profit?"

The two lawyers explained the difference between a non-profit set-up as a 501 (c)(3) versus a 501 (c)(6) and their respective tax implications.

Angela said, "Jeez, talk about getting off point. We all broke the law and need to clean up all the evidence in the crypt."

"She's right," Hillman said, "if it comes out some of us are going to jail. The bed, golden chair, kitchen, bathroom, paintings. Everything goes."

Lewis said. "I checked a week ago and the Supreme Bed alone in now valued at more than seven million. We sell that."

Captain Fitzgerald asked, "Do you guys ever lose money on anything?"

"We lost money on Mario," Lewis said.

Hillman added, "We were going to defend him if a guilty finger ended aimed at him."

"His family's loaded. Rich, the kind we like for a client. But Mario ended up in the clear thanks to DNA."

Chapter 88

Who Needs a Search Warrant?

"Mario's DNA not matching will be a relief to Erin," Brendan said. "She likes that priest."

Captain Fitzgerald said, "Which leaves us four suspects: Mulheye, Lewis, Hillman and Friar Tuck."

"Hillman's results came in with Mario's. No DNA match for the attorney."

"Leaving Mulheye, Lewis and Friar Tuck."

Brendan said, "I spoke earlier to Dooley. He told me Friar Tuck's extremely ill. Diagnosed with an inoperable and malignant brain tumor. The archbishop told me he's accepted his fate. Almost saintly."

"Saintly? He might be killing kids."

"The key to that statement is *might be*."

"How long does he have?"

"Dooley said it's a miracle he's still with us. We need either proof of innocence or a confession."

"Where's he now?" Captain Fitzgerald asked.

"Getting ready to say the Benediction with Monsignor Mulheye. Why not just ask the three clerics for hair samples?"

"Because the firm of Hillman and Lewis LLC stands Constitutional guard at the citadel of Saint Jude's and no one enters without a search warrant. You can't even ask for a toothpick there without getting a lesson on the wonders of the fuckin' Bill of Rights. That's why I'm doing a raid and getting hair sample in those three guys bathrooms."

"If the DNA matches we have no search warrant for the rectory. Won't that screw up—"

Captain Fitzgerald said, "I'll get a new search warrant, go back, get more hair samples and run the DNA test again. Mulheye and Friar Tuck are at the church, Mario's drinking at the saloon and Hillman and Lewis are screaming bloody murder downstairs for being detained. Pretty safe clandestine incursion."

Chapter 89

The Wetback Archbishop

Father Mario walked into the Triple M. Max poured him a cup of coffee and then waved at Angela who had just pushed open the front doors.

The old lady said, "The *San Francisco Chronicle* just ran a special edition. Interesting article above-the-fold." She gave the paper to Father Mario.

Mario stared at the artwork.

A cartoon caricature was of a young man, drenching wet, standing by the edge of a river. His clothes were tattered, but he held the elegant staff and wore the towering miter of an archbishop. A sign near him read: *El Rio Grande.*

The caption beneath the art stated: *The spiritual leader of the City of Saint Francis is an illegal immigrant. No visa. No passport. No green card. just an Irish version of a Mexican wetback.*

The drawing beneath this accusation depicted Dooley as he currently looked, except wearing the white-and-black stripes of a convict. Handcuffed, he was standing on a dock, flanked by two burly policemen. On the left was a sign: *Welcome to Dublin, Ireland, you crook.*

Father Mario said, "Max, pour a shot of brandy in my coffee."

Max looked at the paper and said, "You need a double. Friar Tuck seems to have outdone himself."

"What a hurricane this is going to cause."

"Category Five, I would guess," the bookie cheerfully said.

The door opened and Captain Fitzgerald entered. He pointed at the newspaper. "Dooley phoned the mayor. The mayor phoned the police chief. Dooley wants Friar Tuck arrested for defamation of character."

"Fitz, it's not defamation if it's true," Father Mario said.

Captain Fitzgerald said, "If this is true, then it happened a long time ago. You think Dooley might not have gotten himself phony documentation? And how did Friar Tuck find out he is an illegal?"

Father Mario shrugged. "Might have been me. I have joked a few times over the years about our local religious leader's immigrant status. I get pretty talkative when I occasionally have one or two too many." The priest lifted his coffee cup, drank deeply and added, "As I plan on doing this day."

Angela said, "We can't just stand idly by as that lying blowhard and so-called prince of the church forms a figurative lynch mob to destroy a monk who refuses to talk. Meaning unable to defend himself."

Max said, "Maybe Hillman and Lewis could defend him?"

"How?" Angela asked. "Look at the newspaper. Friar Tuck signed his masterpiece, right down there on the bottom right-hand corner."

Captain Fitzgerald asked, "Where's Friar Tuck now?"

Angela snarled. "Why? Are you going to arrest him for telling the truth?"

"I'm an officer of the court," Captain Fitzgerald said.

"You're also a member of the human race," Angela said. "Friar Tuck's sick. Dying. On his last legs. Even a short incarceration might finish him. "We have to come up with a plan to protect him from Dooley."

Chapter 90

Benediction and Death

Erin stopped by the saloon, showed Mario the search warrant covering the security camera, gave him the key to the safe in the church sacristy and asked him to get the video discs.

Paddy came down the bar and asked his sister where she was going.

She answered, "Saint Jude's. Need to go with Father Mario."

"Police business?"

"Yes, plus they're having the Benediction there."

Paddy said, "Haven't been to one of those in a long time. Who's saying the service?"

"Monsignor Mulheye and Friar Tuck."

"Mind is I tag along?"

Erin, Paddy, Captain Fitzgerald and Angela walked to the church with Father Mario.

Brother and sister sat in the last pew. Fitzgerald stood behind them. Father Mario went around the altar and disappeared. Angela sat in the first pew.

Captain Fitzgerald said, "To much incense, I'm out of here." He left.

There was a large crowd — mostly elderly women.

Monsignor Mulheye performed the Benediction. Friar Tuck served as altar boy. The church's candles were lit; there was a smell of incense in the air. Stereo music played Franz Liszt's Bénédiction de Dieu dans la solitude.

Monsignor Mulheye raised the monstrance, a golden sunburst of rays with the Host in the center of the tabernacle. Covering his shoulders was a humeral veil.

He sang the *O Salutaris Hostia* in a reed-like voice, "O Saving Victim, opening wide, the gate of heaven to man below, our foes press in from every side; Thine aid supply, Thy strength bestow. Captain of the Hosts of Light, overcoming sin's dark blight, ever-glowing splendor bright."

The Benediction ended.

The two priests walked down the center aisle. They stood by the church's doors. Monsignor Mulheye chatted with his parishioners as Friar Tuck made the Sign of the Cross over each.

The last to leave were Angela, Paddy and Erin, who were joined by Father Mario, who had just come out from behind the altar. He gave a video disc to Erin.

They stopped at the entrance to the church.

Erin said, "Monsignor Mulheye, I've forgotten how beautiful a Benediction can be."

"You also seem to have forgotten how to go to Mass," the monsignor said.

Friar Tuck clutched his chest, whispered, "Oh my," stumbled, grasped a pew, steadied himself, stood upright, then went down as if pole-axed.

Angela yelled "Someone call 911."

"No, don't," Father Mario said and waved his arms at a passing cab. "Saint Mary's Hospital is only a few blocks away. Help me carry him."

Friar Tuck was placed in the backseat of the taxi. Father Mario began the Last Rites as the cab driver headed for Saint Mary's Hospital.

Paddy said, "I'm outa here." He stumbled down the church's steps.

Angela said, "So am I. Triple M time."

Erin said, "I'll walk with you. I want to see what's on that security tape."

Chapter 91

Breaking and Entering

After leaving the church, Captain Fitzgerald went to the side door of the rectory. Using his breaking-and-entering-tool kit, he fiddled with the lock and opened the door. He went up the stairs and entered Friar Tuck's room, then Mulheye's and finally Lewis'. In each, using a tweezers, he removed hair samples from either a comb or a shaving razor and inserted hairs into labeled evidence bags.

Captain Fitzgerald started to leave Lewis' room and heard a floorboard creak. Someone was coming up the stairs. He closed Lewis' bedroom door, flattened himself against the wall and waited.

Less than a minute later he heard the creak again, watched his watch's second hand sweep its rotation twice, then peeked out into the hall.

Empty.

He muttered, "Who the hell could that have been?"

Once outside, using his cell phone, Captain Fitzgerald called Park Police Station. A uniformed officer arrived a few minutes later. Fitzgerald handed the three evidence bags to the cop with instructions to have the lab work ASAP and phone the results as each came in to Deputy Chief Brendan cell phone.

The head of homicide walked towards the Triple M Saloon.

Chapter 92

Max's Secret Life

Angela and Erin walked the few blocks to the Triple M Saloon. Inside the bar they ran into Captain Fitzgerald.

Erin asked, "Max, can we use your place upstairs to look at a DVD?"

Max tossed a key on the bar.

Captain Fitzgerald said, "Wait until Father Mario gets back. I want a rock solid chain-of-evidence."

Fifteen minutes later Father Mario entered and said, "Friar Tuck passed away right after I administered the Last Rites."

Captain Fitzgerald said, "What a relief. His latest artwork in the newspaper has just turned a potential raging fire into a tiny tempest in a teapot. Dooley can rage, rage, rage. But at whom? A dead man? People will quickly stop listening."

Erin asked, "Father Mario, you don't seem upset at the death of a friend."

"Friar Tuck was dying — ravaged with cancer. His passing is a relief."

Paddy asked, "I assume he died at the hospital. Are they making the funeral arrangements?"

"All is attended to," Father Mario said.

Erin held up the security videotape and said, "Time to view this."

"I'll watch it later," Captain Fitzgerald said. "I need to wait here until Brendan arrives."

Erin said, "Father Mario, time to go upstairs. Angela, sorry, but this is police business."

"Did I say I care? My friend Friar Tuck is dead. I need a Campari. Actually, I need a lot of Campari."

Father Mario and Erin went upstairs.

Erin was stunned when she entered the bookie's home. Nothing could be in starker contrast from the dump of a saloon below. Furnished with antiques, it was an interior designer's paradise: fresh flowers in antique vases by the entryway, subdued lighting accenting certain artwork, with Persian rugs scattered about.

Father Mario pointed at a bookcase holding hundreds of movie disks. "Max obviously likes flicks."

Erin peered at the vast movie collection. "These are mostly musicals, and a few classics like *Witness for the Prosecution* and *Casablanca*. But I'd estimate eighty percent musicals — from *Around the World in Eighty Days* to *Ziegfeld Follies*. Plus there are a lot of documentaries on things like the life of Placido Domingo and Cole Porter. Not one Western besides *Paint Your Wagon* and *Oklahoma*."

Father Mario said, "Guys who like musicals usually are sensitive. Hint, hint."

"He's still a bookie."

"So what? If you were twenty I'd be counseling you to find a life partner who you could build something with. But you're forty-six, Max a couple of years older. You both have already built a separate life and separate memories. You a failed marriage, his ending in tragedy. Neither union produced a child. So there are similarities, and from watching you both I know there are great overlapping areas of life you both enjoy."

"I don't gamble, except on his God's Bookie Blackboard."

Father Mario said, "You do exercise," and opened a door revealing a fully outfitted gym: Nautilus equipment, free weights, and a stationary exercise bike.

"I've never seen him bicycling outside."

The priest pointed at a treadmill. "Max, on the surface, seems gregarious. Actually, he's shy. But I think if you asked he'd run in the park with you."

"Still playing matchmaker?"

"Love's part of my job description." Mario led her to a bay window looking out at Golden Gate Park. There was a chair, music stand and on an end table a violin case.

Erin asked, "I heard recently that Max plays the violin."

"And you play the cello," the priest said, adding, "lots of classical music written for the violin and cello." He opened another door.

She looked into the kitchen and was stunned. There were two commercial Wolfe ranges, both six burners, three ovens of various sizes, huge woodblock cutting board and prep table,

She sputtered, "I've watched him order take-out, always fast food delivered downstairs."

"Ever seen him eat any of those deliveries? He takes them out back in the alley behind the bar, where he has a trashcan he never uses for garbage. He's been feeding the hungry and homeless ever since I first met him."

One wall of the kitchen held a TV screen and bookcase featuring works by chefs like Rachel Ray and Julia Child.

She asked, "He's a chef?"

"The best meals I've ever eaten have been right here. Both when his wife was alive and after she died."

"He must have loved her deeply."

"Max is a one-woman-at-a-time man. Talk about devotion — the epitome of to cherish, love and honor."

"He never talks of family."

"He's adopted. His adopted parents never should have been parents. Wealthy, wanted a child because it made them look good to their high-society friends, but Max was basically raised by a nanny. I never met her, but Max told me she was the one who instilled a love of cooking in him."

"His wife's family?"

"Also no siblings. Her family was as loving as they come. Talk about sacrifice to make sure their child had the best education. Always giving love, love, love."

"Are they alive?"

"No. They were killed while in Rome, where they went for solace after their daughter died. One of those senseless acts between criminal warring factions that blot out the lives of innocent bystanders."

"How awful."

"Yes, awful. One more room to give you a peek into the most unusual bookie on the planet."

He led her down a hallway and into a large room. One wall held eight flat-screen televisions. They followed horse races, soccer, football and basketball games.

Father Mario said, "Max usually has an employee manning the phones, but he's off today."

She said, "It's just a sophisticated bookie joint."

The priest pushed a button. A small computer screen lit up with a P & L statement for November — showing total profit for the month. There was a computation of twenty-five percent of that profit. After that number were various charities: civil, religious, foreign, and domestic.

Father Mario said, "Every month, without fail, our friend the bookie tithes twenty-five percent of his gambling operation. He also donates one-hundred percent of the rent from the poker parlor."

"You're kidding?"

"The biggest amount goes to orphanages. Second biggest are educational grants for scholarships. Max exudes charity."

"Maybe *he* should have become a priest."

"After his wife died, Max became enraged. He cursed God, but he still maintained that tithe. His wife set all this up decades ago. She had no problem with him being a bookie, but she did have a problem if he didn't help others with the profits. Back then the tithe was ten percent. A few years after she died he raised it to fifteen, then unfortunately twenty-five."

"Unfortunately?"

"I lost a bet to Max. I bet him his wife would live. He took the bet because one, he knew I could afford it and two, he knew that it was a bet he desperately wanted to lose. Each month that she lived Max gave me a percentage of his profits, plus eight grand from the rent on the poker parlor. I did donate that money to various charities. Now I have to match his donations. It keeps me impoverished."

"So *that's* where your money goes."

"Yes. Max is now a man in flux, trying to forget the grief of the past, enjoy the success of the present, and keep open potential for the future."

"Next you'll tell me there's a chapel in here."

"Max lost his faith when his wife died. He's been coming around a bit the past few years, not so much a recluse with his private life, doing things like attending my Golden Gate Park Mass on Mondays."

"I had no idea."

"I think he's ready to start living a full life again."

"Meaning?"

"Max may be a private person. But he is also a man."

Chapter 93

Perhaps a Rat

Deputy Chief Brendan arrived at the Triple M. He led Captain Fitzgerald outside.

Erin joined them and said, "I asked Max to phone me when you both arrived here. Father Mario is upstairs, we have the security tape."

Brendan said, "First the information from the detective who was sent to the Bridge Theater. Lewis's alibi checks out, as far as it goes. *Wages of Fear* was playing at the Bridge Theater and it did start at seven. Need to have his alibi verified by Friar Tuck."

Erin said, "The monk's dead."

The cops absorbed this new information.

Brendan asked, "Where's the body? Still need a DNA run."

Erin said, "I don't know. Ask Father Mario. He's upstairs."

Captain Fitzgerald said, "I want a look at that security tape."

The three cops entered Max's apartment.

Father Mario said, "The monk's passing is going to make a lot of President Trump's local supporters happy."

"Or," Brendan said, "relieved."

Father Mario said, "I know Friar Tuck was working on a new huge poster involving something about POTUS — as usual. Will have to find out, one last political blast at the president in honor of all the others the monk drew. If I find it, maybe hang it at his memorial service. Be TV camera's there — might make national news."

"You don't sound bereaved," Brendan said,

"Or look it," Captain Fitzgerald added.

Father Mario said, "His death was a release from enormous pain."

"Fine," Captain Fitzgerald said, "now once again, where's the body? It needs to be transported to the Hall of Justice morgue."

"Fathers Lewis and Hillman are making the arrangements," Father Mario said and held up the security disc. "Let's watch the video."

They settled into leather armchairs.

Father Mario inserted the disc; the television screen lit up. He said, "Might as well start with the day of the first killing." He looked at the menu, punched in a number and a date appeared in the upper right-hand corner: "Monday 12/22." Initially the screen displayed only snow, then a time code: "5:23 a.m." The black-and-white image of Friar Tuck hurrying down the tunnel appeared.

Captain Fitzgerald asked, "No color?"

"It's a security tape," Father Mario answered, "you expected Cinemascope and surround sound?"

"Why's Friar Tuck going *any*where this early?"

"He was taking the shortcut to the bus stop. He went down to Saint Anthony's soup kitchen every morning to ladle out breakfast to the homeless."

Erin asked, "How did he get out the church doors? I learned they have to be locked from the outside."

"They can be unlocked from the inside. The church is old, and so is its hardware. We should have changed the front door locks ages ago, but the monsignor never seemed to mind having to lock up at night."

The next time code read: "6:12 a.m." The screen showed Monsignor Mulheye, head bowed, walking slowly. He disappeared. Snow appeared.

"No mystery there," Father Mario said. "The monsignor was headed to church to say the six-thirty Mass."

The priest pushed the "Play" button. A few seconds later the screen showed the back of a priest who was obviously Mulheye, walking in the opposite direction. The time code read: "7:06 a.m."

"Slow," Father Mario said, "I can belt out the early Mass in less than eight minutes, right up there with how fast those wonderful renegades said Mass two-thousand years ago when hiding from the Romans."

Snow appeared again. Then: "3:14 p.m." Hillman and Lewis hurried past, oblivious of the camera.

Father Mario said, "After the stock market closes and they finish their physical workouts, their limo driver drives them back to the parish house so they can change from business suits to cassocks. I know where they were going in such a rush: Max's backroom poker parlor downstairs. If they were alive when Christ was crucified, they'd have been in the crap game at the foot of the cross."

Time code read: "3:22 p.m." Monsignor Mulheye walked down the tunnel. Father Mario said, "Off to hear afternoon confessions."

Next time code: "3:31 p.m." The snow dissipated. There was no one there, just an empty corridor. A few seconds later the snow reappeared.

"Strange," Father Mario said, "maybe a rat."

"Not a rat," Captain Fitzgerald muttered.

The next time code was "4:44 p.m." It showed Father Mario walking briskly down the tunnel.

Erin asked, "I thought you always stayed at the Triple M until five?"

"Correct," Father Mario said, "except when I perform my weekly confession. Always go to the monsignor."

Next time code was 5:01 pm. Again, nothing on the screen.

"What's activating the camera?" Brendan asked.

"Who knows?" Captain Fitzgerald said, "but why isn't the monsignor heading back to the rectory? He just finished hearing confessions."

Father Mario answered, "Because he's headed to the saloon to meet me."

Next they watched the entries for all of December. Four more times the camera was activated, but no image of what triggered the motion detector.

Captain Fitzgerald said, "No more to learn here, let's adjourn downstairs."

They all entered the saloon. Sitting in the rear booth was Monsignor Mulheye. Standing next to him were Father Hillman and Father Lewis. The two lawyer priests saw who had just entered and started marching towards the cops.

Captain Fitzgerald said, "Incoming, make that two pissed off legal mouthpieces with intent to sue the PD are incoming. Erin, take the heat — I have something to do."

Captain Fitzgerald took Brendan's arm, led him out the door and a few paces down the street. He said, "Boss, I need to get back in the rectory. I heard someone coming up the stairs. I ducked into a bedroom. Heard some other bedroom door open, then a few seconds later close. Someone had a reason to do this and I want to see if anything's different from when I was just there."

Brendan nodded.

"If the lab calls in with results from the hair samples I swiped from Mulheye, Lewis and Friar Tuck's bathrooms relay the info to me."

"Fitz, what are you up to?"

"Keeping the DNA info just between you and me. Wait for me here."

"Where are you going?"

"Back to the rectory. When I was there someone came, and they must have had a purpose. The only room I know that person did not enter was the one I was hiding in. Need to see if anything's changed in the other four rooms."

Chapter 94

The Journal

Erin listened as Fathers Hillman and Lewis made threats regarding huge lawsuits: against the police department, Fitzgerald, Brendan and her involving illegal detainment.

She felt her Android vibrate, held up the phone and said, "Have to take this, police business," and went outside.

She read:

CALLER I.D. BLOCKED.

Fuck you, you miserable fuckin' bitch. Three kids dead, three!!! You call yourself a cop? I decided strangling is too good for you. I am going to mow you down in the street. I know where you live, I know where you run. The last thing you'll see is my fuckin' truck hurtling towards you — then dead, dead, dead and Hell, Hell, Hell.

An Avenging Angel

***

At the rectory, using his lock picks, Captain Fitzgerald jimmied the same side door he had entered earlier. Knowing all the priests were in the saloon made stealth unnecessary. He went up the stairs and entered Monsignor Mulheye's bedroom first. He carefully studied the scene and thought, *nothing's changed,*

He entered Friar Tuck's bedroom. On top of the writing table was a loose-leaf binder.

Using the tip of a pencil, Captain Fitzgerald opened the journal and read for a few seconds.

He closed the journal and carefully put it in a large plastic evidence bag. Using his cell phone, he called the Hall of Justice and ordered the forensic lab van to meet him in front of the Triple M Saloon ASAP.

Captain Fitzgerald walked back to the saloon and waited outside. When the lab van pulled up, he gave the tech the journal and told him to dust for prints.

The technician did so said, "No prints inside anywhere."

Fitzgerald thanked him, told him to wait — he needed to read the journal and then wanted the technician to take the evidence to the Hall of Justice.

Captain Fitzgerald crossed the street and went to Alvord Lake. He sat on the bench and opened the journal. He read about the harlot turning into a hag, the Nativity scene coming alive, and the hog fighting the angel.

Then he read:

Once again I fell asleep and dreamed a strange dream. I know that these vivid dreams come from the source of the pain in my head.

The dream starts with me at the altar. There's a shriveled old man in the last pew. I feel as if all the deceased members of the Mystical Body strain to see the miracle I am about to perform.

I slide into the pew and ask, "If you want forgiveness you must confess."

The old man nods.

I listen to the vile spewing of a lifetime of corruption. When he's finished I give him absolution and then grab the wrinkled throat and squeeze the life out of the now-cleansed sinner. I gently lift the body and bring it to the altar. Before me my Maker! As He was on the first day and as He shall be on the last.

Astonished, I watch the living Jesus come down from His cross and take the lifeless body from my hands. Christ breaths on the dead man — the breath of love. What was once dead now lives, like Lazarus. The old man kneels and worships the one, true God. He's saved. His reward assured.

I stand humbly before Him. He says, "*In the name of the Holy Spirit, and of the Son, and of the Father.*"

Something's out of place. The wrongness of the blessing hits me. It is backwards, the *devil's blessing*.

Wax runs down the candles on the altar. The hot liquid burns away the white skin of the altar cloth; beneath is black.

What I thought was the Lord smiles and exposes a jagged row of fangs.

The altar turns crimson. I try to flee this obscenity and see a multitude of dancing demons, twisting in the light of the flames and rejoicing.

The Kingdom of the Damned surrounds me.

I moan out an expulsion of agony. I open eyes blinded by dripping blood.

I awaken with a start.

My will crumbles. I know the truth. I've no right to judge. I've no right to kill, I'm wrong. I am condemned.

I'm in mortal sin. The death of my flesh will only be the beginning of an eternal penance. Only Christ can return me to life. No hypocrisy now, I must be sure each element is correct. No priest is here to give me absolution. I must say a perfect act of contrition.

To be truly sorry. I am.

To have a firm purpose of amendment. I do.

To do this because of the love of Christ instead of the fear of Hell.

My eternal punishment blocks my will. Fear makes me sorry. Not love. I helplessly wring my hands. As hard as I try to feel sorry for harming Christ, I cannot rid my mind of the image of my own body, blackened and coarse, roasting in flames forever.

If the third element is not present — if fear is the motive, instead of love — than a priest is needed for true absolution. I must confess.

Fitzgerald closed the journal and muttered, "What a load of fuckin' bull shit."

Chapter 95

The Real Murderer

Captain Fitzgerald walked from Alvord Lake back across the street to the lab van. He removed the first page of the journal, told the tech to wait, walked into the Triple M, sat besides Paddy and said, "I need a favor. Confidential stuff, so I can't use just anyone, need someone I can *trust* to translate something written in Latin."

"Fitz, my Latin's rusty," Paddy said. "Ask Mario."

"It's one lousy paragraph." Captain Fitzgerald handed over a sheet of paper.

Paddy read: *Scribo in lingua latina. Cur non? Latina est apta ad essentiam verbi isti quia est lingua sacerdotorum atque juris periti.*

He translated: "I write in Latin. Why not? Latin's appropriate to the essence of this text as it is the language of priests and lawyers."

Captain Fitzgerald thanked Paddy, went to Brendan and told him he needed a moment outside. The two men stood by the curb.

Captain Fitzgerald said, "Paddy's our murderer."

"You're kidding?"

"Sadly, no. I know his Latin is poor. Yet just now he had no trouble translating a lengthy paragraph in Latin. Why did he have no trouble? Because I think he wrote it."

Brendan said, "That's not proof,"

"A part of me has kept this possibility in mind from the beginning. I had two guys tailing him last night. They followed Paddy from his apartment to the park, watched him talk to Smokey and then watched him pass out. Those two cops were not part of the surveillance teams, they were strictly keeping an eye on Paddy."

"Then why didn't they follow him to Saint Jude's playground?"

"There was a mix-up in communication. I wanted them to continue to watch Paddy's apartment after they took him home. Once they saw him enter they thought they'd completed their assignment and called it a night."

"Can't blame them. They're married, with kids. They wanted to be home for Christmas Eve."

"Whatever, Paddy was free to kill the third kid unobserved. And there are other smaller clues."

"Can you prove Paddy's the murderer?"

"That's going to take more work."

"We still haven't gotten all the DNA results."

"I told those guys down at the lab that if we didn't get them ASAP I was personally going to make it my mission in life to ruin theirs. Need to know where Friar Tuck's body is."

Captain Fitzgerald called Saint Mary's Hospital. He disconnected and said, "The monk's body been transported. The hospital said that a private hearse picked up the body. The transfer was authorized by Fathers Hillman and Lewis."

"Where was the body taken?"

"The hospital said H & L Mortuary, which I wouldn't be surprised stand for Hillman and Lewis Mortuary." Captain Fitzgerald used his cell phone again, learned the number and called the funeral home. He disconnected and said, "Friar Tuck's already been cremated."

"Why the rush?" Brendan asked.

"Beats me. When I have time I will investigate. But the monk's cremation does open up certain possibilities."

Brendan said, "I'm confused. Why would Paddy plant the journal in Friar Tuck's room? Wouldn't any priest do?"

"The other four priests are alive and able to defend themselves. I think Paddy knew the monk was terminal, waited until he died, then planted the damning evidence of the journal."

"What about the Roman collar? The long black dress?"

"I think Paddy dressed up as a priest."

"Dear God."

"Yes, dear God."

"Why not just arrest him and get a sample for DNA testing?"

"I don't have enough for an arrest. Even if I did, I think there are greater ramifications involved."

"Greater ramifications? What are you up to?"

"I'm staying flexible. I'd stay out of the loop on this one, boss."

"I understand, Fitz. If you're right about Paddy this is going to be a mess for the department: retired cop, dressed as priest, murdering kids."

"Maybe not," Captain Fitzgerald said, "I think I have a way out."

"There's only so far I'll go to protect you, if it involves a crime."

"I'll pull this off without committing a crime, least not much of one."

"Is what you're planning let Paddy off the hook as far as punishment?"

"I'd let the department take the broadside before I did that. If guilty that fat fuck is going to be punished one way or the other."

"I know you've successfully trusted your gut instincts for decades. What else do you think stinks?"

"There are no fingerprints on the journal or on its pages — which is what I expected. Who writes a journal that is basically a confession, and wipes down the pages?"

"You better be right."

"The journal explains wiping the pages as a cathartic cleansing. Why? Didn't make sense if it really was a confession. Why get rid of physical evidence, unless that evidence is incriminating to the writer?"

"True."

"There were other things that are not proof a judge would honor, but anyone who knows Paddy will see the links. What first made me suspicious — because I don't like a sudden abnormality in behavior — was Paddy supposedly showing up at the Triple M an hour early. His body's a clock of alcoholic need and gauged to know exactly when to wake. So I asked myself, why's his clock off an hour for the first time in years?"

Brendan said, "No judge will buy that logic as proof of anything."

"There are dreams in this journal: a battle between a boar and an angel, a Nativity scene coming alive, screwing a beautiful woman and then strangling her, and killing an old man to give him redemption. All the dreams are horseshit. None were needed to incriminate Friar Tuck. Just a bunch of crap that is the pure essence of Paddy storytelling bullshit."

Brendan nodded.

"Keep him at the saloon until I phone you."

"Where are you going?"

"No need to know, boss. No matter what, do not let him leave until I call you. Keep buying him drinks."

"You want him drunk?"

"I absolutely want him drunk."

"What if he insists on leaving?"

"Ask him how the tiger escaped. That'll keep him busy for awhile."

Chapter 96

Another Breaking and Entering

Captain Fitzgerald drove a couple of blocks to Paddy's apartment. He removed a burglar kit from his briefcase, jimmied the door and entered. On a table was a laptop. He put on surgical gloves, turned on the laptop and studied the screen. He saw he needed a password.

He typed: "Smirnoff."

Nothing.

"Vodka." Nothing.

"Erin." Zip.

He tried Paddy's mother and father's given names. Nothing. He typed "Police." Again, nothing.

He thought about Paddy and his life as a policeman. He tried, "Horse patrol." Zilch.

He thought about religion and tried "God," then "Christ," and then "Jesus."

He typed "Max," then "Mario," but kept seeing the irritating, blinking message: "Improper password."

He remembered something from a conversation he had listened to between Paddy and Father Mario. Paddy had said, "If you get in trouble do you run to your father or mother? When I get in trouble I always pray to Mary the Blessed Mother."

He typed "Mary."

"Improper password."

He tried "Blessed Mother." Nothing. He tried "BlessedMother." Still nothing.

Irritated, he remembered Paddy sometimes called Erin by her middle name. He typed, "Nonnie."

"Improper password."

Captain Fitzgerald gave the computer screen the finger. He rubbed his face with both hands, stood up and walked about the apartment. On one wall hung a family photograph: Paddy, Erin, their parents and an old lady.

Captain Fitzgerald said, "I remember, the grandmother. She loved Paddy. What was her name?"

He sat in front of the computer. He muttered, "Nope, won't work, grandma's name was Erin's middle name."

He went to the refrigerator, opened the door, took out a bottle of vodka, poured a small amount into a coffee cup and drank.

He went back to the computer and muttered, "I remember. The old lady had a nickname for her grandson."

He typed, "Padre Pio."

"Fuckin' finally," Fitzgerald said as the screen changed signifying password accepted.

He went online, clicked on History and took a look at what Paddy had recently researched. The first sites involved the psychology and symptoms of brain tumors, seizures, and hallucinations.

He noted the dates that files were created. Using his cell phone, he called Brendan and asked, "Paddy still there?"

The deputy chief answered, "Yes. Find anything?"

"The fucker knew Friar Tuck was on his last legs. Paddy prepared evidence to posthumously convict a man he knew was dying."

"Damn," Brendan muttered. "Anything else?"

"He claimed he was in the park on searching for witnesses from eight to midnight. *But no witness names.* I think he made that up to give himself an alibi, because what he was really doing was killing the second kid."

"Why not arrest him?"

"No! Let me explain further. There's another possible agenda. By giving a statement that a witness was at the park the first night at midnight and didn't see anything under the water, created a timeframe to when Paddy knew none of the priests had an alibi."

"I see."

"Also, there are files on his computer he didn't use, but were obviously created to point the finger at Friar Tuck."

"When did he have time to slip back into the rectory and plant that journal?"

"Friar Tuck died right after the Benediction." Captain Fitzgerald started to pace about the apartment. "We know exactly where the other four priests were then. I think it was Paddy I heard on the rectory stairs arriving to plant his journalistic masterpiece."

"How did Paddy get into the locked rectory?"

"Via the tunnel." Captain Fitzgerald opened a door and peered into a closet.

Brendan said, "This is awful."

"He's the killer. I just looked in Paddy's closet; inside a cassock and on a shelf a Roman collar from Saint Jude's. Plus, the dumb shit forgot he picked up a tennis shoe at the scene of the first crime. Sitting right on the floor of the closet. He forgot to bring the shoe with him when he was planting the journal."

"I thought he lost the Roman collar at the first crime scene?"

"He did, but two were missing from Saint Jude's supply room."

"None of this explains the *why*. What motive?"

"And that's the theme of my next assault."

"He's just finishing his drink."

"I need at least another few minutes here in his apartment. Keep him at the saloon until I phone."

"Make sure you bag and tag everything."

"Nope, this search never happened."

"But it will."

"Exactly, maybe."

"Maybe?"

"Maybe."

Chapter 97

Why the Tiger Became Enraged

Brendan bought Paddy another drink. There was a crowd in the saloon. The priests Hillman, Lewis, Mulheye and Mario were discussing where to have the memorial service for Friar Tuck. Two dozen off-duty divorced cops with no where to go on Christmas day were either watching TV or shaking dice for the next round. Angela and Erin were arguing about who should cook Christmas dinner. Max was tending bar.

Paddy said, "Brendan, I should be getting home."

"Have another drink first," Brendan said, motioning to Max. "It's Christmas."

Max poured Paddy vodka over ice.

The deputy chief asked, "Have you figured out why the tiger chose that moment to escape?"

"I need a nap. I really should—"

"Come on, Paddy," Erin said, "you must have figured out *something*."

Other customers gathered around.

Paddy sipped his drink. "I can't remember the names of the two mauled. I'll call them Dick and Harry."

Here we go again, Erin thought.

"They arrive at the zoo's parking lot," Paddy began. "They pay their admission. Then they follow a curving path east and go to the Big Cat Grotto. They stand at the three-foot guardrail. The zoo sign states: 'Home of Natasha, a Siberian tiger, largest of the big cats. Brought here from the San Diego Zoo to breed with the tiger named Tony.'"

Paddy's voice became rhythmical. His audience was no longer in the saloon, but at the zoo.

Dick said, "Aren't there supposed to be two tigers getting it on in there?"

"I don't see any," Harry said, "just a bunch of bushes."

"The sun's setting and they're about to close the zoo; let's get outta here. I came to see a tiger. Is it in the moat, up against the wall, hiding?"

"I'll look," Harry said as he climbed over the guardrail. He went to the grotto's edge and peered over.

"No tiger."

"Let's get going."

Harry said, "Man, I gotta take a leak."

"This place needs a lot more bathrooms. There's one down by the restaurant."

"I ain't walking that far. Gotta go."

Harry went to the edge of the dry moat, stood in the short foliage, unzipped and began to urinate.

In the bushes below, Natasha smelled urine. Someone was challenging her territory! She crept closer to the wall. Through the deepening darkness she saw the man.

And he saw her.

Harry shouted, "Hey, look. The tiger." He directed his yellow stream at the large cat.

Urine hit Natasha in the face. It burned her eyes, soured her mouth, fouled her tongue, enraged her mind. She let out a roar, a bellow erupting from deep within her chest. With a mighty push off her hind legs, she thrust herself up with all claws fully extended. She hit the aging concrete wall, dug claws into a tiny purchase, and pitched herself up, up, up... and over the edge.

"And that," Paddy concluded, "is why I think the tiger chose that particular moment to escape."

Chapter 98

A Way Out

Captain Fitzgerald left Paddy's apartment and went to Alvord Lake. He phoned the saloon on his cell. "Max, is Paddy there?"

"Yes."

"Tell him I need to see him across the street by the lake. One last detail to clear up. Tell him I'm grateful about his helping me solve this case. And tell Brendan I'll meet him around six or so at his home."

Captain Fitzgerald sat at the picnic table overlooking Alvord Lake. He watched the murderer, holding a paper cup, saunter across the street and sit across from him.

Paddy said, "Max said you wanted to see me?"

"When did you first start eavesdropping on the confessionals?"

"What the hell are you talking about?"

"I know from the journal."

"What journal?"

"The journal written by you to make it *seem* as if it was written by Friar Tuck. You knew he was on his last legs. When you realized we were hot on your fat ass, you came up with a plan to pin all this on him once he died."

"Screw you."

Captain Fitzgerald opened his briefcase, removed a pint of vodka, poured some into Paddy's paper cup and said, "Most of the journal is bullshit. There were no dreams, just the demented imagination of your storytelling mind."

"I—"

"You crept into the basement of the church and, like the sick asshole you are, listened to confessions. You pretended you actually were a priest. You fantasized about doing something positive in your sorry excuse of a life like saving a soul."

"How are you going to prove—"

"We have blood scrapings from under the second kid's fingernails. That evidence will match you; the DNA will place you with the second kid."

"You have to have evidence to give to a judge before you can get a sample of my DNA."

"We are going to find the first kid's tennis shoe in your closet. And a cassock and Roman collar."

Paddy asked, "How could you possibly know about the tennis shoe, cassock and collar? Unless you went to my apartment."

"I did go to your apartment."

"Have a search warrant?"

"Nope, being prepared as we speak."

"Then everything you found is inadmissible. A judge will throw it all out."

"You think I won't lie? Even under oath? I was never there. No way to prove I was. I wore surgeons' latex gloves. I repeat you're fucked."

Paddy's chin sank to his chest.

"A supposedly smart asshole like you should have started wondering why all of a sudden I began being polite to your sister."

"You treated her like crap here at the lake."

"Shortly after I realized that soon she might be facing the awful truth that her big brother's a murderer."

"I'm not going to confess, because even if I do I'll still get the death penalty. No way is the DA going to cut me a deal. I understand the political realities of this."

"Good for you." Captain Fitzgerald poured another slug of vodka into the paper cup. It disappeared down Paddy's throat.

"I'll plead insanity," Paddy said.

"The devilish idea behind the journal shows you are not only sane, but had Machiavellian premeditation."

Paddy's held his head in his hands.

Captain Fitzgerald said, "You can go out like a coward or a hero."

"Impossible."

"Anything's possible when you deal with *me*." Fitzgerald removed a pair of handcuffs from his briefcase and held them in front of Paddy's face. "Last thing I want to do is use these."

Captain Fitzgerald tossed the handcuffs into his briefcase. "I haven't read you your rights. Anything you tell me cannot be used as evidence, not that I need any more from what I already have. But my curiosity's running amok. What set you off?"

"I was in the Triple M Saloon as few days ago. A man confessed to Mulheye he was thinking of committing suicide. A drug dealer had given the drunk's daughter a hot load, she ODed. The drunk wanted revenge. That confession depressed me. The kid killed by the tiger compounded this."

"What happened next?"

"In my mind what happened that night was blank at first. Steadily, each day, it's become clearer as I remember. Near midnight I went home, dead drunk. Then took the cassock and collar out of my closet and put it in a paper bag, like I usually did. I went to the park and put on the cassock and collar. Then that shit of a kid verbally assaulted me. The more that I remembered, the more I remembered how angry I became."

Captain Fitzgerald ladled another ounce into the paper cup.

Paddy said, "When that little prick yelled, 'He's touching my pee pee,' I really became pissed. I grabbed his throat. I remember him flailing away, then I shoved him. He hit his head on the edge of the bench. I managed somehow to get home and pass out on my bed. In the morning I saw the tennis shoe on the floor. A tiny flash of memory went through my mind. That's why I went directly back to the lake."

"The stuff in your witness report was bullshit?"

"After I found the kid, most of my thoughts centered on fear... of discovery, of punishment."

"Where you are right now."

"I called Erin because I figured I'd be the last one she'd suspect. My thoughts went towards justification. What I did wasn't really wrong. That punk was so young and already had a mouth like Richard Pryor. I begin to think maybe I did the fucker a favor."

"You were just trying to shut him up?"

"Yes, but the pee pee stuff set me off." Paddy held out his paper cup.

Captain Fitzgerald poured and said, "That first death will be tagged voluntary manslaughter: a person in the heat of passion in response to adequate provocation. Kid gives you the finger, you get pissed, try to strangle him and then shove him. He hits his head and dies. No *intent* to kill. If you had turned yourself in you might have gotten off light. You were a cop for thirty years with a clean record, coupled with the mitigating circumstances that you were drunk. *Except you didn't turn yourself in.*"

Chapter 99

Slaying of the Innocents

Erin stood outside the Triple M Saloon. She noticed a lab van parked in a red zone and knocked on the rear door.

A tech opened it and asked, "You know where Fitz went?"

"No."

"We've finished with this evidence." He held up a plastic bag with the journal inside. "Can you take it and save me a trip downtown? I'd like to get home to my family in time for Christmas dinner."

"Sure." Erin took the bag and signed a receipt for the chain of evidence. She asked, "Has this been dusted for prints?"

The tech nodded.

"What is it?"

"Some sort of journal. Fitz got real excited. He said it proves who the killer of the kids is."

Erin entered the saloon, went to the rear booth and opened the journal.

She read: I was preparing a sermon about the slaughter of the innocence: Rome's soldiers butchering all firstborn in an attempt to kill the King of Kings.

I was tired. I lay down to take a nap. Then the dream began...

Men pour out of huts carrying screaming babies. A large soldier holds a child high in the air, dangling it by its feet. The tiny face looks strange hanging upside down. A sword flashes in the torchlight. The metal gleams as it moves in a perfect arc through the air. The baby's head rolls to the ground, blood gushing from the cavity.

I scream, "What are you doing?"

The soldier wipes his sword and sheathes it. "To kill these innocents, before they are tainted with sin, is an act of mercy."

That dream, that awful nightmare, torments me. Maybe it *is* better, as the Bible says, for a man to have never been born than to lose his immortal soul.

Erin saw Sarah enter the saloon. The wolf whistles started. The psychiatrist worked the room like a politician on the campaign trail — chatting briefly with everyone she knew, smiling at those she didn't know, and flirting with all until she joined Erin in the rear booth.

Angela came over and said, "Private or can I join in."

Erin answered, 'Just for a moment — I need to do some police work with Sarah."

Angela said, "How come when Sarah walks in every guy in here gets hot to trot, but when you walk in, Erin, every male is demurely polite?"

"Two answers," Sarah said. "First: I have the sizzling blood of an Ethiopian boiling in a mixture with the blistering sanguine of a Jamaican. Erin has the northern chill of a hundred percent Irishwoman. No one pictures wild orgies around a raging fire under the full blood red moon when they think reserved Irishwoman."

Erin said, "The second reason?"

"I may be a police head-doctor, but I don't carry a weapon. You, on the other hand, are always packing. Meaning men tread lightly."

"As they should," Erin said.

Sarah looked around the bar. "I love this joint. Makes me think about Damon Runyon and what he might have written if he lived here in the Haight instead of Manhattan's Lower East Side."

Angela said, "He wrote *Guys and Dolls*. Max's favorite musical."

"Runyon wrote a lot more than that," Sarah said. "He liked setting scenes in places like this dump that he filled with cops, pickpockets, crazy people and hookers. This joint's has all that going for it except the hookers."

"Speak for yourself," Angela said. "When I was a young woman in Italy the Nazis were everywhere and took what they wanted. Like my body. Pretty easy decision when you are staring at the lethal end of a Lugar. You either sold yourself or gotten beaten and raped. Or shot. I decided selling was better."

"The Nazis took what they wanted," Sarah said, "but they paid you?"

"Peanuts, a few lira. I think it made those bastards feel like it wasn't really rape if you took a few coins."

Sarah said, "You did what you—"

"I got to enjoy it," Angela said. "Only thing that saved me from walking the streets for a decade or so and ending up a madam was getting sold into an arranged marriage. I believe when a person takes an oath they should stick by it. And I stuck by my marriage vows."

"So you never again—"

"Nope. Straight faithful arrow all the way."

Erin said, "You told me you didn't even like your husband at first."

"Correct. Took years for him to grow on me. But the guy was a raving stallion in bed." The old lady picked up her drink. "I'll leave you two to the grindstone."

Sarah and Erin grinned at each other as Angela toddled away.

Sarah said, "I have picked up bits and pieces of that old gal's life over time, sometimes I think she is fantasizing, then think maybe she isn't."

"I know what you mean," Erin said.

"The mind's a funny thing and capable of remembering what it wants and shaping or shading those memories into what one would have liked to have happened rather than what actually did."

"I catch myself doing exactly that once in awhile, especially when trying to remember why I fell in love with my asshole ex."

"Normal," Sarah said. "When you called you mentioned you needed something from me."

"I remembered while you were post-graduate school at the University of Santa Clara, you once worked part-time for a Silicon Valley firm. Is it possible to override a Caller I.D. Blocked?"

"Not easy."

"Damn," Erin said.

"I still have friends in the industry. Let me make a call. The best nerd I know works out of his house and it's only a couple of blocks away. He has some serious tech stuff in his apartment."

The psychiatrist made the call. A few minutes later a young man entered, listened to the problem, and said, "Should only take an hour or so."

Erin said, "One is marked AAA Investigations. Don't open that one; it will destroy your hard drive. The other one's Caller I.D. Blocked."

He left with Erin's Android.

Sarah asked, "Why do you need to know the caller?"

Erin explained about the threats and her dead parrot De De.

Sarah said, "I advise you to immediately buy another bird."

Chapter 100

A Drive to the Zoo

Paddy choked back a sob as Captain Fitzgerald continued, "Let's look at this from the point of view of duty. You swore an oath when you became a policeman. You joined a proud group — your father and sister among them — and you have a responsibility to protect them from the shattering disgrace at what you've done. The force's reputation, the morale, will go into the tank. But I have way out for you that will be your redemption."

"A way out for me?" Paddy asked. "How's that possible?"

Fitzgerald said, "Let's go to the zoo. I know how much you like that place."

They entered the car and Fitzgerald headed down Kennedy Drive, the primary east-west thoroughfare through Golden Gate Park, and at the Conservatory of Flowers, he turned left on Middle Drive East. "There is a way to redeem yourself."

Paddy said, "You going to give me a lecture on how much good I can do in prison? Maybe teach Bible class. Shit like that?"

"Furthest thing from my mind, lad."

"What then?"

"There's a way if you're brave enough."

Realization dawned as Paddy's eyelids turned to slits. "No, no way. I'm not killing myself."

"Look at it as for family, for your sister."

"I'm not killing myself."

"How about valor?"

"Valor? Bravery? How do you figure?"

"I can arrange things a certain way after the event. I can make you—"

"I'll be dead."

Captain Fitzgerald turned right on Martin Luther King Jr. Drive and passed the Shakespeare Gardens. "I can't figure out how, in just a few days, you wrote so much in that journal."

"I wrote part in the seminary — like the crucifixion. I delivered it at my graduation speech from the minor seminary. It was my favorite."

"You were in the seminary years ago. You're telling me you hung onto some papers you wrote—"

"No. I told you it was my *favorite*. I remember it vividly. I rewrote it a few months ago and created a computer file so that I could print out a copy for Erin. I was going to give it to her on her birthday, because she was at my graduation and told me she thought it was beautiful. But I forgot to give it to her."

"Did other stuff in the journal come from your past?"

"No. All was written after each killing."

"Except for the first kid, what you did was *murder*, not killings. But why?"

"Because if pinning it on Friar Tuck didn't work I was preparing a defense."

"Insanity?"

"What else?"

"I already told you it wouldn't work. Your actions were too precise, your writing too logical."

"Not if I used lawyers like Hillman and Lewis. Those guys can twist things like you can't believe."

Captain Fitzgerald reached the western end of the park, then turned south on The Great Highway, pulling into the small parking lot behind the San Francisco Irish Cultural Center where Paddy's father's body had been found years earlier. "Time to pay respects to your dad."

"Fitz, I thought we were going to the zoo?"

"All in good time, Paddy, all in good time."

The two men stood silent, then Captain Fitzgerald poured yet another ounce of vodka into the cup, gave it to Paddy, lifted the bottle and toasted,

"To a fallen comrade and remembered as a hero who actually was brave enough to commit suicide. "

They both drank, and then reentered the car.

The head of homicide pulled into the zoo's parking lot. The two men walked by the recreation of the Serengeti, past the grazing giraffes and zebras.

Captain Fitzgerald said, "Think about how forgiving God is when a sinner not only accepts responsibility for what they've done, but also accepts punishment."

As they strolled, Captain Fitzgerald's voice became melodious and hypnotic as he spoke of how all the great saints in the Church's history accepted their unjust punishments: Joan of Arc burned at the stake, Samson blinded and chained to a mill's grinding stone, and Shadrach, Meshach and Abednego.

The homicide cop said, "Remember what those three said to King Nebuchadnezzar when they were accused of a crime? 'God will prove our innocence.' Then they went into a red-hot furnace, yet the flames did not scorch them."

Chapter 101

One Sick Fuck

Paddy wiped away tears from his cheeks.

Captain Fitzgerald purred on, "You've broken the most serious of Commandments. But even murder is forgivable. Did you ever read the Old Testament?"

"Yes."

"God considered an eye for an eye as a fair and just punishment."

"I know."

"That's where the death penalty comes from. We don't give it for shoplifting; that's not equitable, not an eye for an eye."

They stopped at the Big Cat Grotto and sat on a bench in front of the empty tiger cage.

Paddy cupped his head in his hands, massaging his temples. "I really wanted to be a priest."

"When did you first start wearing a cassock?"

"Last Halloween, at a party. Mario said he was going dressed as a cop, so I rented a cassock and borrowed a Roman collar from him."

"Did you return the collar?"

"Yes, I gave it back to Mario. Then I went to a rental store and bought a cassock. The Roman collar at the store looked phony. I needed one that was real so I lifted two from Saint Jude's."

"When did you next dress up as a priest?"

"A few weeks later, I'd go to the park. It felt good having people say, 'Hello, Father.'"

"Did you wear a cassock anywhere else?"

"I found out that there are so many priests running around the University of San Francisco — some living there, others visiting, others guest lecturers — they don't all know each other. I discovered I could enter a confessional up there and hear confessions."

Captain Fitzgerald muttered, "Fuckin' holy crap."

"I never knew the person on the other side of the screen, so I wasn't doing anything wrong."

"Anymore than you thought murdering kids was wrong."

"I was almost caught up there, that's when I started going to the basement of Saint Jude's. Just listening made me feel part of the Sacrament. I only went when I knew Mulheye was hearing confessions, Friar Tuck was at the soup kitchen and Mario, Hillman and Lewis were at the saloon. I lifted a key to the side door of the rectory. That gave me access to the tunnel to get to the basement of the church. I knew about the security camera; I was always careful to just edge along the wall."

"You're one sick fuck."

"I think what I did was—"

"Why didn't you just use the church's front doors instead of using the tunnel?"

"Always old ladies in there, they'd see me go behind the altar and report me. Safer to sneak into the rectory."

Captain Fitzgerald poured a drink into Paddy's cup. He spoke about Dante's nine levels of Hell. "The deepest level of hell, the ninth, is where the fallen angel Satan himself resides. When you die you will go to this deepest pit."

"No," mumbled Paddy, "no, no, no."

"Satan's place is furthest removed from the source of all light and warmth. Traitors against God, country and family lament their sins in this frigid pit of despair. And that's what you are, a traitor against God, country and family."

Captain Fitzgerald then explained how forgiving God could be if one accepted their guilt and performed their penance. Then Fitzgerald asked, "Have you read *Crime and Punishment*?"

"Dostoevsky. Raskolnikov considers the common man to be unable to step beyond his conscience."

"And the extraordinary man is able to transgress the law and pave his own way. That how you think, Paddy?"

"I didn't kill an old hag of a pawnbroker."

"No, you killed three kids. But do you remember how Raskolnikov finds salvation? He confesses to his sister Sonia."

"You want me to confess to Erin?"

"No. I mean the symbolism in the Russian tale. The story of Lazarus has taken place, Raskolnikov has been resurrected. You must die before you can be redeemed."

"Screw you, I'm not killing myself."

Another ounce of vodka hit the paper cup and immediately disappeared down Paddy's throat.

Captain Fitzgerald said, "You have an amazing capacity for booze. You should be slurring your words by now."

"I'm about stage eight."

"Which means?"

"When I killed the first kid I was in stage nine — blacked out. Stage ten's passed out."

"Your mind seems fine."

"Sam Johnson wrote, '*Nothing concentrates the mind like the thought of death.*'"

"Paddy, have you thought about what being sent to prison means for a guy like you?"

"I'm not committing suicide."

Chapter 102

The Interpretation of Dreams

"Erin," Dr. Sarah said, "I want to talk about the threats made against you, but first the murders. There is a pattern between people who kill more than one person. First: mass murders. Think James Holmes and the movie theater in Aurora. Think Tucson and Jared Loughner, the guy who shot Gabby Giffords. Mass murderers are either a psychopath, depressed or insane. Your murderer is a serial killer; he kills one person at a time. You have someone who is selecting specific targets, like Bundy or Dahmer — except this killer is selecting children and that's odd."

"Why odd?"

"Serial killers usually go after specific targets — like prostitutes and Washington's Green River murderer. I can't think of any who have targeted children."

"Psychologically, what should I be looking for?"

"There are overlaps between the two type killers. Motivation fed by delusion, depression and a mental disease. Take Dylan Klebold, the Columbine High School shooter." Sarah flipped on her Smartphone, went online, downloaded and read what she found to Erin: "Klebold wrote, 'Such a sad, desolate, lonely unsalvageable I am, not fair! I wanted happiness — I never got it. Let's sum up my life, the most miserable existence in history.'"

"Meaning?"

"I think your serial killer also has the elements of depression that drove Klebold. Here's something else Klebold wrote: 'Glorious, tranquil, radiating with love. Oh, my God, I am sure I am in love.' So this type person has huge swings from manic despair to manic elation."

Erin nodded. "What I think, from reading some of this journal, is the murderer was desperately trying to justify his actions through ridiculous explanations."

"Haven't you ever done anything that you knew afterwards was really stupid and then tried to justify it?"

"You bet, getting married to a cop who was an asshole."

"The person you are searching for may well be going through the same mental gymnastics. I killed, but it wasn't my fault. The hardest part to understand is the victims, and not just that they were so young. They were random. So what's the motive?"

Erin explained about the journal being found in the monk's bedroom.

Sarah said, "Friar Tuck? Mind if I have a look?"

Erin removed from the journal the pages that she had already read and gave them to the psychiatrist, who started to read.

Erin opened the journal and read the next entry involving the harlot and lust.

She thought, *Friar Tuck was tormented by sexual fantasies coupled with a brain filled with a malignant growth destroying logical thought. I didn't think I could ever feel sorry for whoever killed those kids — now I'm not so sure.*

Sarah handed the sheaf of papers back to Erin and said, "Something's not right. Have you ever had a dream that was this long, including dialogue and a coherent storyline?"

Erin shook her head.

"Most dreams are about being chased, or late for something, or something else that is frustrating, but almost always fragmented — disjointed snippets."

"So how do you interpret the dream involving lust?"

"Freud wrote in *The Interpretation of Dreams* that dreams are a form of wish fulfillment — an attempt by the mind to resolve a conflict of some sort. The life of a priest leads to a conflict with one's sexuality."

"My dreams are usually very short," Erin said.

"That's true for most people. Every now and then someone publishes a book about controlling your dreams. Like visualizing what you want to dream about before you fall asleep. And to dream in detail. I've tried this and it does work sometimes."

"Never heard of that."

"And I think whoever wrote this journal has never heard of it either. Lots of attempts at symbolism, which is why I think something is wrong. Many books have been published, such as the *Dream Dictionary,* that give brief descriptions of various symbols. But this dream of lust is specific. Where's the symbolism?"

Erin's phone vibrated. She answered. A lab technician said, "Results for the first DNA finished. No match on Mulheye. Brendan isn't answering his phone. I relayed this info to Fitz — knew he wanted it ASAP."

Erin opened her briefcase and gave the psychiatrist the copies of all the notes and pictures from the avenging angel.

Sarah studied the material. "The second note uses the word fuckin'. Most people don't use a contraction with that word. I can think of one person who always does."

"Captain Fitzgerald! I'm going to—"

"Fitz is a lot of things but stupid is not one of them. He doesn't say 'fuckin'' all the time, just for emphasis. The tough-as-nails cop wouldn't use clichés lifted from books. Speaking of books, have you read any of Fitzgerald's?"

"All of them."

"Same here. They're articulate, well-organized, informative, and nary a curse word."

"Meaning?"

"If I wanted to make you think it was Fitzgerald sending those messages then I might have tried this tactic."

"Back to square one."

"Or maybe it has nothing to do with anything besides someone hates you."

"My ex-husband hates me."

"Isn't your ex a cop?"

Chapter 103

Suicide's a Sin

Sounds floated around the zoo: cackle of a jackal, chatter of chimpanzees, occasional roar of a big cat, and an early nocturnal howl of a coyote.

Captain Fitzgerald's cell phone jangled. He answered, listened then said, "Let me know when the other two are finished." He disconnected.

The cop turned to Paddy, still sitting in front of the empty tiger's grotto, and said, "Lab report in; no DNA match on Mulheye. Mario and Hillman also in the clear. Once all the priests are in the clear half the police force will start nosing around looking for the real killer meaning you."

Paddy sipped his drink.

Captain Fitzgerald said, "Time's running out, zoo closes in half an hour. No matter what, Paddy, you're fucked."

"I was drunk."

"Might lead to mitigating and extenuating circumstances with Saint Peter at the Pearly Gates, but *down here*? Down here, you killed three people."

Paddy sobbed.

"I'm offering a way out for you, a gift of salvation both here on Earth and in Heaven."

"Suicide's a sin."

"So is murder, but both can be forgiven. Is it a sin when a soldier throws himself on a grenade?"

"He's doing it to save others."

"You have an opportunity to hurl yourself on a grenade, figuratively speaking, and become a hero."

"I'm not killing myself. My dad took that way out."

"He was a great policeman."

"After he died I really fell apart."

"What set you off on wanting to be a priest again?"

"When I retired I realized I'd accomplished nothing the whole time I was a cop. More like P.R. than a real policeman. Talk to kids. Stuff like, 'Do you want to pet my horse?' What crap."

"Anything supporting the image of the police as helpful is worthwhile. And now you can once again help police morale by going out a hero."

"Fuck police morale."

Captain Fitzgerald poured a small slug into the paper cup, emptying the pint. He opened his briefcase and took out another. "Think of the boy who died a hero's death right here protecting his friend from a rampaging tiger. Think about what it truly means to do a courageous act and the redemption which can come from the act."

"I'm not killing myself."

"I want you to *redeem* yourself. Remember Daniel and the lion's den? He willingly went into that den of wild beasts to prove one way or the other that what he had done was okay with God."

"The lion kills me, what's that prove? Besides, suicide's a sin."

"You're different than the rest of us, thanks to Mario absolving you in advance for every sin you ever commit. I agree, if you stuck a gun in your mouth and pulled the trigger, it's suicide. The bullet smashes home and no time, not even a millisecond, to repent. But slide into Grotto B and you will have a few seconds to regret your actions — meaning instant absolution thanks to Father Mario. You die in the State of Grace. And what happens next? Let me tell you."

The head of homicide put his arm around Paddy and whispered. When he finished, he said, "And what will be accomplished is it gets the police force, *your* police force, off the hook."

"Fuck the police force."

"What really happened with the second kid?"

"After finding the body by the lake and realizing I had killed a kid, I spent the rest of the day drinking. I tried to justify what I'd done. That stuff in the journal about thinking everyone goes to Hell is true."

"You convinced yourself of what?"

"Killing the first kid was okay. And to prove it I convinced myself I had to kill a second time. And to send that kid to Heaven I baptized him."

"How?"

"I used a water fountain."

"That's why the kid's hair was wet. But that justification doesn't jive with a reason to kill the third kid, the teenager."

"The third kid was the glowing light in the tunnel I saw the first night by Alvord Lake. I jumped to the conclusion that whoever it was had left, but all he did was put out his cigarette."

"I thought you said the light in the tunnel was a guy smoking a cigar?"

"I made that up. I was trying to give myself an alibi for the second kid's death and place the time of the first death when I knew all five priests had no alibi. The guy in the tunnel thought I was a priest. After I left the area he followed me. He saw me remove my cassock. He tailed me to my apartment. The next night he followed me again. He saw me with the second—"

"Paddy, if this is one of your horseshit stories, I swear I am going to shoot you. If some guy knew who you were, why didn't he tell the police?"

"Do you know the Easties Gang?"

"Of course. It's the local gang modeled after Hell's Kitchen's own Jimmy Coonan's murderous Westies Gang."

"This was Murphy, its leader."

"Guy's bad news, made his bones when he was fourteen. By seventeen he controlled drug distribution in half the city."

"The night after I killed the first kid he followed me. When I was throttling the second kid, he suddenly appeared and took a picture of me with his Smartphone. That was the flash of light Smokey saw. I thought it was God giving me a glimpse of the Beatific Vision."

"Why did Murphy do it?"

"Blackmail. He wanted to use my apartment for storing drugs. Thought a retired cop's place was the safest possible. And I didn't kill the second kid; he did. He told me that after I left he felt for a pulse. The kid was alive. Murphy didn't want the kid left as a witness against me, so he used a rock and smashed it into the kid's throat."

"Then you decided to kill Murphy and lured him to—"

"*Lured*? He was eager to meet me. I told him the safest place for him was by the side of the rectory facing the playground as it was private. He laughed at me, said I picked there to make *me* feel safe, not him. I hid behind the maintenance shed. When he arrived I surprised him by hitting him on the back of the head with a rock. He spun around, stunned. I swung again as hard as I could and caught him full in the face."

"No wonder I didn't recognize him, face a mess."

"He was unconscious. I hefted him over the fence and dumped him into the alley. The fall broke his neck, which is what I was hoping."

"That's a death penalty charge; lying in wait."

Chapter 104

Psychobabble

Sarah's Silicon Valley computer nerd friend entered the Triple M.

He handed Erin back her Android and said, "Couldn't get through the Caller I.D. Blocked, It's real sophisticated, but AAA Investigations was a piece of cake."

"It didn't destroy your computer?"

"There are lots of backdoors if you know where to look. This is the phone number of your Avenging Angel."

Erin stared at the ten digits. No surprise on the 415 area code. And, she thought, *I shouldn't be surprised that the number is that of my ex-husband.*

She thanked the computer geek. He went to the front of the bar and chatted with Angela.

Erin wondered if he was the guy who prepared the gadgets for the thirteenth bell, Angela's practical joke.

She told Sarah that the avenging angel was her ex-husband and added, "How can he hate me so much?"

"Some people, when *they* are at fault, no matter how illogical, transfer that fault onto another person. He constantly cheats on you, you leave him. So it's your fault the marriage failed."

Erin said, "I was convinced it was one of the priests trying to distract me — or Fitzgerald trying to get rid of me. I haven't seen my ex in ages."

"Obviously, he's packing a lot of rage towards you."

"My ex, trying to screw me over, was just an unfortunate coincidence with my thinking the killer was trying to throw me off my game."

Sarah said, "I think the timing is not a coincidence. You've been divorced six years. Why do this now? I think because you just got appointed to homicide and handed a sensational case right out of the gate. The ex was jealous of your success. My understanding is his career has languished."

Erin said, "I'm going to nail that asshole's balls to the wall."

"That would be therapeutic, just keep it a fantasy," Sarah said and began to read another dream in the journal.

Angela called to Erin to join her, then bought her and Father Mario glasses of white wine.

The old lady toasted with a hearty, "Merry Christmas," then asked, "Mario, when's the memorial service for Friar Tuck?"

"In a few days. He's already been cremated."

Erin took her wine and returned to the rear booth. Her phone vibrated, she answered and learned the DNA ran on Lewis came up with no match. She relayed the information via cell phone to Fitzgerald. She told Sarah, ending with, "Only one left to run a DNA on is Friar Tuck. Unless there's an explanation for that Roman collar that I've missed, it has to be the monk. Guess the case is settled."

Sarah said, "Do you want me to continue my thoughts? Just finished the one about the boar and angel."

"Sure, what do you think it means?"

"Same problem, too specific. Obviously the writer was fighting with his fears about being punished for what he did."

Erin asked, "Could these dreams have been made up?"

"You mean not dreams at all, just stories?"

"Yes."

"I find that easier to believe than they were dreams. There's a lot of psychobabble out there regarding symbols. Things like dream of a snake or a hammer and it must be about a penis. For instance, the symbol of a boar indicates that you need to look inside to find the answers and secrets about yourself and the people around you. Why should a boar stand for that?"

"What does dreaming about a *bartender* symbolize?"

Sarah grinned, "As I recall from reading the *Dream Dictionary* to dream that you are a bartender suggests that you want to escape from the demands of your daily life. Of course, you didn't mean dreaming about *being* a bar-tender, did you?"

"No."

Sarah said, "And before you ask, I'm not sure about 'bookie,' I guess it has no symbolism. Except whatever symbol you attach to the word in reference to yourself. Back to the journal. The next entry involves an old man and salvation."Sarah quickly read the dream and said, "Same problem. These dreams come across as short stories. In this one, there's a desperate plea for absolution. So the flow of these so-called dreams goes from justification, to realization, to a need to purge."

Chapter 105

State of Grace

As day dissipated and night descended, the zoo's animals settled down. The distant churn of the waves of the Pacific crashing on the sand could faintly be heard. Lighting at the zoo was kept to a minimum so as not to disturb the sleeping needs of the animals.

Captain Fitzgerald disconnected his cell phone and said, "DNA on Lewis now in — surprise, surprise, no match. The noose tightens."

Paddy held out his empty cup.

Fitzgerald poured a shot, checked his notes and said, "There's more light down by Grotto B."

He helped Paddy to his feet and the two men moved to the front of the lions den and sat on a bench.

Captain Fitzgerald shined a pinpoint light on his folder. "At the third murder we never found the weapon. What did you do with it?"

"It was a rock. I saw Murphy's neck was broken. I checked his pockets, found his wallet and cell phone. I deleted the picture of me killing the second kid, then tossed the phone and wallet down a gutter drain. I didn't want him identified quickly. I headed for the saloon. I crossed Stanyan Street and dropped the rock in the park."

"You murdered Murphy to protect yourself against being exposed. You're the ultimate hypocrite, Paddy. You believe you sent the kids you killed to Paradise, but you refuse to send *yourself* there?"

"I didn't kill the second kid, Murphy did."

"You were an accomplice, making you as culpable as him. If you truly believe, then you will sacrifice yourself to prove your premise."

Paddy slurred out, "Not committing suicide."

"Wasn't what Christ did a form of suicide?"

"What?"

"Jesus knew full well when asked, 'Are you the son of God?' that if He answered, 'Yes,' He was going to die. And despite this, He still answered, 'Yes.' That's a good indication, depending on circumstances, that suicide's okay."

"I'm not going to kill myself."

"You don't care about loyalty, society, family, duty, honor or valor. You don't even believe in your own theological justifications, but how about what your life is about to become. Think what comes next. The trial. Imagine the courtroom, crammed with angry, vengeful people screaming for an eye for an eye."

Paddy sobbed.

"Imagine the verdict, absolutely known in advance. Imagine the contorted faces of people yelling in joyful, vengeful triumph when you're found guilty."

Paddy moaned.

"Imagine the penalty phase. The cries for your life's blood coming from the jury, the spectators, even the judge. Imagine a lethal cocktail of fluids entering your bloodstream and rushing to your soon-to-cease-pumping fuckin' heart."

"Oh God."

"Imagine the last thing you will see, the hateful faces staring at you through the window of your death chamber. Imagine the glee of the mothers and fathers of the children you murdered. You'll die with about the same amount of uncaring people witnessing your execution as those who watched Jesus die, except your mother won't be there, no friends will be there, not one person will shed a single tear at your passing into eternity."

"I'm not killing myself."

"Why not? Thanks to Mario, you are always in the State of Grace."

Chapter 106

A Personal Crucifixion

Sarah said, "I repeat, these dreams seem artificial, forced."

"Are you saying these dreams never happened?"

"That's what I suspect."

"What reason is there for Friar Tuck to write this?"

"I have no idea. These dreams aren't dreams at all; they were written with a purpose in mind. Each gives a key to the mind of the author."

"Like how?"

"One: The slaying of the baby, the Roman soldier gives an excuse for what he is doing, an excuse the killer also uses. Two: The Nativity scene coming to life, the baby Jesus shaking an angry fist. The writer is confused about whether what he's done was good or bad. Three: He kills the young woman who has turned into a hag to justify his lust. Four: The boar and the angel. I see this as remorse coupled with fear of punishment. Five: The old man. First saved, then condemned. The killer is confused as to whether what he has done is good or evil."

Erin nodded.

Sarah said, "I think these were written by someone with the intent to convey something to the reader, by using misdirection."

"I still have to read the rest," Erin said and turned the page in the journal. She noticed this was the last entry. She read:

The pain in my head is now constant. The pain emanates out from the center core with a hundred points, as if holes have been drilled in my skull.

My radio mocks me with the sounds of joyful Christmas music. "Oh come all ye faithful, joyful and triumphant."

Erin stopped reading. *Radio? There was no radio in Friar Tuck's room. Something's wrong.*

She continued reading:

I am so afraid. The police are getting close. What if I get caught? The death penalty, unquestionably the death penalty. My mission over, no longer able to bring salvation to the damned. It is time for atonement.

Mortal sin is supposed to be a grievous offense against God. I smash a rock against the face of a rotten and evil murderous teenager and that's a grievous offence against God? And what God are we not supposed to offend — the Old Testament God of fury and fire, or the New Testament God of love? How does anyone know what is an offense against the Almighty?

For all we know a grievous offense against God might be celibacy, or even monogamy.

The shell of my body is exhausted. Sleep will not come. I thought about pills, but shudder at the thought of taking them all. And if I took them all? Vomiting. Defecating. Urinating. A disgusting way to die.

A song comes on the radio reminding me of the hypocrisy of Christmas. "Santa baby, bring me a Cadillac car," is far more honest of the modern truth than "Oh, Little Town of Bethlehem."

Once again I fall asleep and dream.

I am on a hilltop, surrounded by soldiers.

I am naked. I am filthy with muck, perspiration and dried blood.

A wooded cross lies on the ground. It has ropes tied to its crossbars. I am tied to the cross. My back feels the harsh surface, slivers of wood cut into my flesh. The sky, azure blue and brilliantly beautiful, is in sharp contrast to the tremendous terror below.

Erin stopped reading. She realized she had either heard or read this reenactment of the crucifixion before.

Somewhere.

But where? When?

A long time ago.

She read:

My cross thuds into place. I scream. The downward plunge into the supporting hole and subsequent jolt dislocates both my shoulders. I hang from only sinew and muscles.

I feel incredible agony.

I am in the Place of the Skull: Golgotha.

A mob draws nearer.

I watch as Jesus is hurled upon the yoke of His cross. A soldier shouts an order. Others hold His arms to the wooden surface. A spike is placed directly over His wrist. A mallet rises and its sound, as it cracks the iron spike, is the sound of thunder.

The other hand is subjected to the same outrage.

Blood gushes from the wounds, cascading to the earth. Both Christ's hands beat spasmodically against the harsh frame of His cross. The main nerves running down His arms have been severed.

One long nail is violently driven through both of His feet. Jesus makes no sound.

The soldiers drop His cross into its final place.

I hear the twin screams of bone wrenching against bone and shudder at the memory of my own shoulders dislocating.

My mind fills with those recent moments that led up to and after each killing of a child: rancor, reaction, retaliation, remorse, repentance, resurrection.

Erin felt a shiver race down her back like a lightning bolt. What she was reading seemed familiar, *very* familiar, but she couldn't get its nagging familiarity's source to surface in her mind.

Erin remembered another alliteration. When Paddy was talking about the tiger in the saloon, he described its motives to hunt as: scent, saliva, stalk, slay, sate, sleep. The same pattern of alliteration was just used from rancor to resurrection.

With a dread in her heart, she continued to read:

The crowd forms a huge semicircle. People laugh, talk, cast insults — except three: two women and a man.

Christ's head rolls back. Upon His face the rivers of blood ooze from a hundred thorn punctures. His sacred breath rasps from His lungs. Internal hemorrhaging starts, a trickle of crimson runs from His mouth.

The death rattle begins inside His chest.

I shout in a voice choking on sorrow and rage, "Why are You doing this? You are an innocent."

Christ looks at me with eyes that are pools of love. Through blood-caked lips He hoarsely whispers, "For *you* I have done this thing."`

Erin choked back bile. As soon as she read the words, "For you I have done this thing," she remembered. She first heard this at a ceremony at Paddy's Saint Joseph's seminary. Her brother was the top student. He gave a speech about the meaning of giving one's life to Christ. And why. And the *why* was because Christ had given His life for us.

Now full of the knowledge that her brother was a multiple murderer, and through eyes blurred with tears, she read the last three paragraphs in the journal.

I awake and cannot control my writhing. My eyes are full of tears and horror.

I know I am going to die. And because I know this, I have decided to write down everything that has happened.

Maybe someone will understand, if not, I pray Jesus will.

Chapter 107

Redemption

Captain Fitzgerald snapped, "Time's running out."

Paddy held out his empty paper cup. "Vodka."

Fitzgerald poured and said, "No vodka in prison."

Paddy's chin sunk to his chest. Then he brightened. "I know if you have money you can get booze in the joint."

"I'm really getting pissed, so fuck you. I'm going to place you under arrest and here's what's going to happen. You're going to trial. You're going to get the ultimate penalty and end up on Death Row. I want you to imagine what fear is. I have witnessed executions. Have you ever thought about the smell of fear?"

"What do you mean?"

"Imagine you are strapped to the death gurney. The smell of fear is your excrement, which you can't control because you are scared shitless."

"Oh, God."

"The taste of fear is when they start sticking needles in you arm the vomit rising up from your stomach and into your mouth."

"God, God, God."

"The *sound* of fear? It is your own screams as out of the corners of your eyes you see the first plunger pushing the fluid into the tube running to your arm."

"I am so afraid."

"I have heard the most vicious of criminals yelling so hard they ruptured their vocal cords."

"That won't happen. My lawyers will file appeals—"

"Your lawyers will file appeal after appeal while you sit in a cell playing cribbage with some ax murderer—"

"Death row inmates have their own cell."

"The warden is a friend of mine. I'll make sure you're housed with the worst bastard there. You'll be lucky if your cellmate doesn't slit your throat the first night. Even the bad guys hate people who kill kids."

Paddy stared at his hands.

"You'll spend time locked up with some evil asshole. I'll make sure your cellmate's a rapist of men. Even if he doesn't *kill* you, he'll fuck you and fuck you until you either go insane or hang yourself."

"I'm afraid of pain."

"Pain? Then how about this? I kneecap you, making you a cripple. You end up on Death Row not only in *pain* for the rest of your miserable life, but also getting *banged* by some hairy mass murderer."

"You'd end up in prison, too."

"You think I'm dumb? The sun's gone down. Every passing minute it gets darker. I cap both your knees and toss my throw-away revolver into the Pacific. I anonymously phone the cops and tell them I heard shots at the zoo. Then I go home for a well-earned supper. They find you, victim of a violent mugging. You go to the hospital. They get your DNA. Bingo! The child murderer's found. So what's it going to be? A cripple getting fucked on Death Row or a hero?"

Paddy put his head in his hands and sobbed.

Captain Fitzgerald said, "I'll guarantee if you do the right thing I will cover-up everything like I did for your father. You will get a hero's funeral, just like him."

The cop's voice dropped as he whispered his plan.

Paddy asked, "How do I know you'll—"

Once again the cop whispered in a soothing brogue into Paddy's ear.

Tears trickled down Paddy's cheeks. "You know I never wanted to hurt anyone."

"I know, lad."

Paddy asked, "Can I pick the songs I want played?"

"Of course, anything you want."

Another ounce of vodka went briefly into the paper cup before being drained by Paddy. He asked, "Could you sing *Ave Maria?*"

"I can't sing worth fuck all, but I will sing *Ave Maria.*"

Paddy mumbled, "Maybe I should write this down."

"Whatever you want; just dictate it to me."

Captain Fitzgerald removed a notebook and pen from his briefcase.

Paddy explained his last requests. He finished with, "In the park, instead of at Holy Cross, a sunrise service."

Captain Fitzgerald poured another ounce and held out a sheet or paper. "You have to sign this to make it official as far as your requests."

Without bothering to look at the paper, Paddy signed and said, "My whole life could have been different if I had stayed in the seminary. Become a priest. My life could have had meaning, instead of one long bout of drinking."

Paddy took out his rosary. He stared at the tiny figure of Christ nailed to a beam. "I'm afraid of pain."

"You drank more than a fifth of vodka in the past hour or so. I could cut off your arm and I don't think you'd feel pain."

"I'm so afraid."

"As was Christ. In the Garden of Gethsemene He asked His Father to pass this cup away from Him." Fitzgerald poured in the remaining vodka from the second pint. "Drink this and then I'll walk with you."

Paddy gulped down the last few ounces. "Can what I've done be forgiven?"

"We can all be forgiven if we do the right thing in the end."

"I really don't think I can do it."

"Everything you did was a gamble, a murderous gamble to get away with what started out as an accident. Gamble one more time."

"On what?"

"That there's an afterlife."

"I'm too afraid."

Captain Fitzgerald whispered, "Think about the boy killed by the tiger. He wasn't afraid. Think how heroic he was, *imagine* what he went through."

Tears streamed from Paddy's eyes. He mumbled, "I can't do it."

"Brendan told me your idea on how the tiger chose that moment to get out."

Paddy nodded. "Urine."

"Considering the amount of liquid you've inhaled, you must have to relieve yourself."

"I do."

Captain Fitzgerald helped Paddy to his feet.

They went to Grotto B's guardrail, with Captain Fitzgerald steadying a staggering, stumbling Paddy. Inside the animal enclosure were a lion and two lionesses.

The cop said, "*Imagine* the boy climbing over the guardrail. *Imagine* going to the edge and peering into the eyes of that magnificent tiger. Reenact it, imagine what the boy was feeling when he heroically saved his friend."

"No, too dangerous."

"Paddy, you're a storyteller. You already have imagined this and spun the tale to the folks at the saloon. Reenact it. See if your vision was close to what actually happened."

"Too dangerous."

"I thought you had to piss."

"I do."

"Then use the moat." Captain Fitzgerald helped Paddy climb over the guardrail. The retired cop fell down.

Captain Fitzgerald helped him up.

Paddy unzipped and lurched to the edge of the moat. He urinated, swaying back and forth.

Captain Fitzgerald reached out, one hand near Paddy's back, then shook his head and dropped his arm.

Paddy swayed once more, lost his balance, slipped and fell onto the floor of the moat below.

The two lionesses at the edge of the moat peered down at him. Then they lunged.

Chapter 108

A Time to Pray

Erin closed the journal and sobbed uncontrollably. Sarah kept asking her what was the matter but she couldn't answer.

Erin finally managed to stumble to the bar. She asked, "Where's Paddy?"

"Are you all right?" Max asked.

"No, I am not all right. Where's my brother?"

"Awhile ago Fitz phoned and asked me to send Paddy across the street to the lake. Fitz said he had a couple of things to tidy up."

Erin ran across the street to Alvord Lake. No Fitz, no Paddy.

Using her Android, she called Captain Fitzgerald's cell phone.

No answer.

Erin frantically wondered, *what's Fitzgerald up to?* She turned around and Sarah was standing behind her.

The psychiatrist asked, "What's going on?"

"I have to find Fitz; I have to find my brother."

Erin ran to her car. She drove to Paddy's apartment. He wasn't there. She went to Fitzgerald's apartment. He wasn't there.

She went back to her flat. She sat on her sofa. Over and over, she called Fitzgerald's phone.

No answer.

Erin started to pray.

Chapter 109

I'll Take Care of Erin

Captain Fitzgerald entered the deputy chief's home and calmly explained what had happened at the zoo.

Brendan said, "Paddy was mauled to death by lions? How did you talk him into killing himself?"

"I tried family, honor, valor, duty, loyalty, even theology. Just about every fuckin' thing I could think of. I had to tear him apart, then build him back up. I used his own good and evil to show him his life wasn't meaningless, versus his life was utter shit and there was only one way to redeem himself."

Brendan asked, "What finally worked getting Paddy to kill himself?"

"Nothing. I kept circling back, reminding him of what he'd done; and then threatening him again, then being kind to him. The ultimate one-man good cop--bad cop. I used interrogation tactics learned over a lifetime. Even with all that, what actually worked was asking him to play-act what happened with the boy and the tiger in his own mind, and then helping him stagger to the guardrail. I kept whispering *'imagine'* to him. He was in a drunken trance reenacting what happened to the kid who was mauled when he went into the moat."

"Didn't give him assistance? Like a nudge?"

"The thought crossed my mind, but throughout my career I've managed to avoid actually murdering anyone. I didn't want to protect the department that much."

"I wonder what a psychiatrist might make of this."

"You don't need a shrink's opinion on this one. Paddy lived in an ever-growing world that was an illusion. The fantasies in his mind became more and more like realities in his life. He was smart, but the booze got to him. I think until he ladled in a certain amount of liquor, his mind was fine. Then the delusions started. And that's what I was counting on at the zoo."

"What you did is close to a crime. Talking. Lying."

"*Talking* is a crime? Arrest Rush Limbaugh. *Lying*'s a crime? Arrest Donald Trump."

Brendan grinned.

"I need you to do something for me." Captain Fitzgerald explained.

Brendan summed up with, "You want Paddy cremated and a funeral in Golden Gate Park instead of Holy Cross Cemetery. You want a full-dress sendoff. And all this arranged by day after tomorrow as a magnificent tribute for a triple child murderer."

"Exactly; the least I can do is follow through on what I promised him."

"What's the rush?"

"As long as our dearly departed Paddy's body is with us, he's a threat. Cremated first thing tomorrow morning, no autopsy out of respect for his loved ones. No one wants an open coffin to see the tragically mauled and mangled body of one loved and held so heroically dear."

"And the *why*?"

"His DNA and the insidious way it can link him to three murders." Captain Fitzgerald removed a paper. "I had the foresight to get him to sign this. He thought it was a list of songs for his memorial; it's really his cremation release permission."

"There are ways to do a DNA on bone fragments and being cremated leaves fragments. Your plan has another flaw. What about the lab tech who did Friar Tuck's DNA?"

"I've already told him there was a breach in the chain of evidence. A new sample will be delivered."

"A new sample? What does that accomplish?"

"Nothing, because if this works I won't have to send a new sample."

Captain Fitzgerald asked Brendan if he could sleep at his place. When asked why, he said, "The same reason I turned my cell phone off. I have a hunch our newest homicide detective is banging on my front door right about now. And also calling me every five minutes."

"You think Erin knows?"

"Not about her brother's death; I've withheld that information. Plan to release it tomorrow afternoon in time for the five o'clock news. But by now Erin strongly suspects. I phoned Max and he told me she had left for awhile, but then had come back in a rage. Then she left again."

"You mentioned if all works out. What are you planning?"

"No need to know."

"But what if Erin—"

"I'll take care of Erin."

Chapter 110

No One Should Be Alone

Erin sat on her sofa and kept pushing her redial number. No answer from Fitzgerald's phone.

Between hitting her redial number, she printed out all the photos that were destroyed by her ex-husband. She carefully recreated what was once on the corkboard. The last one she pinned up was the shot she had taken of the Golden Gate Bridge, the fog, the freighter, the Great Danes and the girl.

She stared at the photo. *No child for me*, she thought; *no PTA, no soccer games, no teacher conferences, no Great Danes, no helping with homework, no filling lunch boxes, no monitoring TV or the Internet.*

I am going to check out Big Sisters.

A half hour before midnight, she picked up her cello and went to the roof. She sat on a folding chair in the middle of the roof garden. This time of year the plants were barren. In the distance the lights of the Haight-Asbury District shined in companionship with a clear night-sky of stars.

What to play? Something sad like Samuel Barber and his Adagio for strings.

She played, and as she did she felt as if she was a spectator to herself, an entity outside, letting the sadness of the music envelope her.

She was so engrossed she did not hear Angela come onto the roof. The old lady said, "Stop playing something so mournful. I know you're worried about Paddy, but it is still Christmas for a few more minutes. Play something joyful. Your spirit needs uplifting."

Erin played Beethoven's Ode to Joy.

When she neared the end, she sang softly, "Brothers, beyond the star-canopy; must a loving Father dwell. Be embraced, this kiss for the whole world! Joy, beautiful spark of the gods, Daughter of Elysium, joy, beautiful spark of the gods."

She inhaled deeply, then let out a soft keening.

Angela said, "Get a camera — one that also records sound."

"My Android?"

"Whatever, get it and come back to the roof. It's a couple of minutes to midnight."

Erin left, then returned with her Android. "What am I supposed to be recording?"

"Come to the parapet. Turn your phone on. I want to send Christmas out with a bang." Angela removed a gadget from her coat, pointed it at the distant spires of Saint Jude's and pressed some buttons. The sound of the bell resonated across the Haight-Asbury. Fourteen times it boomed out its peeling message of hope and inspiration.

Erin said, "That's *loud*. Usually I can barely hear the church bells."

"This thing has a volume control."

"Why fourteen bells?"

"Went to Mass this morning. They always play music usually sung on Good Friday so I was thinking of the fourteen Stations of the Cross."

"This has to make tomorrow's news."

The two women returned to Erin's flat.

Erin handed Angela a package and said, "Merry Christmas."

Inside were small statues of the Blessed Mother and Jesus.

Angela thanked her and pointed. In the corner was a birdcage, inside were two green parrots about six inches tall. The old lady said, "Those are Spectacled Parrotlets. I moved your cage near the radiator as they like warmth. They have a personality that is outgoing and affectionate."

"*Two* parrots?"

"No one should be alone."

Chapter 111

Miracle of the Bells

Angela entered the saloon at seven the next morning. The only person in there besides Max was Mario. She asked to see the morning paper. She scanned the first page, turned to the second and exclaimed, "Mario, have you read this?"

"Read it to me."

Angela stifled a laugh as she read the headline, "Was There a Miracle in the Haight-Asbury Last Night? At midnight last night Saint Jude's church bell peeled fourteen times. Father Mario, a priest at the parish, said that the church's sound equipment only had a recording of twelve bells. "The priest added that the bells only ring at noon, never at midnight.

"Early this morning, that same priest climbed to the top of the belfry to investigate the odd occurrence. After a careful search of the area, however, no device was found. There is no explanation for the unusual tolling. Maybe miracles do happen?"

Angela put down the paper.

Father Mario said, "You look confused."

"I am."

The priest opened a bag and handed her some gadgets, wire and an antenna. "Last night, when I heard the bell peel, I took a stepladder and a flashlight and went to the top of the belfry. Found all this stuff, most of it hidden. I assume, because of your age, you didn't do the hiding?"

"No."

"You came up with the idea and Erin did the grunt work?"

"Are you going to tell anyone?"

"This neighborhood needs something to make it feel good about itself. And the world needs to believe in miracles even one produced as a practical joke."

Captain Fitzgerald entered the saloon and said, "Need to talk, Mario. Privately."

The two men moved to the rear booth. Captain Fitzgerald asked, "Where's Friar Tuck?"

"Dead," Father Mario answered.

"I know and his body was sent to the Funeral Home of H&L Mortuary. Does H & L stand for Hillman and Lewis?"

"One of their holdings. The monk's been cremated."

"I need the urn."

"Why?"

"A death has occurred and the body whisked away by you."

"Whisked? I raced him to the hospital ASAP."

"Yes. But, after he died did you call the authorities and inform them? As required by law. No, you did not. I want that urn. It will be returned to you after a formal death certificate is issued. Where is it?"

"The rectory."

"Let's go."

The two men went to Saint Jude's. On the dining room table was a large Folger's coffee can.

Captain Fitzgerald said, "A coffee can for an urn? Hillman and Lewis can afford a solid gold urn decorated with emeralds and diamonds. What crap."

"The can was the monk's wish."

The policeman picked up the coffee can. "This will be returned tomorrow."

The priest said, "Where it will be ensconced in the crypt below the church."

Chapter 112

Ashes to Ashes and Dust to Dust

Captain Fitzgerald went to the basement of the Hall of Justice and entered the morgue. He said, "My dear coroner, need a favor."

"What?"

"Paddy cremated."

"Fitz, I haven't done an autopsy yet."

"Of course not, why waste time and the City's money on Paddy? Cause of death: ripped apart by rampaging lions. A rapid cremation is in order."

"What are you up to, Fitz?"

"Why does everybody always think I'm—"

"Because you usually *are*. Besides, I'm slammed with work. Need to run an ASAP DNA test on the remains of Friar Tuck."

Captain Fitzgerald said, "I have already had a DNA run on the monk. Proves he's the guy who killed the three kids."

"What? What! Where's the body?"

"Cremated."

"A proper—"

"Why? He had no relatives. His sins should remain his sins, but the way the media works, when it finds out it will scream for an investigation."

"But a proper—"

"Haters of the church will start whispering about possible child molestation. News hasn't gotten out yet he's the killer. I'd just as soon release this information after our dear, dead monk is installed in the crypt at Saint Jude's."

"And all this sensitive caring involves what?"

"You're truly a suspicious man. I have a special relationship with Archbishop Dooley."

The doctor nodded.

"And my relationship with him will strengthen mightily if I did him and his Church a tremendous favor and kept the media impact of this to a minimum."

"No matter what, Fitz, it's going to be front page news."

"True, but only for a day. Even reporters might go a tad easier tonight writing their stories about Friar Tuck killing innocents as the spirit of Christmas lingers on. Some tiny drop of kindness from the season must reside in those bloodsucking fuckin' pricks."

"And now you want Paddy cremated?"

"Aye."

"I've already looked at Paddy's body. Obviously mauled, but nothing on the news this morning. How was the body transported from the zoo to here without the media finding out?"

"I was at the zoo last night. After the lions were secured in a different area, I brought Paddy's body to the morgue myself, with the help of two other cops."

"You didn't use the coroner's van?"

"No. Paddy's sister hasn't been informed yet. I didn't want her finding out from hearing it on TV."

"So you put him in your car?"

"No, a police van."

"I won't cremate him without a release."

Captain Fitzgerald removed a document and gave it to the doctor. "Signed by Paddy himself; it was his wish."

"Fitz, how did he know he was going to die?"

"Look at the date; signed over a year ago. Apparently he had the foresight to make his own final preparations."

The doctor studied the document, then nodded.

A wooden casket was wheeled to the crematorium and minutes later Paddy achieved the Biblical version of *Ashes to ashes and dust to dust.*

Chapter 113

What Journal?

After tossing and turning, Erin had finally fallen into a troubled sleep at four in the morning. She woke at ten, went to the saloon and asked Max if he had seen Paddy. He hadn't seen him since yesterday afternoon.

Erin went to Fitzgerald's office carrying the journal. He wasn't there. She went to Brendan's office. The deputy chief hadn't seen Paddy or Fitzgerald.

She thought, *if I can't find Fitzgerald or my brother, then there is something else I can do.* She talked to Brendan for ten minutes. When she left he was on the phone.

She knew where to find her ex-husband. She stormed into the vice squad room, saw him joking with a couple of other cops, and went over. "Talk, now, private."

They went to an empty interrogation room. Erin said, "I know what you did. You're my ex, but now you're going to be an ex-cop and an ex-resident of California."

"Fuck you."

"Not anymore, thank God. What you've done is stalking, intimidation, animal mutilation, threatening murder and mayhem. all felonies."

"You have no proof."

"You made a mistake sending me that virus involving Satan in an attempt to destroy my hard drive. You figured it didn't matter if you used your own phone because everything on my end would be toast. Well I didn't use my phone and the sender has been traced back to you."

"Shit."

"You're going to sign an agreement to leave California forever or face prosecution."

"Fuck you."

"If you don't leave I will make sure that instead of living someplace like Tucson or Dallas, you will be living at Folsom or San Quentin. And I will make sure that every prisoner knows you were a cop."

"Fuck you, bitch."

Brendan walked into the interrogation room and said, "Just got off the phone with the D.A. and he has agreed to prosecute you to the full extent of the law."

Erin felt deep warmth enter her heart as her ex's face turned a pale gray.

Brendan continued. "If you resign and leave California, he won't prosecute, unless, of course, you ever return. I will accept your resignation for reasons of health. You need a warmer climate. You have one minute to make up your mind before I arrest you."

"My parents live in—"

"I don't care where your parents live; you don't have to visit them, they can visit you."

"I think—"

"Thirty seconds," Brendan said and removed handcuffs from his belt. "Erin wanted full prosecution; I talked her into reluctantly giving you this break for the good of the department."

"I was just kidding around."

"Fifteen seconds."

"I want to talk to my union rep."

"Ten seconds."

With jaws clenched and veins on his forehead throbbing, he said, "I accept."

Brendan said, "Sign here," and produced a document.

The ex signed and stormed out of the squad room.

Brendan sat besides Erin and said, "Never liked that guy. Now, sadly, there is something I have to tell you."

He explained what happened at the zoo the night before. An accident, Paddy fell into the lion's den.

Stunned and in shock, Erin went to the morgue. The coroner told her Fitzgerald had been there earlier and had Paddy's body cremated. She asked where Captain Fitzgerald was. The coroner informed her he had returned to his office.

Still carrying the journal, she stormed into Fitzgerald's office and shouted, "Why did you drive my brother out to the zoo last night?"

"He asked me to."

Erin slammed the journal on his desk and yelled, "You *knew* Paddy was the murderer and still drove him out to the zoo? You didn't suspect what he was going to do?"

"I am not a soothsayer."

"Why did you rush him into a crematorium?"

"That was his wish." He showed her a copy of the release for cremation signed by her brother. He picked up the journal. "Once this is gone, there will be no evidence left, except for a huge amount that proves Friar Tuck killed those kids."

"What?"

Captain Fitzgerald explained what he was going to do.

"Do you know how many laws you're going to break?"

"I will explain what really happened with those three murders."

After the first minute of Captain Fitzgerald's explanation, Erin was sitting, arms crossed, hugging herself. Two minutes later she was quietly crying. Five minutes later, when he told why the third boy, leader of the Easties, was murdered, she was keening, a low, heart-wrenching expression of her sorrow.

She asked, "You went to the zoo because he *asked*?"

"Correct. I *had* placed him under arrest, but I didn't even bother to handcuff him. Besides, I had two other police officer pals, who waited in the Triple M while I was chatting across the street with your brother, follow us to the zoo in a police van."

"Why the other two cops?"

"Paddy's a lot bigger than me. I didn't want to take a chance that he could overpower me and get away."

"He sits by the Big Cat Grotto and does *what*?"

"He said he wanted to say a prayer for the boy the tiger had mauled to death. I remember feeling I was intruding, so I wandered off a bit. I kind of moseyed on over to the grizzly bear area."

"Then what?"

"I was just heading back. I saw him walking towards Grotto B. There was no one else around except the other two cops. They were about fifty yards away, standing unobtrusively under a tree. That's when this young girl went under the guardrail and walked to the edge of the lion's moat."

"Where are the child's parents?"

Ignoring her, Captain Fitzgerald continued, "Paddy climbed over the guardrail. The girl started to slip into the moat. Paddy hurled himself forward, grabbed her, swung her to safety and fell into the lions den. In the subsequent confusion, after Paddy saved the child and accidentally fell in himself, and what with the lions roaring and us officers trying to decide whether to shoot the animals or not, we had to make an instant decision. Because it was obvious Paddy was already dead, we decided on restraint. During the confusion the girl wandered off. We're still searching for her and her parents."

"You're lying. There's no kid."

"Paddy may have killed three children, but he saved a life at the zoo. Let him go out a hero."

"I think I'm entitled to the truth. Will that girl be found?"

"Obviously not, as she is a figment of my imagination. However, those two pal cops of mine have already signed the report I told them to sign. Which is: Paddy saved a child and lost his life in doing so."

"Somehow you talked Paddy into killing himself. You could have stopped him and saved his life."

"*What* life? His was finished. He went out in a blaze of glory, so to speak, and his name remains unsullied."

"He's dead. And he didn't have to die."

"We all die. The *how* and *why* are what counts. Paddy will be remembered as a hero. His funeral will be dignified. Can you imagine what it'd be like with the relatives of three dead kids screaming obscenities at Paddy's corpse?"

"And if I say something?"

"Against your hero brother? Stay silent and you will rise high and quickly in the police department, the tragic daughter of a dead hero father and sister of a dead hero brother."

"Who killed themselves."

"You had no problem swallowing the same scenario after your father blew his brains out."

"Do you think you can orchestrate any ending you feel like? Reporters—"

"Will do nothing as long as I hand them the most sensational scenario possible. You'll see when you watch this evening's news, which will reveal that the monk committed the crimes, not Paddy.'"

"Friar Tuck's taking the blame for the deaths?"

"Of course, Friar Tuck. Because everybody from the archbishop to the media to the mayor's office knew the monk was bonkers. He also has no living relatives."

"Hardly seems fair, or just."

"The police department comes off looking great; the archdiocese not so good, but not so bad either. Friar Tuck wasn't a secular priest. Dooley will give solace to the families. You know, turn the other cheek, killer dead, closure, all that bullshit. A win–win for everybody."

"What if I talk?"

"Feel free; there's basically no proof in this case."

"The journal?"

"What journal?"

"The one I've been reading."

"And it's *where*?"

The journal was no longer on his desk.

She shouted, "You can't destroy evidence."

"We have conclusive proof that a deranged cleric went off the deep end and killed some kids. Case closed."

She choked back a sob. "Why didn't you destroy the journal and spare me?"

"If the tech hadn't given you the journal I would have destroyed that fuckin' thing. You're a smart cop. I knew you'd start to ask questions, as you've just proven."

She clutched her arms around herself. Tears rolled down both her cheeks. She sobbed, "I loved Paddy."

Chapter 114

Planting a Clue

Captain Fitzgerald watched her leave and then made a phone call. He asked, "Has the warrant for Paddy's apartment been issued?"

"Waiting for you to give the go ahead."

"Forget it; I was mistaken. Shred that warrant."

Having cleared his fallback position in case Paddy refused to die, Captain Fitzgerald next drove to Paddy's apartment, jimmied the door, entered and turned on the computer. Systematically, he deleted all incriminating evidence. Then he went to the closet, removed the tennis shoe, cassock and Roman collar and put them into his briefcase.

He called the Triple M and learned from Max that the remaining Saint Jude's priests were at the saloon.

Captain Fitzgerald drove to Saint Jude's, entered the church, saw that only one old lady was there and she was asleep. He went behind the altar, down the stairs, and walked through the tunnel, being careful to sidle along one wall to avoid the security camera. He went up the stairs of the rectory and entered Friar Tuck's room.

He rubbed the back of his neck and muttered, "Where didn't I look the *first* time around? Father Lewis was watching my every move."

He went into the bathroom, wrapped a towel around the tennis shoe and placed it under the bathroom sink. He opened the closet door. On a shelf were two Roman collars. After carefully wiping it with his handkerchief, he placed the one from Paddy's closet next to them. He hung the cassock in the middle of two others.

Once back downstairs, he carefully opened the side door to the parish house and studied the street. No one in sight. He slipped out and headed for the saloon.

Erin barged through the doors of the Triple M Saloon, sat in the corner by Father Mario and ordered, "Max, vodka on the rocks."

Max glanced at the clock: 4:30 p.m. He asked, "Aren't you still on duty?"

"Just pour the damn drink."

Max said, "Sorry about Paddy; Fitz phoned with the news. Really liked your brother. At least he went out a hero. When's the funeral?"

Father Mario answered, "Paddy's tomorrow. Friar Tuck is getting a Requiem Mass the next day. The archbishop is infuriated that I am holding a sacred service for a triple murderer. However, I am overjoyed that I am sticking it to his so called Excellency Dooley."

"What?" Max said. "Friar Tuck's the murderer?"

Erin said, "Father Mario, how do you know this? Only myself and—-"

"Fitz stopped by and told me," the priest answered. "Paddy's death has been withheld from the media by Fitz who said the announcement will be on the five o'clock news."

Max poured a round for the group and said, "Friar Tuck? I know a majority of the bets went down on him, but I still kept thinking no priest did the crimes."

Father Mario said, "I'm sad about losing my best friend Paddy; I am devastated learning about my fellow priest's crimes. I know how scarred the monk's mind was from what happened to him in the Middle East. Those soldiers he killed wounded his soul. I assume that combined with his illness are what set him off."

Erin swigged down half her drink. The vodka hit her stomach and a glow formed that rose lusciously to her mind. She muttered, "No wonder Paddy liked this stuff so much."

Max asked, "Mario, what time tomorrow for Paddy's memorial?"

"Funeral Mass at sunrise across the street in the park. I plan on wearing my police dress uniform."

"Not your robes?" Erin asked.

"I may be a priest but I am also a policeman. Mulheye, Hillman and Lewis are saying the Requiem Mass tomorrow. I talked to Sarah and she plans on also wearing her dress uniform. We may be burying a friend and a hero, but we are also burying a retired police officer. Paddy's service to the community deserves to be recognized."

Chapter 115

And the Winner is...

Max held out a glass-covered, framed picture of Paddy sitting on a horse. It had obviously been taken at least twenty-five years earlier. Paddy was thin, a smile lighting his face and surrounded by many children. The backdrop was a petting zoo with goats and lambs and bunnies.

Max said, "I'm putting this up behind the bar. Something to make the patrons remember he was a good guy."

At five Max turned on the television. The anchor said, "Today the Bay Area was stunned to learn a monk known as Friar Tuck was the person who killed three children. This cleric has died of a massive heart attack. He was a monastic given a home at Saint Jude's Church by Archbishop Dooley. This generosity was rewarded by what's been called *The Reign of Terror*. Thankfully, this day after Christmas the nightmare is over."

Erin thought, *thankfully? Miraculously is the right word.*

Fitz let out a gruff laugh. "Dooley must be mightily pissed. The monk called him a wetback, dies and the spiritual head of Catholics in San Francisco has no one to vent his wrath on."

The television announcer continued. "Last night, a courageous retired policeman rescued a child at the zoo, preventing a young girl from falling into the lions' den. In doing so he sacrificed his own life. Two deaths, one of a brutal murderer, one of a courageous hero, have softened the sorrow of the death of three innocents."

Max said, "Paddy finally showed his true colors. Talk about bravery. I don't think I'd have done what he did, risk being mauled to death to save a child."

"I'm so proud of him," said Mario, "it kind of balances out the shock of finding Friar Tuck was a killer. I think the monk was always on the verge of that kind of rage, just like he was when in the military. Pent up anger waiting to burst loose. War really is hell and seems to never leave the mind of those who experienced its horrors."

Max said, "Paddy worried so much that he never did anything of value in his life. Then he justified all. I'm sorry about Paddy and I will deeply miss him, but what a way to go. He shone bright last night, like a blazing comet."

Erin thought, *maybe Fitz is right. Maybe this result is the best for all.*

Max went to the God's Bookie blackboard. On it was the following: Monsignor Mulheye 40-1; Father Mario 1-1; Father Hillman 15-1; Father Lewis 15-1; Friar Tuck 1-2. Pool total: $11,100.

Max wrote: *Winning ticket: FRIAR TUCK at 1-2. Payout: Vig $1,110 --. $9,990 to winners. For every $2 bet winners get back $3.*

A group formed at the end of the bar. Max started paying off.

Erin said, "Father Mario, I need to go to confession and I don't want to hide in the shadows and talk to a stranger."

"You want to sit in a bar and talk to an old pal?"

"Exactly."

"Rear booth time."

Chapter 116

Good for the Soul, Hard on the Wallet

Father Mario put on his purple stole and said, "A general confession only. No specifics. Number one: False gods before you?"

"No," Erin said.

"Keep holy the Sabbath?"

"No."

"Use the Lord's name in vain?"

"I occasionally swear, but never use Jesus or Christ."

"No specifics. Did you honor your father and mother?"

"I loved them."

"No specifics. Had any affairs with married men?"

"No."

"Kill anyone?"

Erin paused. That terrible time came back to her when she was sixteen. *How awful*, she thought, *how did I ever let the father talk me into having an abortion?*

She said, "An abortion."

"Jesus Christ! I said no specifics. Just yes or no."

"Didn't you just curse?"

Father Mario looked stunned, then grinned.

She said, "For your penance—"

"Worry more about *your* penance. Steal any drugs out of the property room? Cheat on your taxes, things like that?"

"No."

"Bear false witness?"

"No."

"Never?"

Her confession to Monsignor Mulheye came rushing back and with it her lie of omission about her Dad's suicide and the cover-up that followed.

She said, "I haven't lied since my last confession, except in the line of duty during interrogations, which is lawful."

"You never shaded the truth under oath?"

"No."

"Amazing. Perjury's a serious crime, but a lot of cops and witnesses do it. There is always an excuse like, 'I had to lie under oath, my father was the defendant and his younger brother was suing him.' But no excuse justifies committing perjury."

Erin thought, *I'm not lying under oath, but I am committing a lie of omission, just like I did long ago. I know the monk's not the real killer. I'm costing a charitable foundation half the God's Own Bookie Pot. No one picked Paddy, so there are repercussions in not speaking out..*

Erin did a rapid calculation: pool total 11,100. Foundation gets 1,110 in vig from Max but should have gotten 5,550. *They're short 4,440 bucks because of me.*

She said, "I have to be specific on this one. I learned something during a case. Not speaking out is a lie of omission."

"Would speaking out help someone?"

"No."

"Would speaking out hurt anyone?"

"Yes."

"Then forget it."

A huge feeling of relief flushed through her mind. *I tortured myself after Dad's death, for months and months until Monsignor Mulheye removed the guilt. This time I am forgiven almost from the start.*

Except I can't forget about all of it, a debt is a debt. And four plus grand is not chump change that can be ignored. Restitution must be made but can be made anonymously.

At the bar, pool winners were buying drinks for the losers.

She asked, "Is my confession finished?"

Father Mario said, "The last two Commandments are kind of redundant about adultery and stealing. Did you covet your neighbor's wife or goods?"

"No. Am I absolved?"

"I absolve you in the name of the Father, the Son, and the Holy Spirit. For you penance..." The priest stared off into space.

Oh, oh, Erin thought.

Mario said, "I have to think about it, give me a day."

"Am I forgiven or not?"

"Of course, if God cannot forgive our weaknesses who can? Go and sin no more. Although you *will* sin more, that's all right; you're human."

"I'm definitely flawed."

Chapter 117

Erin Needs to Run

Erin called Sarah and said, "I need to run with someone who sets a killer pace. I also need a pacer who knows how to keep her mouth shut."

Sarah said, "Meaning me."

"Meet me at the Triple M in an hour."

Erin went home, changed into jogging gear, grabbed a check and went back to the saloon.

Sarah stood outside. She bought her athletic clothes from Road Runner Sports. She had glued ruby rhinestones over the toes of her running shoes. Her R-gear On-the-Go woven pants were bright yellow with crimson lightening bolts flashing down each leg. Her sweater was R-gear Recharge Compression Capri colored purple with gold lightening bolts zigzagging down each arm. On the back of the sweater she had knitted, "I love to drink at the Triple Saloon — worst dump in The City."

Erin's jogging outfit was gray sweat pants, gray pullover sweater and gray keds. She said, "Sarah, looking at you makes me think I should go home and get dark glasses."

"If you got it, flaunt it. I repeat, what's up?"

"I need to run. I need to purge what's inside of me."

"You're bereaved. You need to cleanse your mind. Beat yourself up a bit over Paddy's death. You want to run until you're exhausted."

"That and something else."

"What else?" Sarah asked, "and where to?"

Erin took off, calling over her shoulder, "The fox and the hound."

"I'm usually the fox, nice change of pace being a hound."

Sarah caught up to Erin as they passed Alvord Lake. "A hint at what's going on would help."

"Here's a hint. I need a friend who can stop asking questions."

"That's like asking the New York Southern Court to stop asking questions about Trump's shenanigans. I'm a shrink. I ask questions."

They cleared Children's Playground and passed the Bowling Green.

Erin said, "I mentioned I needed a friend; I did not mention I needed a shrink."

They came to 19ᵗʰ Avenue. Erin headed south, leaving the park, and asked, "Sarah, how are you so confident? Nothing ever bothers you."

"My parents loved me."

"So did mine, but..."

"Your parents were both cops. Were they demonstrative?"

"Not really."

"Mine were. I was showered with love. Hence the confidence."

"How did they meet?"

"My Jamaican father thought Halle Salassi was God. He went to Ethiopia in the hopes of meeting this divinity. Instead he was completely devastated when he learned his hero was not a god, but a Catholic. The devastation did not last long because he met a goddess, my mother."

"I know having parents that love you can lead to confidence, but yours is borderline supernatural."

"My father was one of the top Caribbean psychiatrists; my mother was actually an Ethiopian princess. Talk about be raised by two self-assured parents. It helped that they adored each other. Nothing makes a child feel safer than loving parents."

Erin let out a couple of wheezes.

Sarah said, "You're hitting about five-and-a-half-minute miles. Lookin' good, that's about your best short distance pace."

"I know your long distance pace is five-minute miles," Erin said as she picked up speed.

Sarah said, "Can you keep this up?"

"Barely."

"Keep talking," Sarah said, "if you run out of air slow down."

A car went by and a man shouted, "Looking fast, looking hot."

Sarah yelled back, "Because I *am* hot and fast."

Erin barked out a laugh, lost her breath and slowed to a six-mile-an-hour pace, then stopped. She asked, "How do you know that guy was talking about you?"

Sarah smiled, said, "Now that's how to build confidence," and took off in a slow jog.

They arrived at Taraval Street and turned toward the Pacific Ocean. Erin stopped in front of the Taraval Police Station and bent over, her sides heaving as she sucked in air.

Sarah, barely breathing hard, said, "This is where you needed to get to, a police station?"

Erin nodded.

"You know there's a police station three blocks from the Triple M."

"Screw you," Erin said as she entered the station. She wrote a check, gave it to the desk sergeant and said, "Please give this to The Compassionate Friends Foundation."

Erin left the station, handed Sarah her Android and asked, "Need you to take a picture." She stood in front of the police station and added, "Get my mug and the precinct's sign in the photo."

Sarah did as she was told, then said, "Dare I ask why?"

"Just finishing my penance."

Chapter 118

A Funeral

The weather the next morning was appropriate for a funeral: overcast, somber, with wisps of fog clinging like foreboding wraiths to the trees.

Behind a makeshift altar were the priests Mulheye, Hillman and Lewis. Captain Fitzgerald and Brendan had made the necessary phone calls and a couple of hundred people from the PD and DA's office, along with a few politicos, showed up to pay their last respects.

Police officers were in full-dress uniforms, including police officers Sarah, Mario and Erin. They were seated in the front row.

The media had been informed. Television cameras were scattered about to memorialize the event. Archbishop Dooley showed up and insisted that he say the High Mass.

The priests of Saint Jude's refused him with a resounding, "No."

The archbishop nevertheless managed to make a statement about the tragic loss of a heroic policeman to the television cameras. Then Dooley left.

Erin cornered Monsignor Mulheye and said, "I am truly sorry for your lose regarding Friar Tuck."

"As I am truly sorry for the loss of your brother."

"That first night, after the tiger escaped, you and Friar Tuck were in the rear booth of the saloon."

"I remember."

"You were both crying. I thought at the time it was over the death of an animal, but it wasn't was it?"

"Only partly. All death is sad. But Friar Tuck had just heard the doctor's opinion that he had little time left and told me. I was stricken. I still don't believe he was capable of the things you cops are saying."

"Why not?"

"Because that night was the first time I heard him speak. He confessed. He said dying didn't bother him, all die. But he wanted to die with a pure soul. Why would he say that and then kill a few hours later?"

"You'll have to ask a psychiatrist."

Erin noticed a huge banner hanging between two trees. She thought *Friar Tuck's last artwork.*

In the center of the banner was the face of a scowling Donald Trump. Above him were the words: "The president is facing multiple criminal charges in both Washington D.C. and New York." Below the president's portrait was: "PATASS, is this how you make America great again?"

She thought, *I will miss Friar Tuck and his politics. But why have that sign hung at Paddy's memorial service?* She asked Father Mario.

He answered, "We can't drape that banner over the altar at Saint Jude's, now can we?"

Father Mario gave a brief sermon on bravery. Then, with Max on violin and Mario on French horn, *Moonlight Sonata* was played.

Tears streamed down Erin's cheeks. She studied the makeshift altar, the crucifix and a small statue of the Blessed Mother she had brought because Paddy used to tell her, "When you're in trouble, do you run to your father or mother? I run to Queen *Mary.*"

At the altar, Father Lewis consecrated the Host.

She remembered a prayer her mother had taught her: Remember oh most gracious Virgin Mary, that never was it known that any one who fled to thy protection, or sought thy help, was left unaided.

What about Paddy? He was left unaided, alone, forsaken. Now I'm finding my faith again after realizing my brother died to pay for his sins.

A bagpiper stepped out from behind a massive oak tree. His instrument droned out the mournful notes of *Amazing Grace,* filling the air with resonating sorrow.

After the bagpiper finished, Captain Fitzgerald sang, off-key, "*Ave Maria Ave Maria, Gratia plena, Maria, gratia plena.*"

Sarah whispered, "Erin, that guy has the worst singing voice I've ever heard."

Fathers Hillman and Lewis jumped in to help, singing, "*Ave, ave dominus, Dominus tecum, Benedicta tu in mulieribus, Et benedictus.*"

Father Mario gave everyone general absolution for their sins and communion started.

Erin received the Host and thought, *Jesus preached love, so He can forgive Paddy.*

Deputy Chief Brendan gave the order and rifle volleys were fired — a salvo of three shots.

Father Hillman sang, "*Luce che, hai incontrato per strada.*"

Father Lewis answered, "Time to say goodbye. *Paesi che non ho mai veduto e vissuto con te.*"

The memorial service ended.

The crowd followed Erin, who carried the metal urn as she walked to Alvord Lake. She stood by the water's edge.

Tears rolling down her cheeks, she removed the urn's lid and scattered the ashes and bone shards into the lake, just as Captain Fitzgerald had suggested.

Angela said, "Dumping human remains is illegal in this city."

The gang adjoined across the street to the saloon, trailed by Mario, Fitzgerald and Erin, who stopped outside.

Erin asked, "I need a moment alone with Captain Fitzgerald, do you mind, Mario?"

"Of course not, but first your penance. I want you to go to dinner with Max. I've already mentioned this to him and he was receptive to the idea. He even suggested attending the New Year's Eve Ball at the Fairmont. For your penance at dinner I want you and him to have two martinis before the appetizer and at least two glasses of wine with dinner. And, say, a cognac for dessert."

Captain Fitzgerald laughed, "Why not just tell her to have Max over to her house and wear silk lingerie while serving cocktails?"

Father Mario grinned. "Max is partial to colorful flannel, not baby doll negligee."

"Good to know," Erin said.

The priest entered the saloon.

Fitzgerald said, "Your first case is officially over. Not bad, not bad at all."

"*Not bad*? I didn't solve anything. I suspected everyone except the real killer."

"Understandable, considering you loved Paddy."

Erin's eyes watered.

Captain Fitzgerald said, "Homicide, like anything else, is a learning experience. I think you have learned much these past few days. You're observant, you're smart, you don't mind hard work, and you're great at research."

"I didn't solve anything."

"Bullshit. You did a brilliant and imaginative interview with Smokey and got the long black dress clue that linked the two murders. You picked up Hillman's cigarette from the ashtray and eliminated him. You even spotted that the second kid's hair was wet. It didn't solve anything, but it did confirm Paddy baptized the kid, meaning he might have actually believed some of his justifications. And you talked Mario into volunteering a sample of his hair for testing."

"I didn't solve the case."

"I repeat: Bullshit. While I was breaking the law with an illegal search of Paddy's apartment, you were reading the journal. You solved the case, just didn't make the arrest. You knew it was Paddy."

"Because I had heard the crucifixion story years ago, that hardly makes me Sherlock Holmes."

"Yes, but you also started suspecting him because of the duplication regarding alliterated words, the 'sate' and 'remorse' series. That would have sent you on the right path to prove he did it even without the crucifixion story. I think if you had confronted Paddy, he'd have broken down and confessed almost immediately."

She choked back a sob. "It was all there right in front of me, Paddy's incredible ability at BS when telling a story. That alone should have made me suspicious by the second dream. I didn't need Sarah to tell me that dreams are usually disjointed."

"You weren't investigating when you read that journal. You thought Friar Tuck was the guilty party. Besides, police work is teamwork. It's rare one person solves a case."

"*You* did."

"And broke the law. Not proud of what I did, and I wish the ending had come out differently. For your sake."

Chapter 119

It's a Date

Captain Fitzgerald pointed across Stanyan Street at Golden Gate Park, "FYI for you only, the ashes you just scattered from a metal urn was Friar Tuck's."

"What? What!"

"I think I may have accidentally switched the contents in those urns."

"Accidentally?"

"Accidentally, intentionally, you say tomayto, I say tomahto. If a DNA test is ever run on the ashes it will reveal conclusively Friar Tuck's the guilty party."

"You don't give a shit about anything."

The cop said, "I had to tell you, for your sake."

"Why?"

"So when you go to the Requiem Mass tomorrow you can say your actual final goodbyes, and then Paddy will be ensconced in the crypt below."

"For God's sake, why this Goddamn subterfuge?"

"A DNA test may be demanded if the public outcry is as bellowing as I think it might be. That test will reveal that the ashes in that coffee can labeled Friar Tuck are those of the man who caused a Reign of Terror."

"You really are a fucker."

"Part of this I did for you. Go to the Requiem Mass tomorrow to say your actual final goodbyes. Then Paddy will be ensconced in the crypt below."

"Have you no decency, no respect, no shame?"

"Nope, nein, nyet," Captain Fitzgerald said. "And you have to forgive me, and you will in time. What I did switching the remains in the urns was to protect your brother's reputation... and yours. The secret of who the actual killer was is safe."

She sobbed and thought, *I should hate this asshole, but deep inside me I know the fucker is right.*

"And if you want to visit your brother, his is in a simple coffee can now in Saint Jude's sacristy, with a label marking the makeshift urn as Friar Tuck. You can go to the Requiem Mass tomorrow to say your actual final good-byes, and then Paddy will be ensconced in the crypt below."

"Have you no decency, no respect, no shame?"

"Nope, nein, nyet," Captain Fitzgerald said. "And you have to forgive me, and you will in time. What I did switching the remains in the urns was to protect your brother's reputation... and yours, in case a DNA test is ever run on that coffee can's contents. Those remains have the DNA of the killer and are marked as the monk's. The secret is safe."

She nodded.

He said, "At your brother's funeral you should wear the lovely black cocktail dress you wore at the homicide reception for new detectives. You set that fetching dress off nicely with a white string of pearls."

"I will choose what to wear to my brother's funeral."

"Then wear that stunning black outfit on New Year's Eve."

"A suggestion I will use."

"Your first case has come to a close. What do you think of homicide?"

"I think I'd be happy if my second case was a simple domestic murder by an enraged and spurned wife with gleaming and honed butcher knife. Like I've fantasized doing to my ex-husband."

"I'll make sure you get an easy one," the old cop grinned. "And remember that while working any homicide one can find humor in just about every situation."

"You can find humor in this case?"

"Because of Mario giving Paddy eternal absolution, your brother is now in Heaven. That result, considering what he did, is hilarious. The philosopher Voltaire once wrote: 'God's a comedian playing to an audience who's afraid to laugh.' Never be afraid to laugh."

"I'll give you a laugh. For awhile I thought *you* might be the killer."

"Me? Why?"

"I researched your past. No women. I thought you might be a pedophile."

"Just your average misogynist."

"I knew you hated women."

"Not all of them, lass." He gently patted her cheek. "Besides, I'm an asexual person, I have a testosterone level that takes a telescope the size of the Hubble to find anything wiggling. From what I've seen involving lust during my time on Earth, a non-existent sex drive is the greatest fuckin' gift God can give anyone."

She asked, "Why did you try to keep me out of homicide?"

"When you first joined the force I promised your dad I'd look out for you. Homicide can change a person, jade them. But I have watched you this week and I think you have the right stuff."

"Then how come you treated me like shit?"

"Two reasons: I have an image to uphold and I believe in tough love. I used that tough love to make you a better cop."

She said, "Your record hasn't one complaint on file."

"There was once a monumental pile, all expunged when I finished my thirty years. Brendan wanted me to stay on to teach enthusiastic homicide detectives like you lass. I agreed, but only if I could start my next thirty with a clean slate."

Max walked out of the Triple M Saloon. He said, "Erin, the worst and best priest either of us has ever known told me what he gave you as a penance. Are you okay with dinner on New Year's Eve?"

Erin nodded and said, "Max, do you know why Paddy stopped playing duets with me? I know he still played with you and Mario at Mass on Mondays."

"He told me he stopped because it reminded him too much of when you both were young and happy."

"I have the sheet music for Handel's Air in F., a duet for violin and cello."

"From Water Music, I know it well."

She asked, "I learned you are a member of Big Brothers."

"Over the years I've been a Big Brother. In fact, twice. Both are now in their late twenties. College graduates, good family men."

"What do you think about being a Big Brother to a little sister?"

"I didn't think it was allowed."

"You can't, I can."

"You have one?"

"Not yet," she said and smiled.

"We'll discuss it over dinner." He planted a gentle kiss on the back of her hand and reentered his bar.

How much can I tell from the brush on my hand by lips? I can tell gentleness, respect, courtesy. I can also feel reverberations that shoot sonic echoes of response through my hand, my arm, my body, my heart.

Captain Fitzgerald said, "Erin, I know you're pissed at me about Paddy. Give it a week. If you think you can't work with me I'll have you reassigned. I can well understand that staying in homicide now might not have the allure that it did a week ago."

"Still trying to get rid of me?"

"I've grown fond of you; the answer is no."

"That's a relief."

"You and Max make a grand-looking couple."

Her jaw clenched.

"Perfect match."

Her jaw started to hurt.

"There you go, starting to tremble and shake, face all pinched up, looking like a hag over sixty."

She breathed deeply and thought, *he's just trying to get my goat.*

"Come on, lass, let 'er rip. You look like you're going to explode. Expression's good for the soul. Your cheeks are getting all red and blotchy."

Erin shrugged.

"The rage is bursting from your flaming eyes. Yelling 'Fuck you, Fitz,' will release a lot of tension. You can always say, 'Sorry Mom, sorry God,' after.' Go ahead, say it. Yell it. Scream it over and over. I'll understand."

She breathed deeply. *When he said this kind of stuff a few days ago it dripped with sarcasm. Now it's just a friendly ribbing.*

With an affectionate grin, he said, "Dinner on New Year's Eve with Max. Marvelous for the deeply spiritual and widowed bookie and the incredibly flawed and divorced homicide cop who, once dinner's over, plans on wearing a flannel nightgown and serving up herself for dessert."

Erin's mouth formed in a more enigmatic smile than the Mona Lisa's.

Epilogue

Secrets, Spins and Solutions

Captain Fitzgerald entered the saloon by the rear entrance, went to the bar, got his temperature read by Max and removed his mask.

Max asked, "I haven't seen you for a month, quit drinking?"

"No, but the protests over the George Floyd death has put everyone on double shifts."

"When you once walked a beat, did you—"

"That was a million years ago."

"Whatever, but was that knee on the neck used then?"

"Not by me. I am small for a cop. I changed the strap on my nightstick, added one that was four feet long. After a lot of practice, I could hurl that thing like a scud missile at a perp's stomach. It also helped that I drilled a hole on the working end and filled it with a lead rod. Then capped the thing with a plug."

"Was that legal?"

"Don't know, but it worked." Fitzgerald glanced around the bar and asked the bookie, "How things?"

"Let's see, no baseball, no Olympics, no basketball, no horse races, no hockey, pretty much nothing for months including no bar customers except for you guys. To sum up: things for this bookie are pretty awful, but my love life's sensational thanks to Erin."

"Have you got a plan on when you'll reopen?" Fitzgerald asked.

"Not sure. My upstairs bookie operation is all phone-in bets. Once sporting events restart I'll be fine. I don't want to reopen this dump, no matter what the governor or mayor say, until I know things are completely safe."

"You must have time to kill on your hands."

Max grinned. "Not being open means I can spend one hundred percent of my time with Erin when she's off duty."

Erin nodded, smiled and then said, "Fitz, there's something I've been meaning to ask. You told me the urn I dumped into Alvord Lake held the monk's remains. Obviously, I now know that was not true. Who did I toss in the lake?"

Father Mario said, "Fitz didn't lie, he thought it was Friar Tuck's remains. We cremated an Irish Wolfhound that had just died at H & L Pets Unlimited Veterinarian Services and put the dog's ashes in Paddy's metal urn."

"*We?*"

"My fellow priests and I figured Friar Tuck wouldn't last more than a week or so before he died. We hoped we were saving him from the circus that would come when Archbishop Dooley went after him. We thought---"

"You thought wrong, obviously," Erin replied.

Fitzgerald glanced around and asked, "Where's Mulheye?"

Hillman said, "In bed with a cold."

"A cold," Fitzgerald said, "not the virus?"

"We had a doctor test him," Lewis said, "just a common cold."

"Back on point," Mario said, "The timing last Christmas was truly awful. I took the monk to the hospital, but he wouldn't get out of the cab. He wrote on a piece of paper that he wanted to die at the rectory. That's when I got the idea to tell people he actually *had* died."

"Why?" Max asked.

"I knew the archbishop was in a volcano of wrathful vengeance over the monk calling him a wetback in that *Chronicle* published drawing. Dooley wouldn't care if the monk was dying, he would still try to ruin him. But he was stymied once he thought Friar Tuck was dead."

"And you end up stuck with the fact he was alive," Max said.

"I was ready to tell the truth," Mario said. "I went to the Triple M to fortify myself before calling the media, and then learned that Fitz was proclaiming the monk did the killings."

"Yet you still could have—"

"What?" the priest asked. "We'd cremated a dog, placed his remains in an urn marked Friar Tuck. I didn't know at that time that Fitz later switched the urns and the dog was now in the one marked as your brother's and Paddy in the coffee can marked Friar Tuck's. Then we held a phony funeral claiming we were burying Erin's hero brother. We were stuck."

Max said, "Then you moved Friar Tuck into the crypt."

"Not at first," Mario said. "I told Fitz the truth. He suggested creating a living space below the church for the monk, a place where no one would see him. Fitz cautioned that the truth could not only send him scuttling off to prison, but, because we had all participated, me and my fellow priests might go to prison as well."

"It would depend on the public's reaction," Fitzgerald said. "Back then everyone thought the monk was a multiple child killer. We harbored him instead of turning him over to the law. That would enrage the public."

"We held a meeting and decided to do nothing," Father Mario said. "We figured Friar Tuck wouldn't last more than a few days."

"Were you ever wrong," Erin said.

"He was happy. He liked solitude," Angela said and once more went to her shopping cart. She returned and held up a large canvas.

Father Hillman said, "That will make a great cover for one of the coffee table books."

Father Lewis asked, "When did he paint this? He could barely hold a spoon the last few days."

"About two months ago," Angela answered.

Erin said, "Near the end someone must have helped the monk: cooking, cleaning, laundry."

"That was Angela," Mario said.

The old lady said, "Friar Tuck became more and more intense, almost at odds with the way his body was shriveling." She took out a piece of paper and said, "When I read this to him he marched around the crypt waving his fists and moaning."

"What did you show him?"

Angela read, "General James Mattis, Defense Secretary for two years under Trump wrote: We are witnessing the consequences of three years of this deliberate effort. We are witnessing the consequences of three years without mature leadership. We can unite without him, drawing on the strengths inherent in our civil society. This will not be easy, as the past few days have shown, but we owe it to our fellow citizens; to past generations that bled to defend our promise; and to our children."

"Great," Fitzgerald said, "wonderful, brave general, at last someone higher up with balls, but it is not our problem. The monk's cartoons nailing the asshole in the White House isn't going to keep us out of prison and might just be the weapon that sends us there."

"Calm down, Fitz," Max said. "I'll make you a---"

"Just dawned on me," Fitzgerald interrupted, "Max hasn't asked any questions about what's going on. How long has he known about Paddy?"

"I've known for a month that Paddy, not Friar Tuck, was guilty," Max began. "I learned the truth on the night I proposed to Erin. I told her that there would never be a secret between us. Then Erin told me."

"We're getting sidetracked," Hillman said, "our cover-up is in jeopardy."

"Not necessarily," Lewis said. "The drawing in today's *Chronicle* could be merely evidence that someone mimicked Friar Tuck's style."

Hillman asked, "What about the paintings in the church basement? All contain information sensitive to time and date, Meaning all drawn after Friar Tuck was supposed to be dead. And they're all signed."

"Is it a crime to imitate someone else's style?" Max asked.

"Not if you make a full disclosure that you are the artist," Hillman said. "What gets forgers in trouble is passing their efforts off as having been done by famous creators, like Van Gogh or Picasso."

"We have to find someone," Max said, "to claim they painted these."

"I'll do it," Angela said. "You need a beard. The *Chronicle* knows I submitted the Justice Scale art. I'll claim I painted it and *all* the art in the crypt."

"Are you an artist?" Father Mario asked.

"Friar Tuck was teaching me."

Erin said, "To cover this up means more lies and more lies and more lies."

Angela said, "So what?"

The old lady went to her cart and returned with a framed picture. She handed it to Erin.

Angela said, "Trump's the one, as leader, whose set the example of lies, lies and more lies."

Max said, "Shouldn't those numbers on the tombstone be 1776 – 2016? The way you used the dates says truth was born in 'sixteen and died in 'twenty."

"No," Angela said, "the truth is not a person, it cannot die. What I mean by that photo is the truth has been buried for the past four year and, hopefully, will be resurrected in 'twenty-one."

Father Lewis said, "Trump doesn't lie all the time."

"Tell me once when he told the truth."

"When he went for the photo op at Saint John's. He held up a Bible and was asked if it was his. He answered, 'It's a Bible.' He could have lied and said something like, 'This is always on my nightstand besides my bed.'"

Hillman chuckled. "Or maybe he was caught off guard by the question."

Max held up the drawing with the tombstone for the truth and said, "Angela, I thought you were trying to learn from Friar Tuck. He always used his talent to create; he never used photos."

"I did try, Angela said, "I started on paper, like those hands and Adam chastising God about staying six feet away. Then I graduated to canvas ink drawings like this."

She went to her shopping cart, grabbed a canvas and held it up.

The Grim Reaper's Top Ten U.S. Greatest Hits

1) Spanish Flu 1918-1919 — 675,000

2) Civil War—620,000

3) World War II — 405,399

4) World War I — 116,516

5) Flu Pandemic—1957-58 — 116,000

6) Flu Pandemic—1968 — 100,000

7) Vietnam War — 58,220

8) Korean War — 36,574

9) 9/11 War on Terror Ops — 7,024

10) Revolutionary War—4,435

Insert

Grim

Reaper

Here

The Coronavirus in an ongoing event — the total number will not be known until the scourge is brought under control.

And then that number will decide where this Coronavirus belongs on the Grim Reaper's top ten list.

It took less than three months to pass the death toll caused by WWI.

On June 16, 2020, at noon, John Hopkins stated on CNN the
death toll reached 116,567 fatalities.

Who is ultimately responsible for the final number?
As Harry Truman once put it, "The buck stops here."
President Trump, on the other hand and by whatever
twisted logic he claims to be using, stated:
"The death Toll number is a Badge of Honor."

Father Mario asked, "Where's the drawing of the Grim Reaper?"

"I tried and I tried and I tried," Angela said, "but I just couldn't get Trump's face right while peeking out from under the Grim one's black hood. That's why I gave up on ink drawings and switched to Picmonkey, it's a lot easier on my tired old eyes than drawing."

"I'll buy both the Reaper and the Truth's RIP," Max said.

Father Hillman said, "Angela, you can't blame Trump for the virus."

"I can blame him for his initial response," Angela said, "and I can blame him for statements like, 'Drinking Lysol helps cleanse the body,' or peddling false hope that the Malaria drug hydroxychloroquine helps cure the Coronavirus."

Father Lewis said, "Without proof of a specific number of deaths caused by those statements you can't accuse or blame the president."

"I can blame him for withholding funds from WHO, for firing scientists and medical professionals, for muzzling the CDC, for not wearing a mask thinking it makes him macho, for accusing—"

Fitz said, "Forget fuckin' Trump. The point is Angela's style is not anything like the monk's."

"Correct," Lewis said. "Angela, what if you're asked to draw something?"

"I'd tell them to shove it; I don't draw on demand. Let them try to force this feisty little old lady. Everyone knows Friar Tuck and I were friends. I'll claim I did the drawings in his honor. The bigger the lie, the easier it is to believe."

"There'll still be doubters," Lewis said.

"Angela," Hillman said, "Lewis is right. People will ask why you have waited so long before coming forward."

"No problem, the original lie needs to be reinforced," Angela said, "I will explain that I have waited until I had a large enough collection to schedule a complete showing of all the art at a major gallery."

The old lady went back to her shopping cart and returned with a canvas. She said, "This is something Friar Tuck worked on a few weeks ago."

She held up the canvas.

> ANTI FA stands for Anti Fascism
> Donald Trump is calling ANTIFA a terrorist group.
> To be against Anti-fascism it to be pro Fascism.
> Thus it is demonstrated
> Donald Trump is pro-fascist

Angela said, "The monk's wrist was so weak he couldn't continue with drawing the art he wanted. He asked me to draw Hitler shaking hands with Trump, but I am not that good an artist."

"For Christ's sake," Fitzgerald shouted, shoving his arms straight up into the air. "Fuck Trump, fuck Fascists! Quit dicking around and stay on point."

Hillman said. "The original drawings need to be stored in a fireproof safe."

Angela said, "We need to move all the stuff used to create the art from the crypt to my flat. Things like the easel and the brushes. Maybe that six mil bed."

"Correct, Angela, except for the bed," Hillman said. "Anyone else have any suggestions or problems?"

Angela went to her shopping cart and returned with another canvas. She said, "My heart was breaking watching Friar Tuck dying. He tried to draw one when all hell broke loose with the death of George Floyd. He could barely hold his brush. We watched together the assault by military police on the protestors by Lafayette Square. The Friar started to cry. His whole body was shaking. I was terrified his heart would stop he was trembling so much. He kept moaning as Trump strutted through the cleared park. After the charade in front of Saint John's the monk tried to draw something, but couldn't."

The canvas held only ghostly outlines of partly-formed figures.

Fitz said, "Trump's an asshole, but we have a bigger problem than his trying to make himself look like some sort of warrior. Although, in his defense not taking on the looters would have made every policeman in the country look lame."

"Have a heart," Max said. "Forty million people were on unemployment, hanging by a thread. You expect some of them not to fall to the temptation of snatch and grab?"

"Whatever," the veteran policeman said, "it's some other cop's problem. Back to us. Does anyone have a problem with Angela as beard?"

Lewis said, "I do. Too convoluted. People are supposed to believe Angela drew one hundred and fifty works of art in six months?"

"Meaning?" Hillman asked.

"Better to stick as close to the truth as possible. We hold a press conference at Saint Jude's tomorrow morning: radio, TV, newspapers. We show them the crypt. All of it: drawings, easel, even the golden bed."

"Are you nuts?" Fitzgerald sputtered.

"No, he's definitely not," Hillman said. "Continue partner."

"We will tell them we hired a professional artist to emulate the monk's style. We hired him to create a hundred and fifty drawings to be used in upcoming release of five coffee table books and postcards exposing Trump's actions during the potentially greatest threat to lives in this nation's history."

"And to do that you locked the artist in the crypt?" Fitzgerald said. "That's harder to believe than Angela drew the stuff."

"No, it's not," Lewis said. "We claim our deal with the artist was we wanted daily supervision of his progress and we paid dearly for that request."

"The press will want a name," Fitzgerald said, "they always do."

Lewis said, "We will state that as part of the deal we promised anonymity. The artist is a convicted forger, specializing in Dutch masters like Rembrandt and Vermeer. He has served his debt to society, but does not trust the criminal justice system. To protect his name the firm of H and L Enterprises LLC will throw the full weight of its resources to fulfill our promise of anonymity to the artist."

Hillman barked out a laugh. "Bravo, partner, not one of the media outlets in this town will spend an enormous amount of money to try and force *us* to break a promise."

"What about the *Chronicle*?" Fitzgerald asked. "Won't they be screaming that one of your forger's drawings ended up being presented to them as the real thing?"

Hillman answered, "We will rebut that with: In a hurry to release a special edition on Independence Day, instead of verifying facts, the *Chronicle* rushed ahead and printed a salacious suggestion that Friar Tuck might still be alive."

"They'll be lucky if we don't sue them," Lewis said.

Hillman asked, "Angela, you had to get that drawing to the newspaper early this afternoon for them to print their one page Special Edition that hit the streets around four."

"I was watching CNN at noon," Angela said, "and mourning the monk's death. I saw an updated virus death total, then a shot of Trump waving to a crowd and not wearing a mask. I became so angry I took a cab to the *Chronicle*."

"Angela," Lewis said, "what did you say when you dropped the drawing off at the newspaper?"

"I said it was Friar Tuck's art."

"Whom did you tell?" Hillman asked.

"I told the guard at the front desk."

"Spin's easy," Lewis said, "the guard misunderstood you. What you really said was, 'An *example* of Friar Tuck's art."

Fitzgerald barked out a laugh. "Not as outrageous a lie as slingshots and ball bearings in the tiger's cage, just a subtle lying spin on the truth."

"Any thoughts or problems?" Hillman asked.

"I have a problem," Fitzgerald said, "and it's the look of conflict on Erin's face. A concentration that's been there since she said this about our situation and I quote: 'To cover this up means more lies, and more lies, and more lies.'"

"Meaning?" Hillman and Lewis asked simultaneously.

"Meaning our dedicated cop is fighting an internal war," Fitzgerald said, "as we discuss breaking the law."

"I took an oath to uphold the law," Erin said. "I've been wrestling with my own secret involving my participation in hiding Paddy's guilt for six months, not six minutes. That fight was between a lie violating my sacred oath to uphold the law and my love for my brother."

Angela asked, "Erin, are you or are you not going to protect our secret?"

Erin looked from face to face, ending up with Max's. She asked, "Honey, what would you do?"

Max said, "Darling, I trust Mario's judgment. Ask him."

Erin arched an eyebrow and said, "Father?"

"The answer's simple," the priest said. "I used two questions, Erin, when I heard your confession involving a problem you had, which I think involved your knowledge Paddy was the killer and not Friar Tuck, meaning you knew that no one had won the God's Bookie pool. You remember?"

"I remember."

"I will use those same two questions to address this situation involving our secrets. First: would speaking out help anyone? Obviously, it would not. Second: would speaking out hurt anyone? Obviously, yes, it would hurt all of us in this bar. If Paddy's guilt ever came out it would expose a terrible secret that would help no one."

"Look at her face," Captain Fitzgerald said, "Erin's still wrestling with her conscience. Something I thankfully never have a problem with."

A voice cheerfully sang from the rear hallway, "You're all under arrest."

Sarah stood with hands on her hips. She was dressed exactly like Uncle Sam in the famous recruitment poster. She had on white shoes, red and white striped pants, white shirt, blue coat, red bow tie and a white top hat complete with blue band and white star. She had glued a white goatee to her N-95 mask.

The gang in the Triple M collectively gasped.

Fitzgerald asked, "Arrest us for what?"

"Breaking our mayor's legal order that no bar can be open."

The gang in the Triple M stared at Sarah.

"Why so serious people?" Sarah said. "Lighten up, guys, happy Fourth of July."

"How did you get in?" Max asked.

"The rear door. I was jogging over to Erin's place and saw Fitz walking down the alley. Didn't think much of it at first. I went to Angela's and rang Erin's doorbell, then Angela's. Nothing. I thought maybe they're in the saloon celebrating the Fourth."

"How did you know the key code?" Max asked.

"Pretty easy, I've heard you and the priests laughing about the address of Saint Peter's and Paul's, six, six, six, the Devil's number. First thing I tried and bingo. Then I heard Fitz saying he's never had a problem wrestling with his conscience."

The gang in the Triple M collectively sighed in relief.

Sarah went to the bar and got her temperature checked.

Father Mario softly said, "Rear booth time, Erin."

"Why?"

"You need to confess."

"No I don't."

"Yes, you do."

They sat in the rear booth.

Mario said, "Thank God Sarah didn't hear anything crucial."

The other priests, Angela, Fitz and Sarah bellied up to the bar. Max turned on the TV. On the screen fireworks were shooting their rockets red glare and bursting in air into the night sky over the San Francisco Bay.

Father Mario said, "Erin, you admitted you lied and broke a sacred oath to uphold the law."

"You're right," she said. "Bless me, Father, for I have sinned. I have born silent false witness."

"One of the definitions of scrupulous is a person very concerned to avoid doing wrong, like folks who go to confession every day. That is just as much a flaw as the opposite, not giving a damn. For your penance I order you to forget all about this and go on joyously sharing happiness with Max."

"You can't give a penance like that."

"I just did. I'm the one wearing the purple stole. You're off the hook, your conflict over your terrible secret is resolved. Obey your penance. For me, I will find out what kind of rules I've broken when I meet my Maker. That's my worry, not yours."

Erin said softly, "I thank you with all my heart."

~ The End ~

If you wish to contact Joe Harrington his email address shows his affection for Mark Twain, an author who had no problem tweaking those in power by the nose.

mark1clemens@yahoo.com

Author's note: for those of you who assume I must be a flaming, bleeding heart liberal, the reality is I have been a moderate conservative my entire adult life. The first election I voted in I cast my ballot for Barry Goldwater. In the last election I wrote in John Kasich's name, who I think would have made an excellent leader. After waiting two years of hoping POTUS would stop lying I became an angry Independent.